ABOUT TH

Born in Lancashire, Patricia Burton began her working life in the Civil Service before moving to North Wales with her husband and children.

A second career in Education followed, and twenty thoroughly enjoyable years of teaching in a large High School were punctuated by periods of study for degrees from the Universities of Bangor and Keele and by a spell as a visiting college lecturer.

Now, fulfilling her long-held ambitions as an author, she has written a series of three historical romances set in Liverpool. *Captive* is the first of these.

CAPTIVE

BY

PATRICIA BURTON

Best wishes

Patricia Burton

ASHRIDGE PRESS

Published by Ashridge Press
A subsidiary of Country Books
Courtyard Cottage, Little Longstone, Bakewell, Derbyshire DE45 1NN
Tel/Fax: 01629 640670
e-mail: dickrichardson@country-books.co.uk

ISBN 1 901214 54 0

British Library Cataloguing in Publication Data.
A catalogue record for this book is available from the British Library.

*In this work of fiction, the characters, places and events are
either the product of the author's imagination or they
are used entirely fictitiously.*

Printed and bound by:
Gutenberg Press Ltd

For Roy, with all my love.

Acknowledgements

I would like to thank my family and friends for their invaluable support and encouragement.

Special thanks are also due to Monty Mercer for the author photograph.

I am extremely grateful to Dick Richardson of Ashridge Press for his unfailing courtesy and for his professional expertise so willingly shared.

Finally, I wish to acknowledge the assistance given by the staff of Liverpool Central Record Office.

CHAPTER ONE

JAMAICA
NOVEMBER 1790

The sun hammered with unrelenting oppression on the pristine sands, and in the hills behind the crescent-shaped bay, the trees began to sway in ominous warning of an approaching storm. In the far distance, where the horizon shimmered in the heat, the sails of a ship were just visible against the darkening backdrop of massing cloud.

The stench in the hold of the struggling vessel was unendurable. Feeling her way in the fetid darkness, through the press of bodies chained together, the ten-year old girl slipped in the slime of vomit and excreta that covered the heaving floor. Bile rose in her throat and she whimpered softly. Last night, her mother had died and the sailors had tossed the emaciated body over the side. The terrified child had huddled alone for hours in a dark corner of the deck then, as the storm began to build, fear and desperation had driven her below. She knew that somewhere in the cargo of wretched humanity was her only remaining relative, her brother. Whatever happened she had to find him. A sudden lurch threw her sideways and she struck her head against a wooden prop. She slid to the floor, blessedly unconscious, as the ship continued to roll and pitch in the angry swell.

The slaves shifted uneasily, the clank of their chains loud in the confined space, and time crawled by in the heavy darkness.

Consciousness was slow to return to the child. Months of under-nourishment had taken their toll of her weakened system and her mind found relief in her present semi-comatose state. For a few precious moments she could almost imagine that she and her brother were back in their village with their mother and the babies. At the thought of those tiny bodies she whimpered once more, thrusting her fists into her mouth to prevent the rising hysteria. She had learned the hard way that crying brought no comfort, just a greater weariness and the threat of a beating. She lay still as the hateful spectres of the past filtered into her memory.

Life in their tiny village, twenty miles inland from the coast of the Bight of Biafra, had been hard. Food was scarce and the backbreaking efforts needed to coax any yield at all from the arid soil left the whole family exhausted. Their father hunted for meat when he could but, after his death on one such expedition, their lives had become increasingly difficult. Her brother tried to take the part of a man grown, their mother wore herself out in ceaseless labour on their tiny patch of ground and the girl was responsible for all the household chores and the care of the babies. Sometimes, in the darkness of their hut just before sleep claimed her, she wept hot silent tears of misery and self-pity. Why should her father have died? Why did their crop fail? Why was their one scraggy animal sick? Why did her baby sisters wail with hunger, their little bellies distended, their eyes huge in skeletal faces? Why her? Life could not get any worse. But it did.

For years stories had travelled from village to village, whispered on the wind. Tales of spirits that came in the darkness and took away the tribe, leaving only the old and sick to lament in their huts and sing their songs of sadness to the skies. The girl heard the tales, muttered around the fires at night, but her own misery was too acute, too real for her to waste time worrying about what might have happened elsewhere. She was impatient with her brother when he tried to voice his unease.

'You would do better to concern yourself with the living rather than fret about the activities of the spirits of the dead. These are old men's tales. Old men's fears. Unless you can bring meat to our fire, brother, we shall all be dead soon enough. That is my fear and it is a real one.' And then the men had come, big Africans and two white men.

The girl had never seen a face that was not black. In those first shocking moments of the assault, she indeed believed that the invaders were beings from the spirit world. The men had rushed from hut to hut, viciously clubbing any who tried to hinder them as they rounded up every able-bodied person in the village. The girl, with her mother and brother, was herded into the central space beside the communal fire. Old men were thrust aside. A woman who tried to hold on to her son was prised off him and beaten mercilessly into the dust, a shapeless and bloodied heap. The final horror was about to begin.

The men of the village were chained together, arms locked behind them and halters placed around their necks. The women and children were bound with ropes and trailed at the rear. As the dreadful procession left the village, the girl's two baby sisters wailed loudly and began to crawl after them. One of their captors kicked out at the first infant's head. There was a sickening crunch and the child lay still. The girl's mother screamed, a long, undulating note abruptly cut off as the thongs of a whip sliced open the skin of her shoulders. The other baby sat in the dust beside her sister, rocking herself to and fro in silence. The line of prisoners moved away and the cover of darkness descended on the abomination.

All night and for much of the next day they walked. The girl had tried to get closer to her mother, who was trudging onwards in an unseeing daze, but she was forced to the rear with the rest of the children. Her brother was at the front of the line with the men, and she saw that he kept looking back, his eyes straining for a glimpse of his womenfolk. Just once, on a brief stop, he managed a quick word with the girl.

'You are small for your years, sister. Keep your head down. Stare only at the floor. Hunch up your shoulders and stoop a little. Do not look into their faces.' She realised that he was trying to protect her, but did not understand from what. However, she did as she was bidden and lowered her eyes, putting one bleeding foot before the other, stumbling on to the journey's end.

It came with a suddenness and a brilliance that swept away the nightmare, if only for a moment. For the first time in her life the girl beheld the full, awesome wonder of the ocean. The slaves were permitted to hobble across the burning sand and to collapse into the warm, caressing waters of the sea. The gentle waves washed over them, soothing their wounds and refreshing their aching limbs.

That had been the last small happiness that the girl was to know. The respite was short-lived. In the ensuing days, other groups of prisoners limped on to the beach and soon the shore was a heaving mass of captives guarded by men with guns and whips. Day after day, night after night, the girl witnessed scenes of unimaginable cruelty as the depth of man's degradation was revealed. Remembering her brother's warning, she kept herself in the centre of the ever increasing group of children, helping where she could do something practical, comforting where she could not. She kept her head down and tried to shut out the noise of the atrocities around her. Eventually the horrors ceased to shock and became part of her existence. So it went on, until early one morning a neat brigantine appeared off shore and the nightmare of the middle-passage began.

During the appalling journey that followed, from the coast of West Africa to the British island of Jamaica, the girl's one comfort had been that she was able to be close to her mother for at least part of the day. The younger women, whose task was to minister to the needs of the crew, were permitted access on deck and although they were abused and beaten as a matter of course, and were roped together at night, they were grateful for their lot, especially when they had to go into the cargo hold where the men were held. Below decks was a vision of hell. Platforms had been constructed, rather like shelves, in order that greater numbers of slaves could be transported at any one time. The shelves were so low that standing was impossible. Muscles became cramped and wasted, irons rubbed festering holes in skin that refused to heal, disease raged unchecked through the ranks and was compounded by lack of food, water and fresh air. Many of the slaves would have preferred the dignity of death and tried to starve themselves. These rebels were flogged into submission and force-fed by a crew mindful of the value of each item of their human cargo.

After weeks at sea, when men were dying in ever-increasing numbers, things had suddenly improved. The girl learned that they were only days away from their destination and that the remaining slaves were being readied for sale at auction. The prisoners were taken on deck, the filth was hosed from their bodies and they were given fresh water from the barrels and sufficient food to ease the gnawing agony in their stomachs. Amongst one group of prisoners she recognised the gaunt features of her brother; he was moving stiffly, his face lifted to the un-accustomed light of the sun. Relief and gratitude threatened to overwhelm her. Whatever the future held, at least he lived. The three of them had survived. Then came the storm.

It had started quietly enough. The wind slowly strengthened, filling the canvas and whistling through the rigging, causing the ship to skip from wave top to wave top as lightly as a stone skimmed across a river. The girl began to enjoy a sense of freedom as the ship sped along. It seemed to be trying to shake off its shackles. She turned her head away from the spray as her mother's fingers gripped her arm and the feeble voice croaked in her ear.

'Child, if I should not be with you, find your brother. Stay with him so that you may be sold together.'

'But mother, we are almost there. The crew man... he said so. You told me. We shall leave this cursed ship in just a few days. The three of us.'

The girl was filled with a sense of nameless dread. The older woman retched weakly and clutched at her daughter, her legs buckling as she fell back against the ship's rail. Blood-flecked spittle appeared on her lips and only the whites of her eyes were visible. The woman died that same night and her body was tossed over the side before dawn.

The fury of the storm had matched the rage in the girl's heart as the wind grew wilder and the seas more mountainous. A sail ripped from top to bottom and its rags streamed out behind the driven vessel. The swell increased and the ship wallowed in the troughs between the massive waves, struggling to breach each one and then crashing back into the green depths below. The timbers creaked and groaned their protest as the sailors went silently about their work, fear in their eyes.

At the height of the tempest there was a lull and it seemed as if they had come through the worst. They glimpsed land on the starboard side; a crescent curve of sand backed by lush green mountains. Then the sky darkened again and the stalking mass of black cloud caught and swallowed them. The girl saw, on the faces of the crew, that the vessel was doomed. In desperation she scoured the decks until she found one man who had been kind to her. He was a tough wiry sailor from the town of Liverpool, the ship's home port. She fell on her knees and clung to his legs, pointing silently to the hatch over the hold. Time froze. He stared at the waves threatening to swamp the ship then he lurched towards an axe clamped to a mast.

'Aye lass. 'Tis every man for himself now,' he said, and struck the bolt clear with one huge blow. He followed the child into the hell below and began to swing his axe in a frantic attack on the irons that shackled the men together. He stopped, lifting his head and listening, every sense straining in the darkness. Suddenly, the sailor dropped the axe and hauled himself through the hatch. He was followed by the men he had cut free as the screams of those left behind rang out in despair. The child continued to stumble in the blackness of the hold, resolute in her stubborn search for her brother. The last thing that she remembered, before unconsciousness threw its merciful cloak over her, was a bang on her head and an agonising pain that brought with it a new and deeper darkness.

Now, she struggled to leave the past behind and open her eyes. Someone was shaking her.

'Come with me.' It was her brother's frantic voice, dragging her back to reality. 'We must get out of this hole or we perish with the ship.' The boy grabbed his sister and pushed his way through the writhing hordes, trampling bodies underfoot in his primeval fear. Together they struggled up to the listing deck, just as the main mast snapped and came crashing down in a maelstrom of canvas and rigging. The boy found a desperate strength and thrust his sister to one side, clinging grimly to the deck rail. The chaos here was scarcely better than the horror below. Broken bodies lay everywhere. Groaning sailors were pinned down by wreckage and huge waves pounded the ship, sluicing the dead and dying with a grey-green torrent of water. Men and debris together were swept across the pitching deck and over the side.

The ship plunged into a deep trough and for a moment there was a pause in its heaving death throes. Terrifying walls of water towered above them as the vessel wallowed in its deep watery grave. Timbers groaned but violent movement momentarily ceased. Snatching up a rope and using the last of his strength, the boy bound himself and his sister together and lashed them both to a piece of the shattered mast. He knew that he had only moments in which to act. The ship would not live; they were going down. This was their only hope.

By the following morning the storm had spent its vindictive energies, re-gathered its forces and moved on to inflict devastation elsewhere. On the broad terrace of the great house, built in the shady foothills of the mountains that reached to the edge of the sugar-cane fields, Jeremiah Weston inhaled the fresh, gentle air and looked out over the tops of the waving palms towards the sea. Tranquillity had come with the dawn. The centre of the previous day's storm had, it appeared, been out in the waters beyond the bay so only the fringes of the shoreline had sustained any real damage. In the clear light of day, Weston was relieved to see that disruption to his estate had been minimal. It could have been so much worse if the fury had turned inland. But God help any shipping out there. He had lived here in Jamaica for several years but could still be amazed by the speed and ferocity with which a tropical storm was able to turn this serene paradise into a shrieking hell of destruction.

Raising his glass to his eye, Weston scanned the curve of

the distant beach. Many times in the past, in the days following a storm, flotsam worth salvaging had been washed up in the bay. It was a natural repository for the detritus of the sea. Suddenly he froze. He placed the eyeglass down on the balustrade, wiped a shaking hand over his face and turned to the huge man standing patiently at his shoulder.

'Daniel.' He indicated the telescope and stood back.

'What is it, Master? What can you see?' The servant lifted the proffered instrument. His gaze traversed the bay and came to rest on a group of rocks at the far side, where the mountain stream ended its riotous tumble down to the sea. He drew a long, shuddering breath, put down the telescope and stared bleakly at his master. Jeremiah Weston turned briskly away from the shared horror. There was work to do.

'Horses. Get horses, Daniel, and a cart. Me, you, Marcus. We'll pick up two more slaves on our way through the fields as we go down. Hurry now.' His instructions were issued crisply; he was used to being obeyed. He snatched a tricorn hat, crammed it on his head and hurried after his valet who was already rushing down the steps, hurrying away from the house towards the stables.

At a first-floor window, Anne Weston watched the commotion below, one hand on the fair, unruly curls of her four year old son and the other supporting her thumb-sucking daughter against her shoulder. The child had not slept well during the worst excesses of the storm and was fractious and over-warm. The breeze that was fluttering the fine muslin curtains would cool her down. Patting the infant's back, Anne wondered idly what had caused the sudden spurt of activity below. It was unusual for her husband to go out before breakfast. She started as Jeremiah re-appeared around the corner of the house astride his great bay gelding. He rode off in a clatter of noise, closely followed by Daniel on one of the plantation greys and by Marcus, black skin gleaming in the sunlight, whip whistling over the team's heads as the cart rattled down the drive. They disappeared in a cloud of dust that hovered behind them before spiralling silently down to earth. The woman shivered and turned her back on the open window, drawing her children with her into the solid security of their home.

Jeremiah Weston reined in his horse and gazed dumbly at the scene before him. The animal whinnied and pranced uneasily backwards and sideways, shaking it head, harness jangling; it was an alien, cheerful sound in the midst of the grim carnage. Dozens of naked black bodies rolled over and over in the rippling shallows, many bobbing gently in the waves before being deposited carefully on the warm sand. Others had been carried on to the waiting rocks and were draped casually across the boulders, for all the world as if they slept. It was not the presence of death, nor even the magnitude of it that stunned the plantation owner. Weston had spent years in the service of his King's armies and had long been accustomed to sudden demise on a grand scale. No. It was the sight of these men and boys shackled together, one body dragging the next down beneath the clear turquoise waters, that affected him so deeply. It was the thought of the last moments of these doomed men, caught like rats in a trap, that etched itself into his brain. He was conscious of a retching sound behind him and turned around.

His valet was on his knees in the shallows. The man's hands tore at his tightly curled hair as tears poured unchecked down his cheeks. Weston moved towards him and laid a hand on the shaking shoulders.

'Daniel. I am so sorry. It is indeed pitiful. What can I say? I have my slaves, we all do, but to be a party to this. It is monstrous. One of the vessels must have gone down

18

in the storm. A shipment was due in Kingston any day. I know that. It was out of Liverpool.' He looked around, shaking his head in despair. 'Dear God! What chance did they have?'

The slave climbed stiffly to his feet, shrugging away the outstretched hand. 'These people were from the same region as my mother. Look at their features. They... I ...' Stumbling away from his master, he struggled up the beach towards the cart. He snatched an axe and lurched back to the shallows where he began to chop frantically, hysterically at the chains around the dead men's ankles, often slicing through skin and bone in his frenzy. Daniel was unaware of Weston. Images of these men, dying in agony, bound together, filled his head to the exclusion of everything else. The chains and collars that weighed them down were the potent symbol of mankind's ultimate cruelty. It was an abomination. His blood boiled, his hatred raged and he chopped and chopped until his lungs heaved and a red mist danced before his eyes.

Marcus' fist closed over the shaft of the axe as Daniel's aching arms lifted it over his head once more. Four hands on the wood, two black, two brown. The men's gaze locked.

'It surely is enough, man,' said Marcus. 'Yo' needs to help us get 'em into the cart. They must be buried. That be all we can do for them now. Yo' knows it. It be a day's work to clear this beach. They sure can't be left here.' Daniel loosed his grip on the axe and the demented light faded from his eyes. He allowed Marcus to help him to his feet and walked unsteadily towards his master's horse.

Jeremiah was slumped in the saddle, watching his slaves as they set about their gruesome work

'Master?' There was no reply. Daniel spoke again. 'Master?'

Weston looked at his man with an impassive face and his

tone was expressionless as he finally responded. 'You will have to supervise the removal of the bodies and...'

'Massa! Massa!' The voice of one of the field slaves was raised in a high pitched shriek. 'Massa, come quick.' Sliding from his horse Jeremiah followed Daniel, floundering across the sand towards the kneeling man who was trying to haul a great hulk of timber out of the water. Panting, the others crowded round. The slave looked up, his eyes huge, his hands supporting the head of a young girl. 'This one lives, Massa. I swear, this one lives. She moved, I seen it. It's not the water. She moved.' They all stared, repelled by the spectacle before them, each man struggling to contain his emotion. Beneath the crushing weight of the severed section of a ship's mast lay the smashed and broken body of a young man. One arm was lashed by rope to the wood the other was clutched protectively around a girl. As they watched, her body twitched. Once.

Weston reacted first. He drew a knife from his belt and slashed at the ropes binding the pair together. Holding the girl's head, he began to blow air into her slack mouth. She coughed and water dribbled down her chin. She gagged and as Jeremiah turned her upside down she heaved bile and water all over him, staining his breeches and the front of his shirt. Mucus dribbled from his fingers into the sand. Pulling his own smock over his head, Marcus silently handed the garment to his master. Weston nodded his thanks, wrapped it around the girl and, calling Daniel to follow him, set off at a run for his horse.

On the beach, Marcus looked sadly at the crushed body beneath the mast. Not much older than the girl, it was clear that he had died a terrible death. Marcus could envisage the boy forcing his own body beneath the waves to keep the girl's head above water. Their features were alike enough to tell the closeness of their relationship. The boy had indeed done his duty by his sister. Marcus brushed away a futile tear that tracked its way down the furrows of his leathery cheeks. He muttered under his breath. There were evils spirits on these sands and in these rocks. The sooner their task was done, the sooner they could return to the plantation. He bent his back, old scars thrown into stark relief by the sun, and set to work.

Galloping along in his master's wake as they followed the grassy track from the beach to the start of the foothills, Daniel sought to banish the scenes he had just witnessed from his mind. He fixed his gaze on Weston's back but saw only the carnage that had been left behind. He could not escape from the memory of those dark tormented faces, the staring eyes, the emaciated bodies and the dead, dragging weight of the chains. He knew that this day had staked its place in his future. He would never be the same again.

Daniel was beset by guilt, the guilt of his personal heritage. He too was a slave, a house slave. A part of him belonged to the same people as those drowned in the bay. The same people as the child so carefully carried on his master's saddle. But Daniel had never seen the Bight of Biafra, never known the terrors of the middle-passage, the second stage of the trading vessels out from England. He had learned at his mother's knee how the ships brought their merchandise from English ports and used the goods to pay for human life. They then carried their unwilling cargo of kidnapped prisoners to the British West Indies, where they were sold as slaves in exchange for sugar and rum. Finally, the sailors took these commodities back to their home ports of Glasgow, Bristol and Liverpool where they fed the incessant demands of British society.

Daniel knew of this triangle but had never experienced it. He was plantation born and therein lay his burden. He had been fathered by an English plantation manager on an African slave mother. He was the outcome of one of the many mixed blood unions. There were few white women in Jamaica and both owners and managers took concubines who were slaves. In all cases, the child took the status of his mother though the 'coloureds', as they were known, were usually put to work in the house and not in the fields. Daniel, and those like him, was partially white but was born slave. It was this heritage that tore his soul. It had troubled him all his life but never more so than today. His heart bled for those chained captives and for his long-dead mother, but his white man's blood meant that he must accept part of the blame for the wrongs of his father's people. His guilt set him apart. He belonged nowhere.

The beach track ended. They had come to the road that led down to Kingston and, turning away from the town, Jeremiah slowed his horse to a steady walk as he headed for home. The girl, wrapped in Marcus' smock, lay in the crook of his arm. She weighed scarcely more than his own four-year old but he judged her to be between eight and ten. The child was all jutting bone though he could see that she would be quite pretty. Her features were regular and her skin unblemished. Jeremiah had not thought beyond the need to get the child home to Westwinds, where his slaves could take care of her in their own quarters. He would need to leave her with them for he knew that he would have much to do in Kingston later that day.

The Weston plantation was by far the closest to the beach and Jeremiah realised that if the brigantine had gone down, as seemed likely, just off the bay, then most of the bodies and any other survivors would come ashore in the same area. He himself would have to bear the tidings, about the ship and its consignment, to the authorities and merchants in Kingston. Not much of note happened on this peaceful island and all the talk in the clubs and the great houses had been of the expected shipment of new slaves from Africa and the resulting export of sugar and rum to

England. The goods had been stacked on the quay for days, awaiting the first sighting of the vessel off the coast. There would be many disappointed and anxious men in Kingston this night.

Weston also had other concerns; Daniel's response to the dreadful scenes on the beach worried him. The man had lost his reason and all self-control. There had been a naked aggression and an uncharacteristic savagery in his reaction to the horror. His servant was a huge man, six feet four inches in height and seventeen stones of bronze, rippling muscle. He was a gentle giant who had been with the Westons for thirteen years, since being bought by them from a neighbouring plantation at the age of ten. He was a house slave He had been taught to read and write and had eventually been given care of Jeremiah's young son for much of the time. As well as acting as valet to Weston himself, Daniel frequently accompanied Anne to Kingston, assisting her to and from the carriage, carrying her parcels and offering the security of his protection. Jeremiah had never harboured any doubts about Daniel before today. Slavery was an integral part of life on the island and Daniel had seemed to accept his lot with equanimity. But this day, the façade had been stripped bare and the bitterness beneath had been revealed. Jeremiah suddenly felt that he knew nothing at all about the man who had served him these past years.

There were other worries too, worries as yet unacknowledged even to himself. It was well established that these islands took their toll of the white man's health. Most of the plantations were managed, at least for a good part of the year, whilst their wealthy owners returned to England. Jeremiah Weston, a third son of a squire, had needed to make his own way in the world. A small legacy and a government grant enabled him to purchase this plantation but much work had been required to ensure that Westwinds

23

would prosper. He relished the challenge and had thrown himself unsparingly into the task. His efforts had reaped their just reward and he was now the owner of one of the best estates in Jamaica.

Five years earlier, on a rare trip home, he had visited the fashionable spa town of Bath and had met and married Anne Broadwood, daughter of a wealthy Liverpool merchant. He had fallen instantly and irrevocably in love. Whirling through a hectic courtship he had whisked his willing bride back to the Caribbean. They both adored Jamaica and the pretty Mrs Weston had quickly become an indispensable part of Kingston society. The birth of their two children completed their joy. The plantation continued to flourish and Jeremiah's fortune was assured. Lately they had begun to speak of the possibility of a return to England and the purchase of an estate in the country. Anne's parents were dead and she was eager to spend some time with her brother who had taken over the family business in Liverpool. The children too were now at an age where they might benefit from a change of climate and culture. Jeremiah knew that his plantation could safely be left in the hands of a manager, provided that the right man could be found. There was the rub. No one knew better than he that many of the estates were overseen by idle, drunken men who cared nothing for the land and even less for their people. An able, experienced and trustworthy agent was like gold dust in the islands but Weston realised that one must be found, and found soon.

For several weeks now he had been aware of a worrying lethargy and occasional faintness. At first he had put his dizzy spells down to forgetting to wear his hat, but he knew that he was deceiving himself, bouts of constriction in his chest and the loss of strength in his left arm could not be so easily accounted for. Jeremiah became conscious of the now familiar tingling in his hand. He transferred the weight of the child to his other side and rode on. He must get to England and see a doctor. It could be put it off no longer.

CHAPTER TWO

JAMAICA
NOVEMBER 1790

Anne Weston waited in the deep early-morning shadow of the portico, watching for her husband's return. She was a tall slim woman, whose graceful carriage and elegant gestures emphasised the exquisite proportions of her figure. She had soft brown hair and hazel eyes that could reflect brown, amber or flashing green lights, according to her mood. Of a usually calm and unruffled disposition, it was out of character for her serenity to desert her so totally, but on this morning it certainly had. Her disquiet was evident as she paced restlessly up and down; three steps left, turn about, three steps right, pause, turn and begin again. She stopped and mentally shook herself, taking her emotions firmly in hand. There was no cause for such anxiety. What was wrong with her? This would not do. She forced herself to remain still and clasped her hands loosely before her, assuming a tranquillity that she was far from feeling.

When she had first arrived in Jamaica, a romantic twenty-year old bride, each day had begun like this, a constant battle with nerves and apprehension. The house was so much more grand than she had envisaged. How could she, scarcely better than a giddy girl, take control of such an establishment? She would surely say or do quite the wrong thing and Jeremiah would be ashamed of her.

The household seemed to be composed of vast numbers of silent slaves who lowered their eyes whenever she passed. She was the only white woman on the plantation and she had been terrified.

In those early days, her composure had frequently given way to hysterical weeping, and only her husband's patient understanding had enabled her to acquire, at least outwardly, a placid demeanour. Under his watchful guidance she had learned to manage her household in these alien surroundings. She had slowly accustomed herself to the heat and insects, to the sudden tropical storms and the heavy winter rains. Her kindness had soon endeared her to the household and, before long, every slave on the plantation was her willing and devoted servant. The sight of 'Missus' down in the slave quarters with nourishing food or a potion for a sick child became a common feature of the Westwinds estate. For a time it had been the talk of the island. Mrs Weston's largesse did not meet with universal approval.

Anne's relationship with the white population was initially fraught. She had been overwhelmed by the exuberant curiosity of the other plantation owners and their wives. She had not realised that there would be so few women of her own class on the island nor had she any inkling of the excitement and jealousies that a pretty newcomer would induce. She was not prepared and had been petrified. Jeremiah told her to think of the place as a small English village, with the same rigid social structure. The inhabitants of the manor and the landed gentry equated with the plantation owners. The position of the overseer, who represented the absentee landlord, was like the vicar or the doctor. The Officers of the Militia were like officers anywhere in the world. Merchants and traders were equally easily placed. The only really strange phenomenon was the Governor; as the King's representative he should be put on a standing with the Almighty. Anne had giggled at her husband's irreverent imagery and smiled again, now, at the recollection.

She had gradually become accustomed to her new position and if Jeremiah was unaware of her frequently churning stomach and of the mental talking-to that was the necessary prelude to every big social event, then that was as it should be. She had chosen to be his wife and was determined to come to terms with the problems of life in this outpost of English gentility. The birth of Timothy, one year after her arrival in Jamaica, had given her several welcome months of respite from the hectic social round, and after the birth, when the time came for her to resume her activities as a hostess, she had a new-found inner peace and a confidence that was not easily disturbed. So what was wrong today? She mulled over the morning's events. Jeremiah's abrupt departure had given her some concern. The baby's restlessness was a niggling worry and a night of uneasy sleep caused by the storm had not helped. She shook her head. There had to be more than that. Could it be the slaves?

The Maroons, those colonies of runaways who lived in the far reaches of the island, had been indulging in skirmishes recently, and this always had an un-settling effect on all the plantation workers. No. She was unconcerned by these minor rebellions. There was no risk to Westwinds. Jeremiah Weston was known throughout the island for his fair dealing with the slaves. He was a good master and there was a well-organised hierarchy in place. The house slaves and craftsmen were taken from those of mixed race; they were never put to labour on the land and were firmly settled. Even the lowest gang-worker was mostly content. The whip was used sparingly in Weston's fields and there were more people from his estate trading at the Sunday market in Kingston than from any of the other plantations. Jeremiah's slaves had enough free time and sufficient unexpended energy to produce crops on their own small plots or 'polinks'. These fruits, maize and vegetables supplemented their basic diet and the surplus was sold or traded for other goods and trinkets at the weekly market. The Westwinds people were an orderly and generally uncomplaining group. Now that she had become used to them, their proximity posed no threat to her peace of mind and caused her no anxiety. So it was not the slaves, but something was certainly amiss and she was troubled.

Maybe she should look closer to home; not at their people but at themselves. She was blessed in her marriage and regularly gave thanks for her good fortune in securing a husband who was kind, sober, moderate in his habits and who loved her with an unswerving devotion. They had always been happy together and had been lately speaking of purchasing a small estate near Liverpool. Anne sometimes admitted to herself, though not to her husband, that she missed her homeland desperately, so the prospect of leaving Jamaica and returning to England was a source of real joy. Jeremiah too was eager to return home now that he had made his mark and had acquired the means to make a comfortable living for himself and his family. They could ask for nothing more. She sighed.

Did the difficulty lie with Jeremiah? It was true that he seemed distracted of late. There was not a problem with the estate, she was sure of that. It had been a good year; the old crop had been harvested in March and the mill had been working constantly to extract the sugar, the land had been holed for a further spring planting, the rains had caused no damage and the next season's yield was almost guaranteed. Yet something was not as it should be with her husband. He had taken to falling asleep in the library after his dinner, a thing he never used to do. His movements were often laboured and, just occasionally, his speech was slurred.

She dragged her mind away from the unthinkable. She could hear voices. Thank God! At last riders were approaching. As Weston and Daniel appeared in the drive, Anne ran down the broad steps to meet them. The sun scorched the back of her neck and her bare forearms and the fine muslin of her morning gown fluttered gently around her slim ankles. As the men came closer Anne could see that her husband cradled a young girl in his arms. Water dripped from the folds of the stained smock that covered her and from the bedraggled black curls that tumbled around the child's face. Anne looked up at Jeremiah and was shocked by the emptiness in his eyes.

'My dear,' he said on a sigh. 'A slave ship was wrecked in the bay last night. There are bodies on the beach... so many bodies... so very many.' He collected himself. 'This child has survived. She seems to be the only one.' He turned to the man who had dismounted behind him and was waiting, holding his horse's head. He handed over his burden. 'Daniel, take her to the slave quarters and see that someone cares for her.'

Jeremiah moved sluggishly towards the house, his feet scraping the floor as though they were too heavy to lift. He halted, unwillingly, as his wife spoke.

'Wait! Daniel, please take the girl to the kitchen. Give her to Deliah, if you will. I shall come through presently and give instructions myself for her care. Go now, quickly.'

'Mistress.' Daniel inclined his head, cast a rapid glance at his master and hurried off around the side of the house and across the stable yard.

Anne moved towards her husband and laid a hand on his arm. She spoke gently.

'My dearest, we cannot simply abandon that child to the care of the field workers. She is sick, that much was apparent even through the smock.' She laughed softly, trying to lighten the atmosphere. 'She must be returned to health. It may be that we can keep her as a house servant when she is well. After all, do we have any notion as to who has ownership of the girl? It would not be the thing to simply acquire her and put her into the fields. Do you not agree?' There was no response. Anne went on, desperately. 'She must have suffered so. There has to be something that we can do.' She paused again. 'I had considered lately that I should bring over one of the girls from the slave quarters to train as a maid to Margaret's nurse. Deliah is not so young as she was and does need some help. It seems that this waif could be the answer to my dilemma, for I did not know which girl to choose and you know how quickly spite and jealousy can spread on the plantation. May I have her? Please, my dear?'

Jeremiah turned to face his wife, leaning heavily on the balustrade. 'For the love of God, take the girl if that is what you wish. Take her.' And he stumbled up the steps into the welcome coolness of the hall. Anne Weston stared after him in dismay, one hand to her lips the other clenched by her side. She followed him indoors and made her way to the rear of the house.

Approaching the kitchen area, Anne could hear the unaccustomed babble of raised voices. She stood, un-noticed, in the doorway and surveyed the scene before her. The massive bulk of Daniel, still clasping his fragile bundle, dominated the space of the room but the vociferous protest of Deliah, Margaret's nurse, was undoubtedly winning the day. The gist of her argument was evident. The place for a newcomer was in the slave quarters, not here in the house. She, Deliah, would not permit Daniel to introduce this wretch into the kitchen. Who knew what diseases she might carry? Had he taken leave of what little wits he had?

Arms akimbo, black face perspiring, white lace cap askew, she was holding forth loud and long. The other house slaves, even the cook, were in awe of the old woman. She had lived in the big house for longer than any could remember. Rumour had it that she had been concubine to the first Massa, though no one had ever raised the point with Deliah. Later, when younger girls had taken her place in his bed, she had graduated to be house-keeper, a position she had kept when Jeremiah Weston had purchased the property.

Anne, on her arrival from England, had been pleased to have someone experienced in running the house to turn to for advice. She had eventually taken over the household management herself, whilst allowing Deliah to have care of first Timothy and then baby Margaret. Things had worked well and Deliah had never overstepped the bounds of propriety in her dealings with her mistress. She frequently scolded the children, but to Anne she was always punctiliously polite and to Jeremiah, cringingly subservient.

On the surface life was calm, but Anne had long been aware that Deliah's treatment of the other slaves left much to be desired. In the servants' quarters she ruled with an iron fist and everyone, from the youngest maid to Marcus the groom, went in fear of earning her displeasure. There was talk in the town of Deliah being an Obeah priestess. Anne had been made aware of this by some of the other ladies, who had heard the gossip from their maids. She did not like unpleasantness, however, and so long as nothing was done blatantly she was content to turn a blind eye to the communal practices of her servants. They had their own culture, their own form of religion and she was not disposed to interfere.

Daniel was different from the others. He was not afraid of the old woman. He had come to Westwinds at the age of ten, when Jeremiah was still struggling to build up the estate. Anne remembered clearly the account that her husband had given her, one balmy evening, as they sat on the terrace after their dinner. She had only just come to Jamaica and was eager to learn as much as she could about the island ways. Her husband, swirling his brandy around in his glass, had begun his tale.

'Marcus was driving me on a visit to a neighbouring plantation where they had some slaves to sell on. I needed some experienced people to train the new slaves that I was buying as my fields expanded. I never liked Jim Watts, the overseer at Greenways. He was an ignorant man of little education and with few good qualities to speak of. I was told that he had a sadistic streak but had never evidenced it at first hand. We could hear the groaning as we approached the house; we could hear the whistle and crack of the whip too.' Jeremiah stared, unseeingly, into the distance. He looked down at his drink. 'Marcus flinched at every stroke. We knew that Watts was flogging someone, that came as no surprise but we did not expect it to be a woman. She was lying in the dust at his feet and was almost senseless. That brute was enjoying himself, Anne.' Jeremiah stopped and took a quick gulp of his drink. 'We learned later that the woman lived with him. She was his concubine... oh, my dear, do not look so shocked. It is common practice here you know. Many of the Europeans take slaves to their beds. It is the way. It is accepted.' He patted her hand. 'You are an old married woman of the world now. Well, anyway, the woman had been with Watts for years and they had a son, Daniel. Usually the coloureds are well looked after, although of course they are still slaves, but in this instance something had gone wrong. Watts was in a drunken rage and had beaten the boy to within an inch of his life. The mother was trying to run away and take the lad with her.' Jeremiah tossed back the last of his drink, stood up and began a restless wander up and down the terrace. 'There is not much else to tell really. I took the whip from him, knocked him down, put Daniel and his mother in the carriage, threw some money at Watts and Marcus drove us back here. The boy eventually recovered but his mother died not long afterwards. I wrote to England, to the owner of the plantation; he is a kindly man and was horrified to learn how his estate was managed. Watts was dismissed. He scrounged around the island for some months trying to earn enough for his passage home. I heard that he was finally killed in a drunken brawl in Spanish Town, so Daniel was alone. I took him into the house, trained him, taught him to read and write and have never regretted my actions.' He had held out his hand to her and together they had gone into the house.

Thinking back now to that story, Anne was not surprised that Daniel worshipped Weston. He would do anything to serve his master and when Anne herself had arrived to become the lady of Westwinds, Daniel had willingly extended his devotion to her. Her natural kindliness made it a pleasure to serve her, and with her coming a measure of refinement had been added to their lives. There was an elegance in the big house that had previously been lacking, and Daniel was swift to absorb the nuances and manner-isms that distinguished a gentleman's establishment. There had followed a period of quiet contentment but then, less than a year after Timothy had been born, an incident had occurred which helped forge an unbreakable bond between mistress and slave.

Marcus had broken his arm and Daniel was deputed to drive the carriage for Mrs Weston's social call on a neighbour. On the journey home, the carriage had been attacked by two runaways, one armed with a knife and the other with a billhook. At the risk of his life, the unarmed Daniel had launched himself at the two men. The first he had killed with his bare hands, the other had slashed Daniel's arm to the bone with his billhook, before being overpowered and trussed up for delivery to the Militia.

Daniel, one arm bleeding profusely, had somehow managed to drive the carriage back to the estate, hand his swooning mistress over to Jeremiah and describe where he had left the prisoner, before collapsing at his master's feet. For many days it was not known if he would survive the loss of blood, nor if his arm could be saved, but Anne and Jeremiah had nursed him devotedly and eventually his own colossal strength had asserted itself and he had recovered. The runaway had been summarily executed and Daniel's place in the Weston's lives was established.

Now, watching the scene in the kitchen, Anne became aware of all the undercurrents and tensions in her household. With the Massa and Mistress Daniel might reign supreme, but below stairs he was envied and was not seen as one of them. His mixed blood set him apart. For the first time she recognised the loneliness of the man's existence, his isolation. Here, among the slaves, Deliah ruled the roost. The old woman had access upstairs, she had care of young Massa Timothy and Missy Meg, she had the power and the sight and she was one of their own. Anne noticed that the house slaves had ranged themselves alongside Deliah, forming a threatening group. Daniel stood alone.

Anne let the door bang as it closed behind her. She moved deliberately into the middle of the kitchen, forcing Deliah to give ground.

'Daniel, would you please put the girl down here in the chair by the fire. One of you girls go and bring a warming-pan. Don't just stand there. Deliah, if you will get a shawl from my room we can get her out of these sodden rags. Quickly now. The rest of you can get back to work. Master will want his lunch.' The servants bowed their heads in submission but glanced from beneath lowered brows at Deliah's set face. There was a long, long silence.

'Yes, Ma'am.' It was a grudging response. With a collective sigh of relief, the frozen tableau shattered and people began to move. Only Daniel was in a position to see the glitter of malice in the old woman's eyes as she turned away. He drew in his breath and made a surreptitious sign to ward off the evil spirits. He looked at Anne Weston and was afraid for her future.

During the days that followed, an inexplicable apprehension hovered over the house. Outwardly things went on much as before but beneath the surface hidden currents swirled. Anne attempted to ignore the tensions. She paid calls on friends, went shopping in Kingston, was entertained in the island's great houses and took charge, as usual, of her own establishment. Through it all she was aware of the presence of the rescued girl. She knew that Daniel's dead mother had spoken in a similar dialect to the child and that the valet spent many of his free hours with her. Finally, curiosity got the better of the mistress and Daniel was summoned to the morning-room to acquaint her with such information as he had gleaned. Anne sat, pen in hand, thinking things over as she waited for the servant to appear.

It had been established, in the days following the wreck, that the ship was out of the port of Liverpool. She wondered if her brother, Matthew Broadwood, had any investment tied up in the venture. No doubt she would hear from him in due course. News came all the time from England and circulated rapidly amongst the white community. Since the storm, Jeremiah had spent many hours at the Governor's Residence and in the House of Assembly as they debated all the problems connected with the ship's loss. Once, he would have shared this with her, but not now. He no longer even shared her bed but had taken to sleeping in his dressing room, alone. She had tried to broach the matter with him but found that feelings of delicacy prevented her from asking questions. Maybe things would soon improve. She must hope so.

There was a tap at the door.

'Come in, Daniel,' she said, laying down her pen and turning from her writing desk to face him. She never ceased to be amazed at the bulk of his physical presence. Her room was spacious, its ceilings high but he filled it. She smiled and indicated the largest chair she had. 'I want to speak to you at length so please sit down. We have no need of ceremony.'

'Ma'am, you are kind but I would be more comfortable if you permit me to stand, I have been sitting in the library with the Master for most of the morning. We were doing the accounts. I am glad to be on my feet.'

She smiled at this evidence of his innate sense of what was right and proper and did not press the point. 'Ah, yes. I understand that you have taken on the duties of secretary now, as well as valet. We are fortunate to have you in our service, Daniel.' She held up a hand to forestall his protest. 'But enough of your duties. What of the girl? What can you tell me of her?'

'Her name is Sullah. She was taken in the usual way. You know Ma'am.'

'The slavers. Yes, I know. More is the pity.'

'She has had much sorrow. She has lost all her family. The girl thinks that she is ten or eleven years old. In her home village her job was to clean the hut and to care for her two young sisters. She loves children and is happy to have been put to serve in Miss Margaret's nursery but...' He stopped.

'You must tell me what you know. Is it Deliah? Does she make the girl's life difficult? Are there things going on in this house that I should be concerned about?'

Daniel knew that Anne Weston had much on her mind at present and hated the thought of causing her more distress, of adding to her burden. He hastened to reassure her.

'Mistress, you should not worry. Sullah has not complained and Deliah knows that I am watching her. It is probably just the resentment of an old servant for a younger, fresher face. Perhaps the old one thinks that you will turn her from the house and pack her off to the slave quarters once Sullah is trained in her duties.'

'I confess that there have been times, these past weeks, when I would have been glad to be rid of Deliah. There is a malevolence about her that I had not noticed before.' She sighed. 'But then, perhaps I am overwrought. Your master's health is causing me great anxiety.' She looked pleadingly at the giant before her.

Daniel tugged uneasily at his jacket and stared at the floor. 'Mistress… Ma'am… I cannot.'

'I know. You have your master's confidence. I do not ask you to break it. But…. But if there should be anything that you can tell me, anything that I can do to help him…' She sighed again and rose to her feet. 'Thank you, Daniel. Take care of Sullah and keep me informed.' It was a dismissal. He turned reluctantly and left her.

Trudging up the broad sweep of the staircase towards his master's room the slave's preoccupation was absolute. The mistress was right when she spoke of a disquieting atmosphere. A whiff of fear pervaded the whole estate and it had begun with the shipwreck. The field slaves were unsettled. They worked the same hours, completed the same tasks but all was done with a surly countenance and a shifty eye. Daniel, whenever he went near their quarters, was aware of mutterings; sometimes they were curses, sometimes spells to ward off evil.

Inside the house things were even worse. In the kitchen, slaves sidled round the huge table avoiding each other's eye. There were no shuffling dances in the wash-house, no clapping and singing in the dairy. They whispered in corners behind their hands, the talk stopping abruptly whenever Daniel appeared. If Deliah was in the vicinity people suddenly found work that urgently needed doing elsewhere. The woman presided over a great empty silence and seemed to loom larger and larger with each passing day. Her presence permeated every room and the others were afraid.

Marcus had voiced his concerns to Daniel many days earlier. He had been the boy's mentor ever since that long-ago day when he had brought him, beaten half senseless, back to Westwinds. He had been the one who had told Daniel when his mother had died and later had related to him the news of the death of the tyrant who had been his father. He had remained Daniel's only friend amongst the slaves. Marcus, who was now close to forty years of age, had been bought off a slave-ship by the previous owner of the plantation and was purchased by Jeremiah along with the rest of the property. Weston, unlike his predecessor, had recognised the man's qualities and had taken him from the fields, trained him as a groom and given him his own quarters above the stables. Marcus' den had soon become Daniel's place of refuge. He spent much of his time there on Sundays and it was late on one of those evenings that Marcus had spoken of his worries.

'There is trouble brewing, young Daniel. Yo' knows it.'

Daniel nodded. 'Yes, Marcus, I do. It is Sullah. Things have not been right since she came. The master has been sick in his mind ever since that day on the beach. He may have taken a fever, I do not know. He has a fearful lethargy, yet when he lays down his head to sleep he cannot rest.' Daniel was silent.

'It ain't a fever an' it ain't Sullah. An' yo' knows that as well as I. It is Deliah. She be at the bottom of all o' this. She has wished bad magic on Massa, aye an' on Missus if I sees right. Watch them, Daniel, watch them both an' them children an' Sullah too. Watch them.' It was a long speech from the usually taciturn man.

Daniel had indeed watched. Marcus' observations had strengthened his own fears. He too had heard that Deliah was skilled in the black arts and acknowledged the power that this gave her in the household. Sullah bore the brunt of the other slaves' terror; she was the scapegoat. In the main part of the house, nothing really unpleasant could happen. Massa, Missus, or even young Massa Timothy might see. Below stairs, or in the cavernous exile of the attic bed-rooms, things were very different. Sullah's palliasse was frequently soaked in urine, her few clothes were torn, creatures were put in amongst her garments or in her blanket. Her hair was tugged and her arms pinched. She endured it all without complaint, spending as much time as she could in the nursery in sight of the children or tagging along behind either Daniel or Marcus. She regarded both of them as her protectors and gave them a dog-like devotion. Daniel sighed. So many problems. He worried about Sullah, he worried about Deliah but most of all he worried about Jeremiah Weston.

Reaching the top of the stairs, Daniel was brought up sharply. He almost walked into Deliah who was standing silently in the deep shadow. Only the woman's eyes moved. She might have been carved from stone. She stared at Daniel and he felt the hairs on his neck begin to lift. There was a crazed hatred mixed with a wild triumph in her gaze and in that moment he was terrified. He forced his eyes away, breaking the spell. He pushed her out of the way and ran towards his master's room. On the threshold he jerked to a standstill, grasping the door-frame to support himself. The Master was sprawled in his chair, his eyes fearful, his mouth gaping, both hands clutching frantically at the neck of his shirt. Daniel sank to his knees. He did not go in. There was nothing that he could do. The man was dead.

CHAPTER THREE

THE CARIBBEAN
AUGUST 1791

Anne Weston watched as the coast of Jamaica melted into the distance its features blurred by the miles and by the spray hissing from beneath the bows of the ship. Overhead, the wind snapped the great sails into action, filling them and driving the vessel onward, away from the safety of the land and into the vast expanse of the risk-filled future. The passage to England was often dangerous but the weather was set fair and, God willing, in a few weeks they would sight the English coast.

The past months had been fraught with difficulties, and Anne knew that had it not been for her children she would have given herself completely to the ravages of grief. Because of them, such self-indulgence was denied her. There was much to be done. In those first bleak days, arrangements for Jeremiah's burial had occupied her thoughts. People had consulted her as to her wishes and she had given her instructions, moving from place to place like a manipulated puppet and making the appropriate responses to offered condolences in a state of mindless unreality. She had followed the rites of passage for the bereaved with an innate dignity and had emerged with her emotions frozen but her sanity intact.

There were many momentous decisions to be made.

Should she leave or stay? Was it best to sell the estate or arrange management of it? Ought she to go to England and start afresh somewhere new? The problems had chased round and round her muddled head. A woman who had been cherished and protected all her life, she suddenly found herself with total responsibility for close on a hundred souls. It was a daunting prospect but the thoughts of her children's future, a future that only she could now provide, spurred her on.

She had been given assistance. The Governor, his Lady, a couple of the aides, some of the members of the House of Assembly, Jeremiah's Kingston attorney and owners of neighbouring estates had all offered help and advice but the final choice had to be hers. It was hard but she had discovered that once the initial decision to leave the island had been made, other steps followed naturally. She soon realised that she did not wish to sell the plantation. It had been Jeremiah's life's work and his own personal triumph. They had spent virtually all their married life here. On a more prosaic level, it made good business sense to retain the property; it was flourishing. Cane was selling well, exports of sugar were up, recent experiments with coffee were providing interesting results and profits had increased year on year. It was also her young son's heritage. Yet despite her reasons for wishing to keep the property, Anne had no desire to stay on at Westwinds. Without Jeremiah the house was empty, her life here was meaningless. She needed to be with her own kind.

With the help of Ian Macneil, one of the Governor's aides, she had found a manager for the estate and had arranged to take ship for England. She would return to her family in Liverpool. Her brother, Matthew Broadwood, whose wife had passed away, had written urging her to make her home with him and his daughter, Elizabeth. Anne had never been particularly close to her brother, who was twenty years older than herself, but she confessed to a feeling of relief at the thought of the protective mantle of Matthew's secure, comfortable existence descending on her and her children. She would look forward to meeting her niece again. Eliza had been a child of about twelve when Anne had married and she remembered a leggy, impetuous, emotional miss. The girl was motherless now and had no woman to guide her. Anne was sure that they could become good friends. It would be fascinating to see how Eliza had grown up and Anne could help her brother by chaperoning his daughter. They would all benefit.

Anne Weston knew that she was a different woman from the one who had left England six years earlier, bored with the tedium of the prescribed social round, the predictability of business and the trivia of a young lady's life. She had wanted a change, excitement, a new world, a challenge. Well, she had had all those and now wanted nothing more than a tranquil, ordered life in familiar surroundings.

Some of the Westwinds household were to accompany her. She needed a nursemaid for Margaret, a companion and tutor for Timothy and a manservant to see to her luggage and the fetching and carrying that she would need. She also wanted protection for herself and her children on their long journey home. There was no possible way that Anne could contemplate leaving Daniel behind. In the days following Jeremiah's death he had been within call day and night. He had supported her in so many ways, just as she knew he had supported her husband in his last weeks, those weeks when Anne felt that she herself had failed him. She had been surprised to discover the extent of Daniel's knowledge of estate matters and to realise how closely Jeremiah had involved him in business issues. At one stage she had considered appointing him as overseer but had quickly decided that her own and Timothy's need of the man's unswerving devotion and quiet, massive strength, outweighed all other considerations.

Anne had sent for Daniel early one morning as she sat alone in the library. She had set out her proposition briskly, without preamble.

'Daniel, the children and I are going home to England. My brother has offered me a home and I have accepted. He has a house in Liverpool and an estate in the country. It will be wonderful for the children. The plantation is not to be sold. It will be managed. Our... my... people will go on as before, except that Deliah will revert to housekeeper in my absence.' He had looked at the floor, waiting. She continued. 'I find that I cannot contemplate the journey ahead of us without some support. I want you to come with us as tutor to my son and as my secretary.'

To her consternation, Daniel continued to stare at the floor. Then he raised his head. His eyes were damp.

'Ma'am... Ma'am... I... Oh, yes. Yes! Yes!' He beamed through his inarticulate efforts to speak. 'You cannot know how I have dreaded the thought that you would go and that I would have to serve a new master. To be allowed to continue with you and young Master Timothy... It is what I hoped for.' He stood up, towering over her. 'You will never regret it Ma'am.' The decision was made.

Other discussions took place, gaining momentum with every week that passed. Ian Macneil, from the Governor's Residence, was a great help. He introduced the new manager to the workings of the estate and helped her to dispose of those of Jeremiah's effects that Anne did not wish to keep for her son. Ian and his wife Jane were returning home themselves as their tour of duty was finished. He had suggested that Anne book passage on the same ship as them so that she would have companionship on the long voyage. Things were progressing well. Anne had spoken to Daniel about the possibility of Sullah making the trip with them. At first he had been unsure of the wisdom of such a strategy as the girl was very young; however, he knew that the mistress needed someone to care for the children. Sullah was quick, hard-working and would be a familiar face for Margaret in a strange environment. The slave's English had improved beyond recognition and she had quickly assimilated her duties as nursemaid. She would undoubtedly be an asset. When Anne proposed that Marcus too should be included, Daniel had been overjoyed. The days leading up to their embarkation had flown by in a whirl of packing, travel arrangements and nostalgic remembrances. Now they were finally on their way.

Anne drew a shawl about her shoulders and looked around for Daniel. She found him standing by the rail, close to the ship's stern, his face brooding and pre-occupied. As his mistress approached, Daniel turned and inclined his head.

'Yes Ma'am?' he said. Anne hesitated. She was un-comfortable without fully understanding why it should be so. Away from the plantation, the familiar mistress and slave relationship was changed. In the early days of her marriage, she had found the concept of slavery difficult to come to terms with and had never totally accepted it. Now, as the distance lengthened between the island and them-selves, the notion of one person owning another, the 'chattel' culture, seemed unreal. It was inappropriate and she was unsure how to behave.

Daniel waited in silence, watching her face. Anne took refuge in the familiar. There would be time to come to terms with a different social order. Liverpool was many weeks away and they would all get used to new ways eventually.

'I wondered, Daniel, if you had seen Marcus? There are trunks to be taken to our cabin. Sullah cannot find him and we should like to put things to rights.'

'I have not seen him, Ma'am, but I will bring the bags

down myself.'

'That is not what I meant. I did not intend…' But Daniel had already gone to the pile of luggage, hoisted two of the trunks on to his shoulders and disappeared down the steps into the cabin.

In the quarters allocated to the Westons, Timothy was ensconced in his tiny cot. The excitement had exhausted the boy and the unaccustomed motion of the ship had sent both him and his sister to sleep. Margaret was curled up in the bunk that she would share with Sullah and the nurse-maid put one finger to her lips as Daniel blundered into the cramped cabin. The ceiling was low and Sullah stifled the urge to giggle as she signalled him to leave the trunks on the floor and follow her into the passageway outside the door. She quickly became serious, the light in her eyes quenched as she looked around in the gloom.

She shivered, contemplating some private hell. 'I know where Marcus has gone but I could not tell nobody. Yo' must go to him, Daniel. Go now while Missus is at her dinner. Yo' needs to bring him out. He's down in the hold. His head's sure full o' that middle-passage. I knows. I been there too. We never thought ever to be on a ship again. His memories are bad, real bad.' She turned without another word and went into the cabin, shutting the door gently behind her.

Daniel felt his way amongst the barrels and boxes in the airless blackness of the hold.

'Marcus,' he hissed. 'Marcus, where are you?' There was a scuffling sound to his right. As his eyes became accustomed to the darkness, he could distinguish the out-line of sections of cargo firmly lashed in place. Down here, timbers creaked and rats scuttled across the floor; the elusive scent of spices lingered in the air. The sound came again to his right and, turning his head, he saw a shape collapse into itself. Moving lightly for such a big man, Daniel crossed the space between them and groped until he

46

felt the rough cloth of his friend's jacket beneath his hands. He placed an arm about the shaking shoulders, and drew the dark head down to his chest. Neither man spoke.

Daniel knew something of his friend's past, not from Marcus but from snatches of conversations overheard in the house, in the fields and in the Kingston markets. In the early days of his captivity, just off the ship, Marcus had been a rebel and had taken his share of floggings. His reputation as a man who refused to submit to the yoke of slavery had been forged in the horrors of the middle-passage. It had been earned the hard way.

Marcus had been taken from his village when he was about seventeen years of age. He had attempted to escape on the great trek from the interior to the coast but was captured and beaten senseless. On board the ship he had tried to starve himself, preferring death to a lifetime of slavery. He had been strapped to the windlass and the skin of his back flayed with the whip. He had still refused to eat and others, taking courage from his stand, had tried to do the same. A young girl was taken and tied to the mast. She was flogged in front of them all. There were no more protests. Throughout the rest of that tortuous journey, Marcus had tried to stay alive. He had survived and was bought by a plantation owner.

It was three years later that a white sailor from one of the slave-ships was found floating in the dock his head smashed like an egg-shell. It was assumed that he had fallen in, cracking his skull, after a drunken night of debauchery. Few enquiries were made, the ship was due to sail and one crew man more or less was immaterial. The vessel was that which had brought Marcus to Jamaica. The dead sailor was the one who had wielded the whip on the girl. Marcus was known to have left the slave quarters on his plantation and to have been on the quay that night. He was never heard to comment on the incident but the stories about him persisted. He was revered by the other slaves and his wiry strength and phenomenal endurance became a legend on the island.

Daniel remembered and waited. Eventually the sobs ceased and the muffled voice spoke its nightmare.

'I had put it all behind me. Them nights when I waked up screamin', they was long gone. When Massa found me work in his stables an' I was free o' them chains, free o' the lash, I was content. I knows I was. I had shelter, I had food in my belly, I even had money from selling them things what I growed and took to market. The old days, they was all gone. The scars inside, they was all faded like the scars on my back. But when I set foot on this here ship, well, I starts to shake an' can't stop myself. Me. The one them all looks up to. I come down here an' cried like a child. It was not gone away, Daniel. It be still here an' it does chew up my innards.' There was no answer. There could be no easy words to erase the memories, to assuage the hurt, to heal the grief. They were content to sit silently, only their presence giving each other comfort.

Time moved on. Eventually Daniel, leaving the sediment of the past to settle into its own murky depths, began to speak of the future.

'I was once told, by Master Weston, that there are many in England who do not agree with slavery. There have been questions asked in their Government house. There is even a movement set up that calls for ... abolition... I believe that is the word. No slaves at all. Think of that, Marcus. Is it not good to be going to a country where people do not believe in the shackles, or the lash, or the collar? This passage will come to an end and when it does the past will be left behind us.' In the darkness, Daniel felt rather than saw the slow shake of his friend's head.

'Yo' can leave behind a place, yo' can go where you wants but yo' cannot leave yo'self behind. Yo' can't leave man's nature behind neither. There ain't never no escape from that.' Daniel sighed. He put out a hand, helped Marcus to his feet and together they clambered out of the black hole and up to the deck. The sweep of velvet sky was sprinkled with flickering stars and a warm Caribbean breeze caressed the skin. The phosphorescence of the waves glittered beneath the hull as the ship sped on. The slaves stood by the rail, faces turned into the spray and their eyes fixed on the open sea.

Daniel remained on deck long after Marcus had left, dwelling on the torment that his friend, and others like him, had been forced to endure. In comparison with their lives, his own sufferings seemed insignificant and yet in some ways his burden was greater that theirs. He had not been ripped from his home. He had not undergone the agonies of transportation. He had known no life other than that on a plantation. He had never been free. He was a slave and had always been so. Those others, they could hate and despise the white men who traded in human misery and degradation. He was the son of a white man. He hated slavery and all that it stood for but half of him had to accept the confusion that came with his lineage. A slave for a mother, a cruel slave-master for a father. Just as Marcus could not escape his memories, so he, Daniel, could not escape his blood. Jamaica or England, it did not matter.

Sullah tugged gently at his sleeve, startling Daniel and bringing welcome relief from his melancholy intro-spection.

'Them children are fast asleep an' Missus has gone to her bed. Can I stays here for a while with yo'?' she asked.

'I do not think that I am good company, Sullah, but you are welcome to remain if you wish.' She grinned at his precise, pedantic words. He would never speak like the others. He ignored her smile and continued. 'I expect that you have need of some air. Such tiny quarters are sure to be

49

stifling and you have been cooped up for hours. Besides, I am glad that you are not up here alone. It would not be wise.' He looked around, significantly, watching the quiet movements of the few crew members remaining on deck, noticing the surreptitious glances cast in their direction. He turned back to the rail and they stood in companionable silence, conscious of the hiss of the sea and the gentle slap of waves against the wooden sides.

Sullah lifted her chin and leaned back to look at Daniel. Her eyes were troubled.

'Did yo' find him? Did yo' find Marcus?'

'Yes, I did. He was down in the hold as you said. He needed to face his demons. It will be a long journey for Marcus I fear.'

'It will be a long journey for us all. Each time I sees that mast,' she waved a trembling hand at the huge pole that stretched the canvas taut above their heads. 'Every time I sees it, I thinks o' my brother. There is little in my head o' that night, little that I remembers. There is only imaginings. Men an' women screamin' in the sea. Broken planks. Water, always water. Walls of it. Great heights filled with white foam an' a moment of air an' rushing clouds, then down, down. Green then black. Not able to breathe, chokin', chokin' all the time. Fillin' my mouth. Coughin', splutterin', my chest achin' an' the rope cuttin' flesh. But all the time my brother's voice, callin', tellin' me to stretch up, pullin' me round and over him. I wanted to sleep. He never let me be. He shrieked at me over the wind. I hears him in my head. Then for a long time there wasn't no shoutin' nor nothin'. Later, I comes to. I feels sand on my legs rubbin' 'gainst the salt. Hurtin'. Voices shoutin' but not my brother's voice. Other voices. Someone holdin' me, liftin' me up, makin' words that I doesn't understand. But the sounds were kind an' the touch was surely gentle.'

At some stage in the narrative Daniel had unconsciously

taken her hand. He stared at it now in surprise. The fragile, slender, black fingers were comfortably curled and enclosed within his own massive brown paws. He looked down at her tear-stained face.

'Go on, Sullah. Go on,' he encouraged.

'There ain't much else to tell. Yo' knows more o' what followed than I does. I was took to the great house. I ain't seen nothin' like it before. I was put in the fireside chair in the kitchen an' I slept the way them that's dead do sleep. Missus came an' told that Deliah,' the girl's face shadowed and she made the sign to banish evil. 'She came an' told that woman to find me a bed in the attics with the other housemaids. It felt like we slept in the sky.' She laughed and then shrugged. 'But I soon come used to it. Yo' knows everythin' else. Missus and the Massa was kind and the little one, well, she reminds me of my sisters who was gone.' A sly look came over her face. 'The Massa was kind to me. He was a good man. And she done killed him, Daniel. Obeah! That's what it was. I knows.'

Daniel was horrified. He darted a quick glance around but no one was listening.

'Sullah. You must not say such things. It is nonsense. You do not believe in the old bad magic and ill-wishing. Such things are for the ignorant. Master's heart failed him. He had been ill for many weeks. He had worries. Many white men die suddenly in the islands. It is the way.'

The girl simply stared, her dark eyes huge and the whites, great enlarged circles of horror. 'I knows what I knows. I seen it in my village. Folks is wished ill and they fades away. They dies. They can't help it. It is Obeah.'

Daniel released her hand, gripped her shoulders and shook her, roughly. 'You stupid, foolish girl! Listen to me. You will never ever say such things again. Not to anyone. If Missus should hear you, do you think she would let you care for her children so that you could fill their heads with your nonsense? You would be sold. Do you understand? Do you?'

She spoke hypnotically. 'I understands more than yo' think. Yo' white blood denies what yo' knows is true. Yo' pretends to think like them, to feel like them, to believe what they believes. But yo' can't wipe out yo' blood. Yo' is yo' mother's son, one of us. Yo' can talk fine an' dress up, yo' can read their books an' write their words but yo' soul is black, Daniel, black as mine.' She spun on her heel and left him.

Many weeks later, the ship edged its way through the narrow channel that led into Liverpool Bay, sails flapping limply in the fickle wind. Anne Weston had been on deck since dawn. She clutched a damp cloak around her shoulders, her eyes straining through the mist for a first glimpse of home. After weeks at sea she yearned for the feel of solid ground beneath her feet and for the stability of a bed that did not lurch in the night. Most of all, she wanted the warm familiarity of childhood memories, the sights, the smells, the sounds of the town where she had been born.

She had not realised, until now, how much she had missed the kindly voices, the cheerful wit, the sense of bustle and purpose that filled the streets of Liverpool. The Welsh, the Scots, the Irish, the people of the manufacturing towns, they were all here, a teeming mass of generally good-natured humanity. All had come to Liverpool seeking a better life for themselves and for their children, and the town had taken them in with wide open arms and a carefree, casual hospitality. There was a warmth about the people here that accepted diversity, allowed for misfortune and cherished the under-dog. They were tough, hard-living, quarrelsome, but had a generosity of spirit that was unique. Anne was indeed glad to be back. She jigged about at the rail, straining this way and that, a picture of barely suppressed impatience.

Daniel and Marcus, alongside their mistress, exchanged grins. Missus was like an excited child at 'Piganniny Christmas'. It pleased them to see her so happy. The voyage had been tedious once the initial novelty had worn off and there had been many hours for her to brood on the loss of her husband and to worry about the future. The crew had taken a liking to Massa Timothy and the boy had spent much of his time with them, but the baby had sickened soon into the journey and Sullah and Missus had spent days on end cooped up in their quarters with the child. Tempers had frayed, particularly during three storm-tossed nights of plunging seas and howling winds. Sullah had been reduced to a quivering wreck and only the timely re-appearance of blue skies had saved her from total hysteria.

That was all behind them now, and the packing was complete. Sullah joined the others at the ship's rail, baby Margaret held to her body by a tightly wrapped shawl and Timothy attached to the nurse's wrist by a leather thong tied around his middle.

The young Massa was sulking. He blew out his cheeks and stamped his boots on the deck in a ferocious contest of wills.

'I do not want to be tied to Sully. I am not a horse, Mama, to be led on a rein. I am a big boy now. Tell her, Mama. Tell Sully. I am not a baby.'

Marcus intervened. 'Then why does yo' act like one, Massa Timothy? Sullah can't watch yo' an' hold on to little Missy as well. Now don't you go causing yo' Mama no more worry.' The boy glowered, but he stopped complaining. Anne Weston smiled. Marcus had held Timothy on his first pony back in Jamaica. He had let the child hold the reins of the carriage, sitting between his knees, high up on the box. The boy adored the slave and now he slipped a casual hand into the callused black palm and edged closer. Marcus did not look down but nodded once, a smile on his face. Timothy beamed, his anger forgotten and a sudden shaft of sunlight penetrated the grey-white veil of mist, giving them all their first, long-awaited glimpse of land.

'Oh look!' Anne exclaimed. 'Over there! It is Formby Point. I am sure of it. Oh, I do wish this mist would clear. We must be almost there. It is only a few miles to Liverpool. We shall soon be home.' Her voice choked and she turned her head away.

Daniel watched as the swirling curtain lifted. The breeze picked up and the lush vegetation of the coastline became visible, sliding past on both sides of the ship. He too was relieved that the trials of the voyage were behind them but he was worried for the future. The Mistress and her children were sure to be well received but what of himself? What of Marcus and Sullah? They had left a land where a slave culture was the social norm and an economic necessity, where their position in the scheme of things was clearly established. They were going to a place where any reminder of the existence of slaves could be unwelcome to many. People the world over preferred to ignore what they could not justify. They could be an embarrassment. He had read many of the Master's journals and knew that he was right to be concerned.

Slowly, the river closed in on either side and the greenery gave way to ship-building yards, stock-piles of timber and warehouses. A great clamour and din came to them across the water. Bells were ringing and people were shouting and waving from the shore. There was an out-pouring of excitement and joy. The crew swarmed into the rigging and threw their caps into the air, cheering loudly. Daniel felt cold and empty. He gave an involuntary shudder. He was afraid, and he did not know why.

CHAPTER FOUR

LIVERPOOL
OCTOBER 1791

Daniel covered his mouth and half closed his eyes against the clouds of dust that swirled around them as the cart on which he sat bumped and jerked down the rutted lanes in the wake of the Broadwood carriage. He clung to the swaying seat, his teeth rattling with each jolt of the wheels. He risked a quick glance behind him where Marcus, sitting on the floor with his legs splayed, was grimly trying to remain upright whilst attempting to keep Mrs Weston's bouncing trunks within the confines of the cart. On another occasion, Daniel might have seen the humour in the situation but in this instance, he was so enraged that he could think of nothing but the need to hold on to his precarious self-control. He clamped his jaws together until they ached, drew a deep breath and tried to relax the rigid muscles of his shoulders. He was conscious, as he had been ever since they had left the docks, of the swift, side-long glances from the carter. The man kept his head to the front but was aware of every movement made by his passengers. This breakneck drive was a deliberate attempt at provocation and Daniel was determined that he would not rise to the bait.

Things had begun to go wrong the moment they stepped ashore. Anne Weston was delighted to see her brother waiting on the quay and had thrown herself into his arms, laughing and crying at the same time. Matthew Broadwood had patted her on the back, bestowed a cool kiss on her cheek, drawn her hand through the crook of his elbow and escorted her to the waiting carriage.

'There is always business to attend to when a ship docks, my dear. I am sure that you understand. Elizabeth is beside herself with anticipation; she can barely contain her impatience and longs to see you. I shall send you to Fernleigh Hall and we shall talk tomorrow. There is much to discuss.' He halted at a dark green carriage and nodded to the groom who was holding open the door.

Anne was shocked. 'But, brother, could I not wait at the town house for you? We spent our childhood years there before Fernleigh was built and I should be happy to see it again. We could partake of refreshment then travel to the Hall together. Could we not?'

Broadwood flushed a deep, unbecoming red. He looked down at his boots. 'I have made my arrangements, and I should be glad if you would accommodate my wishes. All is in readiness at Fernleigh Hall. It would not do to keep everyone waiting.' Anne bit her lips in dismay but good breeding prevented her from making any further protest.

She climbed into the empty carriage and the two children were lifted in after her. Sullah stood by the step, unsure as to where she should go. She looked questioningly at the groom but his face remained blank. Anne Weston was quick to sense the tension and leaned towards the girl, her clear voice carrying to them all.

'Get in, Sullah, please. If you sit here, across from me, I can hand Margaret over to you. I declare, the child is almost asleep already.' She lifted her chin and addressed the groom, who was still holding the door open. 'Kindly assist my maid and then perhaps we can leave. The horses appear to be rather restive.' She sat back in her seat, a slight frown on her face.

The situation had been observed with interest by Daniel, who was gratified by the way the Mistress had intervened on Sullah's behalf. He looked across at Marcus with a wry smile on his face. It had not taken long for his fears to be realised, and their own experiences which followed only served to increase his apprehension. The carter, a surly individual who stank of sweat and stale ale had stood to one side smirking as Marcus and Daniel struggled to lift Mrs Weston's belongings into the cart. He made no offer of help and insultingly moved right to the end of the seat when Daniel jumped up beside him. He had jerked a thumb at Marcus, indicating that he should clamber over the tailboard and sit on the floor and then whipped up the horses while the slave was still getting himself on board. Marcus had fallen heavily and Daniel needed to lean back with a helping hand before his friend could wedge himself firmly between the trunks. Now, the mean-spirited little man was clearly enjoying watching the dust cloud cover Daniel's jacket and breeches and settle in the ruffled neck of his shirt and the tight curls of his hair.

In the front carriage, Anne Weston tried to make sense of the jumbled impressions that had formed in her mind since she had left the ship. She began with her brother. When Anne left England Matthew had cut a fine figure of a man. Never the dandy, his dress was always sober but was exquisitely tailored in subtle shades of the finest cloth. He had presented an unmistakable impression of long-standing wealth and total reliability. His somewhat dour and pompous manner had often afforded her secret amusement but, even as a girl, she recognised that it was advantageous for a merchant and financier to display such obvious tendencies of stolid dependability.

Now, things had changed. Matthew was still an austere, cold-hearted individual but the confident arrogance and unquestioned superiority had gone. The differences were subtle but they were there. His hair was slightly unkempt and his clothing less than immaculate; his florid face smacked of a degenerate lifestyle. Matthew's bloodshot eyes had refused to meet her own and his response to her request to be allowed to wait for him at the town house was, to say the least, evasive. Anne had always been able to read her brother and, even with the passing years, she had not lost the ability to see behind his public façade. What she found worried her considerably. There was no doubt in her mind that Matthew was a frightened man and that he was drinking heavily.

She had so looked forward to returning home but she was beginning to have doubts about the wisdom of her decision. Six years was a long time and so much had changed. The streets of Liverpool had altered almost beyond recognition. Broad new thoroughfares and sweeping vistas were taking the place of the jumbled houses and twisted alleyways. The ram-shackled yards of the old boat-builders had been edged out by the spacious new docks along the waterfront. There was shipping in the harbour from all over the country, though not much of it seemed to have been built in the home port. She recalled Jeremiah telling her that Liverpool was becoming more focused on providing docking facilities for merchants and traders and less on building new ships. Now she could see what he meant. The town had become a great commercial centre and was evidently prosperous but she felt a sense of nostalgia for the place as it used to be. Anne straightened her shoulders and lifted her chin. This would not do. If she spent all her time looking back, she would lose sight of the way forward. She had made her decision and must accept the consequences.

They had passed familiar landmarks and could not be far from Fernleigh now. At last she saw it, and shaking the nodding Sullah awake she pointed through the window.

'Look, Sullah, there is Fernleigh Hall. Does it not look magnificent?' She blinked away a sudden tear. 'The trees are so beautiful at this time of year. I had quite forgotten the variety of the English seasons. Oh, it is good to be home.' At the sound of his mother's voice, Timothy stirred. He opened a lazy eye and yawned hugely.

'Mama, where is the sea?' he asked. 'Where did it go?' Sullah and her mistress were giggling helplessly as the swaying vehicle halted at the foot of the sweep of steps leading to the open door. Two liveried footmen descended, pace for pace, in perfect unison. Anne composed herself with difficulty and allowed the pair to assist her from the carriage. She looked up at the blank windows on the first and second floor, mentally calculating six from the end, the start of the nursery suite and schoolroom. The windows stared back at her like sightless eyes. Crows cawed around the chimney pots and the sky spun giddily. She stumbled as a gorgeous creature ran towards her.

'Aunt Weston, at last. I declare I thought you were never coming. Oh, what delight, what a joy it is to have company. I cannot possibly call you Aunt Weston. It makes you sound so old. Almost as old as Papa. I shall call you Anne. Oh, it is so good to see you again.' The breathless words tumbled over each other and Anne found herself enveloped in a cloud of perfumed muslin and a confusion of blonde curls and bonnet strings. She laughed, holding her excited niece at arm's length.

'My dear Elizabeth, as impetuous as ever I see. What a wonderful welcome.' She looked the girl up and down. 'But how lovely you are. You look just the thing. That dress, and your bonnet. You are quite the young lady. But let me introduce you to your cousins. This is Timothy.' She drew the reticent boy forward. 'Say good day, Timmy.' He shrank behind his mother's skirts and began to bite on his thumbnail. Anne laughed lightly. 'So much is strange, I fear he will need time to get used to things. But look, here is Margaret. She is the baby.' She drew Sullah, carrying the child in her arms, out of the depths of the carriage.

Elizabeth Broadwood drew in a quick breath. 'Well, Aunt Anne, I was not aware that you were bringing your own … er …servant.' Her eyes widened in surprise and she giggled nervously. 'What did Papa say when he met you on the docks? Have you brought any more?'

Anne spoke more loudly than she intended. 'Three of my slaves have accompanied me and your father did not appear to be in any way disconcerted.'

Eliza's eyes sparkled in mischief and she put up her hand to conceal a smile. 'Well, we shall see. It will make for an interesting time, that is certain. But come, let us go in.'

Accompanying her chattering niece into the house, Anne unobtrusively signalled for Sullah to follow her. The hall was dim after the brilliant clarity of the light outside and seemed more gloomy, less welcoming, than she remembered. A well-corseted, black-clad woman glided from the recesses of the staircase. Anne turned.

'Why, Mrs Edwards, how good to see you. I was not sure that you would still be here after all this time.' Anne's voice was polite, charming even, but lacking its usual warmth.

'Thank you, Ma'am. Where else would I go?' The woman folded her hands and inclined her head but not before she had cast a swift, suspicious glance at Sullah. 'I trust that you had a pleasant journey.'

Anne stifled the urge to snort. Pleasant journey indeed! The woman made it sound as though they had taken a carriage from Chester. What a dismissive way to describe their epic voyage. She gave a strained smile.

'It was trying at times and we are weary. Perhaps you

would show us to our rooms?'

'Of course, Ma'am. The children and your… your…'

'My children's nurse. This is Sullah, my children's nurse.'

'Yes. Well, I thought that the children and their… their servant could occupy the old nursery suite. It is all in readiness. I have put you, Ma'am, in the main guest-chamber. The room you had before your marriage is rather small for your needs now.'

'I am sure that we shall manage very well. Thank you, Mrs Edwards.' Anne smiled at Sullah. 'My brother's housekeeper will conduct you and the children upstairs. I shall go with Miss Elizabeth to my own room and shall come up to the nursery presently.' Giving Mrs Edwards no option but to follow her orders, Anne nodded coolly, lifted her skirts and began to climb the stairs. Lips twisting and eyes downcast, Eliza followed her Aunt past the affronted housekeeper.

In the privacy of the guest-room Eliza leaned with her back against the door, a smile on her face. Anne flung her bonnet on to the counterpane of the bed and began to pace up and down, skirts swishing like the tail of an angry cat.

'That odious woman has definitely not improved with the keeping,' she muttered. 'She was always a sanctimonious, disapproving individual. She could have been a Puritan except that they have charity in their hearts. Did you see the way she looked at Sullah? It was as though I had carried in a piece of dirt on my shoe.' She sank into a chair suddenly unutterable weary. She felt tears prickling at the back of her eyes and shook her head sadly. 'What have I done? What have I done?'

Eliza rushed across the room all levity banished, and threw herself on her knees beside her Aunt's chair. The girl's eyes too swam with sympathetic tears.

'Oh, Anne,' she wailed. 'How positively dreadful. It is

just too much. The loss of poor, dear Uncle Weston, having to leave your beautiful home, that terrible voyage and now this. It will be all right in time. I am sure that it will.' She dabbed ineffectively at her eyes with a scrap of lace-edged frivolity, her volatile emotions once more in evidence. 'It is so sad for you, that you should have to return to live under your brother's roof. I do not know how you can bear it, indeed I do not. I am sure that I should be quite prostrate with grief.'

Anne patted comfortingly at the hand clutching the damp square of cambric. 'I had no choice, my dear, and my lot is not so bad when you consider the lives of others.'

The comment provoked a fresh outburst of tears, although they were now rather more judiciously shed. Eliza could calculate to a nicety exactly when her weeping ceased to be attractive and became disfiguring.

'Aunt, you are so very brave. I do declare that I have never seen such courage. I know how you suffer, but you bear it with such noble fortitude. You think always of others. You think of your children, those poor, dear, father-less babies. Oh, it is too sad.'

Anne jumped briskly to her feet. She had had enough. Such excess of feeling was exhausting. Eliza was even more impassioned than she recalled. The girl would have to be taken in hand. She undoubtedly had a warm heart but needed to learn to curb her talent for exaggerated sensibility. Such wanton displays of unbridled emotion could indeed have serious consequences.

'Let us go to the nursery, Elizabeth.' She gave a wry smile. 'The fatherless babes will surely be hungry and will be wanting their supper!'

Up on the third-floor, Sullah was exploring her domain in a desultory fashion. There was a schoolroom where Daniel could tutor Massa Timothy, a bedroom containing a cot and two single beds and the nursery itself, where the children were firmly encamped on the rug in front of the fire gleefully examining some old toys taken from a dilapidated chest in the corner. The rooms were warm and airy, the furnishings adequate and the barred windows afforded magnificent views over the gardens and surrounding countryside. It was all much more imposing than the home that they had left but Sullah was unhappy.

In Jamaica, the girl had become accustomed to the hostility of Deliah and the other slaves. As a newcomer she accepted that there would be jealousy; nevertheless there had been a comforting security in knowing that she had her place. She understood exactly where she fitted into the household hierarchy. Here, everyone she had come across since leaving the ship, had in some way made her feel unwelcome. More than unwelcome, she felt resented. In addition to coping with their barely concealed hostility, Sullah herself was struggling with the uncertainty of her own position. How would she ever fit in here? What was her place? She was a nursemaid yet not a servant; she was less than a servant. Having already taken note of the conduct of others in the house, Sullah was aware that the indulgent attitude of the Mistress towards her would have to change. She did not doubt that Mrs Weston would always treat her kindly but there would need to be a much more formal relationship now. Everything was different. The girl sighed and went across to the rug to remove a painted soldier from the baby's mouth.

The door was flung open and Eliza Broadwood swept into the room, descended on the children and gathered them into a suffocating embrace. Timothy stood still within the circle of her arms, eyeing her warily. Margaret pulled away and began to wail, holding out her podgy hands to Sullah. The nurse took a step towards her charge and then stopped. She knew instinctively that it would not do to antagonise the young miss. Anne Weston took in the scene with her usual perception and moved forward herself to take the sobbing child from her niece.

'I'm afraid that it has all been too much for the children, Eliza. They are exhausted and quite fractious. They need supper and their beds I think.' She turned to Sullah. 'Has their baggage been brought up yet? I do hope that…' There was a commotion in the passageway outside and Marcus appeared, struggling to fit a huge trunk through the door.

'Ah,' remarked Anne, with a satisfied smile. 'That was indeed well-timed, Marcus.' She broke off, taking in the slave's grim expression and the fluttering, liveried house-boy hovering at his back. She closed her eyes momentarily. What now?

Marcus deposited the trunk with a bang, planted his feet firmly apart and waited for his mistress to speak but it was Eliza who broke the silence. She set Timothy to one side, got to her feet, smoothed down her rumpled skirts and addressed her father's servant.

'There is no difficulty here I trust, John? Mrs Weston's people will form part of this household and will be accepted below stairs by everyone. Do I make myself clear?' The boy nodded, his mouth sullen, his eyes hostile. Eliza continued, icily. 'You will make my orders known to the others. There is to be no bickering amongst the servants. Is that understood? Tell Melchet and Mrs Edwards that I have said so.'

John lifted his head, his face expressionless. 'Yes, Miss.' He flashed one quick glare at Marcus, sniffed and left the room, shutting the door with infinite gentleness.

The dismay in the nursery was evident. Though well-intentioned, Eliza had intervened in the worst way possible. She had given orders to one of the lowest servants to be passed on, by him, to the housekeeper and butler. That in itself was enough to start a riot. She had compounded her error by clearly siding with the newcomers against the established staff. It was the surest way to build a climate of resentment and distrust. Marcus stood with his eyes raised eloquently to the ceiling. Sullah's shoulders were slumped in dejection and Anne wrung her hands as she shook her head slowly.

Eliza was triumphant. She bestowed a bright smile on them all. 'Well, that should settle things,' she announced.

Her Aunt regarded her in disbelief. 'You cannot conceivably think that what you have just done has improved the situation? My dear, I know that you meant well and do thank you for your efforts to protect my servants, but if they are ever to be accepted here then it must be done slowly. You cannot impose an alien people on an already settled group and expect them to fit in at once. Marcus, Sullah and Daniel know that it will take time for them to be part of the household.' She sighed and walked to the window, taking in the familiar, heart-tugging view. 'That boy will be down in the servants' hall at this very moment, stirring up anger and bitterness. Mrs Edwards will be awash with self-righteous indignation. And you say that Melchet is still here?' She received a brief nod from Eliza. 'My brother's butler belongs in the ark, unless he is much changed. If a salt-cellar is moved two inches from its usual place he has a crisis of nerves. It was going to be difficult enough to persuade him to cope with the idea of sharing a roof with three negro slaves. Now it will be impossible. He will be waiting on the steps when Matthew gets home to be certain of being heard first.' She turned to face them all. 'I fear that we have a rough ride ahead of us.' She sighed again. 'Marcus, help Sullah in here for now. I shall speak to Mrs Edwards about sending up some food. It would be best, I think, if you were to avoid the servants' hall for the present. Come niece.' Together, the two women left the nursery, a disconsolate Eliza again reaching for her handkerchief.

Back in the comparative peace of her own room, Anne Weston pressed her hands to her throbbing temples as she struggled to compose herself. Anger would solve nothing. Time would provide a solution and until it did, the least said or done, the better. It was a lesson that Eliza most certainly needed to learn. Anne's mind had raced as they descended to the second-floor chamber. She had rung for a maid and asked the girl to take two trays up to the nursery, one for the children and the other for her own servants. They would all take their meals in the schoolroom for the moment. Anne was certain that Mrs Edwards and Melchet would make a complaint to Matthew, but she had no doubt that, at least until his return, her instructions would be carried out.

Eliza had been subdued since they left the nursery. She was, in some ways, disappointed in her Aunt; she had expected her to come to the defence of her slaves with rather more vigour. Eliza did not doubt of the strength of her own feelings on behalf of her black brothers and sisters. She had recently taken up the abolitionist cause and, in the way of many converts, was most extreme in her views. Her outspoken support for the slaves was a constant source of disagreement between her father and herself; battle lines were drawn, and they were on opposing sides. It was the same in many houses in Liverpool. Several of Eliza's acquaintances had taken up the call to abolish slavery; the revolutionary notion of freeing their fellow man from his shackles appealed to their romantic souls. Their commitment to this new and fashionable crusade gave a purpose to social calls and provided a ready topic of rather risqué conversation at table or in the drawing room. The young people, living in their fine houses, spoke eloquently of equality whilst their weary servants plied them with food and drink. Similarly, they saw nothing ironic in the expectation that footmen and maids would face a wall if they were careless enough to be seen on a corridor by their betters.

Now, watching Anne as she gave instructions for the nursery food, Eliza felt rather misunderstood. She was petulant. She had been trying to help, and to show her support for the slaves. It was unfortunate that her efforts met with so little appreciation. She would leave her Aunt to rest and would go and read some of Mr Roscoe's pamphlets. As she flounced to her feet there was a tap on the door and the largest man that Eliza had ever seen entered the room.

He addressed Anne Weston. 'Ma'am, I have brought your baggage.' He swung a massive trunk easily from his shoulder to the floor. Eliza took in his gleaming bronze skin, his neat dress and his quiet elegance of manner. She was staring.

Anne coughed, her eyes on her niece's face. 'Thank you, Daniel. I have arranged for food to be taken upstairs in the schoolroom. Marcus is already there with Sullah. I am sure that you can find your way. You may leave the trunk here, I will see to it shortly.'

She lowered her head, aware of the momentary flash of hurt in Daniel's eyes as her unexpected coolness registered. He left without speaking, inclining his head first to Anne and then slowly and deliberately to Eliza. The girl blushed furiously and was barely able to resist the urge to respond with a bob and curtsey of her own. What had come over her? The man was a slave. She stared at the floor whilst the watching Anne groaned inwardly.

Upstairs, Daniel ate his meal in silence, a bemused expression on his face. Sullah, thinking that like Marcus and herself he was worrying about their new situation, had offered consoling words; they had no effect. She finally gave up and went, somewhat huffily, to put the children to bed. Marcus, with his closer knowledge of Daniel, had recognised that his friend was preoccupied rather than fearful and was content to wait until confidences were ready to be shared. He knew from past experience that Daniel's long-held need for privacy could make a clam appear forthcoming. He would speak when he was ready and not before. Marcus took out a piece of wood and his knife and, whistling between his teeth, began to whittle a boat from the shapeless block.

Daniel jumped to his feet, Marcus rising more slowly, as Anne Weston pushed open the schoolroom door. She looked tired but was exquisitely gowned in taffeta of palest mauve. Her late husband's gift of pearls was clasped about her throat and the mass of curls, dressed high on her head, revealed matching clips in her ears. She was much more elegantly attired than she had ever been in Jamaica and there was a new reserve in her manner as she looked from one man to the other.

'Marcus, I do believe that Sullah has emptied the trunk and would like to have it removed to the attics. One of the house-boys is waiting outside and will show you where to go.' Daniel moved to accompany his friend but the Mistress held up her hand. 'A moment, Daniel. I should like a word.' The door thudded shut and Anne took a chair at the old table, her finger idly traced the outline of letters that had been scratched in the wood many years earlier. She motioned for Daniel to sit opposite her. 'Not too much ceremony when we are alone, Daniel.' Her voice was troubled and she began an unaccustomed fidgetting with her rings, her reticule and the buttons on the front of her dress. Finally, she appeared to make up her mind, placed both hands on the table in front of her and looked him in the eye. 'It will not do. It will not do at all.' She held up her hand once more, eager to forestall any protest. 'We have known and trusted each other too long for pretence. You know why I wanted to see you. My niece is a very beautiful girl. She is a gorgeously wrapped package of excessive emotion and youthful indiscretion. She will get herself into trouble before long and I do not intend that you should be involved. Years ago I remember her as a very silly child; now she is a very silly young woman who is constantly seeking excitement. Her head is full of romantic nonsense. She spends her days reading poetry and writing sentimental letters; she attends abolitionist meetings and fancies herself as a liberal thinker. The girl imagines that she is free to do as she wishes. She is not yet old enough to realise that by her situation in society she is as much a captive as those she would seek to liberate.'

Anne gnawed at her lip. She pushed back her chair and, as always when worried, began to pace up and down, becoming ever more agitated.

'It was evident that the chit was quite bowled over by the first sight of you. You are indeed a splendid figure, Daniel.' There was no flicker of response to the attempted pleasantry. Anne flushed and pressed on. 'It is, I am certain, self-evident that this ... this... situation must not be permitted to develop.' She looked up again. Still no response. 'I know that I have no need to advise you that it would be most improper for you to be in any way flattered by Miss Broadwood's attempts to be civil. She is not aware, being young and inexperienced and not having a mother to guide her, that her friendliness could be mis-construed and that her anxiety not to set you apart from other people because of the colour of your skin could, by those unused to her ways, be thought to be encouraging.'

Daniel pushed back his chair and drew himself stiffly upright as he looked down at his mistress. 'Mrs Weston, Ma'am, I regret that this matter should have given you any cause for disquiet. There is no situation. The young mistress was startled by my unexpected appearance, that is all. She was unsure of how to respond. Anything else that you may have imagined is quite without foundation. I could not fail to be aware of your niece's beauty, no man could, but it signifies nothing. That picture on the wall has beauty also, but I would never suppose that I could aspire to possess it. I know my place, Ma'am, and I would never, ever, give you cause to worry.'

As always, Anne was struck by the man's immense dignity and she faced him gratefully. 'Well, that is a great relief. I am glad that we have spoken of it. Now I must go and face the lion in his den or, if you prefer, Melchet in the dining-room.' She laughed again and Daniel gave a wooden smile. 'Tomorrow, I shall consult with my brother and we will begin to establish a new order at Fernleigh Hall.'

Daniel watched her leave and resumed his seat at the table. 'I know my place,' he muttered. 'I only wish it were so. What place do I have? Where do I belong?'

Although in some ways he was offended by the Mistress feeling that there was a need to speak of the issue, a secret part of him was flattered that he should have had such an effect on a beautiful young lady of quality that it had given rise to concern. Daniel was honest enough to acknowledge to himself that he had indeed been attracted by Elizabeth Broadwood. He was certainly no monk and had taken several of the Master's house-maids to his bed during the years on the plantation. When a pretty woman indicated that she found him attractive, Daniel had always been quick to recognise the fact and his response could be gratifyingly instantaneous and sometimes alarmingly physical.

This situation was, he knew, quite different. Yes, he admired Miss Eliza's beauty. He would not deny it. She was like a piece of delicate porcelain, a fragile work of art but she was to be set upon a pedestal and adored, not imagined as an outlet for raw, animal passion. He would be content to worship from afar, in the way of those

70

mediaeval knights and troubadors in Jeremiah Weston's book of poetry. He could devote himself to her service. Such a cerebral reaction to physical charms was a new experience for Daniel and was one that delighted him. As well as the lady's loveliness, she clearly had a caring and gentle disposition. This was demonstrated by the way she had leapt to the slaves' defence in the nursery. The incident, related to him by Marcus, had added to his favourable image of her. He felt it was a pity that his usually perceptive mistress was failing to acknowledge her niece's fine qualities. Eliza's was the first act of kindness that had been shown them since their arrival. Impetuous and ultimately unhelpful it may have been, but it was well-meant and Daniel's affection-starved soul responded with gratitude.

CHAPTER FIVE

FERNLEIGH HALL
FEBRUARY 1792

As Anne Weston made her way to the nursery suite, she was quietly content. Those early months in England had been difficult for everyone but as time passed things had improved. She herself, being steeped in the locality from childhood, had quickly picked up the threads of the social life of Liverpool town and its surrounding countryside. Indeed, if truth were told, she found her status as a young widow more enjoyable than even her days as a debutante. She had none of the agonies of the social season to endure but was young enough to still enjoy its pleasures. She was not expected to catch a husband but, as a pretty woman, she could indulge in a little discreet flirtation. Homage could be accepted without obligation, and compliments acknowledged without consequence.

At times, Anne found herself feeling guilty at the satisfaction that she derived from her situation; it seemed disloyal to Jeremiah's memory. Fortunately, she was able to placate her conscience by recalling the necessity for her to attend balls, banquets and house-parties in her role as chaperone to Eliza. She could, after all, hardly ruin her niece's chances of making a good marriage by absenting herself from such conspicuous events.

Anne was aware that her niece delighted in her

company, and that she regarded her Aunt as not at all stuffy. She gladly accompanied Eliza on visits to the girl's existing circle of friends and, since her return to England, had also been able to re-open a whole set of her own socially acceptable connections, made in the years before her marriage. Eliza enjoyed the attention of her new acquaintances and Matthew was delighted. He had been released from the tedium of concerning himself with the supervision of his daughter's coming-out season and was content to leave Eliza's welfare in the competent hands of his sister. To her, he also happily relinquished the running of his household. She had gone out of her way to show consideration to the servants and this proved a great relief to them, particularly in the wake of Miss Elizabeth's unpredictable management of affairs. The establishment now ran smoothly and Anne knew that she was regarded as a Godsend. She paid more than her share of expenses and tried to increase the status of the Broadwood family in the neighbourhood by adding subtle touches of refinement that had been lacking at Fernleigh Hall. Things were going well on the whole and she was pleased.

Reaching the nursery, Anne went in and sat with Margaret on her lap as Sullah made them a pot of tea. The slave hummed happily as she worked.

'Well, Sullah, you seem to have settled here. Tell me, how are you getting on with Mr Broadwood's household?'

Sullah deliberated before answering. 'At first, Missus, they don't like us all. But then they sees that we ain't no different to them and so they let us be.' Anne smiled to herself. She was sure that Sullah, with her quick tongue and prickly nature, had not endeared herself to the others; the housemaids in particular would have bitterly resented a slave occupying a higher position than theirs. Still, things were finding their own level in the servants' hall, just as they had always done.

Sullah set out the cups importantly. This was her domain. She prattled on.

'It surely was a help when you hired that village girl to come in each day to do the housemaid's work in the nursery. Once them downstairs knowed that they did not have to clean the nursery, make up the fire, care for the children's clothes and fetch and carry trays for no black girl, why then they was much less nasty. Some of them young ones even comes up here and talks to me.'

'I am so glad, Sullah, but tell me, what of Marcus? How is he?' The slave was enjoying the unaccustomed chance to gossip with the Mistress. She rolled her eyes, eloquently.

'Why, Missus, he be like Massa Timothy with a new plaything. That there fine lady's carriage that yo' did buy, with a pair of horses to draw it, that little mare that yo' rides yo'self an' a pony for the young Massa as well,' Sullah puffed out her chest. 'That Marcus, he walks round like this all the while. He surely looks important in that smart new livery yo' did get him. Why, I even heard tell that Mrs Edwards and Mr Melchet has been boasting to the neighbours 'bout the grand new Fernleigh rig.' The girl sipped her tea contentedly. 'In the stables they knows that Marcus will work hard. He don't mind if he do all them heavy, dirty horse jobs an' that old Broadwood's groom, why, he's grey enough to be Marcus' grand-daddy. He surely don't say no to another pair of hands.'

Anne finished her tea and left the nursery. Yes, things were going well, at least for three of them; she had no idea about the fourth. He no longer confided in her.

For Daniel, things were indeed very different. Sullah's realm was the nursery suite, Marcus had the stables but Daniel had no space to call his own. He slept in a cupboard-sized room close to the nursery and took his meals with Sullah and the children. In those last months in Jamaica, when his duties had been mainly secretarial, he had become used to dining with the Westons and now he felt it demeaning to be treated on a par with Sullah. The alternative was to take his place in the servants' hall, and that he would have found unendurable. Mr Melchet's narrow-minded bigotry and Mrs Edwards' rigid propriety would have driven him to drink before a week was out.

He spent each morning in the schoolroom with Timothy, who was a bright little chap and eager to learn. Most afternoons too were devoted to the boy; they would take out the carriage to explore the countryside or examine the wildlife on the shore, but by far his favourite hours were those spent with Anne Weston in his capacity as secretary. Then, he could pretend they were still in Jamaica and that all was well in his world. Although the Mistress wrote all of her own social letters, she still needed Daniel's expertise when it came to plantation business. In the early days, Matthew Broadwood had tried to persuade his sister to turn the management of her estate over to him, a suggestion that she had gently but firmly declined. She had come to enjoy her dealings in what was essentially a man's world, and knew that with Daniel's assistance and the occasional input from her solicitor, she was capable of ensuring the continuing prosperity of her son's inheritance.

Unfortunately, these interludes did not happen with any regularity and were quite infrequent compared to what had gone before. Daniel missed the company of his Mistress and the opportunity to demonstrate his own grasp of affairs of business and finance. In the months since their arrival in Liverpool, he had often thought with nostalgia of his time at Westwinds, when he had been secure and had known his place. He watched with envy as first Marcus and then Sullah put down tentative roots in their new environment and began to flourish. He tried to be happy for them in their contentment but had, instead, become twisted and embittered.

It was, perhaps, this sense of personal failure that had made him more receptive than he ought to have been to Miss Eliza's continuing interest in him and his doings. She frequently visited the schoolroom, ostensibly to see how her cousin was progressing, a ploy that would have had more credibility had she displayed a similar concern for baby Margaret's well-being. She would wander around the room, touching things lightly, leaning over to examine Timmy's work but all the time casting fluttering glances in Daniel's direction. There could be no doubt that her behaviour was deliberately flirtatious but she saw nothing untoward in her actions and revelled in the novelty of the situation. She knew that it was beyond belief that anyone should consider that she had a serious interest in her Aunt's slave. She knew it and Daniel knew it. It was a game.

One night soon after the New Year festivities had ended Daniel had gone, as he often did, to spend the evening in Marcus' room above the stable. The night was bitterly cold and flakes of snow were just beginning to fall, drifting gently in the light from the lantern. Daniel, huddled deep in his coat, had stared in amazement at the exquisite patterns forming on his dark sleeve and vanishing as he watched. He had put out his tongue and tried to catch one, laughing like a child. He had burst through Marcus' door in great excitement.

Daniel had stopped, the laughter dying in his throat. The silent, accusatory figures of his two friends were sitting at the table, clearly waiting for him. He stared.

'Sullah?' There was a question in his voice.

'The village girl is watchin' the children, she be stayin' at the Hall tonight. We needs to speak to yo', Daniel. We is both troubled.'

Daniel looked at Marcus one eyebrow raised.

'Sullah speaks it true, Daniel. We needs to talk.'

Daniel knew what was coming, but he kept his face

expressionless and spoke pleasantly.

'This sounds very ominous. What concerns can you both have that you need to share them so urgently with me?'

Marcus shook his head his eyes saddened. 'Now don't yo' come yo' clever words with me. I'se been around too long and seed too much to be taken in with words, Daniel. Sullah here come to see me 'cause you's givin' her worries. But even without her comin' here, I has ideas. I got eyes in my head and I seen what's been goin' on. That there Miss Eliza, she come all around yo', flutterin' an' fussin' an' makin' yo' feel all important. I seen her sort before. It don't mean nothin' to her, but when I sees yo' takin' her on an' makin' back at her, bold as bold, well, I knows that no good will come of it. Trouble. That's what it is. Big trouble and yo' should surely know better.'

Anger surged through Daniel and he had to fight down the urge to beat his old friend senseless. His great fists clenched and unclenched but his face was calm, his voice nonchalant as he answered them.

'It is good of you both to show such concern for me but I need no one to meddle in my affairs. Miss Elizabeth comes to the schoolroom to see Master Timothy and that is all. Her interest does her credit.' Sullah snorted her contempt and Daniel rounded on her, his voice rising. 'You should be ashamed of your nasty thoughts, Sullah. What has the young Mistress ever done to you? You spend too much time with those gossiping housemaids. You have no right to come here carrying your vile tales to Marcus. I know that you…'

Sullah interrupted. 'No. Yo' does not know,' she hissed. 'Yo' does not know nothin'. Yo' don't see how she done look at you. Any woman knows what be in her eyes. She wants yo', Daniel. Oh, she don't want yo' in her bed, she's too much the lady for that. She wants to take yo' soul. Yo' is, by law, the slave of one woman; I sure is surprised yo' wants to be possessed by another.'

Daniel stood up trembling, the blood suffusing his bronze skin. 'You wash your filthy mouth, you slut. There is nothing, nothing wrong in Miss Elizabeth's civility to me. She is a lady. A lady, do you hear me?'

Sullah's eyes filled and she put out a hand. 'Daniel, can yo' not see? It be yo' wish to be part of a white man's world that has brought yo' this. It is makin' yo' blind. Yo' do thinks if a woman like her finds yo' good to look at, then yo' is equal to...' Daniel waited to hear no more. He turned on his heel, clattered down the rickety stair and ran away from the stable and the house, his boots leaving a weaving line of footprints in the settling snow, snow that he did not even see. His breath came in ragged gasps as he fought to put as much distance as he could between himself and the inhabitants of Fernleigh Hall.

After that night, things had never been the same. The matter was not raised again between them and they were carefully polite to each other in their dealings, but Daniel spent his evenings in solitude in his cell-like room and did not seek the company of Marcus in his warm haven over the stable. When Eliza came to the schoolroom, Daniel was careful to keep his eyes lowered and moved as far away from her as the room's dimensions would allow. Fortunately, there were parties and outings to plan and ball-gowns to have made in readiness for the approaching season and as the sport of provoking a reaction in Daniel appeared to be waning, her visits to the nursery dwindled and soon ceased completely. The weeks passed in slowly returning harmony, until one bitterly cold day in February.

Daniel was in the morning-room with Anne Weston, going over the yield figures for last year's plantation crop, when Melchet burst through the door. It was a measure of the man's anxiety that he forgot to wait to be told to enter. Anne looked up from the ledgers, surprise in her eyes.

'What is it Melchet?'

'Mrs Weston, Ma'am. It is Mr Johnson the Master's clerk. He is... he has... there is...,' the old man was babbling incoherently and indicating the hallway behind him.

Anne was scarcely paying attention. She was unusually brusque. 'Daniel, go with Melchet and see what the problem is. I must finish this task today. It has been awaiting completion for weeks. I really cannot be continually pestered by every little crisis that happens in the household.' She returned to her books as Daniel obediently followed the agitated butler into the hall.

He knew Johnson by sight, having once met the man in Heywood's Bank when he had accompanied the Mistress there. Mrs Weston had been delighted to see the elderly retainer and they had spent some time in animated conversation. She had told Daniel, afterwards, that Johnson had been their father's clerk for many years before being handed down to Matthew, and that he knew as much about the Broadwoods' financial affairs as any man alive.

'He is the only person I know who refers to my august brother as "young Master Matthew" and not just behind his back either,' she had laughed.

Mr Johnson followed a rigid code of business conduct and Anne believed that the clerk's word carried as much weight in the town as her brother's. His understanding of finance was universally admired and any of the banking houses would have been delighted to obtain his services but his loyalty had remained with the Broadwoods. He was respected by the entire business community and was known to be sound, God-fearing and totally predictable. It was this very predictability and correctness that made his sudden, dishevelled appearance at the family's private residence so unexpected. Unexpected and worrying.

Daniel quickly took in Johnson's condition and drew him gently into the library, shutting the door on the curious Melchet. The slave gave a sharp neck bow.

'Mr Johnson? Your servant, sir. Did you wish to be received by my Mistress? If so, I will have refreshment brought and conduct Mrs Weston to you.' The old man appeared grateful for Daniel's punctilious greeting, and even in his distressed state was quick to appreciate the way in which the slave had ensured that whatever needed to be said could be said in private. His eyes gleamed and he began to recover his composure. Johnson was a member of the Society of Friends, and believed firmly in the adage that all men were created equal. He recognised Daniel's abilities, and had no difficulty in dealing with the man despite his colour. In addition, Mr Johnson also had a healthy respect for the young Mrs Weston, and if that lady was prepared to give the slave her confidence then that was good enough for him.

Johnson flicked up the tails of his coat, pulled out a chair and indicated a seat across the table to Daniel.

'Mrs Weston will need to be told some of what has happened but as you will see, it would not be the thing for her to become personally involved. Her brother, Mr Broadwood has... ahem... been taken ill. No... no, nothing serious... He is indisposed and is likely to be so for some hours.' Daniel nodded his understanding and Johnson continued. 'He was brought home to the town house and there lies the problem. Ahem... My Master has, for many years had a... a... housekeeper. She resides there. It would not be right for Mrs Weston to meet Mrs Roberts. It would not be right at all. Do you understand?' Daniel nodded again. 'The Master will need to be brought home, but not in such a state as will give rise to servants' gossip. That must be avoided at all costs. It would not do for his reputation in the town to be besmirched. Normally I would not have come here. We would have simply kept him in his bed in the town house until he recovered. The difficulty is that these… ahem… episodes… are becoming more frequent and more violent. Last evening he was brawling in the street. In addition to his drinking there is an underlying malaise brought on by severe worry. His financial problems are considerable and it is these difficulties which Mrs Weston may need to address.'

As the weary clerk slumped in his seat, Daniel moved towards the door.

'I will have refreshment sent in here. You will need to partake of something before you return to town. I will acquaint the Mistress with as much of this as she needs to know for the present, and if it meets with her approval I will go to town with Mrs Weston's own carriage and groom to bring the Master home. It will be dusk by the time we get back and I will see him straight up to his bed. I will take care of him myself until he has recovered. I am certain that like you Mrs Weston would not wish for her brother to be the subject of gossip and conjecture.' Mr Johnson sighed with relief. He had been right to give this capable young man his confidence. The Master would be in good hands. He leaned back in his chair and closed his eyes.

When Daniel returned to the morning-room, Anne Weston looked up impatiently from her ledgers. She was cross and made no attempt to hide her displeasure.

'What a time you have been. What is it? Has my brother left some papers here? Is that why he has sent Johnson? Why is he …?' Her voice died as she registered the concern on Daniel's usually impassive countenance.

'I am afraid, Ma'am, that Mr Broadwood is not himself at the moment. Mr Johnson thinks that he needs to be brought home and taken care of here rather than in town. With your permission, I will take your carriage and collect him from the town house. Marcus and I can do what needs to be done. We can attend to him.'

Anne began to pace up and down. 'Not himself? Taken care of here rather than in town? What, pray, is that supposed to mean? Kindly do not speak in riddles. Is my brother ill or is he simply drunk?' The slave lowered his head. He did not need to answer. Anne stamped her foot and twitched the skirt of her dress behind her with restless hands. 'Do I appear naïve? Have I suddenly lost my sight, my sense of smell, my ability to assess what I see? Do you and Mr Johnson not think that I have known, ever since my return, that my brother has become too fond of the bottle? Dear Lord! He reeks of brandy, sometimes before noon. Can you really believe that I had not noticed? I shall come with you to bring him home.'

Daniel stared at his mistress, aghast. He shuffled his great bulk from one foot to the other, almost hopping in his discomfiture. Anne's lips twitched.

'You need not be so careful of my sensibilities, Daniel,' she said. 'I also know about Mrs Roberts. I have known for weeks. I needed to satisfy my curiosity as to why my dear brother would not allow me to visit our old house. Why he spent several nights there each week instead of coming home in the carriage. It did not require much probing beneath the surface to unearth that particular can of worms; the whole town is aware of it.' She sat down at her desk again and sighed. 'Bring Mr Johnson in here. Unfortunately I fear that there is more to this than my brother's lack of propriety, and if there are further disclosures to be made, then I would prefer to know about them now.' Daniel opened his mouth and shut it again. The Mistress never ceased to amaze him. She was a truly remarkable woman. She was right. There were things that she would need to know. He went to summon Mr Johnson.

Half an hour later the clerk had returned to town, assured that Marcus and Daniel would follow shortly to take the responsibility for Matthew Broadwood from his hands. In the morning-room, Anne Weston was a picture of dejection as she slumped in the window-seat. She watched Daniel take the front steps two at a time and set off at a run round the side of the house to find Marcus in the stables. If Mr Johnson's suppositions were correct, she would have to face a most unpleasant interview with her brother very soon. She stood up. It could have been worse. Eliza had gone to spend a few days with her mother's cousin in Chester and would not be back until the end of the week. It was fortunate indeed that the girl was not at home. Anne moved away from the window. She would go up to the nursery and spend some time with her children. Matthew could be safely left to Daniel for the present. Not for the first time, she thanked God for her slave. She could depend on him absolutely.

The coach drew to a halt in the secrecy of the long winter shadows cast by the three-storied buildings. They stretched across the cobbles of the quay-side and over the grey waters of the Mersey. As Daniel approached the Broadwood house, the door was opened by a rather blowzy female whose age could have been anywhere between thirty-five and fifty years. Her well-fitting bodice of black grosgrain emphasised her ample charms and the sweeping glance that assessed Daniel's huge form contained a hint of speculation. The look spoke of wide experience, yet when she smiled there was a warmth and openness in her expression that struck an immediate chord of empathy in the slave.

'Mr Johnson did say as 'ee would be comin'. I thank 'ee,

for Mr Broadwood do need more lookin' after than I can give him. He be worrit enough to send a body to the grave, an' 'as been these many weeks. But what be I thinkin' of, to keep 'ee standin' on the step like a …like a …' She drifted into silence.

Daniel grinned as he stepped over the threshold, his broad shoulders almost touching the sides of the narrow hall. 'You must be Mrs Roberts. It is a pleasure to meet you, Ma'am, although I would wish that the circumstances were different.' His eyes twinkled as her jaw dropped slightly. The slave's erudite precision was in stark contrast to the lady's own Devonshire speech and was clearly unexpected.

She too was quick to recognise the piquancy of the situation, but her smile quickly faded and she raised trouble-filled eyes to his face. 'Mr Johnson be upstairs with him now. 'Ee will look after him, won't 'ee? I do think as he be sick in 'is body as well as 'is mind and it be not just the drink neither.' Her voice wobbled. 'He be a good man and none shall say different.'

'Rest assured, Ma'am, no one shall know of the Master's indisposition through me. Now, if you would conduct me to his bedchamber, we shall get him back to Fernleigh Hall. Mrs Weston will know what to do. Oh, and the Mistress did ask me to thank you, on her behalf, for taking such good care of her brother's town household. Mr Broadwood could be afflicted for some time but she hopes that you will stay on here and continue with your duties.' The woman nodded her acquiescence but not before a flicker of relief had crossed her face. Daniel felt a surge of pity for her. The position of an ageing paramour was insecure at best, and must be positively perilous if sickness should threaten to remove her protector to the bosom of his family. He followed Mrs Roberts up the steep staircase and into Matthew Broadwood's room.

Nothing had prepared him for the sight that met his eyes. Almost every ornament in the room was smashed. Tables and chairs were overturned, clothing was strewn across the floor and bed-draperies hung drunkenly from their fastenings, shedding swaths of maroon velvet across the carpet. Matthew Broadwood was slumped in a low chair before the fire and Mr Johnson was on his knees, trying to force the Master's uncooperative feet into long boots. Broadwood's face was bruised, his lip cut and one eye swollen and puffy; his good eye glared balefully at his struggling clerk. A stream of abuse poured from his mouth in a vindictive tirade and, as Daniel watched, he kicked out at Johnson. Boradwood struggled to his feet, shifting his one-eyed stare to focus on the figures at the door, his mouth twisting as he recognised Daniel.

'Who the hell sent you here, you black heathen? What brings you into my house? You have no...' The effort required to concentrate, even for a few seconds, was beyond him, and he slid to the floor with his back against the chair and his legs splayed out before him. Mrs Roberts pushed Daniel and Mr Johnson out of the way and sank down beside Matthew, her black skirts billowing around them both. She cradled him in her arms, crooning like a mother comforting a sick child.

'Oh, my dear. My own dear. It is all right. They have come to take 'ee home. 'Ee are not well, my love. Daniel will take care of 'ee. Come, let me help.' She tried to pull him to his feet and he struggled to rise as Daniel moved swiftly towards them.

Broadwood's face was grey, his bruises livid against his sudden pallor. He swayed and would have fallen but for Daniel's supporting arm. The slave took control.

'Perhaps, Sir, you would allow me to assist you to your carriage. Your sister is anxious for your welfare and is waiting for you at Fernleigh Hall.'

The Master made a pathetic attempt to stand upright, unaided but lurched against Daniel's solid bulk, pain and wretchedness creasing his face. Mrs Roberts and Johnson stood together, united in their distress. They watched as the slave gently supported their reeling master from the wreckage that was his bed-chamber, down the stairs and out of his house.

Outside, Marcus held open the carriage door and helped Daniel lift Broadwood into his seat.

'You'd best get in, young Daniel,' Marcus muttered under his breath. 'He might try to get himself out o' there when them horses is at a gallop. He sure don't look like he knows where he is, nor where he be going neither if yo' asks me.' Daniel gave a quick nod and clambered into the stuffy interior, recoiling from the stench of stale wine and vomit. The carriage jerked forward and Broadwood collapsed into the corner of the seat. His head beat a tattoo against the upright as the vehicle clattered over the cobbles and lunged into a faster, swaying motion as the road gave way to the deeply rutted lanes of the countryside.

They were within a mile of Fernleigh Hall when Matthew, for the first time that day, returned completely to his senses. He was silent for a while as he gathered his thoughts, shifting his position and pushing himself upright on the seat. When he spoke, his voice was thin and tired but his words came clearly.

'How did I come to be here?'

'You have been … unwell, Sir, Mr Johnson was concerned for your health and came to see Mrs Weston to ask what should be done. The Mistress sent Marcus and myself to escort you home.' There was an embarrassed pause as Broadwood examined his stained clothing and his grazed hands. He fingered his swollen lip and winced as he traced the line of his bruised cheekbone and felt the damaged tissue around his eye. Daniel lowered his gaze.

The silence resumed and eventually Matthew continued, his voice stronger now and more decisive.

'I shall not inflict myself upon my sister this evening. Tell her I regret that she has been put to such trouble on my account. When we get home, keep those jabbering busy-bodies out of the way and help me upstairs. All else can wait.'

By the time that the carriage swept across the gravel in front of the house, Broadwood's attempt at bravado had vanished. He shrank into his seat at the sight of Melchet, Mrs Edwards and a gaggle of housemaids waiting at the top of the steps. Daniel snatched off his own cloak and draped it over the wilting figure. He jumped down almost before the carriage had rolled to a stop, deposited the Master on the floor and half carried him into the house, brushing everyone aside. They were through the hall and part way up the stairs before any of the onlookers had moved. Mrs Edwards and Melchet stared at each other and with one accord, made to follow them up the staircase. Anne Weston appeared, her imperious voice halting their steps and silencing the buzzing housemaids.

'Mr Melchet, a word in the library if you please. Mrs Edwards, would you kindly arrange for dinner to be served on a tray in my own room this evening. Mr Broadwood is unwell; we shall not be dining formally today. You girls have work to do I should imagine.' She stared at them all and reluctantly the group broke up to do her bidding.

Upstairs, Daniel removed Matthew's soiled clothing, bathed his face and hands, set a warming pan in the bed and kindled the fire. Broadwood sagged in his chair, a furred dressing gown wrapped around his shaking shoulders and his trembling hands held out towards the comforting warmth of the blaze. Daniel had prepared a soothing cordial and gradually Matthew began to relax. His eyes were heavy and reality, thankfully, seemed to be a long way away.

'I shall see my sister in the morning. Tell her… tell her not to worry.' He nodded slowly to himself. Daniel could scarcely catch his muttered words. 'There is one way out. The only way. Bentinck.' His head drooped forward on his chest and he slipped into an uneasy doze. Daniel stayed awake. He could not sleep. He was waiting for the morning.

CHAPTER SIX

FERNLEIGH HALL
MARCH 1792

It was two days before Matthew Broadwood could be persuaded to leave his chamber and during that time the only person whom he would allow near him was Daniel. Melchet complained vociferously to Anne Weston but was told, in no uncertain terms, that however Mr Broadwood saw fit to arrange his affairs it was not the butler's place to question his decisions. A mutinous Melchet retired to the servants' hall, muttering about them folk from foreign places not knowing how a gentleman's residence should be run, and those who came with high-falutin ideas above their station, but it was to no avail. Daniel had gained the Master's confidence and remained ensconced in his rooms.

Eventually, when he could no longer put off the evil moment, Broadwood descended to the library and sent for his sister. He was rested, had not been near the bottle and had dressed with care. Anne was delighted to see him looking so much like his former self and tears sparkled on her lashes as she went to greet him. He suffered her embrace with his customary impatience and edged away to take his seat. He nodded at Daniel.

'A drink, I think, Daniel,' he ordered, rubbing his hands together. 'See to it man.'

'Tea, Sir, or coffee?'

Broadwood glared and gave an exasperated sigh. The slave had wilfully misunderstood and now he could not ask for brandy without incurring his sister's displeasure. It had been neatly done.

'Coffee then,' he snapped. 'And get a move on.' Daniel raised a quizzical eyebrow at Anne who was struggling to hide her amusement.

'For me too, please,' she smiled. Daniel bowed and left brother and sister alone.

Matthew searched desperately for a safe topic of conversation. He dreaded the coming discussion and was eager to postpone it for as long as he could. He shifted in his seat.

'Hrrmph,' he grunted. 'Good man you have there, sister. Gets things done. No fuss. Not like that damned Melchet, flapping around, gossiping everywhere and blathering about every little thing. Sound. Aye, sound. That's what he is. Forget he's coloured half the time. Aye. Pity really.'

Anne refused to be diverted. 'Yes, Matthew, Daniel is indeed a good servant and you can rely on his discretion, which is just as well in the circumstances. Would you not agree?'

'Always did have a sharp tongue on you, even as a girl,' he blustered. 'Not sure I know what you mean.'

Anne jumped to her feet and began her usual restless pacing up and down the length of the room. She was not deceived by her brother's manner. Matthew was a worried man.

'You know as well as I do what I mean. Let us have done with this pretence. I am a Broadwood too, and if there is anything going on that will affect this family I have a right to know. I am no longer your little sister, Matthew. I am a grown woman, a widow with money and estates under my control. I am well versed in the ways of the world and in the shortcomings of men too, if it comes to that. Now let us discuss this openly and honestly. What has gone wrong? Where do we stand?'

There was a tap at the door and Daniel entered bearing a heavy silver tray; he provided a welcome diversion for Matthew Broadwood.

'Set it down there, man, and then put yourself on the other side of that door. I would not put it past those chits in the kitchen to have their ear to the keyhole. No, nor Melchet neither. Nosy beggars the lot of them. Stay there until you are called and let no one in.' Daniel set down the tray and held Anne Weston's chair as she resumed her seat.

'Thank you, Daniel. I'll pour. You may go.'

'Wait!' The sudden command came from Matthew Broadwood. He stared at Daniel. 'You take down correspondence for Mrs Weston don't you?' Daniel nodded. 'And you have doings with the estate in Jamaica too?' He nodded again. 'And you have a fair grasp of business according to your Mistress. Is that so?'

Anne answered for an embarrassed Daniel. 'Yes. He does all that, and he also administered the plantation affairs for Jeremiah. My husband always insisted that Daniel was the best secretary he had ever had.'

'Aye, well, I need someone to help me here if I am going to be working at Fernleigh for a while. Can't expect old Johnson to keep on coming out all this way.' He cast a sly glance in Anne's direction. She kept her face expressionless but she understood perfectly. Johnson's clerking days were over; he had seen too much. Besides, she knew that Matthew could not conduct his business from the town house for much longer, for if Mr Johnson spoke the truth the family home was heavily mortgaged and would have to go. The Master addressed Daniel once more. 'You know how to keep your trap shut. I've seen proof of that, so you can do some work for me. You can start now. Check that door and then sit yourself over there. Get a move on. What are you waiting for?' Daniel, receiving an almost imperceptible nod from the Mistress, checked outside the door, closed it firmly and took his place to one side of the desk, listening attentively.

Broadwood cleared his throat and gathered his thoughts; he wondered where to begin. He had, throughout his life, been top dog. The only son of a wealthy Liverpool merchant, his mother had been the daughter of an important banking family. Matthew had always led a life of privileged luxury; a house in a prime position on the waterfront, an army of servants, a fine carriage and the best horses, decent clothes and pleasant friends of similar social standing. The death of his mother, when he was twelve, had been the only scar on his early life. He had missed her dreadfully, and had not been pleased when after an interval of only three years his father had married again. Matthew was dispatched to Oxford to grow up, but an unfortunate episode with the daughter of a porter had resulted in his hasty recall.

During a season with his Aunt in London, Matthew had met and married the rather plain daughter of an aspiring Lord Mayor and had brought his new wife and her substantial dowry home in triumph to Liverpool. On his return he had been disconcerted to discover that his young step-mother was pregnant, but the birth of a daughter, Anne, who would not threaten his inheritance, had ensured that Matthew's tranquil existence would continue undiminished. His great sadness was that his own wife had only produced one healthy child, a female who had been named Elizabeth. They had continued to try for a male heir but the birth of their fourth still-born son had resulted in Matthew being left a widower.

He had thrown himself into the business wholeheartedly and the Broadwood fortune had gone from strength to strength, expanding year by year as Liverpool's prosperity increased and her shipping carried manufactured goods across the world. Old Mr Broadwood had invested wisely and his interests were diversified. Matthew, less astute and less inclined to work than his father, had quickly discovered that the slave trade produced the greatest profit for the least effort. Once he had acquired his trading partners and purchased his share in the ships, he was content to sit back and count his money without considering any alternative options.

He sighed as he remembered those heady days, but Anne was becoming impatient. She set down her empty cup and drummed her fingers on the arm of her chair.

'Well, Matthew,' she prompted. He sighed again, closed his eyes and began his tale.

'All was well until the war in the Colonies. We had ships taking slaves to America and there was a goodly profit to be made here on the cotton they brought back. At that time, anything sold to Europe from America had to come through our ports. It was a good living. But then, His Glorious Majesty,' Broadwood lifted his cup in an ironic toast and banged it down, rattling the saucer. 'The King decided to lose the Colonies. Oh, it made no difference to him, or his German cronies, but it almost finished half the men in Liverpool. Trade vanished over night and if you did get ships out, there were privateers waiting to snatch the prize. It was a bad time, but I was lucky. I managed to buy into a ship bound for the West Indies. You know all about that. Took all kinds of goods to Africa we did. We had all the manufacturing in the North of England at our backs, all wanting to come through Liverpool. Aye, goods were shipped out as fast as they came in. They took them to Africa, as I said, then carried people from there to work on the plantations in the Caribbean.'

'The middle-passage,' murmured Anne distractedly, glancing across at Daniel's set face.

Matthew went on as if he had not heard. 'There was a lot of money to be made. Oh aye, a fortune. Everyone in Liverpool town was buying a share in a ship or was sending goods out. We could scarce keep up. We bought more ships, invested more money. Then it started to go wrong. One vessel lost more slaves than normal through some sort of vile disease that they carried from the interior. We scarce covered our costs on that trip. Three months later, one of our ships went down in the Irish Sea; loaded with goods from Manchester that was. Why, they had hardly cleared land when it was wrecked. We got part of our money back eventually, but the insurers don't rush themselves to pay out and we had to borrow to keep going.'

Matthew began to flounder and Anne, who knew him so well, realised that he was about to recount his own errors.

'Go on,' she said quietly. 'What next?'

'Yes, well. It was no fault of mine. No, none at all. The insurers wanted too much money; the premiums were out of all reason. It was eating away at the profits. It was not easy. It was not my fault I say. Indeed it was not.'

'You went to sea without insurance? Is that what you are saying? You invested Broadwood money without cover?' Anne was horrified.

Matthew scrambled to his feet and thumped the table. 'You have no idea what it was like, sister. They were taking too long to pay out. We could not put to sea. Don't you criticise me.' Daniel too stood up as the irate man marched across the room and straddled the fireplace, his hands clasped behind his back, his coat tails lifted and his face red with mortification. He was anxious now to finish, to get it over. 'I invested once more. Almost everything I had. One last throw. Lightning would not strike the same place twice. It could not.'

'You didn't,' whispered Anne. 'Oh, brother, you surely did not send out another ship without insurance.'

94

'Aye, and this time we reached Africa. We had almost reached Jamaica. That blasted hurricane, the whole ocean and it had to hit my ship. Late for hurricanes too it was. Not the proper season. Twelve months last November. I shall never forget it. Within sight of land, or so I understand. Nearly every soul lost, and my fortune with it.'

Anne and Daniel exchanged glances. 'Sullah,' muttered the Mistress. 'I knew it. I knew it at the time. We all knew it from the first if truth be told. The only ship due into Kingston was the Liverpool ship.' Anne watched her brother as he resumed his seat. He was obviously not going to mention the gambling debts, the drinking, the fighting. Neither was he about to admit that the town house had been secured against a loan, and Fernleigh Hall too for all she knew, although Mr Johnson had not said as much. She sighed. 'So what is there to do, brother? I can purchase a house, not on a grand scale but adequate for our needs, and you are welcome to make your home with me.'

A shifty expression flitted across Matthew's features and he refused to meet his sister's gaze. 'Let us not be hasty, my dear. I think I can keep a roof over our heads. Oh, aye, I believe that our family will stay at Fernleigh Hall. My daughter is about to be wed. She will marry Henry Bentinck. He is a friend of mine and has been these many years. He is a well set up man of business, with estates here and in the low countries. His money is in land as well as trade. Old money, Dutch money. Family came over with King William. Aye, to be sure, Bentinck is a wealthy man and with good connections. He will keep those debtors off my back and see this family's fortunes turned around. He met Elizabeth five years ago, when she was but a child; now he is looking for a bride and wants her hand. And he shall have it with my blessing.'

Anne was surprised. 'I had no notion,' she mused. 'Eliza told me nothing of this. It was my understanding that she

95

was to have a season in London.'

Matthew Broadwood stroked his chin and chuckled. It was not a pleasant sound. 'It is no surprise that she has told you nothing. The girl does not know. Not yet. But by God, she soon will.'

The following day, Elizabeth Broadwood returned to Fernleigh Hall. She whirled through the front door in a fluff of feathery bonnet and a state of high excitement. She was in love, again, but this time it was for ever.

'Bring in my bags, Marcus. Take them upstairs. One of the maids can unpack and I will wear the new sprigged muslin this evening. It is possible that someone might call. Ah, Melchet, there you are. Where is Mrs Weston? Is she in the morning-room?'

The butler wore the pained expression that his dealings with the young Mistress usually induced. 'Beg your pardon, Miss, but the Master asked to be informed when you returned. I believe he will wish to see you.'

'Yes, yes. By all means tell Papa that I have arrived, but I must see my Aunt. You will find me in the morning-room, if that is where she is.' Melchet nodded wearily and went in search of the Master. He knew from long experience that it was useless to try to persuade Miss Elizabeth to relinquish a course that she had decided upon.

Eliza burst into the morning-room, dropping her bonnet and gloves on a chair, and flew across the carpet to Anne Weston, enveloping her in an enthusiastic embrace and causing the papers that she had been working on to scatter like autumn leaves. Daniel, who was standing beside the desk, bent to retrieve them, allowing himself a quick glance at the girl's excited expression. Eliza was looking her best. Her conventional, fair-haired prettiness was enhanced by animation and her glowing face and sparkling eyes reflected her obvious well-being.

Daniel had no time to consider whether to withdraw; the girl launched into immediate and rapturous explanation of her happiness.

'Oh, Anne. My dear Aunt. You cannot possibly believe what has occurred. That it should be so sudden. That it should happen to me. I can scarcely credit it myself. It was at a supper, on my very first night in Chester. He was there and we were introduced. Oh, Aunt, it was so wonderful. I feel as if I have known him all of my life. Within five minutes, I knew. He is so fine a figure in his uniform that he makes me want to weep. He is so tall, so strong, such a handsome man. But then, looks are not everything. His taste,' she raised eloquent eyes to the ceiling. 'His taste supersedes all. It is exquisite. Why, every little thing he does, every gesture, every movement is perfect. And his speech. He is so sensitive, has such compassion. And when we talked, we found that we enjoy absolutely the same things.' She paused for breath.

'You appear to have discovered a great deal about the man after only one meeting,' commented Anne, dryly. 'Or have you seen this paragon more than just the once?'

Eliza frowned and pouted. Her Aunt's reaction was not at all what she had hoped for. Such scepticism was not for those in love. But then, Anne was really quite old. She must be almost thirty. Eliza conferred a dazzling smile on Daniel.

'He stands almost as tall as you do, Daniel, although he does not have your breadth of shoulder.' She turned again to Anne. 'We met every day during my stay with Mama's cousin. He paid a call each morning and he was most complimentary about my sketching. He thinks that I have a rare talent. In the afternoons, he was found to be walking in just the very places that I had determined to explore.'

'What an amazing coincidence,' murmured Anne.

Eliza prattled on, undeterred. 'In the evenings, we dined

at the same houses, and he thought that my playing of the pianoforte was quite the finest that he had heard in any drawing-room. What do you think of that, Aunt? Was that not a most generous compliment?'

'Generous indeed. He would seem to be a most resourceful young man. And tell me, does this delightful person have a name?'

Eliza's laugh tinkled. 'I declare I am such a scatter-brain.' She stood up, flushing. 'His name is Captain Edward Stanton and later today or perhaps tomorrow he will call and leave his card.' She clapped her hands, delightedly. 'Oh, Aunt, I do so long for you to meet him.'

Anne Weston's face clouded and her eyes became sombre. She took her niece's hands.

'Have you seen your father, my dear? Have you spoken to him since your return? I believe he has something to...'

The door opened and Melchet coughed discreetly. 'Pardon me, Ma'am, Miss, the Master wants to see you both in the library. Would you come with me? He asks that you do not keep him waiting.'

Eliza's troubled gaze travelled from the butler, to Daniel, to her Aunt. 'What is it?' she asked. 'What is wrong?' Her voice was wary. Anne did not answer. She linked her arm through that of the girl and drew her into the hall. In the doorway, she glanced back over her shoulder at Daniel and gave a slight shake of the head. The slave put his crumpled papers on the desk and tried vainly to smooth them out. He felt so sorry for the girl. Her happiness was infectious. She had been so joyful. What would she say when she discovered that she was to be sold to the highest bidder? A lady of quality, and she was no more free than he was.

The tension in the library was palpable.

'I will not do it! I will not, I say. You cannot make me do it. I cannot be expected to marry a man I have seen only once. And he is old, so very old. Why, he must be at least forty. What is all this about? I had no thought of marriage. Why are you saying such things? Papa? Aunt?' The tear-stained, dishevelled girl held out an appealing hand and Anne Weston put an arm around her shoulders, glowering at her brother.

Matthew was beside himself with temper. He stood with his feet apart, his eyes glittering in his mottled face as he hovered threateningly over his daughter.

'You will not! You dare to say so to me? You are not too old to have the strap taken to you, chit. Not too old at all. And do not think for a moment that I would not do it. I have reared you, clothed you in all your fine gee-gaws, educated you, given you everything you ever asked for. And what have I had in return, eh? Answer me that. What have you ever done for me? Nothing. Nothing, ever.' His stubby fingers stabbed the air only inches away from his daughter's face. The girl flinched. 'You take. That is all you have ever done. Take! Take! Take!' He roared his abuse into her face, spittle forming on his lips.

Broadwood took his accustomed place in front of the fire and resumed more quietly.

'Henry Bentinck is one of the quality. His family is indeed one of the best connected in London. London, are you listening wench? This is no Liverpool merchant you are being offered. This is a man who can command a place at the best tables in the capital.' He stared at his sobbing daughter and his exasperation exploded into a roaring diatribe. 'You stupid, stupid girl! I have found you a good match. Better than you could have hoped for. What more do you want? I will say this but one more time, you will wed where I say. You will marry Henry Bentinck. And as soon as possible.'

Anne took her niece by the arm. 'Let me take you to your room, Eliza. It will not do for you to upset yourself so. You are distraught.'

'Distraught! Pah!' bellowed Broadwood. 'You have been told what is to happen and you will do as you are bid. I am your father and you will obey me. Do you hear me, girl? You will obey. Let there be no mistake.' Eliza covered her face with trembling hands, tore herself free of her Aunt's grasp and ran sobbing from the room.

There was silence for a time and then Anne Weston gave an exasperated groan.

'You foolish man. Do you never learn? Now look what you have done.'

'She had to be told damn it. She had to know. It had to be done.'

'Yes, brother, but there are ways of doing things. For the love of God, leave the girl to me. You have done quite enough.' She stalked out and went in search of her niece. Matthew snatched up a decanter and poured a generous measure of brandy, gulping it down. He poured a second glass more slowly and carried it to the window, staring out across the garden. It would work out. The girl would come round. She had to. It was the only hope he had left.

In her own room, a woebegone Eliza poured out her feelings on to a sheet of paper. She was being forced into a wealthy marriage to save her family's honour. She and her dearest Edward were at the mercy of their fates, and they must bear their burden with fortitude just as other star-crossed lovers in history had done. She would always remember their short time together and would never give her heart to anyone else. She could see no way out, unless her darling should suggest that they run away. She would go with him anywhere. To be sure, she would forfeit her inheritance and be cut off from her family but she would not mind being poor as long as they were together. He could send a reply with her servant. She sealed the letter and hurried to the nursery suite in search of a messenger.

Eliza pressed her letter into Daniel's hands.

'Daniel, I am relying on you to deliver this to Captain Stanton in Chester. If you were to take the horse at once, no one would see you; it is getting late and you will not be missed. I know that you will do this small service for me.' She held his hand, urgently, looking up at him with tears brimming in her eyes. 'And, Daniel, no one must know. Not my Aunt, not Sullah, no one. Bring me his reply. I will stay awake.' She turned and with a whisper of silk skirts and a last, pleading look over her shoulder, she left him.

A glimmer of daylight was hovering on the horizon before Daniel returned from Chester. He had told Marcus of his errand before he set out and his old friend had done everything possible to dissuade him. Once he had seen however that Daniel was adamant, he had put food and drink in the saddle-bag and the horse had been ready when Daniel appeared. Now, the groom was waiting as the exhausted animal returned home. One look at Daniel's face told Marcus that things had not gone well but he asked no questions; there were some things that he would rather know nothing about. He stood, patting the horse's steaming neck as he watched Daniel trudge off towards the silent house. The faintest glimmer of a pale face showed for a moment at one of the second floor windows but when he looked again it had gone.

In the darkened schoolroom, Daniel was met by a breathless Eliza.

'Well? Where is my letter? Where is Captain Stanton's reply? Oh, Daniel, do not tell me that you did not find him? I was so certain that I could rely on you.'

'Miss Eliza, please.' Daniel put his hands on her

shoulders, feeling the heat of her skin though the fine cloth. 'It was too late. Captain Stanton's regiment had left for the coast. There is much trouble across the Channel and many troops are on the move. There was hardly anyone left in the barracks at Chester. I am sorry.'

Eliza nodded slowly, unwillingly. 'He would have come for me if he had known. I am sure of it.' She sighed. 'Thank you, Daniel. You did your best.' She left the room, her shawl trailing dejectedly behind her, her fair hair tumbling loosely down her back.

Daniel hunched over the nursery table, his head in his hands. He was wretched. He had not told the truth. Yes, the regiment was on the move but he had reached Stanton in time, tracking him down to an inn on the outskirts of the city. The man was tipsy and had read Eliza's letter out loud to his two drinking companions, laughing at her lovelorn phrases.

'Two dances, a couple of strolls, a few whispered nothings in the drawing-room, a kiss and a quick fumble and the girl thinks she is at the altar. Mind, if her father had made it worth my while... Well, I could certainly do worse... she's a pretty little piece and could be taught to please, I'll be bound.' Daniel had kept his head lowered and his hands clenched by his sides as the three men sniggered. The red mist was descending again and he heard Stanton's words as though from a great distance. 'Does she really think that I would take her penniless? On a Captain's pay? How does the silly creature think to live?' He had yawned, languidly. 'Here you, boy.'

'Yes, Sir.'

'Tell your Mistress that I had left. Do you understand? Tell her you couldn't find me.' He had dropped Eliza's message on the floor and staggered from the inn with his companions, leaving Daniel to grovel in the dust for Eliza's letter.

CHAPTER SEVEN

CHESTER
MAY 1792

Henry Bentick sat back in his seat as the coachman cracked his whip and the carriage lumbered away from the front of Rossmere Hall. His half-sister, Mary, continued to flutter a dutiful hand out of the window until the horses had completed their circle and set off down the long drive. His aunt's house was an impressive example of late Tudor architecture, with two magnificent towers and a mass of tall intricate chimneys. As a specimen of comfortable lodgings it left much to the imagination; however, it was most convenient. Apart from the fact that his mother's sister was wealthy and the only member of the older generation left, she was also their only family in this part of the country, so it had been sensible to spend a few days here on the outskirts of Chester on their way to Fernleigh Hall. Sensible, but hardly enjoyable. Henry always called on his Aunt Pimblett when business necessitated a visit to Liverpool but he usually contrived to stay at an inn in Chester itself. On this occasion, Mary's presence had meant that Rossmere Hall was the obvious place to break their journey.

Aunt Pimblett led the existence one would expect of a rich, unmarried gentlewoman of more than seventy years. She kept an adequate table of plain wholesome food, an impoverished cellar left over from her father's day and she entertained on the smallest scale possible. Her needs were met by three elderly retainers and her sole friend, apart from a toothless King Charles spaniel, was an equally ancient companion who rejoiced in the unlikely name of Rosamund Beauchamp. Mealtime conversation was restricted to prolonged discussion of the state of the weather.

'It has been a fine day for the time of year. Has it not, Ma'am?'

'Indeed, Rosamund. It has been exceptionally fine. Do you not agree, Henry?'

'Oh yes, Aunt, extremely fine.'

'And do you not think so, Miss Bentinck? Would you not admit to it being a very fine spell of weather for such an early month?'

'Most certainly, Miss Beauchamp. I quite agree. In fact, I would go so far as to say that I cannot ever recall so fine a spell before.'

And so it had gone on. Henry had been able to plead the excuse of business. He had retired to the solitude of the library after dinner with a cigar and a glass of magnificent old Cognac that he had discovered in a cobweb-strewn corner of the cellar, and which he now kept secreted behind the heavy velvet curtains. Mary, he knew, had been almost demented by the end of her first evening in the drawing-room and had only been persuaded to remain by the unavailability of any other viable option.

His stern expression softened as he regarded his young sister; a cold, callous man, she was the one individual, throughout his entire adult life, for whom he entertained any affection. She was offspring of his father's second marriage; her mother had died of consumption when the child was only four years old and Mary had been left very much to her own devices until Henry had taken her under his wing. The pair intuitively recognised similarities in their character and neither had ever presumed to judge the other in the light of normal standards of propriety and social acceptability.

Mary was aware of the intensity of her brother's gaze and she turned her head towards him, a smile lifting the corners of her mouth.

'Well, brother, away at last. I do swear that I should have died of boredom if I had been forced to endure one moment more of your Aunt Pimblett's wretched hospitality. Do you realise that on our last evening I resorted to counting how many different ways there were of commenting on the fineness of the weather? I had to do something to prevent myself from banging my long-suffering head against the nearest wall. It was really too much to expect.'

'I do apologise, my dear, but I could hardly take you to the inn. Besides, my Aunt has no female relatives and she owns some exquisite pieces of jewellery that have been handed down from her grandmother. It would do you no harm to cultivate that particular relationship; you know how you love jewels. Come now, let us be more cheerful. I do assure you that Fernleigh will be much more to your taste. The Broadwoods spared no expense when building the Hall. It is only the aristocracy who have such little regard for their creature comforts; the merchant class have very different priorities.'

'I own that I shall be glad to be pampered after the past few days and I am looking forward to seeing Elizabeth, but I do confess that I very much miss life in town.' She sighed. 'I do not have high expectations of Liverpool society. It really was too bad of you to become involved in a scandal, Henry,' she went on waspishly. 'Now we are exiled to this social wilderness for Lord knows how long. You were extremely foolish.' She lapsed into a sulky silence and stared out of the carriage window at the unravelling panorama of the Cheshire countryside.

Bentinck closed his eyes, determined that his sister would be given no further opportunity to foster her discontent. It was a measure of her exasperation that she had seen fit to criticise him at all. However, she was right, he had been foolish. In the past he had always been so careful. His proclivity for young boys had been an affliction for many years. It stemmed, he was sure, from his own mother's rejection of him. How old had he been, six, seven? Just because the stupid dog had died. He had enjoyed making the animal suffer but he had never intended that it should die. He had not thought to kill his mother's pet. He shrugged the memory away; it was all so long ago. But his mother had avoided contact with him after that, right up to her death, and he was convinced that all his ensuing acts of violence had been to attract her attention and to punish her for ceasing to love him. His Papa had not seemed to be unduly concerned. Not until the episode in his early teens, when he had thrashed the much younger son of an estate worker with a whip. The incident had been hushed up and he was severely beaten. There had been nothing else until he had left for a tour of the Continent at the age of eighteen.

Henry smiled as he recalled those two years spent in Europe. Papa had hired a former army officer as his mentor, convinced that the man's military background and worldly experience would protect his son from the worst excesses of his natural inclinations. Papa had got it wrong. Compton was indeed worldly, was indeed experienced, but Henry knew that his father's unimaginative Dutch soul would have been revolted by the lessons that his son had been taught. Henry's mentor had introduced him to a range of perverted practices to which he had rapidly become addicted. Practices that would outrage human decency and which pandered to the sadistic streak that had always formed a large part of the boy's make-up.

When his son returned to England, Henry's father gave him charge of the family shipping in the port of Bristol. He hoped that by keeping the boy away from London society for most of the year he would keep him out of temptation's reach. Unfortunately, the cosmopolitan habits of the waterfront had only served to strengthen Henry's baser instincts, and the fond Mamas of Bristol had been thrown into disarray by his consistent refusal to involve himself in the annual lottery of finding a partner in the marriage stakes. Henry's natural inclination was to remained unwed and the Bentinck fortune had stayed safe despite the grasping machinations of the womenfolk.

On the death of his father, soon after Henry's thirtieth birthday, the young man had installed a manager on the family's country estates and had moved with his half-sister and her governess to the London house in Portman Square. Their share in the shipping business had grown out of all recognition under Henry's guidance. With none of his father's long-held scruples to deter him Henry invested heavily in slaving, and when the focus of that trade moved to Liverpool he rapidly acquired contacts in the town, basing most of his ships in that flourishing port. One of his first partners was Matthew Broadwood, and on an early visit to Fernleigh Hall he had met the young Eliza.

Bentinck opened his eyes to find his sister watching him with a predatory interest.

'Tell me, Henry,' she asked, without preamble. 'What attractions does Elizabeth Broadwood possess to draw you to her, when you have so steadfastly refused to be caught by any of the other nets that have been spread for you? I must admit to extreme curiosity.'

'The advantages of a match with the Broadwood girl are many. Think for a moment. So far away from London there will have been no hint of a scandal. The girl is young and impressionable. She will also, no doubt, be biddable. When I first saw her, five years ago, she was undeniably pretty; fair hair, blue eyes, slender, she reminded me very much of my Mama.' He paused and cleared his throat. 'Matthew Broadwood is almost penniless but, if properly managed, his shipping interests could be revived. His is one of the proudest names in this part of the country and he has well-established and influential contacts. Do not forget that Liverpool has all the industrial manufacturers clamouring for an outlet for their goods. There is a fortune to be made here with the right man at the helm. Elizabeth's dowry will be her father's business. You want to return to London do you not? What better way to lay the ghost of that stupid scandal than by my turning up with a beautiful young wife?'

Mary eyed her brother with a speculative expression and gave a cynical smile. 'Let us hope that the beautiful young wife appreciates her good fortune. What if she should hear of your misdeeds when we return to Portman Square?'

Colour suffused Bentinck's pale face. 'Once we are wed, it will be of little consequence. I will own the father and I will own the daughter. As a married man I can take my place in society again. The gossip will be forgotten. It will be put down to exaggeration and Huntingdon's youth.'

Henry closed his eyes once more bringing all further conversation to an end, but his thoughts were busy. Who would have imagined that Huntingdon, in his cups, would have confessed all to his father? Fancy telling the old man all about the goings on in the house by the Thames. And then, for the father to challenge him to a duel! It was as well that someone had seen fit to whisper in the ear of the Duke; His Royal Highness, anxious to avoid scandal, had soon put a stop to the notion. Even so, Henry had been advised that it was an opportune moment to leave the

108

capital. A few months out of society and the gossips would soon discover a new target for their barbs. He had misjudged that young idiot, Huntingdon; he must ensure that he did not misjudge the Broadwoods.

In the gardens of Fernleigh Hall, the pale blossom floated on a light breeze and settled in a carpet on the grass. Eliza Broadwood got to her feet, shaking stray petals from her skirt as she drifted across the park towards the ornamental lake, her mind on the expected visitors. She heard a splash and spotted Daniel and Sullah, with the two Weston children, tossing bread into the lake. A brood of ducklings made their ungainly way down the slope and flopped into the water in their mother's wake, gliding eagerly towards the source of food. The children's giggles rang across the park. Eliza stood watching for a moment; her cousins were growing up; so too was Sullah. There was a new self-conscious elegance about the slave-girl's movements. How old was she? Thirteen, fourteen, maybe more. There was certainly nothing of the child in the way she was looking at Daniel.

Eliza was annoyed.

'Daniel,' she called. 'Daniel, would you get my shawl from the house. It is cooler than I thought and I am sure that Sullah can manage very well without you for a short time.' The slave hastened up the grassy bank. On this warm afternoon he was wearing only breeches and a fine lawn shirt open at the neck. He looked even larger without his jacket. Eliza smiled up at him. 'Please bring it to the seat in the herb garden for me. I do so like to sit there. It is so private and sheltered.' She watched as he dashed away, delighted to do her bidding.

Young Margaret gave a startled cry. 'Hurting. Sully, you hurting Meg.'

'Sullah is sorry, my pet.' She bent and hugged the child, releasing her hand. 'I just wasn't thinkin'. Look, lets us give that there Mammy duck some bread. All them little ducks have took everythin' for themselves. They be greedy, that's what they be.'

'Greedy, greedy,' chanted Timothy as Sullah stared at Eliza, with defiant eyes. The young Mistress turned away and strolled across the lawns towards a distant hedge. The sun disappeared behind a cloud and Sullah shivered.

Carrying the soft, woollen shawl over his arm, Daniel was conscious of a twinge of apprehension. During the past months, he had endeavoured to temper his feelings of admiration for Eliza by reminding himself of the trust placed in him by the girl's aunt and, more recently, by her father. Since the day when Daniel and Marcus had brought him back to Fernleigh Hall, Matthew Broadwood had overcome his initial disinclination to be reminded of his links with slavery and had accepted them both as valued servants in his home. Daniel's secretarial work had multiplied and the Master had come to rely on him more and more. As his understanding of the family's affairs increased, Daniel had been horrified by the examples he uncovered of Broadwood's feckless approach to business and his recklessness in financial dealings. He feared that the Master was right when he asserted that a massive investment of funds was needed if the Broadwoods were to continue as a respected force among the merchants of Liverpool. The money that would be forthcoming from Eliza's marriage was indeed necessary to save not only the family fortunes but also its reputation.

The slave approached the herb garden with considerable caution. It was not often these days that he was required to perform any service for Eliza. He had never been alone with her since the night that he had been sent to deliver her letter to Captain Stanton. Whilst part of him regretted that she no longer came to the schoolroom, he was in many ways relieved that the turmoil inevitably caused by her presence had ceased. Now, he was bothered. He knew the young Mistress well enough to recognise that she was in a peculiar frame of mind, and whilst the prospect of a private encounter with her excited him, he was also aware that her tendency towards unpredictable behaviour could be a source of trouble. She had deliberately engineered this situation and, although flattered by the attention, he could not help being mindful of the impropriety of her actions.

There had been a worrying irresponsibility about Eliza's conduct in recent weeks. In the days following the delivery of her father's ultimatum, the girl had remained shut in her room, eating little and becoming increasingly hysterical. Anne Weston had spent hours with her niece and had eventually coaxed her into a more rational state, although relations between Matthew and his daughter had continued to be fraught. She appeared to be seeking to annoy her Papa at every opportunity and conversation at dinner frequently resulted in one or the other of them stomping from the room. Eliza's loudly aired views about abolition and the wickedness of those merchants who saw fit to trade in human flesh were designed to provoke an angry response; so too were her veiled barbs about seemingly respectable men who kept secret establishments where they lived with women of a certain reputation. There was a simmering tension in the atmosphere and everyone in the house was aware of it. The last thing that Daniel wanted was further problems.

Eliza was sitting in her favourite retreat. The seat was sheltered from the wind by a laurel hedge and the sunken garden basked in the warmth of the May sunshine. The relaxing scent of lavender and thyme lingered on the still air. As Daniel approached, his steps crunching on the gravel path, he could see that Eliza was weeping. The tears fell unheeded as her restless fingers twisted her handkerchief into knots. He hesitated, loathe to impose himself on her misery, yet equally reluctant to turn aside from such obvious distress. The dilemma was solved by the young woman herself.

'Oh, Daniel, what am I to do?' Eliza wailed, looking up at him as he towered over her. 'Do sit down. I feel so wretched. I must confide in someone and you are one of the few people in this house that I can trust. I know that you will always stand by me. I had thought that Aunt Weston would be my friend but she can only preach obedience to Papa and point out the benefits of this... this... arrangement. They both make my marriage sound like a business proposition. What of mutual affection? What of love?' Daniel flushed and she patted the bench beside her as she took her shawl from his arms and draped it around her shoulders. He sat down at her side, careful to keep as much distance between them as was practicable. Eliza's eyes flashed in the face of his evident reluctance, before she recalled that she was distressed. She gave a stifled sob and touched her crumpled handkerchief to her face. Daniel found himself reaching involuntarily for her hand and capturing it inside his own. He was careful not to look at her as his stomach churned and his senses swam.

They sat in silence for some time. Eliza's sobs ceased and she cast sidelong glances at the slave's troubled face.

'I feel quite, quite abandoned,' she murmured. 'As though there is no one who can appreciate my deepest feelings. Only you, Daniel. You understand. Do you not? Why should I be forced to marry against my will? I have not seen Henry Bentinck since I was little more than a child. Why, I do believe it is all of five years since he was here at Fernleigh. I can scarcely recall what the man looks like. If my father's mismanagement has brought the family to ruin, then he should pay the price, not I.' She paused in expectation but Daniel made no response. Her callous disregard for the position of Matthew Broadwood surprised him. His disappointment in her was evident and she continued with rather less patience than before. 'If only you had found Captain Stanton that night, I would have been safely wed by this time and Papa would have had to look elsewhere for salvation, but I am to be sold like some chattel. Surely, Daniel, you of all people will know how I must loathe the thought.' She turned her appealing eyes to his face. There was a long silence.

Daniel's reply, when it came, was careful and considered.

'Miss Eliza, I would never willingly do or say anything that would bring hurt to you or to your family. I owe everything to Mrs Weston. I have a high regard for Mr Broadwood and I ...well... you must be aware... you are held above all in my estimation. But because of my position... well... I have no notion of a person thinking that they can place themselves where they alone see fit. I cannot have. Whatever my blood, I was born slave and will surely die so. As such, I go where I am sent. I do as I am bid, and I have no right to wife or family without the agreement of my Master or Mistress. Whilst I regret that this proposal should bring you such unhappiness, in my culture it would be expected. There would be no other way. Indeed, even here in England I believe that your father has the right to dispose of you in marriage as he wishes. It is only a widow who has the entitlement to arrange her own affairs. Is that not so?'

Eliza jumped to her feet, snatching her hand away.

'But you know that my heart belongs elsewhere.' She kicked angrily at the gravel, sending up a shower of stones. 'You know that Captain Stanton and I were to be married.' Her lip wobbled and her voice broke pitifully. Daniel got up and opened his mouth to reply but Eliza swept on. 'I know that he would have come for me. We would have gone away. Papa would have forgiven us eventually. But it was not to be. You did not find him and I am to be sold. I hate Papa! But I tell you this, Daniel, if I am to be forced to wed, then I shall take from the situation anything that I can get. If I am to be bought, then I shall make sure that the price comes high.' And turning on her heel she hurried away, out of the fragrant oasis of warmth into the chill wind that was now blowing around the house.

The Master of Fernleigh took up his usual stance, straddled in front of the blazing library fire. He had heard the sound of the carriage and was waiting for Melchet to follow his orders and conduct the guests in here. Anne was on a low chair by the window, reading a book of poems. Each of them was busy with their own thoughts. Matthew was conscious of an overwhelming feeling of relief that Bentinck had finally arrived, and he intended to waste no time in settling the details of Eliza's marriage so that the betrothal could be announced at dinner the following night. He had asked Anne to take Mary to her own sitting-room and to entertain her there until the business side of the affair could be concluded. His expression was benign as he regarded his sister. He could rely on her to do the right thing, unlike Eliza, who had elected to be indisposed and was staying in her room. His brows lowered as he acknowledged that he would have to make his daughter's excuses to Bentinck. He could only hope that the chit's insatiable curiosity would get the better of her reluctance and that she would appear at dinner.

Anne's face was calm but her mind was uneasy. Matthew had planned a grand house-party for the weekend to celebrate his daughter's betrothal, but Anne was too uncertain of her niece's present state of mind to feel in any way relaxed about the affair. All the domestic arrangements were in hand; rooms were prepared, food was ordered and the kitchen had been in a state of siege for a week. Extra staff had been engaged and all was in readiness. Unfortunately, Eliza's fitful disposition left no room for complacency. If only Matthew had consented to his daughter's request that she should at least enjoy a few days of Mr Bentinck's company before any agreement was finalised. Anne was sure that when faced with evidence of her suitor's vast fortune and impeccable social standing the girl's acquisitive nature would have ensured that she would consent to the marriage. As it was, she had serious reservations about Eliza's intention to cooperate.

'Mr Henry Bentinck and Miss Mary Bentinck, Sir.' Melchet's voice boomed out. He stepped aside and Anne put down her book to greet their visitors.

Matthew introduced her. 'May I present to you my sister, Mrs Weston.' Anne closed her eyes, just for an instant, as a tide of relief swept over her. Her gaze was fixed on Henry Bentinck and only the slightest tremor of the hand that she held out to him betrayed the intensity of her emotion. She had not realised how tense she had been, but now she felt that she could relax at last. There was nothing here to cause Eliza upset or distress. The man was middling tall with fine bones and a good, if somewhat sallow, skin. He looked, if anything, younger than his years and his expertly tailored clothes were dashingly cut, although not in any exaggerated fashion. His appearance bespoke a monied, elegant lifestyle and the only fault that Anne could find was his eyes. They were rather protuberant and set closely together, giving his face an unfortunately shifty look. More than this, they were devoid of all expression. A dead fish, was the thought that sprang, unbidden, to Anne's mind.

The humour of the comparison caused Anne's smile to

deepen, increasing the cordiality of her welcome.

'Mr Bentinck, I am delighted to make your acquaintance,' she declared.

'It is a pleasure that I return in full, Ma'am,' he responded, taking her proffered hand and raising it to his lips with perfect courtesy. His voice had a musical quality, which served to disguise the lack of true warmth in his manner. Anne's initial assessment of his character was of a self-possessed, rather aloof but exquisitely mannered individual and she felt a moment of disquiet at the thought of her niece's sentimental, impulsive nature. Still, perhaps the pair would be good for each other.

She turned to Mary as Henry moved on to speak to his host. The expensive simplicity of the other woman's travelling habit was not lost on Anne. She immediately felt dowdy, although she had dressed with particular care for the occasion. From her feathered bonnet to her delightfully shod feet, Mary's entire ensemble exuded quality, refinement and good taste. Yet, somehow, there was a suggestion of overt femininity that Anne knew any man would instantly recognise. Mary Bentinck had her eyes modestly downcast; her voice, musical like her brother's, was softly modulated; her movements were stylish and restrained, but, there was that about her that caused Anne great unease. She felt her heart flutter in her chest, like a sparrow confronted by the threatening presence of a bird of prey. Mary raised her eyes to meet Anne's gaze; there was a flash of acknowledgement in their depths as she observed the older woman's apprehension but it vanished so speedily that Anne doubted that it had been there at all.

'I have so longed to meet you, Ma'am,' she purred. 'I do hope that our visit will not inconvenience you in any way.'

Anne was embarrassed by her involuntary reaction to Mary's demeanour. It was unlike her to be so uncharitable.

She smiled and, in her anxiety to make amends, greeted her guest with more enthusiasm than politeness required. She was conscious of the other's amusement and became extremely flustered.

'I am so very delighted to have you here,' she gushed. 'Of course you will be no trouble. Let us go to my sitting-room. I am sure that you are in need of refreshment after such a long journey. Everything is in readiness. It will be a pleasure.' She listened with horror to the sound of her own brittle, prattling voice; even Matthew was looking at her strangely. What was the matter with her? She was no gauche, inexperienced girl. Anne drew a deep breath and took herself firmly in hand. 'Let us leave the gentlemen to their discussions, Mary. I may call you Mary, I trust? And please, you must call me Anne.' With a regal inclination of her head in the direction of the menfolk, she swept past the other woman and out of the door, fighting down the urge to pick up her skirts and run from the house.

CHAPTER EIGHT

FERNLEIGH HALL
MAY 1792

Elizabeth Broadwood stood at the window of her chamber, gazing out across the lawns of Fernleigh Hall. She had always thought that her home looked most attractive in the spring, and in the purple dusk of this May evening it was truly beautiful. Her eyes filled; her volatile emotions were, as ever, close to the surface. Part of her wished that the weather could have been cold and wet, with rain dripping from disconsolate branches and blossom battered by chill winds. That would have been in keeping with her mood; it would have reflected her misery. Another part of her was glad that the Hall was at its best, since it made the acceptance of her father's demands easier to bear. She could never see her home sold to strangers, and the thought of her Papa being known throughout the area as a discredited debtor was not to be tolerated. She knew that there really was no choice, but her sentimental soul was determined to wallow in the magnitude of her self-sacrifice.

Eliza was almost prepared to believe in her own nobility; almost, but not quite. If truth be told, there was a ruthless streak of realism deep beneath the girl's frothy sensibilities. She had an undiluted instinct for self-preservation and was honest enough, at least in her own mind, to acknowledge it. It was this aspect of her character that recent events had brought to the fore. Whatever happened, Eliza would survive. More than merely survive; she would emerge at the top of the heap.

A long rejected memory of an encounter with her grandfather surfaced, unbidden, into her consciousness. The old man had been sitting with her on his lap and had declared,

'If I was stranded on a desert island with this Miss, I should be up a tree throwing coconuts, for I swear that if only one of us were to survive it would this little one.' They had all laughed as he had set her down but there had been a sadness, a disappointment in the old eyes and the moment had stayed with her ever since. It was odd, she mused, that her maternal Grandpapa, who saw her so seldom, should be the one to see her so clearly. Maybe that was why he had been such a successful man.

She knew herself well enough by now to see that Grandpapa had been right. She would withstand life's difficulties, and could see nothing wrong in seeking to assure herself of all its creature comforts. She shuddered at the thought of those wretched, down-trodden, shawl-draped women of the manufacturing towns, whom she sometimes passed in the carriage. She did not know how anyone could bear to live in such conditions. All the Fernleigh servants, even Aunt Weston's slaves, had a better existence than those workers. Eliza had been born into pampered luxury and unquestioned wealth and she was determined that it should continue.

Her thoughts were interrupted by a gentle tap on the door and her maid slid into the room.

'Beg pardon, Miss, but the Master is waiting for you in the library. He has the other gentleman with him.' The girl's eyes were avid with curiosity as she stared, awestruck, at Eliza. 'Eh, Miss, it bain't be my place to say so, but 'ee don't 'alf look grand.' She flushed, aware that in her excitement she had lapsed into the broad, flat speech of her home village. She lowered her head and mumbled again. 'Beg pardon, Miss,' before bolting through the door.

Eliza rose, smoothing down the silk of her gown. She was looking 'grand' and she knew it. There was no room for false modesty in her world. If her father had neither title nor wealth, then Eliza had only her beauty to commend her. It was up to her to make the most of her attributes. She studied her appearance for a moment and then nodded in satisfaction. Her hair was dressed in a youthful style, with one or two artless ringlets 'escaping' casually from their coils. Her dress was simplicity itself but the quality of the fabric and the cut was perfect. Her only jewel was a single pearl on a fine gold chain that nestled tantalisingly in the hollow of her throat. Her face was becomingly pale. She took up her wrap, drew a long breath and cast a last look out of the window, where the dusk had deepened and the first flickering stars had begun to appear.

Reaching the top of the staircase, Eliza was startled by a sudden noise and her hand flew to her mouth as Daniel stepped from the shadows.

'Forgive me, Miss Eliza, but I had to see you….I wished to make sure… I had to discover… Are you all right?… Is there anything that I can do for you?' A surge of gratitude swept over the young woman as she saw the anxious expression on the face of her Aunt's slave. She had some notion of what it had cost him to approach her in this way and she experienced a rare moment of humility in the face of such devotion. She bit back her first impatient retort and answered him with a new gentleness and a surprising kindness.

'It is good to know that I am in your thoughts, Daniel. I do thank you for your care. I am quite well and I am prepared to accept what must be.' She pressed his hand, her touch burning his ice-cold skin, and moved past him down the wide staircase, steadying herself with one hand on the balustrade.

In the silence of the library, Matthew Broadwood, back to the fire, chewed on his cigar. Shreds of tobacco drifted down the front of his jacket as he darted anxious glances towards the door. Henry Bentinck was also standing but his posture demonstrated only a nonchalant elegance as he examined the local landscapes that adorned the walls.

His perambulations put him behind the door as it opened to admit Melchet whose bland announcement, 'Miss Broadwood, Sir,' preceded Eliza's agitated entrance. He was able to study the girl in the seconds before she registered an awareness of his presence. She was the epitome of youthful, bewitching innocence and his senses were stirred by her girlish prettiness and natural charm. He could see nothing calculated or sensual in her appeal, and he rejoiced inwardly at his good fortune as he struggled to compose his features before Matthew's glance directed the girl's attention towards him.

Broadwood appeared the devoted Papa as he kissed his daughter's pale cheek, but Bentinck's shrewd eyes did not miss the slight turn of her head away from her father's embrace. There had obviously been disagreement and he had no doubts as to its cause.

'My dear, may I present to you my very good friend, Henry Bentinck? Bentinck, my daughter, Elizabeth.'

'I am pleased to have the opportunity to renew your acquaintance, Miss Broadwood,' murmured Bentinck in his well-modulated voice. 'May I be permitted to say how well you look? You have certainly grown up since our last meeting.'

The open admiration in his eyes flattered Eliza and she found herself almost smiling as she inclined her head, bobbed a pretty curtsey and extended gloved fingers for him to take. In a gesture that was more European than English, he captured her hand in both his own. He conveyed it to within an inch of his lips, where, with his eyes on hers, he planted a hint of a kiss in the air, fractionally above her glove. It was an act of seductive deliberation. Eliza felt the blood rush to her face, and she snatched back her hand as though she had been burned. Mentally she chastised herself for her gauche behaviour but her reaction had been instinctive. She was glad to take the seat indicated by her father and sank into it with relief.

Matthew was speaking but Eliza had to force herself to concentrate. Every nerve end twitched and she had to keep her eyes fixed on the floor as her stomach fluttered and the pulse in her neck beat a remorseless tattoo. She was very much afraid. This man had a disturbing physical effect on her. Heat seemed to radiate through her body and she had to clasp her fingers together to still their trembling. She was acutely aware of Henry Bentinck's disturbing presence. Her mind was in turmoil. Dare she defy her father? Did she still want to? The warmth receded, leaving her icy-cold.

'I am sorry, Papa. Forgive me, but would you mind repeating what you were saying. I fear that my thoughts were elsewhere.'

Broadwood cleared his throat. Was the child playing fast and loose with him? He looked at her agitated face and decided that she was probably overcome by the moment.

He began again. 'Mr Bentinck has asked me for your hand, Elizabeth. I have given my consent to the match providing, of course, that you wish to accept his offer.' He smiled to indicate that he had made a joke, and that his statement was not to be taken seriously. 'I shall leave you to discuss the matter,' he continued and, duty done, he tossed his mangled cigar into the fire, bent to kiss his daughter once more, nodded at Henry and scuttled from the library breathing an audible sigh of relief.

Bentinck came to stand in front of Eliza. He placed one finger beneath her chin and tilted up her lovely face. There was a long silence. Eliza started to tremble once more.

'You would make me an exceedingly happy man, Miss Broadwood, if you would consent to become my wife. I may say that I have the utmost admiration for you, and find myself overwhelmed by your beauty.' He watched the swift colour rush into her face, and noted the apprehensive flicker in her eyes before they were modestly lowered. He was tempted to laugh out loud. The girl was incapable of pretence. Her fear was evident but equally, there could be no doubt that she was stimulated by his attentions. He waited in silence, his eyes never leaving her face. What would she do?

Her response was breathless. 'Mr Bentinck, I should be honoured to accept your proposal,' she whispered.

Bentinck took his place beside her on the sofa extracting a plain box from his pocket. He gained possession of her hand and drew off her glove, his gaze dwelling all the time on her face. Eliza felt light-headed and there was a noise like hissing surf in her ears. Henry opened the box and lifted out a circle of magnificent diamonds, which sparkled and glittered in the reflection of the fire. She drew a gasping breath at this evidence of his wealth.

'We are famous in Holland for the quality of our stones and these have been in my family for almost two hundred years,' he declared. Slowly, he slid the ring on her finger, turned over her hand and set the lightest of kisses in the centre of her palm. He stood up, pulling her to her feet and, drawing her shaking arm through his, he led her out of the library towards the dining-room. She accompanied him like the proverbial lamb to the slaughter, his cold diamonds scintillating on her hand where it rested against the sumptuous velvet of his jacket.

A bemused Eliza remembered little of the evening that

followed. She was battered by conflicting emotions. Her betrothed appeared to be everything that a woman could desire. His looks were pleasing, his dress stylish but avoiding ostentation; he was a cultured and much-travelled man yet did not seek to impose his undoubted superiority upon those with a less extensive knowledge than his own. He allowed discussion of poetry, art and music and was charming to everyone. He was fervent in his admiration of Eliza's beauty, listened avidly to her discourse and was thoroughly attentive to her playing of the pianoforte. He had even accompanied her, singing in a most pleasant baritone, although he disclaimed any talent for music and insisted that it was Eliza's playing which made him appear in better voice than he actually was. The girl, despite herself, had thawed towards him and Papa, in his relief, had become happily inebriated, although by no means disgracefully so.

Mary Bentinck, at their first meeting, professed herself to be overjoyed at the enticing prospect of acquiring such a pretty sister-in-law, and Eliza was flattered and intrigued by the attention of Henry's flamboyant sister. The Bentincks were indeed a fascinating pair. Mary had spoken of house-parties at which a Royal Duke was present, of hunt balls, of many a sojourn in Bath and of their glamorous neighbours in Portman Square. She hinted at delicious scandals concerning ladies of her acquaintance and laughed at the latest absurdities of the King and his wife. She painted an exciting picture of her social landscape, and Eliza's interest and curiosity was aroused. The girls' conversation had become highly improper and Anne Weston was relieved when Matthew and Henry had at last joined the ladies for coffee.

Now, the evening was over and Eliza was free to consider her new position in the privacy of her room. After all her worries, it was possible that the future could be less dreadful than she had imagined. She was both fascinated and repelled by her betrothed. There were things about him that frightened her, yet her apprehension was tinged with excitement. She was certainly not indifferent to him. A sense of power, of animal magnetism emanated from the man, making him impossible to ignore. In addition, she could scarcely fail to be impressed by the magnificence of his lifestyle. She freely acknowledged the acquisitive side of her nature, which would ensure that she enjoyed to the full the privileges that went with becoming Mrs Henry Bentinck. For that, she was prepared to pay the price.

'Eliza, may I come in?' The request was accompanied by a gentle tap at the door.

'Why, Aunt, I am delighted to see you. I am far too agitated to sleep. It has been a strange day. Has it not? Tell me, how do you find Mr Bentinck?'

Anne Weston moved Eliza's discarded gown aside and perched on an overflowing chest. She hesitated before addressing her niece in her usual quiet voice. 'I find him an… an… educated man, and your Papa believes that he is a most suitable match. He has great wealth and a good social position; he will make excellent provision for your future. Life in London will most certainly be to your taste.' She smiled. 'But I do have one concern, my dear; I know that you are always quick to give your friendship, but pray do not allow yourself to be so easily impressed by city tittle-tattle, nor to be so disparaging about life in the provinces. I do not speak of Mr Bentinck but of his sister. I fear that Miss Bentinck may not prove to be the best of companions for you in your new station. She is not quite the thing you know.'

Eliza rounded on her Aunt, angry at this slighting reference to her new friend. 'I really have no way to please you do I Aunt Weston? As I recall, it was you who urged me to accept this marriage with good grace. For the sake of my father and my family's reputation you were willing to send me to the altar in wretched misery. Now, when I find someone who is to my liking, and who can help me in my new life, you criticise her manner in such away as to be sure to spoil my pleasure. I feel sorry for you, Aunt. You are so bound by what you consider to be proper that you have ceased to find any joy in life.' A calculating gleam appeared for a moment in the girl's eyes. 'This marriage may not be the love match for which I had hoped, but Mr Bentinck is not displeasing to me and I shall undoubtedly be well recompensed for what I do. Can you be certain that your anxiety on my account is not driven by envy, Aunt?' she asked.

Anne stumbled to her feet. Her lips were compressed, her face pale. She was dismayed at this latest example of her niece's shallow nature. 'Goodnight, Elizabeth,' she muttered and turned away.

Eliza was immediately contrite. 'Anne... Aunt... I... I am sorry... I did not mean...' She was stammering to an empty room. Flinging herself on the bed, she wept copious tears of rage, confusion and exhaustion, until she drifted into a troubled sleep.

The darkness of the house closed about Anne as she climbed the stairs to the nursery floor, seeking solace as always in the comforting proximity of her children. She too was exhausted; the last weeks had taken their toll and her emotions were drained. She felt that it had been a long, long time since she had known any true peace of mind. Passing the schoolroom, she heard a slight scuffling and the fine hairs on her arms lifted in reaction to the unexpected noise. She stopped, took hold of the knob and turned it carefully. Her mouth was dry.

'Who is it?' she whispered. 'Who's there?'

'Mrs Weston, Ma'am, it is only me.' Daniel's soft voice immediately calmed her. The sound of his gentle Jamaican lilt brought sudden tears of homesickness to her eyes. She went into the darkened room, shutting the door on the sleeping house.

At first, Anne was barely able to discern her slave's shape but as her eyes became accustomed to the gloom, she could make out a denser dark mass against the back-drop of shadows. Without speaking she joined Daniel at the bare table, the scrape of her chair on the floor sounding unnaturally loud in the silence. There was no need for words; each of them drew comfort from the presence of the other. The moments ticked by. Eventually Anne spoke, her reluctant voice, even in a whisper, shattering the peace.

'I suppose that we could sit here all night, but I fear that it would solve nothing and we would both be the worse for our vigil in the morning. I must confess, Daniel, that I came up here looking for comfort. I wished to be near my children. I did not expect to find you up so late. Why are you not asleep?'

Daniel stretched his arms above his head, yawning mightily. 'You are right, Ma'am. To stay here would do no good. Tomorrow must be faced and it would be better dealt with by a rested mind. The problem is that I have never been able to learn the facility of falling asleep to order. I only wish that I could.' He smiled, his teeth gleaming in the darkness. 'Marcus can sleep anywhere, at any time. I have even seen him dozing in the saddle.'

Daniel's Mistress appreciated his attempt to lighten the atmosphere and she too smiled, albeit fleetingly.

'I thought that we could all be happy here. When my husband died it seemed the logical thing to do, to return to the protection of my brother in the town where I spent my early years. Why has it not worked out as I thought? What could I have done to improve things? I feel so useless here. There is little purpose in the social round; I am too old to be distracted by designs for pretty clothes. The gossip of the drawing-room is not to my taste. My brother thought he needed a housekeeper but the servants at Fernleigh were running this establishment very well without my intervention, and my niece will have no further need for a chaperone in a month or two. What is the point?'

She jumped to her feet and began her usual agitated pacing up and down. Daniel grinned, in spite of himself.

'Has Liverpool changed so much, or is it I who have changed? In Jamaica, there was a purpose in my life. Even without Jeremiah I was occupied and felt needed. The people on the estate relied on me, and all their problems became my problems; their successes were my own.' Anne flung herself back into her seat and dropped her head on her arms. Her voice was muffled. 'Perhaps that is the answer. Maybe we should go back home... There. You see,' she declared in triumph. 'That is it. I still regard Jamaica as my home. Is that where we should have stayed, Daniel? Is it? Should we look to return once my niece is safely wed? What do you think?'

Daniel's head spun. To go home to the island of his birth, where he had a place, a recognised place in society. To return where he belonged. Not to have to stay here and watch Miss Eliza depart for her new life in London, a life in which she had no need of his devotion. He was sure that once he was back in the Caribbean his world would right itself and its present turbulence would be only a memory. Daniel was grateful for the concealing darkness. He tried desperately to keep his voice steady, non-committal. More than ever before, he would need to give his Mistress an honest and considered opinion.

'It is possible, Ma'am, that a return to the island would be the answer to your present despair, but are you certain that it would be best, in the long term, for you and your children?' Daniel forced himself to continue. 'It is an action that once taken would be difficult to retrieve. It might be best considered in the light of day and perhaps even later, when things have settled into a pattern after Miss Elizabeth's wedding. You certainly could not think of leaving before that event. Would it not be more judicious to let the decision wait until then?'

'Thank you, dear Daniel,' murmured Anne. 'I know what it cost you to give me such sound advice. Your longing to go home was in your voice, even if I am unable to see your face. What you say is right, of course. The middle of a tiring night, at the end of a long day and after so many fraught months, is scarcely an opportune time to take such momentous decisions. I declare, I am becoming as emotional as my brother's child.' She climbed stiffly to her feet and wandered across the room. In the lighter oblong of the open doorway she paused. 'I will always be grateful for your support,' she said, and left him. It was only when Anne had reached the welcome sanctuary of her own room and had wearily undressed, that she remembered that she had not discovered why Daniel was still awake.

The following morning was a perfect English day. Eliza, Henry and Mary had breakfasted early and had taken the carriage into Liverpool, where Bentinck had business matters to transact. The ladies were intent upon purchasing lace, ribbon, hair ornaments and other frivolous necessities from the smart establishments that had sprung up in the town. Anne was checking final domestic arrangements with Mrs Edwards and Sullah had organised Marcus to drive her and the children to the shore. In the library, Daniel and Matthew Broadwood were taking down details of a new cargo from a Manchester manufacturer.

'Mr Broadwood, Sir, are you well?' Daniel put aside his pen and moved around the desk to the Master's chair.

Matthew was easing a finger around his neck, seeking to loosen the constricting folds of his cravat. His face was puce and his breathing laboured. He waved the slave back to his seat. After interminable moments, the angry colour faded from Broadwood's cheeks and his breath came more normally. He relaxed, his heavy head drooping on his chest. The ticking clock punctuated the silence.

The old man's pain-filled eyes studied Daniel. His voice was strained and hoarse.

'You have proved yourself to be trustworthy these past weeks, Daniel,' he said gruffly. 'My sister was right about you. You do not fuss and you know when to keep a still tongue in that head of yours. This is not the first of these attacks that has come my way in recent months.' He waved a vague hand in the direction of the copious paper-work. 'The business, the worry, the estate. You know.'

'Yes, Sir, there has been much to concern you of late.'

'But the others must not be told anything of my indisposition. I must see Elizabeth safely wed. The girl seems to have accepted her lot and Bentinck is a good catch, but he is a businessman to his boots. If he should scent a weakness, well, he will surely drive a harder bargain. I cannot afford for him to know that I will probably not see out the year.'

Daniel gasped. 'But, Sir...'

Broadwood continued, his voice becoming agitated. 'No. Let me finish, man. I must see my daughter settled and the family affairs on a sound footing. Whatever it costs. Do you understand me? Do you?'

The dangerous colour was beginning to flood Broadwood's features again, and Daniel hastened to reassure him. 'I do understand, Sir, and I shall say nothing if that is what you wish, but should you not see a Doctor?'

'Pah! Doctors! They are only good for cutting up dead bodies, man. They cannot do any damage then. I would as soon let a witch doctor loose on my ailments than one of those butchers.' He gave a short bark of laughter. 'And you would know all about witch doctors, Daniel.' He laughed again, pleased with his own joke.

'If you are sure, Mr Broadwood,' murmured the slave. 'But what of Mrs Weston? Will you not at least take her into your confidence?'

'No!' The response was emphatic. 'My sister came here, after the death of her husband, to seek my protection. She is not to be given further cause for worry.'

Daniel nodded his agreement. 'Then can I get you anything, Master?'

'Aye, a brandy, and a stiff one. And you need not look at the clock. I know it is early. Get me a drink and then leave me to rest a while. We can finish these manifests later. Our first guest does not arrive until tomorrow. He should be an interesting companion at the dinner table to be sure. A Mr Barton, George Barton. From the Colonies… Oh, no… I must not call them that. We lost those. Did we not? The gentleman is from America. Virginia or Georgia, I believe.' He put back his head and closed his eyes. Daniel let himself out of the library, pleased to see the Master more animated, and made his way to the schoolroom.

He had scarcely set out Timothy's books for the next lesson, when the door crashed open and Sullah tore into the room, clutching a sobbing Margaret in her arms. She was closely followed by Marcus, who was dragging Timothy by the hand.

'What has happened? What is wrong?' Daniel leaped to his feet and sent the chair crashing to the floor behind him.

Sullah was almost incoherent with rage. She jerked a thumb at Marcus as she pushed against the door of the children's bedroom. 'Ask him,' she panted. 'Ask Marcus.' She snatched Timothy's hand and gathered both of the infants into her arms. 'Come to Sully, my pets. A nice warm drink and a little nap be what yo' pair needs. Everythin' be all right now. Don't you go frettin'. That nasty man be all gone now.' She pulled them into the sanctuary of the nursery and closed the door firmly at her back.

Daniel set his chair to rights and pulled up a stool for Marcus.

'What is all that about? Sullah is clearly angry, and Miss Meg is upset. Even Master Timmy is scared. What is the boy afraid of? What has happened?'

Marcus' lips were pressed together in a thin, tight line; his face was impassive but his eyes blazed.

'It is that Bentinck. The man Miss Eliza is goin' to marry. He almost ran us off the road. He be one misbegotten son of a God-forsaken whore!' Daniel's jaw dropped. He had never heard Marcus bad-mouth anyone in all the years that he had known him, and to speak in such a way about one of the Master's guests was so out of character as to be beyond belief. He stared at his friend in consternation.

The door flew open once more and a distracted Anne Weston rushed across the room to clutch at her coachman's arm.

'Elizabeth told me that there was an accident. What happened, Marcus?' Her voice rose shrilly. 'What has happened to my children?'

Sullah appeared at the nursery door, a warning finger to her lips. 'Shh,' she whispered. 'Missy Meg is fast asleep an' Massa Timmy be dozin'. They is both all right, Ma'am. You has no cause to fret no more.'

Anne's face was ashen 'Tell me. Someone tell me what has happened. You, Marcus. You tell me.' She looked around helplessly before sinking into the chair vacated by Daniel.

'We had all been down to the shore. It was a fine

mornin'.' The slave sat forward, his strong arms on the table and began to pick at his finger nails. 'We was lookin' for shells an' them children was havin' a good time, for sure. I knows they was. Well, we was all comin' home, an' I could see the big gate to the Hall, just a ways along the lane. We was comin' from one side and that Mr Bentinck, he was comin' from the other side, drivin' his own carriage with them two ladies in. We was much closer to the turn for the gate than he was, Missus.'

'That sure be the truth,' interrupted Sullah.

'Quiet, Sullah. Do go on, Marcus,' pleaded Anne.

'Well, Ma'am, when he sees me, he done whip up his horses to get to the turn afore us. He was stood up an' crackin' his whip, an' laughin' all the while. Miss Eliza, she was half upset an' half excited, but the other lady, why, she was real pleased. Her eyes, they was all a-glitter. Well, I has to pull back on my horses, Ma'am, an' I pulls back as hard as I can. The little mare, she done hurt her leg an' the carriage bucks an' rocks like a live thing. Missy Meg bumped her face, and the young Massa, he fell off the seat an' bangs his arm. They was real scared, Ma'am. Well, when we gets through the big gate they was all a long ways down the drive, laughin' an' wavin' they was. Like nothin' was wrong.'

The pause stretched into endless minutes as the three slaves watched the Mistress in silence. Her eyes were closed and her fists clenched. When she spoke, she had to force the words through gritted teeth.

'Thank you, Marcus, and you too, Sullah. The children will recover and there would seem to be no harm done. It is most important to Mr Broadwood, and to my niece, that this weekend should pass without disruption. It must go well. It will be best, therefore, if nothing further is said about this incident for the present. It was a... a... mis-judgement on Mr Bentinck's part. He would not have meant any harm to come to the children. Poor judgement and high spirits. That is all.' She smiled, a bright, empty smile and left them.

The slaves stared at each other. Sullah was the one to break the silence.

'It was not poor judgement an' it was not high spirits neither. He knowed exactly what he was doin' an' he enjoyed it.'

Marcus nodded. 'We could all have been hurt an' hurt bad but that man, he was not goin' to be beat to that there gate. Not by a black man. No sir, not if he had to kill for it. That Bentinck, he be evil an' his sister too. Wicked folks, that's what they is. No good will come o' this here weddin'. I knows it. An' Missus, she knows it too. I got a real bad feelin' 'bout this.' There was fear in Marcus' eyes and both he and Sullah made the familiar sign to fend off evil spirits.

Daniel wandered across to the schoolroom window, rubbing abstractedly at the old wound on his arm. He gazed outside. 'There is nothing that we can do. Nothing,' he declared, and laid his forehead against the cool glass. 'There is nothing that anyone can do.'

CHAPTER NINE

FERNLEIGH HALL
MAY 1792

The early-morning sun flooded through the half-open door of the stable, picking out scraps of hay on the cobbled floor and outlining the dark shape of a man working on the gleaming coat of a small bay mare. The horse whinnied blowing gently down her muzzle as she nudged the man's shoulder. His bronze skin glistened with sweat and the muscles of his back rippled with each rhythmic stroke of the brush. Daniel allowed the scent of warm hay, the sweet breath of the animals and the hypnotic movement of his arms to fill his mind, penetrating its troubled corners and soothing its restless surface. Marcus had been sent to work in the garden and Daniel had offered to help in the stable, finding a healing peace in grooming the horses. The animals accepted a man as they found him with no notion of colour, wealth or social standing; there was no need, here, to concern himself with questions as to where he belonged.

Daniel was mildly surprised to find himself speaking to the horses in the language of his early childhood.

'There you is. You sure is fine now, my beauty. No need to be fussin' yourself an' gettin' in a fidget. You be a beautiful missy. You sure is. I knows. Daniel knows my lovely.' He smiled, feeling a rare warmth at the memory of his days with his slave mother that the words invoked. It was astonishing, but those very early years on Jim Watts' plantation had seemed happy and secure. That was before he knew that he was different, before he was told who was his father; it was before the realisation of the mixture of his black and white blood drowned his personality in confusion. He could remember being content, playing with the chickens in the dust. He put down his brush, revelling for the first time in the comfort of early memories of his mother.

The beginnings of an acceptance of who he was stirred somewhere deep in his being and he had an unaccustomed sense of satisfaction with his lot. Whistling, he went outside to wash at the pump in the yard. He plucked wisps of straw from his hair, enjoying the feel of a cool breeze on his skin. He worked the handle of the pump, dousing his head and upper body beneath the stream of icy water, coming up spluttering and panting as his hand fumbled for his discarded shirt on which to dry himself.

Daniel dashed the water from his eyes and blinked as a voice startled him.

'Is this what you want?' Mary Bentinck was standing less than a yard away, the slave's shirt dangling from her fingers. Her velvet riding habit was marked by splashes of water, her head was on one side and the tip of her tongue was just visible through parted lips. Her dark eyes flicked over Daniel's dripping head and chest before she returned her gaze to his face. The look in her eyes shook him to the core. A gleam of desire smouldered and flickered for an instant and then disappeared but the signal had been clear and unmistakable. In that moment, Daniel knew that his fleeting contentment was gone, and he was again filled with bitterness, anger and confusion. He was certain that this woman was about to toy with him, like a cat with a captive bird, and there was nothing that he could do to avoid it.

Mary Bentinck tapped her whip against the folds of her skirt and moved towards the stables. She looked over her shoulder at Daniel who was struggling into his damp shirt.

'I shall need my horse to be saddled,' she ordered, passing into the dimness of the barn. He followed reluctantly, keeping his eyes on the floor. Daniel again found himself thinking of his early years, and he could hear his mother's soft, melodic voice.

'Never look them in the face, child. If yo' looks cowed they will soon find other sport. Yo' looks into their eyes an' they won't be happy 'til they've broken yo' spirit.'

He gathered together saddle, stirrups and bridle, his movements quick, economical and unconsciously graceful. The horse sensed his unease and moved her feet in a restive side-step. Daniel kept the animal between the woman and himself, and when he had finished he led the creature outside and stood at its head, stroking the long muzzle and murmuring in its ears.

Mary Bentinck appeared at his elbow. She put her hands on his shoulders and turned him to face her, stepping right up against him.

'Help me up then,' she murmured. Daniel obediently held the stirrup as she lifted her skirt and placed her foot. Her eyes met his. 'Help me mount.' He placed both hands on her waist lifting her effortlessly into the saddle. He stepped back at once, his gaze lowered. The woman stared at the top of his head. Deliberately she opened her hand and the whip clattered to the floor. Daniel bent down, retrieved it and, without raising his head, he offered it to her. She took it from him and immediately released it again. As it rolled across the cobbles, it came to rest against a gleaming black boot. Daniel scrabbled to pick it up, biting back a yelp of pain as the heel of the boot was driven hard on to his hand. He drew back and looked up into the sallow, cruel face of Henry Bentinck.

Daniel was sickened as he realised that this was the man to whom Eliza was betrothed. He recalled Marcus' account of the carriage accident the previous day and knew that he must somehow get out of the stable yard.

Bentinck looked into the dark eyes, and when he spoke his voice was full of menace. 'Pick it up, boy.'

Daniel's lashes lowered, hiding his expression. 'Yes, Master,' he mumbled, and extended his numbed hand. He heard a clatter of hooves and a stranger appeared in the shadow of the arch leading from the drive. Bentinck, with his back to the new arrival, stamped down again with his foot and Daniel gritted his teeth against the agony.

'I said pick it up.'

'Excuse me,' smiled the newcomer as he dismounted. 'I don't think the man can do as you ask. The lady's crop appears to be caught under your boot. If you will permit me?' He bent down and pulled the whip from beneath Bentinck's foot, presented it to Mary with the merest inclination of his head and looked at Daniel. 'Could you attend to my horse? He has had a good workout this morning and needs to be fed and watered.' He turned to Bentinck, holding out his hand. 'George Barton, at your service, Sir,' he drawled. 'From the state of Georgia originally although presently lodged in Liverpool town. Are you a guest here too?'

Bentinck struggled to contain his anger.

'If I may be allowed to introduce myself, Sir? I am Henry Bentinck; this lady is my sister, Miss Mary Bentinck. In answer to your question, yes, we are guests of Mr Broadwood. Now, if you will excuse me. I have things to do.' He turned on his heel, and stalked out of the yard his boots echoing loudly on the cobbles.

'I too have dallied rather longer than I should,' said Mary. 'I shall see you some other time, Daniel,' and

138

wheeling her horse about, she galloped through the gate, pulling hard on the bridle.

George Barton watched them leave, a pensive expression on his pleasant features.

'Neither of those two has a gentle hand, it seems to me,' he murmured wryly. He turned to Daniel. 'I should run those fingers under the tap if I were you,' he advised. 'Then, if will you point me at the house, I really should go and find my host. I have met Mr Broadwood on several occasions but this is the first time that I have had the pleasure of staying at Fernleigh Hall. It is a real pretty house, that's for sure.' He looked curiously at Daniel. 'Have you been here long?'

Daniel was nonplussed. He had become unused to such open friendliness since leaving the Caribbean.

'No, Sir,' he murmured. 'Only for a few months. Three of us came from Jamaica with our Mistress. Mrs Weston is sister to Mr Broadwood and she came back to her old home when her husband died.'

'Yes, I seem to have heard that he had a widowed sister. And you are obviously the groom here. Right?'

'No, Sir,' corrected Daniel. 'I am tutor to Mrs Weston's son. I also assist both the Mistress and Mr Broadwood with their correspondence and some of their business dealings. I am just helping a friend with the horses.'

Barton considered the slave's reply. 'Yes, I see.' He nodded. 'It cannot have been an easy transition. I spent some time in Jamaica as a young man and know something of how things work over there. Society sure is a lot different here.' He gave a brief inclination of his head, handed over the reins of his horse and moved briskly beneath the arch, setting off in the direction of the house. Daniel watched him go, comforted by the man's unexpected insight.

Anne Weston was crossing the hall as Melchet opened

the front door. She paused, listening.

'Good morning, Sir. Mr Barton, is it not?' Melchet's gloomy tones echoed in the silence.

Anne moved forward. 'Mr Barton?' She extended her hand, smiling a warm greeting. 'I am Anne Weston, Matthew's sister. We were expecting you. Welcome to Fernleigh Hall.' She turned to the outraged Melchet. 'I will conduct this gentleman to the drawing-room myself, please inform Mr Broadwood that his guest has arrived and then...' She raised a quizzical eyebrow in Barton's direction. 'Coffee perhaps?'

'Coffee will be just fine Ma'am,' he drawled, his mouth quirking at the corner as Melchet inclined his head and withdrew in a rustle of outraged propriety. Barton gave a conspiratorial grin. 'I am afraid that our Colonial manners appear to be generating considerable disapproval.'

'I know,' she confided, smiling once more. 'Whoever heard of the mistress of a house receiving guests at the door herself.' She sighed. 'I fear that Melchet has always brought out the mischief in me. I really cannot resist shocking him. If only he were not so... so eternally pompous!'

Barton nodded his agreement. 'I can see why he makes you react like that but, you know, it could be his way of dealing with his own insecurity. Perhaps he can only function in a fixed framework.'

As she preceded him into the drawing-room, a smile lurked on Anne's lips; George Barton was a complete surprise. She had expected her brother's business associate to be old, stuffy and deadly dull. Instead, she had introduced herself to a stranger with whom she had established instant rapport and empathy. She knew nothing about him and yet felt as though he had been a friend for years. It was most odd. She realised that her face was flushed and her eyes bright as she conducted him to a chair close to the low fire. Settling herself on the sofa across from him, she watched as he studied the room with open curiosity. Anne was exhilarated. She had not realised just how stifled she had been by the formality of her brother's home and by the wearisome round of social engagements that had become her life. She felt alive for the first time in months. George Barton was certainly a refreshing change.

As Melchet brought in the tray and she busied herself with the ritual of cups, jugs and coffee pots, Anne found herself examining the visitor with a candid interest. About ten years older than herself, he was moderately tall, taller than Matthew but without Daniel's great height. The shoulders beneath his perfectly cut jacket were broad, but his trim waist and narrow hips gave the lie to any suggestion of grossness. He gave the impression of a man whose life was lived not in banks or drawing-rooms but in wide open spaces. She nodded to herself. Yes, America was right for him, a heroic new world of adventure and enterprise.

The blue eyes twinkled at her and Anne blushed like a young girl. She gave a slight shrug, acknowledging that she had been staring quite unashamedly. Passing him a cup, she made a detailed study of the toe of her shoe.

'You must think me exceedingly rude, Sir. I confess to ill-mannered curiosity. I have not met an American gentleman before.'

'Why, don't apologise, Ma'am. I had no little curiosity of my own to be fulfilled. You are the first lady that I have met since coming to England who has not reminded me of my maiden aunt.' He settled back into his chair, one elegant leg crossed over the other. 'My father died when I was a boy, and when my mother remarried I was sent to England to live with her sister for a time. Can you just imagine that? An American boy, brought up on a cotton plantation by a black-mammy nurse; I played with all sorts of youngsters back then and never did learn to curb my tongue. I got into scraps the whole time. Then I was set down with this spinster lady and was taught my manners. Trouble was I was dead set against learning the lessons. I was beaten regularly I can tell you. I was mighty glad when I was sent away to school.' He laughed, his eyes crinkling at the corners. 'Mind you, Ma'am, I think that my Aunt Jackson was even more pleased; we neither of us much looked forward to the holidays, that's for sure. As soon as I was old enough, I took ship for the West Indies. I did some attorney work in Jamaica for a spell, and then when Mama's second husband died I went back home to Georgia.' He sipped his coffee, watching Anne over the rim of his cup. They regarded each other in companionable silence.

Matthew Broadwood bustled through the door, disturbing their bemused reflections. Anne could have sworn that regret flickered for a moment on Barton's face, before he jumped to his feet, bowing to the older man.

'Mr Broadwood, Sir. May I say how delighted I am to be here. It was so very kind of you to invite me to be a guest in your very fine home.' Anne smiled as she noted the way in which the American extended every old-fashioned courtesy to his host.

Matthew's chest swelled with pride and he beamed his delight. 'The pleasure is all mine I can assure you, Barton.' He turned reproachfully to Anne. 'I do hope that my sister has received you with due regard to proprieties?' he enquired. Anne ground her teeth; Melchet had been carrying tales again.

'Why my dear Sir, I have never been received so well anywhere. Your sister has extended the most gracious hospitality,' intervened Barton. He threw a cryptic smile in Anne's direction. 'I must say, that if the people that I have met so far at Fernleigh Hall are anything to go by, why, I shall look forward to a most entertaining weekend.'

'Excellent, Sir, excellent,' declaimed a relieved Matthew, taking up his usual stance in front of the fire. 'We can safely leave our business until tomorrow. Perhaps Anne will show you around the place this afternoon and you can meet everyone else at dinner. I think we can promise you an enjoyable evening.' He stomped from the room, leaving the two of them alone again.

'Shall we begin with the house, Mr Barton, or do you prefer the garden?' Anne asked, rising and shaking out her skirts.

George offered her his arm with a bow. 'At least the garden has the advantage of being outside Melchet's range,' he suggested, and was rewarded by a quick gurgle of laughter. Together they strolled through the front door, deep in animated discussion.

It was late in the evening as Matthew Broadwood surveyed his guests from his position at the head of the table; it had been a long time since twenty people had sat down in this room. Half the party was made up of his business acquaintances and their dreary wives. He smiled grimly. It would do no harm for them to see him entertaining on this scale, particularly considering the rumours buzzing around Liverpool about his financial state. The Rector and his lady were always on anyone's guest list. Matthew would be surprised if they dined at home on any more than one day each week and, having partaken of their food, he could scarcely blame them for eating out whenever they had the opportunity. Old Blundell's nephew had brought his new bride along; pity she was such an insipid piece. He compared the unfortunate young woman with Mary Bentinck, sitting near her. What a contrast. One so straight-laced and the other anything but. It was odd, mused

Matthew, that a cold, repressed place like Holland could produce such a voluptuous wench; she was more like a Mediterranean beauty than an offspring of the low countries.

Matthew took a hasty swig of his wine and turned his lustful thoughts away from Mary Bentinck as he studied his own womenfolk. Anne was looking surprisingly well this evening. She had a higher colour than usual and appeared to have recovered some of her old vivacity. She was certainly managing to charm both young Blundell on her left and George Barton on her right. He supposed that his sister's unorthodox manners might well appeal to the American fellow. He gulped more of his wine, indicating to the hovering Melchet that he should refill the glasses.

Broadwood gazed, with bleary eyes, the length of the table to where his daughter occupied the seat opposite his own. The girl still seemed to be a little pale, but she had clearly set out to be an attentive hostess and was looking quite serene. Composure suited her fragile beauty rather better than her normal volatile and somewhat noisy manners. She had acquired a new self-possession and elegance that made her seem older than her years and a more suitable partner for Henry Bentinck. He shied away from any contemplation of Bentinck's personality. Disturbing rumours had come his way in recent days, from Mrs Roberts in the town house. He had put most of it down to malicious gossip, but seeds of doubt had been sown. Still, it was too late now. He and Bentinck had agreed terms for Eliza's marriage. Money had changed hands, and the family's honour had been upheld.

That was enough. He would not allow himself to dwell on anything else. He rose stiffly to his feet and banged on the table.

'Ladies and gentlemen, I have an announcement to make which gives me great delight. My daughter,

Elizabeth, has accepted a proposal of marriage from my friend Mr Henry Bentinck, a union to which I have been pleased to give my consent.' There was a smatter of polite applause. Eliza's face paled and she stared at her plate. 'I ask you all to join with me in drinking to the health and happiness of Elizabeth and her future husband, Henry Bentinck.'

In the universal pushing back of chairs and happy chatter that followed, most of the guests missed the young woman's swift intake of breath as her betrothed reached for her hand and carried it to his lips. George Barton's sharp eyes noticed that Bentinck had, apparently unknowingly, squeezed the girl's fingers, crushing his diamond ring into the soft flesh of her hand.

'Elizabeth and Mr Bentinck,' chorused the guests, smiling at a benign Henry and his future wife. Only Mary did not echo the toast.

She raised her glass solely to her brother, mouthing the words. 'To you, dear Henry.' Her gaze flickered over Eliza and she smiled.

Anne Weston watched the pair and shivered. Surely she had imagined that look of contempt on Bentinck's face as he had bent to his betrothed. She must have, mustn't she? For an instant, the man had appeared to actually hate either Eliza, himself or both of them. It was unnatural. Anne turned to George Barton at her side and, as she saw his expression, she realised that she had not been mistaken. He had seen it too. There was much here that she did not understand but Anne knew, with a sick feeling of dread, that her niece would have little joy of her union with Henry Bentinck.

In the darkness of his cupboard-like room, Daniel tossed restlessly, trying to empty his mind, but sleep eluded him.

He was afraid, afraid for Miss Eliza and afraid for himself. He knew that Henry Bentinck was his enemy. Had it not been for the intervention of the other gentleman, Mr Barton, who knew how far Bentinck may have pushed him? How far could the man have gone before Daniel's pride would have demanded that he retaliate? The slave had witnessed behaviour like this before, on the island. Some of the plantation managers, even some of the owners, had delighted in abasing their slaves, in stripping them of all dignity. He had seen it, to his eternal shame, in his own father. He had listened to Marcus speaking of crewmen on the middle-passage who had the same perverted nature, and had heard his friend insist that it was possible to withdraw within yourself, into an inner core where your tormentors could not reach. Then, no matter what they did, you still had ownership of your own soul.

Daniel had heard all this but had never been sure that he would be able to endure the humiliation. For almost all of his life, he had been aware that within his personality lay the seeds of the mindless animal rage that had dominated his father's final years. His loathing of this tendency had made him learn to suppress it in his youth and now he nearly always had control of the demon. He was however, on rare occasions, conscious of it hovering on the edge of his sanity, waiting to take over his mind and his body. It was like a gun to his head and today, in the stable, the trigger had been close to being pulled.

He sighed. How much of his problem was due to his father's character and how much due to his own? His greatest fault, he knew, was his overbearing pride. Why should that be so? Was it his mixed blood that was responsible for his arrogance? Was he the man he had become because of his ancestry, or would he still have had the same nature no matter what the colour of his skin? How often, over the years, had he pondered this question?

Yet he had never come anywhere near the answer. Nor had he ever been really put to the test before, not like other slaves, not like Marcus and Sullah. Was it his determination not to be like the others that drove him? Was he so ashamed of his black blood that any attempt to humiliate him resulted in this surge of blind rage? He clutched the blanket close around his shoulders and shut his eyes, but his fears would not be laid to rest.

He was afraid of the feelings that Henry Bentinck could arouse; worried for himself but more so for Miss Eliza. He groaned and hammered his fist into the palm of his hand, seeking relief from the aggression that was threatening to choke him. Here, in his own room, he could acknowledge that he loved Elizabeth. He knew that it was wrong, that it was impossible. It was not the physical love of a man for a woman; it was more the love of a knight for his lady, a worship, an adoration, but nonetheless strong for that. The thought of her father making that high-spirited girl the captive of such a callous and cruel man was beyond belief. To push her into such a marriage, and to do it for money, was no better than selling your own child. She would be as much Bentinck's chattel as any slave; the man would be entitled to do with her as he willed. So it was with any husband, he knew that, but this man was evil. Any creature in his power would bring out the worst in him. Daniel had seen that at first hand.

He clambered angrily from his bed and began to pace the floor. He had to find some way to dissipate this soul-destroying rage. Tugging on his breeches, and carrying his shoes in his hand, he slipped down the silent stairs, through the kitchen and out into the velvet darkness of the night. The dark shadow ran wildly across the lawn and disappeared into the sanctuary of the trees.

Blood surged through Daniel's veins. His breath came in great heaving gasps, and pain beat against his temples in time with his pounding feet. Deep in the enfolding blackness of the wood, the slave flung himself on to the dew-covered ground. A fitful moon broke through the cloud and bathed the trees in an almost translucent light. Gradually he regained his breath and with it, a modicum of his composure. He hauled himself upright, leaning his back against the tree and enjoying the feel of rough bark on his skin. He had discovered his body again. He was no longer simply a tortured mind.

'This has to stop!' He deliberately spoke out loud, seeking to establish contact with his physical self. 'Bentinck is not a devil. The man cannot do anything to you that you are unable to overcome. There are laws in England. Think about the slave ships. What you are asked to tolerate is nothing. Nothing. Accept your black blood. Accept yourself for what you are.' His fingers traced the raised skin of the scar on his arm and he was back in the steaming heat of Jamaica. He closed his eyes. 'Accept it. Be proud of your slave heritage. Think of your own Mammy. She was a good woman, she was strong, she had spirit but she was wise too. Think of the torment she endured, the kidnapping from her home in Africa and then the middle-passage with all its horrors. Consider the hardship of plantation fields and the worse hardship of life with your father. Think of her, Daniel. She survived and so can you.' His breathing slowed and he continued to give voice to his troubled thoughts. 'As for Miss Eliza, well, she is no different to all the other women who must marry where their family bids. It is the way things are, the way they have always been. She has no choice. Few women have. She is a prisoner of her social class. There is no cause for worry. Bentinck will not treat his wife badly. He has a position to keep. She will be safe.'

Daniel nodded in satisfaction at his own reasoning. It was having an effect. Hearing the words spoken gave them a reality that they did not have inside his head. He was calmer now and, stumbling to his feet, he began the weary trudge back to the house. Somewhere, deep in his mind, a demon was whispering.

And the sister? What of Mary Bentinck? What of her, Daniel? She cannot be ignored. She will not go away. What do your clever words say about her?

He shook his head and broke into a jog. The huge shadow of Fernleigh Hall loomed ever closer.

CHAPTER TEN

LIVERPOOL
JULY 1792

It had been many years since the old church of Saint Nicholas on the waterfront had witnessed an event of such social significance. The carriages of the merchants, financiers, foundry owners, members of the Corporation, even the local Member of Parliament, Colonel Tarleton and his brother, the Mayor, had been arriving for the past hour. They formed a straggling procession down past the dry basin, across the front of George's Dock and almost to the start of Strand Street. The inhabitants of coaches that had halted alongside the Fish Market, held handkerchiefs to their noses. They retired as far as possible into the recesses of their vehicles to escape both the smell and the raucous calls of the fish-wives, as the carriages waited to move closer to the gate of the church, where the passengers could safely alight.

The bells rang out across the Mersey and the sunlight sparkled on the water, as a playful breeze ruffled the feathers in the ladies' bonnets and tugged at the fabric of their fine gowns. Within the sanctity of the churchyard, bare-footed, ragamuffin children squealed and chased each other around, luxuriating in the unaccustomed pleasure of a break in their daily grind. Their lank-haired mothers, shawls crossed beneath their sagging breasts and babies clutching their legs, stared at the parade of finery before them with speculative and hostile eyes.

Finally, all the guests were within and the restive crowd awaited the arrival of the bride. Matthew Broadwood and his daughter were known to many. The girl's grandfather had built up a sound business in the town, and before the family had moved to the grand new place out in the countryside, they had been a familiar sight around the quays. Their reputation had suffered of late, what with Matthew's drinking and gambling and the girl's involvement with the abolitionist meetings, but they were still the gentry and still an object of curiosity.

''Er shouldn't be long now,' called one scraggy crone to her neighbour. 'Though why 'er should be wantin' t' get 'ersel' 'itched is beyond the likes o' me.'

'Aye,' retorted the other. 'An' if it were yo' Bill as 'er were gettin' 'itched to, it 'ud be beyond reason an' all.' This witticism was greeted with hoots of derision and provoked a further sally from the first woman.

'Well, it stands to sense don't it, them Broadwoods must be daft, else why'd they go an' live out at t' back o' beyond when they've 'ad a perfectly good 'ouse right 'ere in t' town.'

'Shurrup Lizzie! 'Er's comin'. Look. 'Ers arrived. Ee, God bless thee, lass, good luck t' thee,' and the women drew back as Matthew Broadwood climbed out of his carriage and turned to assist his daughter.

There was a hiss of in-drawn breath followed by the satisfied 'aahh,' of universal approval, as the bride halted at the gate and smoothed the folds of her skirts. Her dress was of a delicate cream silk that gleamed and shimmered in the sunlight. Loose curls framed her face beneath the brim of her nonsense-trimmed bonnet. She clutched a posy of cream and white blossoms and their bell-shaped heads nodded and danced in her trembling hands. Her face was ashen and the blue eyes expressionless as she watched her father tug his cravat into place, straighten his jacket and offer her his arm.

'Well then, girl, are we ready?' he enquired heartily.

'Yes, Papa,' she replied. 'Let us get it done,' and placing her fingers on his sleeve, she moved through the now silent women, out of the sunlight and into the deep shadow of the church, passing beneath the portal and into the gloom beyond.

The bells pealed and the bridal couple appeared in the church doorway to the sound of a few ragged cheers and a babble of voices.

'Tha's done it now, lass, there bain't be no road back,' advised one, with cynical relish.

'Good luck charm, lady, buy a good luck charm to start yer new life?' wheedled a toothless hag, pressing close to Eliza with her grubby basket and waving assorted items under her nose. She turned to Henry Bentinck. ''Ow 'bout 'ee, Sir?' she begged. 'Will 'ee buy my lucky charm fer yer new lady-wife?' She looked up into his eyes and her voice faded. She backed away, her face pale beneath its coating of grime. Muttering under her breath, the old crone pushed her way through the crowd, putting as much distance as possible between herself and the church. At the corner of Chapel Street she stopped and looked back over her shoulder. 'Eeh, that poor maid,' she mumbled. ''Er will surely need some luck,' and, shaking her grizzled head, she disappeared into the warren of twisted alleyways.

Anne Weston stood beside her brother, watching Henry hand Eliza into his carriage. The girl had recovered some of her colour and even smiled nervously at the well-wishers. Anne squeezed Matthew's arm.

'They are not going to be too long away, brother. Poor

Eliza, there can be no Continental wedding journey for her, not with the way things are with the French. At least Scotland is not too far to travel. It should be pretty at this time of year and quite warm. I believe that the moors are a wonderful sight in August and there will be much gun sport for Henry to enjoy. Why, I am told that half of London society has taken to spending the summer months in Scotland. There are sure to be many balls and parties for Eliza to attend and to display all her new clothes.' She glanced sideways at her silent brother and continued rather desperately. 'We both know how much she will enjoy that, do we not?' There was still no response. 'Come along,' Anne murmured, becoming exasperated. 'You are not the first Papa to lose his daughter to marriage, you know. And it was, after all, a union that you wanted.'

'Aye,' responded Broadwood, heavily. 'But what of the girl? What did she want, eh?'

Some of the impatient guests pushed forward from behind as the carriage began to move and Anne and Matthew were swept along in its wake. Anne waved her handkerchief, blinking back tears as Eliza's fingers fluttered from the window and Henry leaned out beyond her, hat raised in one hand and the other resting possessively on his bride's shoulder. Matthew Broadwood stood to one side, panting heavily, as the younger guests and the urchins ran after the coach as it gathered speed. His sister watched him with concern.

'Matthew, are you all right? What is wrong?'

He smiled, nodding his head. 'There is nothing wrong, sister. Nothing that a stiff drink will not cure. It is all this wedding nonsense. The house is full of people all the time. Why, we have had no peace for months. I shall be glad to return to a less frantic existence. It is a rest I need, that is all. Look, I believe that is Marcus with our carriage. Let us get out of here and get home. Once this lot has partaken of all the refreshment that Mrs Edwards has organised, they will leave and then we shall have Fernleigh to ourselves again.' He cast a swift glance around and noticed Mary Bentinck laughing with a group of young men who had flocked around her. 'Well, almost to ourselves,' he said, dryly. 'It is a pity that Bentinck could not take his sister to Scotland with them. Still, I don't suppose it would be quite the thing, would it?'

Mary said her farewells and moved to join Anne and Matthew. The carriage stopped and Marcus assisted the two women in and turned to help his Master. Broadwood slumped in the seat across from Mary and Anne. He was still pale, and his sister watched him in silence as he closed his eyes and appeared to be snoozing. Mary Bentinck stared out of the window, making no attempt at civil conversation; she was totally preoccupied. The swaying motion of the carriage made Anne feel sleepy. It had been a busy few weeks since Eliza's betrothal and she was exhausted. She too closed her eyes and allowed her thoughts to drift idly over the recent events.

There had been a simmering tension hanging like a cloud over Fernleigh Hall, and not all of it could be explained by the sultry heat of an unseasonably oppressive June. Eliza's mood had been strange. She vacillated between a giddy, hysterical excitement, usually when she was in the presence of Mary Bentinck, and a pained and sullen silence whenever her new friend was absent. Both girls had gloried in the selecting of fabrics and designs for Eliza's new gowns and even appeared to enjoy the tedium of endless fittings. Anne, whose own patience with feminine frippery had always been in short supply, was astonished by the amount of time deemed necessary to decide between a blue lover's knot, a mauve bow or a snippet of lace. Still, she had been relieved to see Eliza happy about at least one aspect of her forthcoming wedding.

Anne had tried to broach the subject of the impending marriage on one occasion when she had been alone with her niece in the garden. The Bentincks had retired to their Aunt's Chester home for a few days and Mr Barton was visiting manufacturers in Manchester. For once, Fernleigh was without guests. The house had been stifling all day and the two women had determined to take a turn around the lawns, leaving Matthew to snooze away the effects of his dinner.

'Eliza, my dear,' Anne had laid a gentle hand on her niece's arm. 'I cannot help but be concerned about you. You do not seem happy nor even resigned to this marriage. If you truly are totally wretched, well, I am sure that it is not too late. We can speak to your Papa. Perhaps things could be delayed for a little while. After all, you are still very young.' The girl continued walking, forcing her Aunt to hurry after her. Anne tried once more. 'Mr Bentinck is not an ill-favoured gentleman and you will become accustomed to his ways.' She gave a brief smile. 'When I married dear Jeremiah, I well recall that I too was full of doubt. It is to be expected; it happens to us all, to all brides, but we get over it. Why, it is not so many years ago that girls were forced to wed men they had never even seen. Can you imagine that?' Eliza did not reply. 'What is it? What is troubling you?' Anne persisted. 'Can you not confide in me, my dear? I am sure that it would help for you to talk about your concerns. If you keep on brooding about things as you have been wont to do, you are going to make yourself ill. You are already so dreadfully thin and pale. Please, Eliza. Will you not talk to me?'

In the silence, the piercing call of a cuckoo echoed through the trees and faded away across the darkening lawn. Anne's eyes filled with tears. It was such a quintessentially English sound. It evoked memories of that romantic and magical summer when it had seemed as though herself and Jeremiah were the only two people in the world. The sounds had been clearer, the colours brighter and the scents headier. She had never felt more alive. Anne looked at her niece with pity in her eyes. It was so unfair. Why should Eliza not have the right to feel that same kind of joy? Why should the girl not have the chance of experiencing that same happiness? It was wrong. The whole system was wrong. Why could a woman not control her own destiny, determine her own future? The girl's bitterness was understandable and suddenly, on this glorious summer's evening, Anne felt ashamed that she had been so intolerant of Eliza's misery. Could she really have forgotten the insecurities of her own youth? Could she have lost so easily the memory of her own ideals and hopes and dreams? Putting out a comforting hand towards her niece Anne leaned forward.

'I am so sorry, dear Eliza. I have failed you badly. I should have understood. It seems a long time since I was your age and much has happened to me since then, but it does not excuse my hard-hearted words and actions. I am truly sorry.'

Eliza laid her head on her Aunt's shoulder and wept unchecked floods of bitter tears. It seemed an age before she sniffed and eventually lifted her head.

'What an absolute fright I must look,' she blurted. 'But it is such a relief to let go at last. I have felt that I should burst during these past days. There have always been guests about and people around me. I have had to play a part and it has been hard, so very hard.' She began to cry again, great shaking sobs. Anne drew her towards a seat, sheltered by a tall hedge of stately yew. She pressed her own handkerchief into the girl's unresisting fingers but made no move to curb the passionate outpourings. The tears would provide blessed relief and an easing of tension. There would be time for words later, when the flow had ceased and all the suppressed feelings were finally released.

As the sobs subsided, Eliza leaned against the back of the seat, her face a wan oval in the deepening twilight. Her husky voice floated out of the silence, soft and pensive.

'The difficulty, dear Aunt, is that I am not certain myself how I feel.' The words were hesitant as she sought to probe her own emotions, trying to give expression to her hidden thoughts. 'When I am with Mary and she is describing the life that they live in London, their famous neighbours, politicians, courtiers, titled folk and the like, it all seems so exciting. A great and splendid adventure. The balls and musical evenings, the banquets, the rides and shooting-parties and picnics... and... and... so many interesting events. When I compare the life I shall have in London with the dull, dreary round of morning calls that we have here, well, I am quite captivated. I begin to like the notion of becoming Mrs Henry Bentinck.' She paused and Anne caught the sheen of tears in her eyes before she turned her face away. Nothing stirred in the silent garden.

Eliza shifted in her seat and faced her Aunt again.

'There, you see. I have been totally honest with myself at last. I sound most mercenary. Do I not? Quite the money grubber.'

Anne pressed her hand. 'Go on, my dear, go on,' she encouraged.

Eliza drew a deep, unsteady breath. 'The problem is that I am captivated by the notion of this marriage, but I am afraid of the reality of it. Wait, do not interrupt, for I declare, if I do not go on with this now, I shall never be able to bring myself to utter it again. There is something... something... I do not know what it is, but there is that in Henry which terrifies me. When I am with him, sometimes he excites me.' The girl flushed and lowered her head. 'He can be fascinating and, as you know, I have always been susceptible to a gentleman's charms. But this is different. He arouses feelings that I did not know I possessed. At these times, I can consider my marriage with, if not joy, at least with some interest.' She smiled at her Aunt's discomfiture. 'If you are determined to be the recipient of girlish confidences, Aunt, you cannot allow yourself the luxury of being so easily shocked.' Eliza was unable to remain in her seat. She stood up and turned away from Anne who had to strain to hear her next words. 'There are other times when we are together, when he looks at me and... and... I am mindful of how a snake might hold its victim captive by its stare. His eyes can be so cold, so empty. They shrivel me to my very soul. He seems like two different people.'

'He has not hurt you?' Anne too jumped up, grasping her niece's arm and turning the girl to face her. 'If he has harmed you, your Papa would never, never let you marry him.'

'No. No,' Eliza answered, tonelessly. 'He has done nothing. Nothing. He has been attentive, charming, complimentary. He has bought me gifts, paid for my clothes, given me jewellery. I can have no complaints. Why,' she laughed, a cracked, brittle sound. 'He even told me that he knew that I would be his wife more than five years ago, when we first met. I was only a girl. I had not even put up my hair, and he has waited all this time.'

'Then, my dear, he must care for you deeply. Would you not agree?'

'Well, perhaps so. He... he... said that he had to marry me because I reminded him of his Mama.' She shivered. 'It is getting cool, Aunt Anne. Let us join Papa. We have talked enough for one night.' Eliza had turned and made her forlorn way back to the house. Her Aunt had followed her, convinced that nothing at all had been resolved.

The carriage jolted over a rut, causing Anne to snap out

of her reverie and to glance out of the window to see where they were. Matthew snoozed on, his mouth opening noisily as he slid ever more deeply into the cushioned bench. Mary Bentinck was regarding Anne with some curiosity.

'You were lost in thought, Mrs Weston. Are you missing your niece already, or is it perhaps the disappearance of the amiable Mr Barton that is the cause of your abstraction?'

'As a widow of less than two years, Miss Bentinck, I could scarcely be expected to be concerned by the departure of any gentleman from my brother's house,' Anne snapped, and instantly regretted allowing herself to be provoked. She wondered how it was that the other woman's barbed comments always seemed to be able to pierce her shell.

Anne was ashamed to admit that George Barton's return to America had indeed left her feeling desolate. Just before he set off, he had followed her out on to the terrace one evening after dinner and had taken her hand, turning it over and stroking her palm.

'Mrs Weston,' he declared, 'I would not wish to be guilty of any impropriety towards a lady who has been widowed and who still mourns her husband, but I have not much time. I cannot avoid returning to America. I am needed there and my business in England has been satisfactorily concluded. I have already stayed longer than I should. I can clearly say nothing at present; both you and your children need time to become used to your new situation. However, I would wish you to know that you have my undying admiration and that I hold you in the highest esteem. I would hope to return to this country next year and would like your consent to call upon you then.' It had been as much a declaration as it was possible for him to make and it had been enough. But now she was missing his comforting presence in her life and Mary was aware of it.

That Miss Bentinck recognised her victory was obvious by her discretely murmured comment.

'Why, please do not be cross with me, dear Madam. You must forgive my ill- manners if I have given the slightest offence, for be assured that none was intended. You are so brave and bear your sorrow with such fortitude that I forgot that your husband has so recently passed away. I do think that excessive mourning is an indulgence and is in such bad taste. Would you not agree?'

Anne was again stung into ill-considered self-justification. 'I have two young children whose care is my first priority. I would not wish to burden them with my own sadness. I have no need of outward trappings to remind me of my grief, Miss Bentinck.'

'Why of course,' purred the other. 'I did not wish to imply any want of proper feeling or delicacy on your part. To be sure, your devotion to your late husband's memory is all that it should be. Your attention to Mr George Barton was, I am certain, no more than your duty in fulfilling your obligations as your brother's hostess.' She smiled at Anne whose fury mounted. How dared Mary presume to pass judgement on her own conduct? She seethed at the temerity of the woman. This must stop.

Anne kicked out at Matthew's ankle, causing him to jerk awake and pull himself upright.

'Eh? What? Where are we? Er... What was I just saying?... Er... Anne, my dear, what was it that I just this moment remarked?' he observed, blinking owlishly.

'I believe you pointed out that we were almost home, brother, and that we must be ready to receive the wedding guests. At least we appear to have got here first,' and she gathered together her gloves and purse as the coach rolled to a stop. It rocked gently as Marcus jumped down from his box and opened the door. Anne was handed down from the carriage and preceded her brother and Mary Bentinck into Fernleigh Hall. The house was looking its best and its Master felt a warming glow of satisfaction as he gave his hat to the waiting Melchet and prepared to receive Liverpool's most notable citizens with lavish hospitality. No one would ever be able to accuse Matthew Broadwood of stinting on the wedding of his only child.

It was after midnight before the last guest had departed and an exhausted Anne Weston could drag herself upstairs to the nursery floor. She knew that, tired as she was, sleep would not come easily that night. Her brain seethed and simmered, the fragile state of her emotions making her restless and uneasy. It brought back memories of her bereavement, and produced a state of mind that she had thought to have put behind her. She was dizzy and faintly nauseous. Her jaw was clenched and her hunched shoulders ached with tension. She longed for the comfort of Jeremiah's arms about her, yearned to give herself up to being cherished and protected. Reaching the schoolroom door, she sighed and straightened her back.

Inside, Daniel sat in his usual place at the table with books and maps laid neatly before him. He gave the appearance of having been working but his writing paper was blank and his pen dry. He stood up, holding out a chair for his Mistress, taking in her pallor, the dark circles beneath lacklustre eyes and her distracted air. His concern made him rather more familiar than was normal lately.

'Can I do anything for you, Ma'am? You look tired. A glass of wine perhaps, or a little of the Master's brandy? A cup of hot chocolate? Anything at all. You have only to ask.'

The slave's solicitude was more than she could bear in her over-wrought state, and with a surge of relief Anne took the proffered seat, laid her head on her arms and gave vent to months of pent-up strain and stress. Great shuddering sobs shook her shoulders as Daniel hovered helplessly at her side. He put out a consoling hand, but snatched it back as though he had been scalded. His natural instinct was to give comfort; he wanted to hold her, to soothe her fears, dry her eyes and take away her worries, but it was not his place. He remained standing as close to her as he dared, trying, by his very proximity, to convey his devotion and the depth of his feeling for her. She raised her swollen eyes to his face, shaking her head in wordless anguish.

It was too much! Daniel dropped to his knees beside her chair. He took her hand in his, murmuring calm, meaningless sounds in her ear. He gentled her as he would a fretful horse, stroking and patting her back, easing the stiffness from her shoulders. She clung on desperately, her fingers digging into his palm. Imperceptibly, she began to relax, the sobs subsided and her breathing became calm, quiet. Daniel wondered if she was asleep but then she spoke in a muffled voice.

'Forgive me, Daniel, but I did need your comfort. You cannot know how much your support has meant to me since the death of my husband, and never was it more needed than at present.' She raised her head again. 'I am so very tired and have been so worried. I cannot carry it all any longer.' She sniffed and blew her nose. 'Did you make mention of hot chocolate? I think I should like that. Put another log on the fire, bring a drink and let us sit for a while. I am so weary that I can barely hold myself upright but I know that the moment I lay my head on the pillow my thoughts will twist and turn and grow to torment me. I feel suffocated when I lie down. I cannot go to bed. I simply cannot. Not yet. So yes, chocolate, if you please.'

Fifteen minutes later, Anne had repaired her ravaged appearance and had regained her normal, graceful demeanour. Only the slightest tremor of her hands betrayed her anxiety. In the time that Daniel had been away, she had considered how far she was prepared to confide in her slave. It was not, perhaps, the thing to do but she knew that unless she discussed her worries with someone, unless she gave voice to her fears, they would continue to gnaw at her mind and disturb her sleep until her sanity was threatened. She did not doubt Daniel's devotion, nor his discretion. She trusted him absolutely. He was more than a slave; more than a servant; he was a friend.

She had once toyed with the notion of confiding in Sullah, as another woman, but was aware that the young girl would be unable to discern the nature of the problems in the way that Daniel, with his quick, incisive mind, was able to do. Sullah and Marcus were both good and loyal people but neither had Daniel's understanding, nor his sensitivity. There was her brother, but she had long accepted that Matthew was the last person with whom she could discuss her worries. Whilst she was convinced that he shared many of her concerns, she also knew that he wanted his suspicions about Bentinck denied, not confirmed. She could not bring herself to add to his woes; his mental state was precarious enough, God knew, and she had evidence already of how soon he could descend into alcohol dependency. No, there was no support to be gained from that quarter.

The only other possible confidante in the house was Mary Bentinck and Anne was not slow to acknowledge that Henry's sister was indeed part of the problem. The woman's ill-natured gossip, her insidious comments, her blatant sensuality and her vulgar manner had rung warning bells from their first meeting. Her presence in the house was a cause for disquiet, although with the departure of Eliza her capacity for creating mischief had been severely curtailed.

'Mrs Weston.' Daniel touched her elbow as he placed a cup of steaming chocolate on the table. 'Are you recovered, Ma'am?'

Anne nodded, a slight, sad gesture and looked appealingly up at him. 'Take the other chair, Daniel. We have to talk. I must speak to someone.' Her voice cracked and she took a hasty sip of her drink, wincing as the hot liquid burned her lips. 'I know that you share many of my concerns. It is... I am bothered by... I do not know what...' She inhaled deeply and let out the words in a great rush. 'I fear that we have married my niece to a monster.' Anne sat back, relieved. At last she had given voice to her worst fears. A log fell and sent up a shower of sparks as it settled deeper into the fire, leaving a living, red hole where flames flickered and danced. Anne stared at the glowing heat, mesmerised.

She gathered her thoughts together and now her words came freely.

'He seemed to be an ideal match. A good family, wealthy, well-connected, not too old; he is just about the right age to curb Eliza's impulsive youth and help her to settle down. So much promise. But then, after I met him it all changed. It is in his face, in his eyes. There is a coldness, a want of feeling, a lack of humanity, a rigidity of manner, a watchfulness. Oh, it is impossible to explain. Do you understand what I am saying, Daniel? What do you think? What are your impressions? Do your thoughts agree with mine or is it all in my imagination? Am I being foolish?' There was an unconscious pathos in her appeal. Her hands were held out before her, spread wide, palms up.

Daniel gave a sorrowful shake of his head.

'No, Ma'am. It is not in your mind. I have seen it for myself and so have Marcus and Sullah. We have all spoken of it. There is a cruelty in him. I know it and I fear for Miss Eliza because of it. I have seen such a look on a face before.' His eyes darkened as he looked into his own past. 'But there is more, Mistress.' He hesitated, reluctant to add to her misery. 'I would not have told you... but I... well, we...' His voice trailed away.

Anne stood up shakily and paced across the room, pausing to rest her burning forehead against the cool glass of the window. There was silence and the logs stirred in the fire once more. She turned her tired gaze on Daniel's face.

'Go on,' she ordered. 'You must tell me. You cannot stop now.'

'It is Sullah, Ma'am. She went into town only last week. She has got herself into gossiping with some of the servants from the town houses. It seems... well, according to what she was told... there is talk that Mr Bentinck and his sister were forced to leave London because of some scandal in high places. It was real bad gossip so Sullah says, though the maids would not say exactly what it was that he had done. Something to do with a young lordling and Mr Bentinck and a group of his friends and a club of some kind that they belongs to.' As he became animated, Daniel's voice lapsed into the rhythm and cadence of his native Jamaica. 'Whatever it was, there sure was a lot of bad talk and that man and his sister, they had to leave until it all died down.' He waited, glad to have shared his unwanted knowledge.

Anne took another sip of her drink, her eyes thoughtful.

'That would certainly explain much that has puzzled me,' she mused. 'Why would they stay with an elderly Aunt in Chester at the height of the season? Especially someone like Mary. I can understand that Henry might have to come North for business reasons but why inflict the provinces on his sister? She is so obviously a social animal. And this wedding journey too. Despite all his protestations about the sport and shooting, Scotland is hardly a favoured spot for newly weds. I appreciate that they could scarcely go to Europe but why not Surrey or Sussex or even Bath? Of course, if the larger part of society is frequenting those places and Bentinck has been involved in a scandal, then he would need to take his bride elsewhere.' There was a pause. 'Yes, I do see.' She was silent for a time. 'My poor niece. It is to be hoped that Mr Bentinck has learned from whatever ills overtook him in London and has mended his ways. I am certain that it will be so. Scandals always die down. A new source of gossip will soon be found. Who knows, perhaps his marriage will be the means of his return to social acceptability.'

'Yes Ma'am,' nodded Daniel, but his voice carried little conviction. 'We can only wait and trust that things improve with the passing of time.'

Anne finished her drink and stood up, stretching her aching back. She could perhaps sleep now.

'Good night, Daniel, and I do thank you. I feel better for unburdening myself.' She smiled gently. Daniel held open the door and watched his Mistress disappear along the gloomy corridor. She had said that she felt better but he did not think that it was true. Like him her concerns were deep-rooted. It would be a long night.

CHAPTER ELEVEN

FERNLEIGH HALL
AUGUST 1794

Two years passed peaceably at Fernleigh Hall. Eliza's occasional letters were rather formal, stilted accounts of her life in London, and were peppered with references to the great and the notorious personages who made up the cream of society. The only mention of her husband always appeared in the final sentence of each letter, and was always worded in exactly the same way. 'Mr Bentinck keeps in good health and sends his felicitations to you all.' Of Mary's doings, there was no observation. More news, however, was to be had from Mr Trimble, Bentinck's office clerk, who travelled to Liverpool whenever business transactions were required.

From Trimble, who was frequently garrulous after only two glasses of wine at dinner, and who could be relied upon to be shockingly indiscreet, they learned that the Bentinck town house in Portman Square had been opened up again. It was the setting for many well-attended, though somewhat riotous parties. Eliza and Henry seemed to be at the centre of a circle of younger people who had more energy than sense and more money than breeding. Mr Trimble also confided the news that Mary had become Mrs Harrison. She had rushed into an ill-advised union with a Captain Andrew Harrison; a gentleman who had been less than honest about the size of both his family's Irish estates and his own ensuing income.

It was perhaps fortunate that Mary had not been required to endure life on an Irish farm for many months before word had come through of her husband's demise in a drunken riding accident involving a fellow officer. She had returned to her brother's home as the tragic widow of a dashing Captain. Even though nothing specific was said, important subversive action in and around France was certainly hinted at. Mary was becomingly modest about the hero's exploits and wore her black with zest and style. According to Trimble, who recounted his tale with many meaningful glances and much tapping of the side of his nose, she had quickly become the focus of attention. After all, as a lady who had already had a husband, she was subject to none of those constraints on her conduct that had regulated her unmarried status. The freedom suited her.

For Anne Weston, the past two years had provided a period of stability and necessary recuperation. All thoughts of a return to the Caribbean had gone; she devoted her life to the care of her children, the management of her brother's household and good works amongst the poor of Liverpool. She had established a fine reputation in the town and had become a leading member of respectable society. The sight of Mrs Weston in her carriage, attended by her three slaves and her delightful children, was greeted along the quay and in the newly furbished thoroughfares of Castle Street, Dale Street and Water Street, by gracious nods, courtly bows and genuinely smiling faces. She was still a beautiful woman, and more than one town gallant had sought to pursue her favour. All had been courteously but firmly rejected. Anne was content to wait for the return to England of George Barton.

Almost every ship that slipped into the Mersey from America carried a packet of letters for Anne. Word had been sent that Mr Barton's mother had suffered a long and painful illness for more than a year and was not expected to survive for many more months. The result of her incapacity was that George had been unable to leave America to return to Liverpool as he had intended. Instead, he had been forced to content himself with ever more committed messages to the waiting Anne, letters to which she had happily responded in the same tone. They had established a firm understanding and she was happy to wait until he should be released from his obligations.

Matthew Broadwood too had benefited from this prolonged period of stress-free normality. His debts were paid by his son-in-law and his ships, even allowing for the war with France that had finally been declared in February of 1793, had prospered. Indeed, several of the privateers, in which he had a large share, had returned a considerable profit as a direct result of the hostilities. With the limitation of his alcohol consumption, his health had improved to the extent that he had resumed his visits to Mrs Roberts in the town house on one, or sometimes two afternoons each week. However, mindful of his previous near disastrous experience, he took care to return home every evening for his dinner and spent each night in the respectable security of his own bed.

The family fortunes had continued to flourish and Matthew had been much involved in the planning and financing for the building of the new Queen's Dock. Work had already begun although it would be a year, probably two, before it was complete. That he had money to invest in such a project was largely due to Daniel's efficiency. The slave's efforts resulted in a stable, well-run company whose assets were diversified and whose borrowings were kept within manageable limits. There were still occasions when Matthew felt pains in his chest and experienced a shortage of breath, but he now functioned only within his limitations. He relied more and more upon his sister's slave to advise and care for him. His business was secure; his family name was again respected in the town; his wayward daughter was no longer his responsibility and he was regarded as the epitome of a prosperous and worthy member of the merchant or 'middling' class. Day succeeded day in comfortable complacency, then everything changed.

Daniel, Marcus and Sullah were spending an amiable Sunday afternoon chatting in a desultory fashion as they sat in an unfrequented and sheltered corner of the garden which Marcus had made his own. In the past year, they had taken to spending their free Sundays together. In winter they were cosily ensconced in the room above the stable, and in summer they went outside in the pleasing warmth of the English sunshine. Conversation turned, as it so often did, to their days in Jamaica, with Marcus in particular reviving nostalgic memories of his old home that were, to say the least, selective.

'It surely was a good sort of life, an' I knows it,' he recalled. 'The bustle of the market in that ol' Kingston, the sale of stuff you had grown with yo' own hand, the chance to pocket a coin or two, an' all the time, the gossip an' chatter o' them there womenfolk.' He rolled his eyes in comic horror.

'But, Marcus, the market here in Liverpool town is surely just as interestin'. Why the folks there can teach anyone 'bout gossip. An' not just the women, neither,' laughed Sullah.

Marcus shook his grizzled head. 'Yo' young folks don't know how things was. But I knows. Jamaica was a good place to be, an' our own kind was there. Our own people. Not like here. We wasn't welcome when we first come here. I knows we wasn't.'

Daniel lounged a little apart from the other two, idly scattering blades of grass and watching as they floated through the air. He smiled at his friend.

'I sometimes miss the island too, Marcus, but life here has improved since we first arrived. I don't feel so strange now when I go to the town. There are more like us than there used to be, many more of the gentry are employing black domestics and the townsfolk don't see us as a threat no more. They are accustomed to us now. This town is a boiling pot for all kinds of people and the best thing is that they will accept you even if you are different. They will share their town. The poorer they are, the more generous their spirit. That is what I have found.' Daniel paused to collect his thoughts. 'Many of the labourers and those in the manufactories, well, they are in favour of abolition. They want to see us all as free men. They have sympathy for us even though, in some ways, we are better off than many of them. There are preachers that I have heard speak and they have been and seen for themselves what the middle-passage does to people. The townsfolk did not know before how bad it was. Now that they do know, many of them are coming out against slavery. There is even talk of a bill in Parliament to stop slave trading altogether and making us just like other servants with a wage and all. Can you imagine that?'

Daniel's face was shining, his voice was animated. Sullah, watching him, felt her stomach contract. She lowered her gaze in case her face should give her away. She had loved Daniel for all of her life but in recent months had come to acknowledge a growing passion that had nothing whatsoever to do with hero worship from afar. Her skin felt warm and she had to resist the urge to jump up and dance around wildly in an effort to dissipate the churning energy in her insides. She felt their eyes on her

171

and looked up, startled.

'What? What is it? What did yo' say?'

'Yo' needs to wash out yo' ears, young Sullah, as yo' is always saying to Massa Timothy,' said Marcus. 'Daniel asked if yo' is happy here.'

Sullah smiled. 'I has care o' them children, Missus is kind to me, I has good food, a place to sleep, I goes to town, I has friends. What else is there?'

'Yes,' nodded Daniel. 'We can certainly...' He broke off in consternation. 'Something is wrong.'

The slave leaped to his feet and hurried towards Melchet who was lurching across the lawn, waving his arms and struggling for breath. The old man clung to Daniel's supporting arm as he doubled over, his shoulders heaving.

'The Master,' he gasped. 'The Master. Quickly! He is ill!' Daniel raced across the grass, leaving Melchet in the care of Marcus and Sullah, a sick feeling of dread driving him faster and faster. The hall was silent but the library door, unusually, stood open wide. On the threshold Daniel pulled up short, his eyes taking a moment to accustom themselves to the gloom after the brilliance of the sunlight outside. He was dimly aware of the sound of the carriage rattling past the front of the house and subconsciously registered that Marcus was already on his way to bring Mr Broadwood's physician. He moved forward into the over-warm room. It was the stuff of his nightmares; a repetition of the day that he had discovered Jeremiah Weston, his Master, dead in his chair. This time it was Matthew Broadwood lying back against the cushions, his face ashen, his eyes staring, one arm hanging lifeless by his side.

There was a flicker in the eyes and the sound of a rasping breath. Daniel felt the hairs lift on the back of his neck. He had been so certain that he was looking at a corpse. For a moment he remained still, carved from stone, then he forced his unwilling legs towards the windows, wrenching up the sashes one by one and bringing in reviving draughts of air. He turned to the figure in the chair. The Master's mouth was twisted in a semblance of a grimace and the corner of one eye was pulled down. His throat rattled as he tried to speak. Daniel dropped to his knees and took hold of Matthew's hands. One was warm and gripped furiously, not knowing its own strength. The other was flaccid, dead.

The slave put his face close to the Master's.

'Marcus has gone for your physician, Sir. He will be here before long. Try to rest and leave everything to me. You will soon feel better. Try to rest. I will stay with you.' The desperation faded from Broadwood's eyes and the gripping fingers relaxed slightly. The sick man made a guttural noise. 'Please, Sir, do not try to speak, not yet. You will overtax yourself. Is it Mrs Weston?' The eyes flickered. 'She has gone in a friend's carriage to take their children to the shore. It is such a beautiful day and they enjoy playing with others of their own age. She will be back before long. Please, Master, get some rest. I will wake you as soon as she arrives.'

Daniel placed cushions behind the lolling head, brought water to wet the dry lips and took up his position again on the floor beside the chair. The Master's hands were held tightly in his own; neither man was willing to release the other. The minutes ticked slowly by, each one an eternity and all the time Daniel prayed quietly.

'Not again, Lord. Dear God, please, not again. I cannot tell the Mistress. Not again.' The long shadows crept across the floor, reaching out towards the kneeling slave and the restless figure in the chair. Faintly, through the open window, came the jingle of harness and the rumble of carriage wheels. Farther away, carried on the still air, the sound of church bells could be heard tolling for Evensong.

By the next afternoon, Matthew's chamber had taken on all the trappings of a sick-room. The physician had examined him the previous day and had told a distraught Anne that her brother would not recover from his disabilities and that another attack was possible at any time. Such an attack would most likely result in death. Daniel had carried the invalid upstairs and gently put him to bed; he sat up with the Master all that night but now, a nurse had been employed and Daniel was released. He joined the Mistress in the library where she was writing to tell Eliza that the doctor had advised that she should come home with all possible haste.

Anne rubbed a hand over her aching eyes, throwing down her pen and sitting back in her brother's chair in exasperation.

'Oh, Daniel,' she groaned. 'What a difficult task. How do I tell the girl that her Papa is dying, that he is so sick and is incapable of speech or movement? Eliza is still so young. How will she bear it? She will have such a journey to face and not to know what is at the end of it. And how if she does not arrive in time? What then?'

'Remember, Ma'am, Miss El... beg pardon, Mrs Bentinck... is no longer alone. She has a husband to give her support and I am sure that he will accompany her from London. He will not allow her to travel alone on such a sad errand. Your letter will be there within a few days and they could be at Fernleigh before next week is out. The Master is no worse at present. You must write your letter, Ma'am and wait. It is out of your hands.'

'You are right.' She picked up her pen once more. 'You are right as usual. Where would we be without you?' She gave him a weary smile. 'Now then, what shall I... Yes, Melchet? What is it?' She turned in enquiry to the butler who was hovering in the doorway, a package in his hand.

'Excuse me, Mrs Weston. It is a letter from London.

From Mrs Bentinck. It has just arrived by special messenger. It did not come on the mail-coach.'

Anne snatched it from him, her eyes fearful. 'What a coincidence,' she whispered. 'At just such a time. But a special messenger? Pray that it is not more ill-tidings.' She opened her letter with shaking hands and Daniel followed her eyes as she scanned line after line, moving steadily down the page. At last she stopped, nerveless fingers dropping the paper and allowing it to drift to the floor.

'Madam?' said Melchet.

'Mrs Weston, Ma'am?' Daniel prompted.

She stared from one to the other. 'They are coming,' she managed at last. 'They are on their way here and are only hours behind the messenger.' She slumped back in her chair, the colour draining from her face as the startling news and the effects of a sleepless night combined to take their toll.

'Brandy please Mr Melchet,' instructed Daniel, already halfway across the room to open the windows. 'And then, could you ask Mrs Edwards to prepare rooms for the guests and send someone for Sullah? She must come and attend to her Mistress.'

Melchet moved towards the side table, his old legs shuffling, his rheumy eyes glistening with the sheen of tears. 'Eh, lad, I don't know what things be comin' to. I really don't. Whatever next, eh? Whatever next?'

Daniel patted him awkwardly on the shoulder. The old man's lapse into his native Lancashire dialect was a measure of the strain that he was under. He had been with Matthew Broadwood for so many years.

'The Master can rely on you to see to things during his incapacity I am sure, Mr Melchet. Now, if you will pass me that brandy for Mrs Weston, I know that you and Mrs Edwards will be able to cope without her for a while. Sullah will take the Mistress to lie down and I will see to

175

things in here. It may be that Mr Bentinck will wish to acquaint himself with the Master's business affairs and I must ensure that all is in good order.' Melchet nodded slowly and trudged towards the door. He turned to face Daniel, one hand on the knob.

'You are a good man,' he said. 'A good servant to the Master,' and he gave a dignified bow before letting himself out.

Daniel continued to chafe Anne Weston's hand as he watched her take tiny sips of the brandy. The breath caught in her throat and she coughed.

'Why are they returning to Liverpool after all these months, and why in such haste? They cannot know about Matthew's illness. Their coming would appear to be providential. It is most opportune. Why then am I so apprehensive? Why do I fear the worst?' Daniel did not answer. He too was afraid of the return of Henry Bentinck.

It was almost dark before the Bentinck coach drew to a halt at the bottom of the steps. Anne was waiting in the drawing-room and watched from the window as Henry alighted and turned to help his wife. Anne's hand flew to her mouth to stifle her exclamation of horror as the light, spilling from the front door, caught the face of her niece. Eliza had always been slender. She was now skeletal. Her cheeks were gaunt and her eyes appeared to be sunk into her head.

'She is ill, she must be ill,' muttered Anne, as Elizabeth passed out of her line of vision. 'The girl is sick.' She half turned to go and greet her niece then turned back to the window. 'Oh, no,' she sighed, as she saw Henry reach once more into his carriage and give his arm to the distinctively stylish, black-clad figure of his sister. 'Not Mary as well.' Then, instantly regretting her lack of empathy, she recollected that Mrs Harrison, as she must now be called, was only recently widowed and she felt ashamed.

The door opened and Melchet's hushed voice announced, 'Mrs Bentinck, Ma'am.' Eliza drifted behind him like a wraith. There was a smile on her face but the effort was pitiful to see.

'My dear Aunt, you have no notion of how good it is to be home,' she murmured. 'It is a delight to see you again. It has been far too long.' She held out her hands to the glow of the small fire in the grate. 'Where is Papa?'

'Eliza, sit here. Sit where you can be warm.' Anne guided her unresisting niece into a chair, looking at her helplessly. 'You could not know, but I was writing to send for you. Matthew has had some kind of attack and he is not at all well. He is very ill, and the physician insisted that you should be sent for. It is indeed fortunate that you elected to visit just now. When you have refreshed yourself I will take you up to him.' There was no response from the younger woman. 'Eliza?' Anne spoke sharply.

'Yes, I heard you, Aunt. By all means let us go and see Papa,' and she got to her feet like an obedient child.

Anne was at her wits end. Eliza appeared to be viewing the world from a distance. She was hearing what was said, speaking words of her own, but seemed to be totally disconnected from reality. She stood in the centre of the room, waiting to be conducted upstairs.

The door opened abruptly and Henry Bentinck appeared. He looked from one woman to the other before moving quickly to Eliza's side. Anne did not miss the way her niece appeared to shrink from him, trying to make herself smaller.

'What is happening? Good evening Mrs Weston, or I suppose I should call you Aunt Weston.' His voice echoed around the walls, grating on the silence. He stared at Anne. 'What is amiss here? Where is Mr Broadwood? Why this strangeness?' He strode to the door, almost colliding with his sister who was loitering in the hall. 'Melchet?' he bellowed. He turned to glare at his wife and then at Anne. His eyes narrowed. 'What have you been hearing? Who has been carrying tales?' he hissed. 'Is that why there is no proper greeting?' He moved threateningly towards Anne.

'Pardon me, Sir.' It was Daniel. Bentinck's head rotated slowly. His cold eyes took in the size of the slave and the sight of Melchet and Mrs Edwards clustered behind him. He cast a swift glance at his wife and addressed Anne in a more normal tone.

'There would appear to be something that you wish to tell us Mrs Weston,' he said and threw himself into a chair. 'Pray, do speak.' He waited.

Anne clasped her shaking hands together. She addressed her niece but her eyes never left Bentinck's face.

'Eliza, I am so sorry, my dear, but as I was saying, your Papa is seriously ill. I am glad that you have come.' With an effort, she tore her gaze away from Eliza's husband and took her niece's arm. This time, the meaning of her words seemed to penetrate the girl's mind and the first spark of emotion kindled in her eyes. She clutched at Anne in a gesture of desperation.

'Take me to him,' she pleaded. 'Take me to Papa.' And clinging to her Aunt she stumbled past Bentinck as though he did not exist.

They reached Matthew's chamber. The door creaked open and the two women crept towards the bed. Already there was the unmistakable odour of the sick-room, a sweet, decaying smell that seemed to hang in the cloying air. It was stifling. The figure propped on the high pillows seemed curiously shrunken and frail. His hair was sparse, like that of a very old man and was plastered to his head by perspiration, allowing the pink of his scalp to shine through. The blue-veined hands had a new transparency, one plucking restlessly at the counterpane and the other lying motionless, like a piece of meat on a butcher's slab.

Eliza took in the horrors of her father's twisted features, his empty eyes. She threw herself on her knees, and buried her head in his covers as paroxysms of grief shook her thin frame. Anne stood to one side, helpless in her own vulnerability. She ached with pity and despair; she had already learned enough of Eliza and her husband to realise that the young woman probably needed her father's protection more now than at any time since her childhood. Most of all, however, her anguish was for Matthew. It was cruel that her brother should be stricken in such a way. He was still comparatively youthful, certainly not ancient, and for a man of his stature to be reduced to a state of helpless imbecility, well, it seemed unjust.

A draught caused the candles to flicker and a puff of smoke to belch from the smouldering fire. She turned as Henry Bentinck sidled into the room. His cold eyes took in the wretched figure on the bed, his prostrate wife and Anne's own tear-stained face. She gasped. Just for an instant, she could have sworn that a smile hovered on his thin lips. Now it was gone; it must have been the uncertain light. She was mistaken. Bentinck inclined his head in her direction and, without speaking, he turned and left, the door clicking shut behind him.

Anne lifted her sobbing niece to her feet, drawing her gently away from the bed and putting a comforting arm about her shoulders.

'Elizabeth, you must come with me now. There is nothing that you can do for him. You are becoming too distressed and will make yourself ill if you go on in this fashion. We will go to my room and I will have refreshment brought. No one will disturb us there. We can be alone.' She stressed again. 'We shall not be disturbed. We must talk, my dear. We really must talk.' She took

Eliza's arm and led her, unresisting, down the passageway to her private sitting-room.

Melchet deposited the tray on a low table, casting a horrified, sidelong glance at Eliza. He tore away his gaze with difficulty. What had become of his pretty young mistress?

'Will that be all, Mrs Weston?'

'Thank you, Melchet.' She nodded her dismissal, following him to the door and closing it firmly. She sat beside her niece, taking hold of both of the girl's hands. 'Now then. What is wrong? What in the name of God has happened to you? Are you sick also, my dear? Please talk to me. There must be something that I can do to help you.' She poured a drink and handed it to Eliza.

The girl's eyes were downcast, her hands trembled and the cup clinked against her teeth. She returned it carefully to the saucer and finally raised a despairing face to Anne.

'There is nothing that anyone can do now. Perhaps Papa would have been... but not now... I will have to... it is so dreadful.' The disjointed phrases jerked from her, almost against her will.

'Take your time, Elizabeth. Take all the time you need. Tell me what you can. Let me at least try to help. You are home now. We are all your friends here.' At that, the tears began to flow again. In between wrenching sobs, Eliza told her story.

'I knew when I married that my husband was a man of many contradictions. He could be charming but callous. He could stir up passions yet remain cold and aloof. He had position and wealth, but was clearly hiding something in his past. There were so many signs. If only I had taken the warnings. But there was Papa and the family's reputation to consider. Henry was to be his lifeline. He told me that if I consented to become his wife then my father's debts would be paid. If I did not, he would see him ruined.

What else could I do but marry him?' She stared at her Aunt with unseeing eyes and took a quick gulp of her tea.

'Let me fill up your cup,' said Anne, picking up the silver teapot and allowing the younger woman time to gather her thoughts. Eliza was more relaxed now and the words came in a rush. It was a tale needing to be told.

'It has taken months to put it all together. My husband has told me nothing, but gossip from the maids and so-called friends, scraps of conversations that I was not meant to hear, circulating cartoons that I was not supposed to see and the barbed hints of my sister-in-law, eventually painted the true picture. Henry was always cruel, especially to the weak.' The statement was made in such a matter-of-fact way that Anne recoiled. Eliza continued. 'He adored his mother. It appears that she looked much like myself when she was young. She was always worried by her son's mean nature, then when she was ill he killed her pet dog. Oh, they gave out that it was an accident but I do not believe that was the case. His mother withdrew from him totally and right up to her death would not have him anywhere near her. Her rejection of him only made him worse and he grew from a nasty boy into a sadistic man. A man who hates women and who must dominate anyone weaker than himself.' Her eyes were filled with revulsion and bitter knowledge. 'I think you can imagine what life has been like as the wife of such a man.'

Anne Weston did not know what to say. What words of hers could bring comfort in the face of such misery? She shook her head sadly.

'Eliza, you poor, poor child. I am so very sorry. But things will surely improve now that you are home.' She paused as a thought struck her. 'Why did you come back? What made you leave the capital with such haste?'

Eliza bit at her lip and a speck of blood glistened. 'When Henry was last here with his sister, when they visited his

Aunt in Chester, well, he had been forced to leave London then. It was because of a gaming scandal. Some say that there was more to it than money but I cannot know for sure. Whatever the truth of it, there was the most dreadful gossip at the time and the Bentincks were shunned by all society. Word was out about the activities of Henry and his friends. They belong to a club that meets each month. It has its own warped rules and customs; it caters for the worst excesses imaginable. All the members are sworn to secrecy.' The silence stretched between them. 'The problem is,' continued Eliza, 'that when the worst of the scandal had died down and we had returned from our wedding journey to Scotland, the entire thing began again. Many of the sons of the nobility are members of this club and Henry is a leading figure. He is older than them and more experienced. Then, two weeks ago, Huntingdon committed suicide. He was at the centre of the first scandal and was foolish enough to become involved again. Now, tales of the worst kind are rampant in society. Anyone who had anything to do with the club has been forced to leave town. So you see, Aunt, we may be here for some time.'

The door crashed back against the wall, making both women leap to their feet.

'Mrs Weston, Miss Eliza,' it was Daniel. 'Come quickly. It is the Master. You must come at once!' Anne, with a swift glance at her slave's face, knew the worst. Matthew Broadwood was dead.

CHAPTER TWELVE

FERNLEIGH HALL
SEPTEMBER 1794

In the three weeks that had passed since the death of Matthew Broadwood, things had changed out of all recognition at Fernleigh Hall. No one was in any doubt that Henry Bentinck was the new master. Henry had ordered his things to be put in the main bedroom on the morning after Matthew's funeral. He had also given instructions that Eliza's mother's rooms should be opened up for his wife, despite her protestations that she preferred to remain where she was, in the familiar room that had been hers for most of her life. Melchet had already left, going to live with his widowed sister in her small house across the river and Mrs Edwards had asked Anne Weston for a reference and was actively seeking another situation. Bentinck had sent for some of his own staff from Portman Square, and an atmosphere of tension pervaded the house. It resembled a battlefield before the commencement of hostilities, as the old staff lined up against the new.

Eliza was distraught at her father's death and for many days they had feared for her sanity. Slowly however, under her Aunt's watchful eye, she had begun to recover and had recently taken to accompanying Anne on afternoon outings in the mellow September sunshine. The fresh sea air and gentle warmth had brought a little colour to the girl's cheeks and though her eyes still bore the dark smudges of many sleepless nights, and unexplained bruises were often to be glimpsed on her arms and shoulders if her shawl slipped, Eliza appeared to derive a quiet pleasure from these hours spent away from the Hall. When the drives had first been suggested Bentinck had demurred, but Mrs Weston had enlisted the aid of the physician. He insisted that a short drive in the countryside each day, in the company of her Aunt, was just the thing to help the young Mrs Bentinck recover her health. Henry had been forced to yield but it was the only concession that he made.

Daniel stood at the nursery window watching as Marcus handed Anne and Eliza into the carriage. Even from such a distance the younger woman's pallor and frailty were clearly evident, and the slave's outrage, never far from the surface since the death of Matthew Broadwood, threatened to explode. Every servant in the house knew of Bentinck's cruelty towards his young wife. The maids gossiped freely about her injuries and tear-swollen eyes. In addition, during the silence of the nights following Matthew Broadwood's death, when a restive Daniel had prowled the dark corridors, he had heard for himself the muffled screams and sobs that came from her rooms.

All his old protective instincts towards Eliza had been aroused. The urge to beat the life out of the ruthless man who had become Master of Fernleigh, was almost impossible to control. As far as possible, Daniel kept away from Henry's vicinity, remaining within the schoolroom during the day and avoiding the company of all except Marcus and Sullah. Anne Weston, well aware of the dangers inherent in any open conflict between the two men, came upstairs to the nursery suite whenever she wished to consult with Daniel on business matters and did her best to deflect any questions by Bentinck as to how her slaves occupied their time. She was astute enough to realise that a time of reckoning would come and she went in fear of the outcome.

Her nephew by marriage had made it clear, immediately after Matthew's funeral, that he would accept no responsibility for Anne, her children or her slaves and had done his best to provoke her into leaving Fernleigh Hall. Anne confessed to Daniel that were it not for Eliza's precarious health she would have been more than happy to quit her old home. She would enjoy a small establishment of her own. However, as things were, she felt obliged to care for her brother's child as best she could.

Watching now, as the carriage pulled away from the front of the house, Daniel cracked his knuckles violently; his rage simmered and bubbled but could find no outlet.

'There be no use yo' frettin' yo'self, Daniel,' murmured Sullah, who had glided up unseen and was standing behind him. 'The woman has got herself a husband an' he can do as he pleases. He is her master, jus' like Mr Weston was mine. There is nothin' for yo' to do 'bout it. Why, even the Missus, she knows how that man do treat his wife an' there is nothin' that she can do neither.' She jerked her head at Timothy who was patiently waiting for Daniel to look at his work. 'Yo' would do better to forget all 'bout young Missus an' look after Massa Timothy likes yo' is supposed to.'

Daniel scowled but his inherent sense of fairness made him hold up a placatory hand.

'Yes, Sullah, I do know and I have no need of anyone to point it out. I know…' He was interrupted by a banging on the door, and moved quickly away from the window as one of Bentinck's servants came in. The man eyed Sullah up and down, turned his head and stared at Daniel with a sneer on his face.

'What a pity to disturb you.' He leered at Sullah again. 'A great pity.'

Daniel took a step forward, fists clenched at his side but the girl stepped between them, holding out a hand to Timothy.

'Come with me Massa Timmy. Yo's finished work for today.'

Bentinck's man made for the door in her wake, turning again to Daniel. 'Your Master wants you, boy. He wants you now. In the library. And I would not keep him waiting if I were you.'

Daniel stayed in the schoolroom, breathing deeply. He had been expecting a summons for several days and was certain that Bentinck would seek to humiliate him and goad him into some kind of reaction. He had never forgotten the incident in the stable and knew that Eliza's husband would, eventually, turn his vindictive attention to the Weston slaves. It was no accident that Anne had just left. Daniel ran his fingers through his hair and dropped his head. Would he be able to retain his self-control? He sighed.

The slave sensed, rather than heard, someone come into the room. He raised his eyes, thinking that Sullah had returned. Henry's sister was watching him from the doorway. Mary swayed across the floor, stopping just in front of him, the heady smell of her perfume invading his nostrils.

'Well, Daniel. It has been a long time. Has it not?' She put out a hand and touched his arm, running her fingers along his sleeve. Her eyes were fixed on his face, her lips parted. 'It would seem that my brother has sent for you. Perhaps he wishes to send you away. I must confess that I should be sorry to see you leave. I should be very sorry indeed.'

Daniel stepped away from her, lowering his gaze. 'If you will excuse me, Madam, I must not keep Mr Bentinck waiting.' He kept his voice level and his tone deferential. He knew that he could ill afford to play Mary's games. Bentinck was dangerous but his sister was lethal.

Mary's mouth curved. One hand plucked lazily at the black ribbon round her throat.

'I know now where to find you. Is that not so? I am sure that there is much that you could teach me here in your schoolroom. My education has been sadly neglected since the death of my dear husband. I am a lonely widow and have become aware of the need of a strong arm to... to comfort me.' She moved to one side, ensuring that he would have to brush against her as he passed. Her voice was husky. 'But I must not delay you. My brother has sent for you and you must do as you are bid. You are merely a slave after all.' She smiled again as her thrust went home and a spark flashed in Daniel's eyes. 'There will be other times. You need not be fearful of me. I can be most gracious to those who give me pleasure, and I have never doubted your ability to please.' Daniel bobbed his head and blundered towards the door.

The woman was like a reversed mirror image of her brother. With him, a cold exterior hid a terrifying and secretive passion; in her, a very obvious ardour concealed a calculating soul that was incapable of true feeling. Brother and sister displayed a world-weary malevolence that was only assuaged by new experiences or by preying on those in no position to defend themselves. It was clear to Daniel that Henry was already bored with his young wife. Tormenting Eliza had become too easy. He was looking for a new victim and what better targets for his cruelty than the household's three slaves.

As Daniel approached the library, he knew that the coming confrontation would only be the first of many. If he wished to emerge intact from these initial skirmishes, he would need to bury his pride deep within himself where

Bentinck could not reach. Such control would demand much of him, but his concern for Mrs Weston, Eliza and Sullah, all of whom were, to some extent, at this man's mercy, must over-ride his personal feelings. The women needed his protection. He could not allow himself to be provoked by anything that Bentinck said or did. Any loss of temper was a luxury that could cost the others dear.

Schooling his features into a semblance of respectful obedience, he tapped gently on the door.

'Enter.'

'You sent for me, Master.' Daniel waited with his head bowed. His inclination was to address Henry as Mr Bentinck, since the title of 'Master' still seemed to belong to Matthew Broadwood, but he rightly assumed that any refusal to acknowledge Henry's status in the household would immediately antagonise the man.

'I am pleased to see a proper attitude of respect from you,' sneered Bentinck. 'You would seem to have discovered some sense, or perhaps it is simply that you have a healthy instinct for the preservation of your own hide.' Daniel did not reply and continued to stare at the floor. Bentinck resumed. 'It is my view that you have been allowed to move far above your station in this house. You took advantage of a weak and stupid woman who was left without a husband in a heathen land. You wormed your way into her confidence and took upon yourself tasks unsuited to one of your status and colour.' Daniel gnawed at his cheek and felt the warm blood trickle into his mouth. He focused on the pain and tried to blot out Bentinck's remorseless voice. He kept his head down and, seeing the other man glance at his huge hands, he slowly uncurled his fists and let them hang loosely by his sides.

Since the slave apparently presented no threat, Bentinck rose from behind the desk and moved to stand behind Daniel.

'I can understand how you managed to inveigle yourself into the good offices of my wife's Aunt, but what exactly did you have on Broadwood, eh?' He poked his finger in Daniel's back. 'The old man was a downy bird, and not one to be taken in by the likes of you. What secret shame were you party to? Answer me!' The last words were shouted and Bentinck strutted around the slave's massive bulk, halting immediately in front of him.

Anger blazed through Daniel as he fought desperately to retain his subservient pose. He had known before he entered the library that his control would be tested to its limits, but he had drawn upon lessons learned, at a great price, at his mother's side. Never look a white bully in the eyes. Never show courage. Never display anger. If there was no challenge then there was no sport. If there was no pride to subdue, there could be no humiliation. No matter how restrained Daniel was, however, it was clear that Bentinck would not be satisfied until he was rid of him. The slave's quiet strength, his quickness of mind, his business acumen and the reliance placed upon him by others in the household all served to irritate the new Master. Beyond that, Daniel suspected that Henry was aware of his devotion to Eliza and was determined to punish him for it. What the man would be capable of should he ever discover the fact of his own sister's oblique approaches to a coloured man, brought Daniel out in a cold sweat of terror.

Bentinck was unaware of Daniel's thoughts but seemed able to smell the scent of his fear and had noted the beads of perspiration on his forehead. He gave a satisfied smirk, content to have pierced the slave's protective shell. He struck again.

'You should not be living inside the house. From today you will occupy the stable with the other one. All your so-called secretarial duties are to cease immediately. Your kind should undertake only menial tasks. You will assist the gardener and clean the carriages. Your tuition of my wife's nephew is finished. The boy is being brought up like an infant. What can he learn from a slave? He will go away to school. Everyone will need to recognise that things have changed in this house. There is a new Master here.'

The seconds dragged by in heavy silence. Bentinck waited for some response. Daniel lifted a humble head, veiling the expression in his eyes. His voice was a mumble, his words barely distinguishable.

'Will that be all, Master?'

Glancing through the window, Bentinck saw that the Rector's carriage was drawing up in front of the house. His sport was over for the day. He waved an indolent hand in Daniel's direction.

'Get out, boy. Take yourself off to the stables.'

Daniel walked stiffly from the library, through the kitchen quarters and out of the servants' entrance. Once outside he hurried through the trees until he reached a secluded spot. He leaned forward, retching and spat out a stream of blood and bile. His raw cheek throbbed un-mercifully but he had held on to his self-control. Bentinck had not beaten him. He sank down to the ground, holding his head. He had an ominous sense of impending disaster. His troubles, he knew, had scarcely begun.

Less than a week later, on Sunday afternoon, the three slaves were in the room above the stables discussing the changes at Fernleigh Hall. The unease between Anne Weston and Bentinck was obvious to them all. Their Mistress had tried to object when Henry had insisted that it was time for Timothy to go away to school, but he was adamant. He had played on her natural fear that she may be guilty of trying to compensate her son for the loss of his father, and was not allowing the boy to grow up as quickly as he should. So, Timmy had left and Daniel had moved out of the schoolroom.

Strangely, he had discovered that in some ways he preferred the heavy, manual work to his former duties. He gained satisfaction from testing his massive strength and the physical exertion certainly made it easier to sleep at night. In addition, he enjoyed the straightforward company of Marcus much more than having to negotiate the intricacies of precedence in the servants' hall. Perhaps more importantly, here in the stables he was less likely to come into Mary Harrison's orbit and all three slaves were well aware of the danger of crossing that particular path.

Sullah lounged in Marcus' chair. Her pose was deliberately provocative and the older man grinned to himself as he watched her lift her skirt slightly and point her toe, arching a foot and displaying a very pretty ankle. She too was thinking of Bentinck's sister.

'That Missus Harrison, she come up to the schoolroom last week.' The girl gave a malicious grin and tossed her head. 'I sure don' know why. I can't think she come to see me. No, nor Missy Meg neither. Who yo' think she come to see, Daniel?'

'It is possible that Mrs Harrison came to look for Mrs Weston. She is often upstairs with her daughter, is that not so?' Daniel's precise speech irritated Sullah.

'Well, be that as it might be, Miss Eliza, I do mean Missus Bentinck, she don' come up there too,' she drawled. 'She come up two times. An' she asked me where you was Daniel, so we knows jus' who she was lookin' for, don' we?'

Marcus stood up and banged his cup on the table.

'Will yo' both stop all that. I knows that them two women will bring trouble, an' before too long. Yo' marks my words. I knows it. I is goin' to see to my animals. They got more sense than the pair o' you.' He stomped down stairs and they heard the jingle of harness and the restless stirring of the horses.

Daniel coughed. He found himself growing slightly warm. For the first time, he was conscious of Sullah as a woman and not as the little girl whom he had rescued from the Jamaican beach. She must be almost sixteen he supposed. He shot a surreptitious glance in her direction, taking in her shapely outline and flawless skin. He coughed again. This was ridiculous. How could he possibly be tongue-tied with Sullah? The child had been around him for years... and that of course was the difficulty. Unnoticed, the child had become a very attractive woman.

Watching his discomfiture through narrowed lids, Sullah was well pleased. She arched her back and gave a fabricated yawn, stretching her arms above her head.

'It surely is hotter than an oven in here. I thinks I'll take a walk by the lake. It will be good to be out in the clean air.'

Daniel jumped to his feet. 'I do not think it advisable for you to go alone, Sullah. If you should come across Mr Bentinck... well... I...' The expected insistence that she could manage very well on her own did not materialise.

'Why, that's real nice, Daniel. I surely would be glad o' some company,' and smiling at his stupefied expression she preceded him down the ladder.

In the stable, Marcus, who had heard the entire exchange, whistled as he energetically groomed an already gleaming horse.

'Er... we... Sullah and I... Sullah wishes to walk out and I do not think that it is fitting that she should go alone,' stammered Daniel.

'Quite right too,' asserted Marcus gravely. 'I knows jus' what yo' means,' and his shoulders shook with mirth.

Daniel felt himself growing hot again, and was almost prepared to go back up the ladder when he caught his friend's eye. Marcus was nodding his grizzled head. His voice became serious. 'I does think that Sullah should not be goin' out in them there woods on her own. I done tol' her so already. The Mistress, well, she knows it too. She keeps a good eye on who do go up to that nursery now yo' don' live up there no more, Daniel. The Missus wants that we should look out for each other. She did tell me so an' I knows it.' It was a long speech for Marcus and he grunted to signify that he had nothing more to add. He attacked the shining coat with renewed vigour as Daniel took Sullah's arm and led her out into the sunlight.

Marcus was at the tap, filling the horse's bucket, when Henry Bentinck clattered into the yard. His animal was frothing at the mouth and the slave winced to see flecks of blood on the creature's heaving sides. His disgust was plain to see and Bentinck's eyes narrowed. He unfurled his whip and cracked it on the cobbles of the yard. The slave gave an involuntary flinch at the sound of the lash. The rider smiled as Marcus turned back to his water bucket. The lash flicked out, tearing the sleeve of his shirt and raising a weal on the black skin.

'Don't you ever turn your back on me again,' hissed Bentinck. 'Do you hear me? I shall flay the skin off you if you do not remember how to treat your betters. Perhaps then you will know who is Master here. Your kind is all the same. You understand only one thing.' He rode the horse towards Marcus, drawing back the whip once more. The animal's hooves caught the bucket and sent it clattering across the yard. The startled horse reared and Bentinck slid ignominiously to the floor, just as Mary, Eliza and Anne Weston came through the arch.

Henry scrambled to his feet, his face a livid mask of hate, his eyes blazing and his mouth a twisted snarl. His breeches were wet and his jacket splattered with mud. Through a red haze, he heard his sister laugh. He drew back his hand and with all the force at his command, lashed out at Marcus' face. The slave threw up his arm in an instinctively protective gesture, and the soft underside skin was lacerated to the bone as it took the full force of the whip. Eliza screamed and Anne Weston's voice rang out.

'Enough! That is enough I say.' She ran across the yard to the injured man as his hand dropped to his side and the blood dripped on to the cobbles. Tearing off her silk shawl, she bound it tightly around the wound and clasped Marcus' other hand to hold the blood-soaked fabric against his chest. Putting herself between the two men, she glared at her niece's husband. 'You may be Master here, but this is my slave and you will not touch him again. Come, Marcus. Let me help you upstairs and we shall send Daniel for the physician.' She looked around the yard. 'Where is Daniel?' she asked.

Marcus gripped his injured arm, trying to prevent it from shaking. Great beads of sweat poured down his face as he struggled to reply.

'He took Sullah for a stroll in the woods, Ma'am,' he muttered thickly. 'An' I do thank God that he was not here.'

Anne Weston nodded bleakly. 'So do I,' she whispered, so that only her slave could hear. 'So do I, or murder would have been done.' She led Marcus past the weeping Eliza as Bentinck and his sister turned to make their way to the house.

Henry looked back. 'The slave will answer for this day's work,' he promised.

In the upstairs room, Mrs Weston was trying desperately to staunch the flow of blood as Marcus slumped in the chair, his face grey. There was the sound of running feet and

Daniel appeared at the top of the ladder.

'What has happened?' he begged. 'Eliza came to fetch me. She said there had been an accident.' Even in her distress, Anne noticed the man's unconscious use of her niece's given name and her tone was cool as she turned to face him.

'Marcus has a badly gashed arm. We need to get him to the physician without delay. There is not time to bring the man here. There has been a great deal of blood lost. Help me get Marcus down the ladder and into the carriage. I shall come with you myself in case of any difficulties.' She did not spell out what problems there might be but they were all aware that the doctor would be reluctant to treat a slave. However, the appearance of a servant brought in personally by the much respected Mrs Weston, was a different matter. Daniel pulled Marcus to his feet and put him across his broad shoulders. He edged his way as carefully as possible down the ladder, but by the time they had reached the ground the injured man was bleeding freely and was barely conscious.

Daniel pushed his friend on to the seat of the carriage and left his Mistress to climb in alone as he ran to hitch up the horses. Eliza and Sullah stood in the shadows, watching in fear as the coach rattled across the yard and down the drive.

'What happened to Marcus?' the girl asked accusingly. 'You was here.'

Eliza began to weep again. 'My... my husband... he hit him... with the whip.' Sullah's hand covered her mouth. In that instant she knew that nothing could ever be the same again. Apart from the pain of the injury, the fact that Marcus had been flogged was a deliberate attempt to degrade him, to remind him of his slavery.

'This will not be the end of it,' she prophesied. She stared at Eliza, her eyes seeing something far beyond them both. 'Yo' marks my words. This is just the start. I says before an' I says again, no good will come of us bein' here.'

As the sun set behind the trees, the two women walked together into the shadow of the house. At the bottom of the front steps they paused.

'What are you going to do now, Sullah?' Eliza asked.

'I needs to let the village girl who looks after Missy Meg, get off home,' she replied. 'Then I'll wait 'til the Missus do come back an' she will tell me 'bout Marcus. He is sure to be all right. Daniel will look out for him. They do always look out for each other.' She glanced quickly at the frail young woman beside her. 'It surely ain't my place to say, Missus, but it's my belief that yo' needs to look out for yo'self too. That man o' yours be in a towerin' rage an' his sort be always after hurtin' someone.' She pressed her lips together, determined that she would say no more.

'I do thank you for your concern, Sullah, but you must not worry.' Eliza was grateful. 'My position dictates my husband's treatment of me. His abuse can only go so far and I have already experienced the worst that he can do.' She had disclosed more than she had intended, and lowering her head she hurried up the steps into the hall. Sullah turned her feet towards the servants' entrance, brooding on the un-palatable truth that Eliza Bentinck, and other women like her, were no more free than she was.

From the library window, Henry watched his wife and the slave with their heads close together, their ready sympathy for each other apparent in their demeanour. He ground his teeth together and looked down in surprise as the wine glass, which he was gripping ever more tightly in his hand, shattered. The liquid dripped from his fingers and he was reminded of the sight of the slave's blood flowing on to the cobbles in the yard. Henry knew, without any doubt, that if the women had not appeared when they did,

Marcus would have died. The man was fortunate that he had been spared, but someone would suffer for Bentinck's humiliation. Opening the door, he caught a glimpse of Eliza as she disappeared in the direction of her room. There was no doubt that she had sided with the slaves. She had run for Daniel. His eyes narrowed and he pressed his lips tightly together. She would need to learn the error of her ways. He snatched up a thin cane from his desk, flexed it in his hands and moved silently up the stairs after his wife.

CHAPTER THIRTEEN

LIVERPOOL
OCTOBER 1794

Marcus took a deep breath and heaved the bale of silk into the cart; he rested for a moment against the wooden sides. A month had passed since his altercation with Henry Bentinck but the pain in his arm was still considerable and the massive loss of blood had sapped both his physical energy and his mental strength. His hair and his face appeared grey in the harsh October light and the chill wind blowing off the Mersey seemed to penetrate to his very bones. He pulled up the collar of his jacket and climbed on board. He would be glad to reach the warmth of the stables.

As his tongue clicked the horse forward, he rested his hands lightly on the reins and reflected upon the uneasy peace that had descended on Fernleigh Hall. Henry Bentinck had left for Chester two weeks ago, taking his wife and sister with him. Anne Weston and her slaves had breathed a concerted sigh of relief and had settled down to enjoy a welcome period of domestic harmony. Then, only yesterday, the even tenor of their days had been shattered by the receipt of a letter from America. It had informed the Mistress that Mr George Barton's mother had finally passed away and that he intended taking the next ship for England. Marcus grinned as he recalled Mrs Weston's girlish blush and glowing eyes as she had told them the news, then her hectic excitement and the suddenly discovered necessity for new fabrics, bonnets and gee-gaws. Nothing would do but that Daniel should be sent at once to bring the seamstress from the village. Sullah started to occupy herself with new trimmings and frills, and Marcus went immediately to fetch a bale of mauve silk that his Mistress had ordered weeks ago. The fabric had fortuitously just arrived in town. It was good to see the Missus looking happy again and as he set the horse's head for home, Marcus began whistling tunelessly through his teeth.

Less than a mile from Fernleigh, the slave was forced to tighten his grip on the reins. His gentle, authoritative voice calmed the horse as it tossed its head and skittered within the shafts. Like the startled animal, Marcus could hear, behind him, the rattle and rumble of a much faster and heavier vehicle being driven relentlessly in his wake. The lane was scarcely wide enough here for two coaches to pass but there was nowhere to pull over.

The sound of the rushing hooves thundered on the hard ground and with a sickening stab of fear, Marcus knew; without even looking over his shoulder, he knew. He risked a quick glance back. It was the Bentinck coach. Henry was standing up; the reins were held high in one hand and the long whip curled above his head to crack along the flanks of his steaming horses. A demonic grin split his face as he realised that Marcus had seen him.

Inside the lurching carriage, a white-faced Eliza clung desperately to the hand-strap as she was thrown from side to side, and even Mary was showing signs of fear. It seemed almost certain that they would turn over.

'For the love of God!' Eliza panted. 'Your brother has finally lost his mind. What has got into him? This is insanity!' She cried out as her head struck the frame of the door and Mary's eyes widened in panic as the coach swayed and plunged in the rutted lane.

From the corner of his eye, Marcus saw the foam-filled mouths of the two horses as they began to draw alongside. The clatter of the heavy coach filled the air with thunder, and choking clouds of dust gave a dream-like quality to the scene. Everything seemed to happen in slow motion. There was a screech of clashing wood and metal, a scream of fear-maddened horses and from somewhere deep in his chest Marcus emitted a bellow of rage. The wagon began to tilt. For a moment the slave thought that he had righted it and that Bentinck's carriage had got through, but a wheel hit one of the rocks at the side of the lane. As his horse went down with a final, piercing scream, Marcus was conscious only of a blur of sky, trees, grass and the hard roadway. He felt an agonising pain in his back as he was thrown to the ground. The huge bulk of the cart loomed over him, blotting out the light. Then it toppled and there was nothing.

The Bentinck carriage drew to a shuddering halt; the terrified horses trembled in their harness, their blood-streaked flanks heaving and their eyes rolling wildly. Henry climbed stiffly down from the box, his pale face expressionless. Only his burning eyes betrayed his wild euphoria. Pushing open the door of the coach Mary looked back along the lane. The demented horse was thrashing wildly on its back and struggling to get to its feet but the unnatural angle of its foreleg told its own sorry tale. The cart lay upside down in the ditch. One wheel had broken off and was lying in pieces on the grass. The other spun silently in a cloud of choking dust.

Mary's eyes narrowed as she looked down at her brother.

'It was deliberate, Henry. Was it not? You set out to run him off the road.' She spoke thoughtfully; there was no accusation in her tone.

Henry lifted his gaze to her face. 'The creature insulted me. He had to die. He was of no consequence.' He reached up to the driving seat, took a pistol from the box and moved briskly towards the wreckage behind them. Mary watched as he approached the panic-stricken horse, put the gun to its head and pulled the trigger. A flock of birds rose in a squawking cacophony of noise from the trees beside the road, their wings beating the air as they veered away. The echoes died. The dust settled. The turning wheel slowed and finally stopped. A smothering silence enfolded them like a blanket.

Eliza opened her eyes, aware that the danger was over and the coach had halted. She groaned as she moved her throbbing head, wincing as her probing fingers touched the already discolouring bruise on the side of her face. She struggled to sit upright and noticed the still figure of her sister-in-law, curiously immobile in the open doorway.

'What is it? What has happened?' Her shrill voice echoed in the eerie silence. She fought to suppress her rising panic as Mary gave no sign of having heard. 'Answer me,' she insisted. 'What has happened here?' Mary stepped down and walked away without a word. Eliza stumbled from the carriage, clinging desperately to its side as the devastation in the lane became apparent. She watched in horror as Mary joined her brother, who was standing in mute contemplation of an object in the ditch.

With a sob of fear, Eliza floundered towards the pair. One name rang in her head. Daniel. Daniel. Daniel. She halted staring down for long, relentless moments, her eyes registering the nightmare. The body was not Daniel. It was Marcus. Eliza turned to her husband, her voice seeming to belong to someone else. She wanted to scream but could not. The mundane rationality of her question surprised her. It was bizarre.

'Was it an accident, Henry?' she asked.

Brother and sister exchanged a rapid glance. 'Something frightened the horses. They bolted. We came round the corner and the cart was in the centre of the road. We hit it. The wheel is broken. There. See.' Henry pointed. Mary began to draw her sister-in-law away from the carnage.

Eliza's shuffling feet moved once and then she stopped. 'Marcus,' she pleaded. 'We cannot leave him there.'

Henry took her other arm. 'My dear, both you and my sister have had a dreadful shock. There is nothing to be done for the slave. I must get you both home to Fernleigh. We are almost there. I will send someone back to do what needs be done.' Together, they bundled Eliza into the carriage. Henry jumped on to the box and they moved off at a slow, careful pace towards the Hall.

Anne Weston and Sullah were all but hidden by the mass of tumbled gowns, jackets, blouses and skirts that littered every available inch of the chamber. Anne's wardrobe was undergoing a thorough overhaul in readiness for the return of Mr George Barton. The unrelieved black that had been worn out of respect for a dear brother could now, quite properly, be discarded in favour of the less intense mourning shades of mauve, lilac and grey. Mistress and slave were gossiping happily and it was a moment or two before either of them became aware of the presence of Eliza.

It was a faint breath of draught on her cheek, rather than any intrusive noise, that caused Anne to lift her head. The words of welcome died on her lips as she took in her niece's stricken features. In the past weeks and months she had become accustomed to Eliza's unhealthy pallor, brow-beaten demeanour and abject misery. Never before, how-ever, had she seen an expression of such unmitigated horror on the young woman's face. Anne rose unsteadily, her heart thudding, blood pounding in her ears. She shivered in fearful premonition. What could have happened to her niece? What tragic news had the girl brought?

With difficulty, Anne found her voice.

'There is something wrong, Eliza?' It was more of a statement than a question. She drew the younger woman into the room. 'You must tell me. What is it? ... It is not George, is it? It is not Mr Barton?' Eliza continued to stare and Anne shook her by the shoulders in exasperation, her tone rising hysterically. 'For the love of God, niece, what is the matter with you? Tell me!'

Eliza shook her head in bewilderment. 'George?... George?... Who do you mean?... Oh, Mr Barton... No... It is not him... It is...' She glanced wildly at Sullah. The slave laid down the black silk that she held. Her face was a carved ebony mask.

'It is Marcus. That is what yo' is sayin', Miss,' she asserted. 'It is Marcus.' There was certainty in the dark eyes. Sullah needed no confirmation. No one dared breathe. A sudden gust of wind rattled the ivy leaves against the window, splattering a few drops of rain on the glass and shattering the silence.

'Yes,' whispered Eliza. 'The carriage... coming back from Chester... Henry said the horses bolted... We crashed into Marcus... An accident... He is dead.'

Anne was ashamed. Her first feeling had been one of relief that the bad tidings did not concern George Barton. Now, she was angry that her instinctive emotions did not do justice to the unswerving loyalty and devotion of her slave. Marcus deserved better. Glancing at Sullah's haunted face she caught a glimpse of the stunned, bereft child who had been rescued from horrors of that beach in Jamaica so long ago. Marcus would not lack for grieving.

He would be mourned as deeply as any man could be mourned. Sullah and Daniel would... *Daniel... Oh, dear Lord!* Anne grabbed her niece, jerking the girl like a rag doll in her anxiety.

'Has anyone told Daniel? Say something! Daniel, does he know?'

Eliza's head moved slowly from side to side. 'My husband has sent his own groom to bring back... to fetch... the body. Daniel was not in the stables.' She looked around in helpless indecision. 'I did not think to tell... He was not there... Where is he...?' Sullah was half way across the room. The schoolroom. If Daniel was not in the stables nor the garden, then that was where he would be found. It was the one place in the house where he was unlikely to come across any of the Bentinck servants. He would be there and Sullah would find him. She had to.

The slave girl had not had the time to work out the reasoning behind her automatic reaction to the news. If she had, she would have realised that Daniel would need to be protected against himself in the next few hours. Anne Weston, however, had been quick to appreciate the fact and, as Sullah paused at the door, she urged the girl forward.

'Yes! Go to him, Sullah. Find him. Make sure that he is alone when you tell him, and whatever happens, do not let him leave the schoolroom. He must be kept away from the stables, at least for the moment.' Anne thrust aside the insistent voice in her head that added, *and away from Henry.*

Sullah's hand hovered over the door knob; she did not want to go in. Taking a deep, steadying breath she allowed her natural practicality to assert itself. Someone, at some time, would have to break the news to Daniel. Who better to do it than herself, the third member of their tight-knit group? As a threesome they had been forged by their early experiences in Jamaica, each of them drawing strength from the other two. Together they had overcome most of the difficulties of their new life in Liverpool and had gradually made for themselves a small haven of companionship. Their Sundays off had acquired a regular pattern of long, shared hours of gossip, reminiscences and un-demanding friendship. Each of them was aware that they did not stand alone, that the other two would be there in support, no matter what happened at the Hall.

Since the advent of Henry Bentinck and Mary, the controlled strength and placid acceptance displayed by Marcus had been increasingly important. It was odd that Daniel, who prided himself on behaving in a measured, mannered and socially acceptable way, should be the one most affected by Bentinck's tormenting. Marcus, on the other hand, who had borne the brunt of the new Master's dislike, had been a calming and restraining influence on his friend's increasing bitterness. For weeks, the older man's wise counsel had protected Daniel from the force of his own feelings. Now he was gone. How would Daniel react?

Sullah pushed open the door and slid into the room. At first she did not see Daniel who was kneeling by a pile of books in the corner, sorting and stacking them neatly.

He looked up and grinned. 'You do creep about, Sullah. I ought to put a bell around your neck.' He flushed, embarrassed by his lack of thought. The wearing of a slave collar was buried too deep in Sullah's psyche for her not to be hurt by such a comment. There was silence. Daniel looked at the girl in surprise. He had expected an instant, angry reaction. His eyes narrowed. 'You are upset,' he said. 'What is it? What is wrong?'

Sullah dropped to her knees beside Daniel, her long fingers reaching out to grasp both his hands.

'There ain't no good way to tell you.' She shook her

head sadly, her eyes filling with tears. She blinked them back; weeping never helped anyone. 'It is Marcus. He is dead, Daniel.' She gripped hard, her nails digging deep into his flesh.

'How?' The single word was forced through clenched teeth.

'An accident. There was an accident on the road from Liverpool. The cart... the carriage... a crash... I don't know how... but Marcus... he died.'

The kneeling man closed his eyes, swallowing his pain. His mentor, the man who had been as a brother to him ...He would never see him again, never talk to him. He would never be able to tell him how much his advice was valued. It was too late. Why had he not said how much their friendship meant? Daniel began to sway, rocking gently backwards and forwards, as grief rolled over him. He slumped on his heels and squeezed his eyelids together. Scenes from the past paraded across his vision; Daniel and Marcus, Marcus and Daniel, scenes from Jamaica and memories of their sea voyage to Liverpool; happy hours in the secure warmth of the stable loft. So much to remember, so much to grieve for, but much to be thankful for too.

A faint smile tugged at the corner of Daniel's mouth. That last thought was worthy of Marcus himself. Carefully he released Sullah's clinging hands and opened his eyes, gazing into the dark pools of misery so close to his face. He brought his palms together on either side of her head, his thumbs gently smoothing her frowning brow.

'It is all right, dear Sullah,' he murmured. 'It is all right. We must all die at our appointed time and an accident could happen to anyone.' He hesitated, watching her intently. The girl felt herself growing hot under his probing gaze. She looked away and made to stand. Grabbing her wrists in a painful grip, Daniel pulled her down beside him, his face implacable as his eyes bored into hers. 'What is it that you are not saying? There is more to this. I see it in your face. Tell me, Sullah. Tell me all of it.'

'The Bentinck coach was in the lane as well, so I been told.' Her voice was resigned. 'Massa Bentinck, he was drivin' and Miss Eliza an' that other one was inside the carriage. The Massa, he do say as the horses took fright an' run wild. That be what he says. They crashed into the cart an' it went off the road an' Marcus... Marcus died.' Her head drooped.

Daniel's massive frame began to tremble violently. He climbed stiffly to his feet and stumbled to the window, looking down into the stable yard. He straddled his legs wide, seeking to keep his balance, his great hands curling and uncurling of their own volition as the sinews of his neck stood out like knotted rope. Sullah watched in terror. There was something primeval about such anger. It was made even more terrifying by its silence. The big man fought his own demons. He breathed heavily... in... out... in... out, battling for control of mind and body. He stared unseeingly at the activity below.

After endless, agonising minutes the tension seemed to ease and Sullah sagged thankfully. He had found himself again. Praise be! Daniel turned, a black silhouette against the light. She could not see his features; they were in deep shadow.

'I must see him. Where have they taken him Sullah?' His words were calm and quiet.

'I do think that they said the Massa's man was goin' to bring him home. They was takin' him to the stable, so the Missus tol' me. We will both go, Daniel. We will go together.' She was almost eager in her relief. He had taken it better than she had dared to hope. The worst was over.

Daniel stepped away from the window and Sullah gave a gasp of horror, her hand at her mouth to stifle a scream.

Never had she seen such naked hatred in any human face. She was staring, not at a fellow being but at an instrument of implacable vengeance. Ice dripped in her veins, travelling the length of her body and leaving her weak and shivering. It was not over. It had not yet begun.

As she staggered after Daniel down the back stairs, Sullah fought to shake off the mind-numbing fear that was all but immobilising her. In all the years that she had known Daniel she had never had cause to be afraid of him. Now, he was a different man, an unknown quantity. He was like one possessed. She caught up to him as they crossed the yard, her timid hand tugging at his sleeve.

'Please, Daniel, wait… I… I needs to get my head right before I goes in there… I needs a moment. Jus' wait a while.' As she had hoped, her entreaty for time for herself slowed his headlong rush and they both came to a halt beneath the arch. The door was open, the stable dim and dark, holding its secrets. They drew close together, seeking comfort.

An agitated Anne Weston appeared in the doorway.

'There you are.' Her voice was unnaturally loud, even harsh, her eyes reddened and her hands gripped tightly in front of her bodice. She cleared her throat and continued in a more normal tone. 'He is in here… They have brought him… I don't know what… I am not sure who will… Oh dear.' She choked and stood to one side.

Daniel and Sullah edged through the opening, the girl curling her fingers into the man's hand. Marcus was lying on an old door set on two trestles. In death he was strangely diminished. It seemed that his bulk had ebbed away along with his life-blood. Sullah hung back but Daniel pulled away the cloth that covered the body from the waist down. The girl gave a horrified gasp at the sight of the mangled wreckage. The bones of her hand cracked as an unknowing Daniel ground her fingers together. His throat convulsed as he stared at what remained of his friend. A long sigh shuddered through his frame as he drew the cloth back over the body, over the face, over the tortured, sightless eyes. The fabric settled, moulding itself to the lifeless contours beneath.

Releasing Sullah's hand, Daniel moved one rigid step backwards, then two, then three. He turned to the Mistress who hovered half in and half out of the entrance.

'I will go to the place where he died, Ma'am. I have to see for myself what happened there. When I come back I will do what must be done for Marcus.' He looked at Sullah and asked gently, 'Will you do the woman's part for him? It will not be easy. He did not die quiet. Can you do it?'

'He was my friend too. I can do what I must.' Her dignified response almost shattered Daniel's fragile control. Giving her arm a quick squeeze he left the stable and began to jog across the yard and down the long drive.

The smashed wagon still rested on its side in the ditch, the broken wheel lying like a marker, in silent accusation at the side of the road. Apart from the rasping of Daniel's heaving lungs the silence was complete. Immobile leaves hung from the trees, the long grass was still and no birds sang. It had become a desolate spot. Goose-bumps rose on Daniel's skin and the hairs prickled on the back of his neck. He jerked into motion seeking to dismiss his superstitious fears in a burst of determined activity. He knelt in the lane examining the tracks. He studied the fractured wheel and clambered on top of the over-turned cart. Only when he saw the flattened, blood-soaked indentations beneath the heavy vehicle did his imagination bring him to a gut-wrenching halt.

Tears etched rivers in the dust on his face, streaking where he rubbed his eyes with ineffectual fists, in the way of a child. From deep within him came a groan, a rumble of noise that congealed into comprehensible words.

'This was no accident. It was a killing!' The sounds hammered in his head as he dragged himself away from that soulless place, back along the road that led to Fernleigh Hall.

Less than a week later, Henry Bentinck stood before the fireplace in the library as he attempted to explain to Peter Blundell what had happened. Someone had indeed been quick to spread the story of the incident in the neighbourhood. Bentinck's voice was angry, acrimonious.

'That wretch was almost responsible for a tragic accident,' he snapped. 'There he was, right on a bend, straddling across the middle of the lane. I came around the corner and was right on top of him. I had the devil's own job to keep my carriage on the road. What might have happened to my wife, or to Mrs Harrison, I cannot think.' He stopped, aware of the expression of distaste on the face of his neighbour. He continued in a more conciliatory tone, 'Oh, I know the man is dead and I regret that it should have happened, but let there be no mistake in this, the slave's blood is not on my hands. He was at fault and he alone.'

Peter Blundell turned mildly enquiring eyes towards Eliza, who was sitting by the window staring blankly out into the garden. 'It must have been a dreadful ordeal for you, Ma'am. I trust that you are recovered.'

Eliza's voice was expressionless. 'You are most kind, Mr Blundell.' She rose. 'If you will excuse me, I have a headache,' she murmured, and drifted like a wraith to the door.

Blundell rushed to hold it open. 'I hope to see you in better health before too long, Elizabeth.' The older man turned a stern face to Henry. 'Forgive the familiarity, Sir, but I have known Matthew Broadwood's daughter since she was a small child. I feel a duty of concern towards this dear lady.' He laid a gentle hand on the young woman's shoulder and spoke to her quietly, turning his back on the figure by the fireplace. 'Take care of yourself, Ma'am. Do remember that if you ever wish for a change of scene for a day or two, my wife would indeed be pleased to have you stay with us.'

Blundell's kindness pierced Eliza's shell of indifference and her eyes filled as she tried to smile at her father's old friend.

'You were always good to me, Sir, as was your lady and I thank you for your solicitude. I do not often pay calls since my marriage but be assured that I shall remember your offer with gratitude.' Inclining her head, she left the library and moved wearily up the stairs.

Peter Blundell resumed his seat, refusing to meet Bentinck's eye. He took out his snuff-box and inhaled deeply as he stalled to gain some time before his next words. Finally, he too stood up and faced his host. A straightforward and honest man, he saw no reason to prevaricate now that Eliza had left the room. He came straight to the point.

'I have been hearing things, Bentinck. There have been rumours about your activities circulating in Liverpool for some months. They are common gossip in London and are known in Chester too. I have tried to ignore them for the sake of my old friend's good name but I can do so no more. There is also the state of your wife, Sir. Her fear, her tears, her bruises, they have been noted. Good God man, what are you? And now, this incident with the slave. I have spoken with Matthew's sister and I have to say that Mrs Weston does not believe your version of what occurred in the lane. The tracks of the two carriages… Well, we do not need to go into details but… things are not right. Not right at all.'

Bentinck interrupted, incredulously. 'You do not mean to tell me that you have been out there examining the road? Do you doubt my word, Sir?'

'Mrs Weston's man, the other slave... he went to look. He insists that the tracks show that the cart was run off the road. It was never in the middle. It was forced off.'

'And you would take the word of a slave against me? Is that what you are saying? The word of a black heathen against a gentleman?' He threw himself into a chair.

Blundell sighed and went to the door. He stopped with his hand on the polished knob and addressed Henry Bentinck.

'Nothing can be proved of course. The truth will never be known. There will be no public enquiry. I had hoped that it would not come to this, but I am afraid that I must ask you to withdraw from those business ventures of mine in which you have an interest. I shall ensure that you do not lose financially. You will be reimbursed, but I would not wish to be associated with you in the future and you are no longer welcome in my home. I bid you good day.'

Bentinck was left alone, anger threatening to choke him. He prowled the library like a caged tiger, his raw fury at odds with the restful ambience of Matthew Broadwood's sanctum. His mind teemed with bitterness as he raged against his fate. He had been driven from the capital by gossip and rumour, and had thought to make a new life here in this thriving town. Had he not taken Fernleigh Hall and built on the fading Broadwood reputation? Had he not forsaken most of his old friends and the life that he had enjoyed to gain the favour of this Puritanical society? Now it was over. He faced social ruin. He had failed, and all because of two slaves. Damn them! Damn them all! They would pay. One had already paid but the other one... the clever one... the one who had thought to rise above his station, worming his way into old Broadwood's trust and

Eliza's good graces... He was still here and a heavy price would be exacted for this day's work. It would indeed.

The man poured a glass of brandy, draining it in a single gulp. He knew that once word of Blundell's actions leaked out, as it was bound to do, he would be ostracised. He was finished in Liverpool. He stared out of the window as the red mist faded leaving him empty of all emotion except a cold and lethal need for revenge.

CHAPTER FOURTEEN

Fernleigh Hall
November 1794

In the days that followed the tragedy, life at Fernleigh Hall slowly returned to an outward semblance of normality. The family attended St. Nicholas' Church on Sundays and Eliza took afternoon drives into the countryside accompanied by her sister-in-law, although she could never step into the carriage without a shudder. The women often strolled along the waterfront enjoying the sea air and the bustle of the quays. Henry Bentinck was sometimes seen boarding the stage or the Eastham boat to Chester in pursuance of new business ventures. Anne Weston and Sullah revived their interest in new gowns for Mr Barton's visit. If they were less enthusiastic than before, at least the occupation kept their minds away from the awful emptiness of the loft above the stables.

Yet for all the appearance of commonplace activity, an air of suffocating menace hung like a fog over the Hall. Servants sidled around the rooms, carrying out their duties in a sullen silence. The usual light-hearted banter in the below-stairs warren was absent. Maids trod softly, and eyes were not raised from the floor. The threat was tangible. Storm clouds were gathering and fear stalked the corridors. Mixed with the fear was guilt and guilt had never made a comfortable bed-fellow. The three slaves had not been truly accepted by the staff at Fernleigh, but in the face of their rejection Marcus had remained cheerful, unfailingly civil and had worked harder than any of them. To their surprise his presence was missed. He had almost become one of their own and the manner of his death offended their sense of justice. They muttered together in corners and made belated and self-conscious overtures of friendship towards the other two slaves. Sullah responded but Daniel was different.

Daniel had built a wall of silence around himself and had retreated into a self-imposed isolation born of despair. In the immediate aftermath of his friend's death, he had given loud and angry voice to his worst suspicions, insisting that Marcus had been callously and brutally murdered. He had written down his findings from the scene of the 'accident' and Anne Weston had delivered the document to Blundell Hall. Daniel was aware that Mr Blundell had been to see Bentinck, but as day succeeded day and nothing happened, he was forced to the conclusion that the concept of white justice for a black slave was as unlikely here as it had been in Jamaica. He brooded, working himself to exhaustion during the long days and walking the woods and gardens in the sleepless hours of the night.

Very early one morning, in the misty time that precedes daylight, Sullah found Daniel slumped on a bank near the lake. He was staring with vacant eyes at the skeletal trees wreathed in ghostly vapour.

She stood before him, imposing herself on his vision. 'When yo' goin' to get yo' head around this, Daniel?' she urged. 'He is gone an' all this wailin' an' anger won't get him back. I been watchin' yo' an' yo' will be under the dirt jus' like he is if yo' goes on like this.' She dropped to her knees beside the cold figure and reached for his hand, her voice losing its hectoring tone and her dark eyes brimming as she pleaded with him. 'Daniel, my dear Daniel, yo' cannot keep hurtin' this bad. I needs you. Missus needs you. We all has to die. We all has to accept it. Yo' surely cannot think that Marcus would want it to be like this.'

Daniel flinched as her warm tears fell on his hand. He absently stroked the girl's hair, pulling her head down to rest on his chest and slipping an arm around her thin shoulders. Sullah scarcely dared to breathe in case she destroyed the intimacy of the moment.

'You don't understand,' he muttered thickly. 'It is not his death. It is not even the manner of his death. God knows I have seen much worse. It is that I cannot get justice for him; there is no justice for a black slave. The evil that destroyed a good man is still here in this house and it will destroy us all.'

The girl raised her head, she felt years older than Daniel. There had never been room for ideals in the harsh reality of her world. She had to make him see.

'But yo's wrong. It ain't nothin' to do with black an' white. Any Massa who is the cause of a servant's death, in any place, would never be took before a judge an' made to pay. We all knows that. If any servant was killed it would have been no different. It ain't colour, Daniel. It ain't skin. It is... sta...status. Yes, status, that is the word. I have heard yo' say it lots of times. It's all 'bout master an' servant not black man an' white. This ain't Jamaica and the white blood in yo' carries no blame for his death. Can yo' not see?'

The clear light of the early winter sun touched her face, tingeing the delicate features with gold and gleaming on the braids of her hair but Daniel was impervious to her appeal. He continued to stare out across the lake and did not seem to have heard.

'The evil is still here,' he persisted. 'We shall all have to pay, the Mistress, you, me and most of all, El... Mrs Bentinck. I have seen how he uses her. We have all seen it.' He gripped Sullah's shoulders, his fingers digging into the delicate bones. He did not see her features twist in pain. 'We have seen her bruises. We have all heard her cries. We have seen her change from a joyful girl into a beaten victim.' His voice rose and he stood up, dragging Sullah with him. He shook her. 'You know, everyone knows what is happening and he is getting away with it. No one can stop him.'

Anger, frustration and bitter disappointment welled up in Sullah's head and she pulled away.

'So!' she spat. 'So now we knows the truth of it. Now we sees the real Daniel. Yo' pretends to be all cut up 'bout dear Marcus but yo' don't care. Yo' only cares for her. Yo' don't worry 'bout the Missus, no, nor 'bout me neither. Oh yes, yo' got fine words. Yo' always has fine words but yo' can't see nothin' but that... that... woman. Yo' wants her. Yo've always wanted her. Ever since we done come here. Oh yes, yo' thinks to fool yo'self and us all too but yo' don't fool nobody, Daniel. Yo' wants that woman so as yo' is the son of a white man an' not a black slave. All them fancy words an' fancy ways, they won't make yo' any other colour than what yo' are. Yo' is so mixed up. I feels sorry for yo'. But I feels even more sorry for Marcus. He deserved a better friend.' She spun on her heel and ran up the bank towards the house, trailing the last vestige of early mist in her wake. She left a stunned Daniel to drop back on to the grass in consternation, his head sunk in his hands.

The days stretched into weeks and inexorably things began to change, fraying the edges of the social life at Fernleigh

Hall. The initial drip, drip of minor slights steadily increased, swelling into a spate of insults that could not be ignored. Conversations outside the church terminated abruptly when the Bentincks appeared. Bows and greetings on the quay were not acknowledged. Calls paid were not returned, and it appeared that all the ladies of the fine town-houses were no longer to be found at home in the mornings. Even the poverty-stricken Rector and his wife discovered that they were unable to find a free evening when a dinner invitation could be accepted. Tradesmen's bills, demanding instant settlement of accounts, threatened to engulf the Hall. The honest citizens of Liverpool made their displeasure known in clear and unequivocal terms.

Each and every humiliation was marked by Henry Bentinck. He feigned indifference to the outside world, but he responded to the insults by growing ever more vicious towards those around him. Only Mary was exempt from his mindless fury and, as ever, Eliza bore the brunt of his savage depravity. In the past, only the prospect of an unexpected guest catching a glimpse of his wife's bruises or her tear-stained face had curbed Bentinck's worst excesses. Now, with the Hall in socially imposed quarantine, all restrictions on his behaviour were removed. Henry's abuse became ever more sadistic and Eliza refused to leave her room. All Anne Weston's attempts to see her niece were thwarted and she was powerless to intervene between a man and his wife in their own home, no matter what atrocities were taking place. Eventually, however, Eliza's passive acceptance of his ill-treatment impinged upon his satisfaction. There was little sport to be had in plaguing a spirit already crushed beyond recovery, nor was there any delight in tormenting a body that no longer responded to pain. He was thwarted at home and took to the waterfront brothels in search of more spirited victims.

Hundreds of stars spangled the inky blackness above the walled kitchen garden and a full moon bathed the cobbled paths in the blue-white light of an early December frost.

Residual seed-heads sparkled and icy diamonds glinted on the remnants of fading herbs. The magic was lost on the frail figure huddling deep in her cloak and slumped on a solitary bench in the corner farthest away from the house. Eliza had ventured out for the first time in many days but was exhausted by the unaccustomed exercise and immune to the beauty of her surroundings. Her eyes registered the vague outline of her shallow breath on the cold air and her thoughts drifted in the same formless patterns.

In the shadow of the wall a sentinel watched and waited, unwilling to disturb her solitude. Daniel often came to the garden in those hours when the all-seeing windows of the house were blind in their night-time shutters. He had heard her soft footsteps and had known instinctively who it was. She too became aware of another person in the garden.

She spoke, her voice a mere rustle on the air, a whisper of barely formed sounds.

'Who is it? Who is there? Daniel, is it you?' The black shadow detached itself from the conniving darkness.

'Why are you here?' His gentle voice drifted towards her. 'I had heard... I believed you to be unwell... sick... They said you do not leave your room.'

'Do sit. I cannot look up at you.' She waved a hand, thin to the point of transparency, in his direction. The effort drained her and she shivered. Daniel stripped off his jacket, draping it around her shoulders. He moved carefully to the end of the bench and turned to look at her. He stared, gnawing at his bottom lip as his nails dug deep into the flesh of his palms. She had always been lovely but now, with her features pared down to their immaculate bone-structure, her beauty was ethereal. Her teeth chattered and her body shook.

Daniel could contain himself no longer. He slid from the bench and knelt at her feet, taking her hands and covering them with his own. The dam burst.

'Eliza...My dearest.' The yearning of three long, help-less years poured out. Status, background, creed, colour, blood were all forgotten. She needed his protection. He stood in one swift, fluid movement and lifted her bodily from the seat, cradling her like an infant in his arms, her head nestling against his shoulder. He strode out of the walled enclosure, underneath the arch, across the yard and into the comparative warmth of the stable. Two of the animals shifted uneasily as Daniel moved past their stalls, past the ladder leading to the empty loft and down to the tack room at the end of the block. Here, in a tiny cubicle was the space he had called his own ever since Marcus had died.

Gently, Daniel set Eliza down in the battered comfort of a discarded sofa, and snatching up a blanket from his pallet he tucked it around her shivering body. His massive bulk loomed over her and he touched her hair, her face, her eyelids with long, tender fingers. She sighed softly.

'Daniel?' It was a question. She was child-like in her helplessness.

'What has that brute done to you? What has he done? How has he hurt you?' His words were slurred and his vision misted.

'Daniel?' She opened her eyes and she swayed towards him, his blanket slipping from her shoulders. 'He is not here. Henry is not at home,' she murmured. 'He is gone to Bristol on business. He left yesterday. He will be gone for weeks.' She reached out a tentative hand and stroked his arm, her fingers tracing the old scar. At her touch his breathing stopped. His face burned and his eyes blazed. The fitful glimmer of light in the cubicle vanished as a shadow blocked the doorway.

'Daniel!' Anne Weston's voice sliced the air between them. 'Elizabeth! For the love of God! Have you both taken leave of your wits? What have you…?' She stepped forward, holding her lantern high, taking in the scene in the cubicle. She almost swooned in relief. They were not too late. Anne turned to the hovering figure at her back. 'Sullah, take the light and see Mrs Bentinck back to her room. She is not well. Stay with her.' She wrapped the blanket around her niece and pushed both women, un-ceremoniously, through the door. Daniel, clinging to the last vestige of self-control, slid down on to the straw.

Grateful for the enfolding gloom, Anne Weston took the sofa and watched her slave with mixed emotions.

'Daniel, look at me,' she commanded. 'Look and listen for I intend to have my say. Sullah and I have watched you ever since we arrived in England. You have always been attracted to my niece.' She held up a cautionary hand. 'Listen! It is time the truth was spoken.' She continued more gently. 'You were taken by her beauty, her freshness, her charm and her apparent concern for the cause of slaves. You adored everything about her. In a way, you transferred all the admiration that you had once felt for me, to Elizabeth.' Anne drew a ragged breath. 'I believe that you have a need to admire a woman whose skin is white. I have always thought this, even back in Jamaica and Jeremiah agreed with me. You cannot be attracted by another slave, because a part of you has ever been in denial of your mother's heritage. In your mind, if you could attract a white woman, then that would prove your worth.'

Daniel jumped to his feet his face suffused with suppressed anger. 'There is nothing wrong in my admiration for the young Mistress. You never found fault when it was you that was the focus of my devotion. Did you, Ma'am?'

Anne lowered her eyes. She was forced to acknowledge the truth of Daniel's accusations. She had been flattered by the young man's attention and it had amused her to accept his worship from afar.

'But, Daniel, this is different. Eliza is not what you think. She is shallow, and feckless. She has no self-discipline and at present she is vulnerable. She is looking for any means of escape from her situation. Should you persist in your attentions, she will yield, and what then? Have you considered the future? It cannot be and you know it. You are a slave, Daniel. And there is Henry. Since Marcus was killed, you two have contrived to stay out of each other's way and we have all been thankful for it. But such restraint will not last. He wants revenge and so do you. Can you imagine what would happen if he knew of this night's events?' She shuddered.

'But she does care for me, and I would never hurt her…'

'She is grateful for your affection, but you mean nothing to her. She will use you and then discard you. Now let us put an end to this.'

'She does care. I swear that she does. You are unjust to speak of her as you do, Mistress, and I never thought you to be cruel. He beats her. Look at her. Look at what he has done to her. She is your own flesh and blood. How can you stand by and allow him to torment and humiliate her?'

'This is England and a wife belongs to her husband in almost the same way as my slaves belong to me. A woman has no rights and precious little freedom. It has always been so. You are not the only captive here. A good, kind husband is as much a blessing to a wife as a gentle master is to a slave.'

The silence lengthened and stretched; the horses next door stamped their feet and morning light began to filter into the cubicle. The tension seeped away in moments of passive reflection. They had travelled a hard road. Anne

Weston struggled to her feet, accepting Daniel's proffered hand.

'One last thing, Ma'am. How did you know she was here?'

'Sullah. It was Sullah. She has worried for weeks. She saw Eliza leave the house and she knew that you would be pacing the gardens as usual. She watched and when you came in here, she ran for me. You should be grateful to her, Daniel. Deal with her gently for she loves you dearly.' She smiled as she turned to leave. 'Now there is a union that I would happily sanction.'

It was late the following afternoon before Daniel saw Eliza again. He had been working on the hard ground in the vegetable garden for most of the day, double-digging in preparation for the spring planting. It seemed a pointless task. He knew that he would not be here to see the seeds sown; Anne Weston had finally determined to leave Fernleigh Hall and set up her own establishment on the outskirts of Liverpool. She had divulged her plans to Daniel and Sullah earlier that day.

'Things here are becoming quite impossible,' she declared, pacing the bare floor of the schoolroom to where both slaves had been summoned. 'I cannot rest for fear of what may happen next. I stayed, after my brother's death, out of a sense of duty to my niece but she is a grown woman, a married woman and I am unable to intervene between husband and wife, no matter how much I might wish to do so.' She halted in front of Sullah. 'I am concerned that my nephew-in-law may turn his attentions to you, Sullah, and before too long. He has bullied his wife to such a degree that there is no sport to be had there any more. You are different. I have seen how he looks at you. You would be a natural choice as his victim. You have

223

youth, beauty and are high-spirited, but because of your status you would have no redress, no matter what he might do. You were also a dear friend of Marcus and, perhaps more importantly, are under the protection of Daniel.' Anne bit her lip and laid a hand on the girl's shoulder. 'He would enjoy using you, my dear, and through you he could provoke Daniel. Daniel would kill to protect you and Henry Bentinck knows it.'

The large-fingered nursery clock ticked away the minutes. A whirring sound startled them all and the hour chimed, leaving an uneasy quiet in its wake. Anne cleared her throat and moved to the window, scrubbing at a pane and staring down the empty drive. Her back remained turned on her two servants.

'We all know, do we not, that his intended victim is you, Daniel.' She spun round to face them, her eyes brimming with unshed tears. 'Let there be no pretence. You have been his target ever since we got here. I have had one slave killed. I will not lose another.'

Daniel shrugged his mighty shoulders. 'Ma'am, of course we go wherever you say, and I know that you speak truly about his intentions, but I can take care of Sullah and of myself too.' He rubbed a tired hand across his eyes. 'Are you certain that it would be right to desert your own flesh and blood in this way? As you say, you cannot interfere between a man and his wife but your very presence in this house affords her some protection and prevents the worst of his violence towards her. If we leave, she will have no one to care for her welfare. She will be at that man's mercy. Is that what you would wish, Ma'am?'

Sullah snatched his arm and dragged him round to face her fury. Her eyes blazed.

'How can it be that yo' never learn? Was Marcus' death not enough? Must that evil man have another life jus' so she can be protected? If we stays here yo' will surely go the way of Marcus. Is that what yo' really wants, Daniel? Will that satisfy that load o' guilt that sits on yo' shoulder like a parrot?' She appealed to her mistress. 'Missus, make him see. Tell him how it is.' The girl's voice broke.

Anne held out a hand towards Daniel. 'I do feel bad about Eliza. I have tried, you know that I have tried but it has made no difference. We will not be far away, at least not for some time. She will call on us and we can make sure that she is well. It will be somewhere for her to visit, away from the Hall. My mind is made up. We leave this place as soon as arrangements can be made for me to take a house in town.'

The slave inclined his head, his face set. 'Then there is no more to be said. By your leave, Madam, I will go back to my winter digging.'

Daniel left the room, his shoulders slumped, his heavy footsteps echoing down the back stairs. His brain seemed to rattle in his head as he stumbled out of the kitchen and into the garden. He snatched up the spade and began a frenzy of digging, chopping up the hard, unyielding earth, breath hissing from his lungs to hang in great clouds on the frosty air. Dig, turn, move one step, dig, turn, move one step. He set up a punishing, relentless rhythm. Sweat streamed down his face blinding him, his muscles screaming their protest as he tried to blot out all semblance of thought in mindless activity.

All day he dug, and in the afternoon Eliza came to him. She drifted silently into the walled enclosure, a ghost in the gathering gloom, her velvet cape and hood cloaking her in the darkness of anonymity. He did not look up but was aware of her presence from the moment that she had entered the garden. Whenever she occupied the same space as himself, he knew. His breath quickened, his skin tingled and finally he raised his head to find her standing only feet away. She was watching his labours with unremitting concentration.

Just for a moment, Daniel thought that he had surprised a knowing, cunning glint in her eyes but he was surely mistaken. Her expression was the same as ever, sweet, guileless, innocent. Catching his gaze with her own, she blushed prettily.

'Good afternoon, Daniel. Pray do not let me disturb you.' He started to deny that she had ever disturbed him but choked on the convention and instead, straightening his back, he thrust the spade deep into the soil and waited. 'I had to see you,' she whispered, shyly. 'Yesterday, we… I… You must not think ill of me. You really must not.' She opened her blue eyes wide, twisting her fingers convincingly together. 'I have been aware that you admire me, Daniel. I have always known it and if only things had been different, well… You are an attractive man and I have need of… but… but there is nothing to be done.' She dabbed at her eyes with a scrap of a handkerchief, allowing the hood to slide from her hair. She shivered. 'It is so cold here… Is it not? May we…? Perhaps we could talk…? The stables will be… I must confide in someone.' She turned, pausing for an effective moment before slipping through the gateway.

A mesmerised Daniel closed his eyes in an agony of disbelief. She had looked for him. She had sought his company. She found him attractive. She had said so. Daniel blundered across the yard pushing open the creaking stable door. He passed the horses' stalls, passed the carriage and passed the foot of Marcus' ladder. He froze. There was a rustling sound. Behind him, a horse snorted and the slave let out his breath in a noisy gasp. He turned into his cabin, his frame filling the doorway.

Eliza was ensconced on the sofa, feet firmly together, hands clasped in her lap, back straight and her head modestly lowered. She lifted purple-veined, heavy lids and

226

allowed her eyes to travel over him.

'Daniel?' It was a prompt.

He dropped to his knees at her feet, his hands reaching out to push back the concealing hood and reveal the glory of her hair. She looked different. The brow-beaten victim had gone. He could see that she had taken trouble with her appearance and there was a glimpse of the old Eliza, the carefree young girl that she had once been. He could not trust himself to speak but feasted his eyes on her delicate features, swallowing hard. She sat immobile as he raised his hands again, his clumsy fingers fumbling with the clasp of her cloak whilst the blood drummed in his ears.

The sounds of a sea-shanty drifted across Daniel's consciousness.

'Heave ho, row lads row. Mmmm... mmmm... Row lads row.' It was unreal. He blinked, shaking his head, but the sound would not go away. 'Heave ho, row lads row.' The tuneless singing was now accompanied by other noises. There was banging and clattering in the room above, a sliding screech as something was dragged across the floor. The room had belonged to Marcus. The song was one that Marcus used to sing. Daniel shook in primeval fear.

'Daniel? Daniel, is that yo'?' It was Sullah's voice, penetrating, piercing, insistent. It seeped through cracks in the floor. 'Is yo' there, Daniel?' His eyes flickered to Eliza's still figure. Her face was shuttered. She drew the folds of the cape about her shoulders and pulled the hood up over her hair.

Daniel barged out of the cramped room and up the rickety ladder into the loft.

'What are you doing?' he panted. 'Why are you here? How long have you been hiding? Do you think to spy on me? Do you?' He grabbed Sullah by the arms and shook her viciously. The girl's head flopped from side to side as she tried to pull away from him. He slapped her face, flinging her across the room. She clattered into Marcus' chair, knocking it over and lay cowering in a corner, her eyes rolling in abject terror.

Her voice floated towards him, muffled by the dust. 'I did not spy. I was here before yo' even came. Yo' an' her. I surely did hear yo but I was no spy, Daniel. I often comes here. I feels close to Marcus. An' today I was movin' his things so they be ready for when the Missus takes us away.' Two great tears squeezed from her eyes and rolled in silent protest down her cheeks. 'I won't come again. I doesn't want to come here no more.' She scrabbled, crab-like across the floor and disappeared through the trapdoor. Daniel followed her down, his dead friend's spirit an accusing weight on his shoulders.

His cabin was empty, the silence oppressive. Daniel threw himself on to the sagging sofa, despair threatening to overwhelm him. Why was it that nothing in his life was ever as it seemed? Not Eliza, not Sullah, not even himself.

CHAPTER FIFTEEN

LIVERPOOL
DECEMBER 1794

The clutter of masts bobbed and swayed in the harbour as a squally wind sloshed the grey, muddy waters of the Mersey against the ships' sides, pushing them together and forcing them apart in a ragged dance. Anne Weston stopped and pointed at the scene.

'Look at that. Those ships resemble nothing so much as a group of drunken sailors weaving their way out of Mother Redcap's cottage after depositing their ill-gotten gains.' Eliza smiled and linked her arm more firmly into the crook of her Aunt's elbow. Anne shot her a quick look, nodding her satisfaction. The girl had been so much better since Henry's departure for Bristol. It had been a slow recovery but she was improving by the day. She had become more animated and if the old vivacity was lacking, well, her present demeanour was certainly more appropriate to a married woman. Her niece was looking pretty again; she was still too slender, still delicate but she had lost that dreadful pallor and the air of cowed submission that had dragged her down for so long.

They strolled long, enjoying the fresh breeze.

'It is so good to see you nearly well again, my dear. I do declare that I have never been more bothered in my life.' Eliza's eyes clouded for a moment and her step faltered then she lifted her chin, breathed deeply and they walked on.

'Miss Broadwood! It is surely Miss Broadwood. It can be no other.' An exquisitely uniformed officer impeded their progress. He doffed his hat and his bow included them both but his eyes were only for Eliza. He straightened up, laughing at the girl's bemused expression.

Anne stared from one to the other. She intervened quickly.

'I regret, Sir, but I do not have the advantage of knowing whom I address. However, you are in error I fear. My niece was Miss Broadwood but has been Mrs Henry Bentinck these many months.'

The man acknowledged his mistake with a dismissive gesture. 'I must indeed beg pardon but I have been in France and have only recently returned. This lady and I are dear friends. We met in Chester when my regiment was lodged there. Our acquaintance was most cruelly curtailed by the advent of hostilities.' He shifted his gaze to Eliza, who was staring at him, enraptured. 'Is it not so, Ma'am? Pray tell your... Aunt... that I am not over-forward in paying my respects. As I recall, we were most definitely introduced.'

Anne Weston found herself supporting her niece as the girl slumped against her.

'This is no time for civilities, Sir. I beg of you, give Mrs Bentinck your arm on the other side, she has been most unwell recently and today's exertions have been too much for her. Our carriage is just along the quay... If you could assist me?' Together they half-carried the silent girl towards the waiting coach. The footman, whom Anne always used instead of Daniel now if a journey with Eliza was involved, saw their stumbling approach and came to help. They lifted Eliza on to the seat and a relieved Anne climbed in beside her. Leaning through the window, she held out her hand. 'I still do not know whom I address, Sir, but I do indeed thank you for your timely assistance.'

'Edward. His name is Edward. Captain Edward Stanton.'

The words came from behind her and Anne turned in surprise at the tone of suppressed excitement in her niece's voice. The girl appeared to be quite recovered from her temporary indisposition and her glowing face and sparkling eyes gave the lie to any suggestion of sickness or frailty. Warning bells clanged in the older woman's head as the Captain's amused glance ranged from one lady to the other. Anne did not like him; he was clearly enjoying her discomfiture and she certainly did not approve of the warmth of the manner in which he was regarding her niece.

'Perhaps, Ma'am, you will permit me to introduce myself to you, in the absence of anyone else to perform the duty. After all, we must observe the proprieties, must we not? I am indeed Captain Edward Stanton, at your service. I am delighted to make your acquaintance.'

'This is my Aunt... Mrs Anne Weston,' Eliza breathed. 'She is... was, my late father's sister.'

He was instantly contrite. 'Forgive me. I was not aware that Mr Broadwood had passed away. My deepest condolences to you both.' There was an uncomfortable pause and then Stanton and Eliza spoke together. 'May I...?'

'My husband is...' They laughed.

'Ladies must always take priority. Please go on,' he insisted.

'I was about to remark...' Eliza was incoherent in her eagerness. 'Although Mr Bentinck is away at present, my Aunt is living at Fernleigh Hall with us... even though today we have been looking at properties that she might wish to take... you see she is to set up her own establishment... and...'

'My dear, our business is of no interest to Captain

231

Stanton. I think that we should return home.' Anne leaned out to the coachman but was forestalled.

'Yes of course, Aunt, but as I was saying to Edward… to the Captain… I am sure that my husband would insist on such an old friend partaking of our hospitality whilst he is in the area.' She turned to Stanton, offering her hand. 'I insist. You must call on us.'

He clasped her fingers, holding them longer than etiquette demanded before raising them to his lips. 'I should be honoured, Mrs Bentinck. Until tomorrow then.' He bowed to both ladies, signalled to the driver and watched the carriage bowl away.

There was silence inside the coach. Each woman was preoccupied with her own thoughts. Eliza was giddy with excitement. The initial shock of seeing Edward Stanton again was giving way to feelings of intense longing for what might have been. Her insides churned and she felt as though her heart was being squeezed; she had difficulty breathing. Outside the window, the grey afternoon had become a bright kaleidoscope of vivid colour and the horses' hooves beat out a glorious message… *He is here … he is here… Edward is here… Edward… Edward.*

She closed her eyes, casting her mind back to the wonderful weeks in Chester, those weeks before her betrothal to Henry. She could recall her heady delight when the gallant officer had led her out in the dance and had promptly torn up her card and claimed her for his own for the duration of the evening, raising murmurs of out-raged disapproval from the dowagers. She remembered the so-called shopping trips to Chester, chaperoned by an elderly maid who had been persuaded to sit in the public gardens whilst her charge strolled along the banks of the Dee in delightfully unsupervised walks. She would never forget his promises, his whispered words of love, nor the liberties he had taken with her person before she had stayed his wandering hands. If only Daniel had not been too late with her letter. If only Edward's regiment had not chosen that particular time to move off to Dover.

Eliza sighed, dreaming of how different her life would have been. Edward would have married her. She would have been an army wife. They may have been poor for a while but neither of them would have minded that. It would not have mattered. Papa could never stay angry with her for long and he would have accepted Edward, she knew he would. Given time, her father would have found a way out of his troubles, a way that did not depend upon the good offices of Henry Bentinck. At the thought of the man she had married Eliza's eyes filled. It was cruel, too cruel. Why had she been forced to pay for Papa's mistakes? Why had she been made to suffer so? It had all been for nothing. Her father was dead and his reputation no longer mattered. Henry's magnificent life in London, his enviable social connections, her opportunity to shine in the salons of the capital had all faded away. So much had been promised and it was all gone. It was unfair. Everything had gone wrong in her life. Everything. Why should she have been forced into marriage against her will? A tiny, insidious voice dropped words in her ear. *You have not been treated justly. Why should you not take some happiness? Why should you not do as you please for once? Who is to stop you?* Eliza nodded to herself, put back her head and pretended to doze.

Anne Weston clung to the strap as the coach lurched towards Fernleigh Hall. There was a hollow, sinking feeling in the pit of her stomach. There had been more than a casual acquaintance between those two, she was sure of it, and it was not over. She knew Eliza well enough to recognise the resurgence of the girl's former, self-obsessed vanity. Her niece would do whatever she wanted without thought for either responsibilities or consequences. It was evident that her emotions had been stirred by the encounter with Stanton and she was in the right frame of mind to revel in all the intrigue of an affair.

That an affair was about to be embarked upon Anne had no doubt. But what could she do? Only that very day she had signed a year's lease on a property in Everton Hill. She had to get away from Fernleigh. She had outstayed her welcome. Besides, the mail had brought news that George Barton was already bound for Liverpool and she could scarcely entertain him in Henry Bentinck's house for any length of time. She sighed. Perhaps Bentinck would soon be home. He could surely not remain in Bristol for many more weeks? Then Eliza would be his responsibility and not hers.

Mary Harrison sat at the desk in the library, toying with a letter opener. Pen and ink were ready but the sheet of paper before her remained blank. The woman's gaze was fixed on the window and a smile played along the edge of her voluptuous mouth. She had been watching Daniel as he hacked dead wood from the shrubbery and tossed the branches in a heap at his feet. She had observed his actions for some time and knew exactly what his next movements would entail. She slid from her chair and left the library, running up the stairs and snatching a heavy cloak from the chest in her room. The door clicked behind her as she hurried along the passage, down the back stairs and out into the garden. She looked neither right nor left as she made her way to the far end of the shrubbery, turning into a green-walled enclosure of almost impenetrable bushes. The remains of a fire smouldered in the centre, sending a thin spiral of smoke into the dank air. Mary sat on an upturned box, poking her toe at the twisted pile of blackened twigs. She heard Daniel crashing through the bushes long before he came into view. Her breath quickened, her eyes blazed and her tongue flicked out to moisten dry lips. She waited.

The slave staggered into the clearing, his arms full of branches. He noticed nothing as he dropped them on to the grass. As he released his burden he bent double, coughing. It was a loud, harsh, rasping sound. His legs were trembling and his head swam. He was impatient with this recent, unexplained weakness and he muttered under his breath in the old Jamaican dialect.

'Calls yo'self a man, Danny boy? What's wrong then? Can't lift a few twigs no more? Why's yo'...' He stopped as he saw Mary, a silent, immobile figure sitting on his box. He straightened up, conscious that he had been over-heard and embarrassed by it. He was also aware of his dirt-streaked hands and face, his stained trousers, torn shirt and mud-caked boots. He ducked his head, resuming his normal, pedantic form of speech.

'Excuse me, Mrs Harrison Ma'am. I did not realise that you were here. May I help you? Is there anything that I can do?' It was a pathetic attempt to retrieve his dignity.

Mary stood and swayed towards him. Lifting her skirts high, she stretched out one elegant foot across the smouldering fire that stood between them. She stopped inches from his chest and put her head back to see his face. She could hear his breathing, smell the sweat from his labours, the smoke on his clothes but most of all she could sense his fear.

Her voice caught in her throat, deep, sensuous, husky. 'Yes, Daniel. Oh yes, you may help me. There is most definitely something that you can do.' Her eyes dropped to his feet and her burning gaze travelled all the way up his body. Perspiration formed in beads on his forehead and he ground his teeth together. She continued. 'There is no one here. No one at home. Henry is still in Bristol, the women have gone to town and Sullah has taken young Margaret for a ride to the shore in the cart. We shall not be disturbed.'

She unfastened her cloak and stepped even closer until their bodies touched. Her arms hung at her sides as she thrust herself against him. For an endless moment Daniel did not move and she lifted a hand to his neck pulling his head down, her eyes never leaving his face. Her other hand slid along his arm, her fingers resting on the raised scar. With a strength born of fear Daniel thrust her away, lifting her bodily over the fire and sending her tumbling into the bushes. Gasping in horror, he turned and fled, crashing through the trees as tangled branches scratched and tore at his clothes, his face, his hands. Mary lay where she had fallen the breath knocked from her body.

She began to tremble as if from an ague, her teeth chattering as she turned her face into the damp earth. Sobs of frustration racked her and she pummelled the ground with angry fists. Eventually, exhausted, she dragged herself to her feet and staggered back to the house. In the sanctuary of her room she stripped off her clothes, wrapped herself in a coverlet from the bed and lay down. Outside, the afternoon light faded and the sounds of the household beginning preparations for the evening meal drifted into the quietness. Mary lay in the gloom, nursing her bruises and planning her revenge. Her head throbbed with one, remorseless message. *The price of her humiliation would be paid, and paid in full.*

Daniel's feet slowed as he approached the stables. The noise of horses' harness, animated voices and a child's squeals of delight mingled with the chimes as the clock above the arch struck four. Passing through the opening, he could scarcely connect the normality of the scene before him with the events from which he had just fled in terror. He was repelled by Mary Bentinck, as he still thought of

236

her, but much of his horror and his disgust was centred upon himself. He despised all that she and her brother stood for, he knew of her depravity, her cruelty, but he had still been tempted. He was afraid because he recognised how close he had been to yielding to her seduction and he loathed himself for his weakness.

Daniel struggled to compose himself, trying to speak normally as he addressed his Mistress.

'Pardon me, Mrs Weston Ma'am, I did not realise that you had all returned or I should have kept away.' He indicated his dishevelled appearance. 'I am in no state to be seen by ladies.'

Anne smiled ruefully. 'You certainly speak the truth. Look at you. I do hope that the garden is in better condition than you are.' She turned to the others, lifting young Margaret down from the cart where she sat beside Sullah and leading the way towards the house. Eliza drifted after her, giving no indication that she had even noticed Daniel's presence. Sullah scrambled down from her seat, handing the reins to Bentinck's servant. She stared anxiously at Daniel.

'What has happened now?' she hissed. She looked him up and down and Daniel's eyes flicked to the coachman who was standing by the horse's head listening avidly.

'I will speak to you later, Sullah.'

The man thrust the reins into Daniel's hand 'Beg pardon I'm sure. I don't want to hear your doings, some of us got work to do at the house.' He waved at the two vehicles and the horses. 'All this lot is up to the necks in mud.' He gave a satisfied smirk. 'I reckon it will keep you out of mischief for a good few hours.' He turned to Sullah. 'An' I think you'd best get on with your work as well, missy. Come on.' Without waiting for her reply he led the way out of the yard. With a last troubled glance at Daniel's set face, the girl stumbled after him.

It was late the following morning when Edward Stanton came to Fernleigh Hall, cantering into the stable yard and dragging round his horse's head as he reared to a showy halt in front of Daniel. The slave had been carrying water across the yard and was startled by the unexpected visitor. What was Stanton doing here? He put down his buckets and waited silently, his eyes taking in the beautiful lines of the prancing grey and noting the flecks of blood on its sides and the cruel pull of the bit in its mouth. The rider might cut a dashing figure on this fine animal but he was no true horseman, that was certain. He had iron hands and made heavy use of both whip and spur. Daniel felt a pang of sympathy for the beast.

Stanton coloured under the slave's disapproving scrutiny and leaped from the saddle, flipping a coin across the yard.

'Make sure you take proper care of him.' The coin rolled on the cobbles before falling flat at Daniel's feet. He made no attempt to pick it up.

'I cannot accept your money, Sir, but I shall be glad to look after this fellow. He is indeed a fine animal.' Stanton's mouth tightened at the precise vocabulary and refined tone but he could find no fault in the slave's manner. He grunted and turned away, striding towards the steps that led to the front door of the Hall.

From her window, Eliza watched his approach. She had been in a fever of impatience since early morning. Her maid had been driven to distraction by countless contradictions of hairstyle and changes of gown. The effort had, however, been worthwhile and Eliza knew that her newly acquired sophistication was displayed to its best advantage. She stepped back as Stanton glanced up but then returned, laughingly, to her former position. He would know that she had been looking for him. Why pretend? Time was too short. She did not wait to be summoned but hurried along the passage and down the staircase, arriving just as the servant opened the door to admit her guest.

'That will be all right, Jackson,' she said. 'Captain Stanton is expected. Coffee I think, in my sitting-room.'

The footman's jaw dropped. 'The library, Madam, you mean the library.'

'No. I mean my sitting-room. Captain Stanton, this way if you please.' She turned away and led him up the stairs, noting the unexpected speed of Jackson's departure as he scuttled off to the nether regions to impart his momentous news. Behind her she heard Edward's admiring laughter. She threw a quick smile over her shoulder, her eyes dancing with mischief as she gave a carefree shrug.

It was more than an hour before the pair emerged from Eliza's sitting-room. They crossed the gravel in front of the house, deep in conversation but fully aware of the watching eyes at almost every window. Their body language spoke volumes; he bending attentively towards her, she tossing her head and swishing her skirts, conscious, so very conscious of her own beauty and his admiration. Daniel heard them coming and had Stanton's horse ready. He handed over the reins and stood back as the man mounted flashily, skittering his animal from side to side in a fine display of exaggerated skill. Eliza watched with flattering absorption. She turned to Daniel, tapping his arm sharply with her riding crop. Stanton's eyes narrowed as the slave flinched.

'Do hurry, Daniel. Get my horse.'

'Your horse, Madam?'

'My horse. What is wrong with you? Are you stupid all of a sudden? The Captain and I are going riding.'

'But Mrs Bentinck…'

'Are you deaf, boy, as well as stupid? Did you not hear your Mistress? Get her horse and get it now.'

'It will take me a moment to change, Ma'am. You will,

of course, wish me to accompany you.'

Eliza smiled at Stanton before turning to the slave. 'Oh no. I have no need of your services.' Daniel veiled his eyes, hiding his dismay.

He stood beneath the arch, watching as the huge grey pranced down the drive beside the delicate mare. The sound of laughter floated back as they rounded the corner and disappeared from view. Daniel sighed and returned to work. There was much to do this morning, and later in the day he was commissioned to take Mrs Weston over to her new house in Everton Hill. Now that the Mistress had made up her mind to leave he knew that there would be no respite until everything had been packed away, transported and installed in the new establishment. He sighed again. He would be glad to go.

In the weeks that followed, it was as well that Mrs Weston and her servants were fully occupied by the need to transfer all their belongings to the new house. Anne was spending a large part of every day at Everton Hall with Sullah, Margaret and young Timothy, who had returned home from school for the winter break. The boy had grown out of all recognition and his proud Mama could scarcely keep her eyes from him. In the evenings, back at Fernleigh after a long day, she had her meal in the nursery with Sullah and her children before taking a quick turn around the garden and having an early night. She had set up this new regime partly because she wished to spend as much time as possible with her son; she had missed him sorely during his time in school. It also gave her an excuse to avoid those degrading scenes in the dining-room.

Captain Stanton dined every night, sitting between Mary at one end of the long table and Eliza at the other. On the only occasion that she had shared their meal Anne had been most uncomfortable and felt that she could not condone their risqué conversation by remaining a part of it. The sound of their mocking laughter had followed her up the stairs as she left them, and she had not returned to the dining-room again.

The day that Anne was due to take possession of her new home, she was sitting with Sullah packing the final few items of Margaret's clothing. The slave coughed.

'Missus, can I asks yo' somethin'? Somethin' 'bout the ladies?' Anne knew that she should not allow her servants to gossip and certainly not to herself, but Sullah's face was contorted with worry and she had been chewing her thumb-nail with savage intensity. Their peaceful companionship lent itself to confidences so she nodded and waited. 'Well, Ma'am, not many days ago, them two was both lustin' after our Daniel like bitches on heat.' Anne gulped. 'It got so's he couldn't put his head thro' the door without one or other o' them chattin' him up, makin' big eyes an' comin on all coy. Now they's like a couple o' alley cats 'bout this new army man an' don' hardly give Daniel a look no more. I doesn't understand fine ladies. Indeed I doesn't. An' that Miss Mary, she's worse than Miss Eliza. She looks like she wants to put a knife in Daniel's back. The way she stares at him reminds me o' that Mr Bentinck. Like a cat with a bird. An' the footman don' tol' me that at the dinner table they is both tryin' to catch the Captain's eye. They do say in the kitchen that their necklines is gettin' lower an' lower every day, an' yesterday yo' could all but see Miss Mary's ...'

'Sullah, that will do!' Anne fought to suppress a smile. It was not a matter for levity. She herself had been told twice this week, by ladies of her acquaintance, that Mrs Bentinck and her new beau were the talk of the town. They did not appear to mind who saw them together. And the same man had been seen escorting Mrs Harrison. The

Rector had asked her, rather pointedly, when her niece's husband was due to return from Bristol.

Anne sighed, straightening her aching back. Yes, the sooner Henry returned the better and she had never thought to say that. He would soon send Stanton packing and hopefully there would be no harm done. Her mouth twisted in a wry grimace. The one consolation in all this was that as Mary and Eliza went about their pursuit of the gallant Captain, Daniel was left in peace to get on with his work. For that, she was deeply grateful.

As if on cue, Daniel rapped on the door.

'Is this the last lot for the carriage, Ma'am? The children are already up on the box and ready to go.' He smiled proudly. 'Master Timothy is holding the reins, and a fine job he's doing too. That boy loves horses and the animals know it. They always know.' Sullah heaped the bags and packages in his outstretched arms and turned to hold open the door. She glanced anxiously at Daniel as he gave a hastily smothered cough.

'That's it now, Missus. There be just us to go when yo's ready. I could go with Da…' A harassed-looking footman, appeared at Daniel's shoulder, bringing the conversation to an abrupt halt. Anne Weston closed her eyes in despair. What now?

'A gentleman to see you, Mrs Weston. He is in the library.'

'A gentleman, Jackson?' Anne was puzzled. George Barton's ship was not due in Liverpool until the New Year. She got to her feet, flicking the dust from her shoulders and attempting to smooth her crumpled gown. She went downstairs.

As Anne approached the library door it was flung open and the astonished footman was treated to the amazing spectacle of the old Master's widowed sister running like a young girl into waiting arms, her skirts twirling to reveal a

242

very nicely-turned ankle and her hair tumbling down her back as she was lifted off her feet and swung around by the American gentleman in a blur of laughter and tears. Jackson stood on the threshold, his head on one side and a daft grin on his face until, with an apologetic shrug, the gentleman closed the door in his face. For the second time, the normally pedestrian servant bolted for the kitchen to shock the cook with unimaginable gossip about their betters.

Inside the library, Anne was firmly ensconced on George Barton's lap. She scrabbled ineffectually with the grips in her hair but gave up the task to which she was completely unequal. She pulled away with a rather belated concern for propriety, but was promptly put back where she belonged.

'I still do not understand, my dearest. Your ship is not due in Liverpool until after the year's end. How can it be? Oh, I do not care how you got here. I am just so very, very happy to see you.'

'Yes indeed,' he drawled. 'My ship for Liverpool is still on the high seas, to be sure, but the moment I knew I could get passage on an earlier boat bound for Bristol, why, nothing would keep me away. But say, Anne, things have gone well with you, haven't they? You are truly pleased to see me? Why the tears, my love? Shall I go away again?'

'No one in the world was ever more glad to see anyone than I was to see you, George.' She spoke with such simple sincerity that he instantly regretted his jest and kept an arm firmly around her waist as the fire went out and the room grew cold.

When, hours later, Barton learned of recent events at Fernleigh Hall, he insisted that they dine that evening at his hotel in town and that Anne and her children should leave at once for the safety of Everton Hill. George was aware, as a result of his two days spent in Bristol, that

Henry Bentinck was, by now, on his way home. He had no intention of allowing his betrothed to be in the house when its master discovered Edward Stanton's presence.

The storm clouds massed overhead as George Barton helped Anne into her own carriage before jumping on to the box beside a thoughtful Daniel. To the American, the thunder and lightning that crashed over the chimneys seemed to provide an appropriate setting for what was likely to happen at the Hall. The horses pulled away and as the coach gathered speed down the drive, only Daniel looked back.

CHAPTER SIXTEEN

EVERTON HILL
JANUARY 1795

On a gloomy afternoon in early January, George Barton and Anne were huddled by the fire in the morning-room. With the closing of the old year and a change of surroundings, Anne Weston was revelling in the freedom that comes with a new beginning. Only now, with hindsight, was she able to appreciate the enormity of the problems that she had had to face since leaving Jamaica. She sighed luxuriously.

'You know, my dear, I feel really hopeful for the first time in months. It has been a difficult journey in more ways than one.' She took his hand shyly. 'I felt so lonely and so very inadequate when Jeremiah died. You cannot imagine. Such responsibility, and so many momentous decisions.' George lay a comforting arm across her shoulders and Anne felt a warmth in her face that owed nothing to the heat of the fire. At first she had found some of his American manners faintly shocking but now she was more relaxed, at least when they were alone. She leaned against him and continued her reminiscences.

'I cannot recall those endless weeks at sea on the journey from Jamaica without a shudder. The children were bored and Marcus and Sullah carried the ghosts of the middle-passage on their backs. I cannot think what I would have done without Daniel.'

Barton nodded. 'He has indeed been your mainstay for a long while and for that we must be grateful to him but he sure is a complex character. It seems to me that he has had more problems than your other slaves in adjusting to life away from Jamaica. Is it just a colour problem, Anne? There does seem to be more to it than that.'

'I believe his colour is at the root of his difficulties. He does not know where he belongs. You see, in the islands 'coloureds' as opposed to black slaves were treated differently. It seemed natural there. They were always in the house and not in the fields. They had positions of trust and responsibility. Many, like Daniel, had some education and, before his death, Jeremiah used him more as a secretary than a servant. Perhaps we ourselves caused his problems? I don't know.' She sighed. 'He has such a good mind. He is quick, methodical and so very loyal and discreet. What are we to do with Daniel when we get to Georgia, my love? What do you suggest?'

Barton deliberated for a time. 'I guess I can find him work in the estate office, but I hope that you will distance yourself from him when we get home. He has become too close over the years, Anne, and if it should continue in my house there will be trouble with my own slaves. They too have their hierarchy and are easily upset.' He put another log on the fire and stood with his feet apart and his back to the flames. For a moment Anne was reminded of her brother and felt tears pricking at her eyelids.

George was instantly contrite, dropping to his knees and taking her hands.

'Oh, my dear. I have spoken too forcefully. I am sorry. I forget that you have been used to ordering your own affairs. Do forgive me.'

Anne smiled through her tears. 'It is not that. I was just thinking of Matthew. Poor man, and poor Eliza. It is odd, but when I first came I had hoped that my niece would be a source of comfort and friendship. Instead she was a great disappointment and has caused me many hours of sleepless anxiety. She has been over-indulged, I fear. She is emotional and feckless and I soon realised that there could be no hope of true and equal companionship. I had to resign myself to concerns and responsibilities that were neither sought nor deserved. There were so many troubles; her fascination with Daniel, her ill-conceived marriage and then this infatuation with Edward Stanton. She has indeed caused me much heartache.'

George resumed his seat at her side.

'Don't fret. It is over now. You can rid yourself of responsibility for those at Fernleigh Hall. You will have someone to care for your welfare in the future.'

She nodded, dabbing at her eyes. 'I know that I am being foolish. It must be pre-marriage nerves. I am aware of my good fortune. My children are happy. Meg adores you. You permit her to climb all over you and answer all her prattling questions with exactly the right mixture of nonsense and gravity.' She gave an indulgent laugh. 'Timothy too is thrilled to be attending school in Liverpool and to be returning home each night. You have brought us all such happiness.' A silence descended on the room as each of them reflected on the past and contemplated their future. The dusk crept up to the house and slowly darkened the windows.

They had been in the Everton Hill house for three weeks, when Anne Weston summoned Daniel and Sullah to the morning-room. She turned from the window as they came in and extended a hand to each of them.

'You have to be the first to know. Mr Barton and I are to be married the month after next. We shall all be leaving

England and returning to his estates in America. I am certain that you will both love it in Georgia. After all, we are all used to plantation life are we not? His holdings are vast and I am told that his house is the first word in elegance. If the crop is cotton rather than sugar or coffee, well, it matters not. It will be like being home again.' Anne smiled happily from one dark face to the other.

Sullah's eyes sparkled and a grin threatened to split her face. 'Why, Missus, that sure is the best news I heard in years. To feel the sun again after all these months in this rain-soaked place. I declare, I don' care where I goes jes' as long as it be warmer than Liverpool in January.' She giggled, sharing in Anne's delight.

Both women looked at Daniel, waiting for his reaction. A faint smile played around his mouth but it did not reach his eyes.

'Daniel?' Anne asked. 'Are you not pleased also? I would have thought that you of all people would have been glad to shake the mud of Liverpool off your feet. We all know that you have had your share of troubles here. A new land, a fresh start, is that not what you want?' She was puzzled.

Recognising the importance of his answer, Daniel spoke with a fierce integrity. He would not respond merely to please, he would speak the truth.

'For you, Ma'am, for your children, for Mr Barton and yes, probably for Sullah too, I believe this to be the right thing. For Miss Eliza, I think it will feel like an abandonment. She should not be left here alone. As for me, well, it matters not where I am. But, Mistress, how will you feel afterwards, when you are safe and secure in America? What of your conscience? Can you turn your back on your own flesh and blood? Can you walk away and leave her to her fate? Do you not feel any responsibility for her? Any compassion?'

Daniel had unerringly touched a raw nerve and Anne was angry. She wanted no more difficulties. No more problems.

'My niece forfeited any right to my concern and compassion when she ceased to behave in a reputable manner. She is a grown woman, a married woman and has no need of a nursemaid. She has made her own choice this time and must take the consequences.' She turned to Sullah. 'Come. There is much to be done.' The door slammed behind them and the noise echoed in the silent chamber.

Daniel was left gnawing his fists in frustration. *Why could he not dissemble? Would he never learn? Now the Mistress was upset and Sullah too, and for what? Just so that he could speak his mind. Why could he not be like Marcus used to be and learn to accept what came his way? Surely then life would be easier?* A sudden bout of coughing bent him double. He wiped his mouth with a piece of rag, glanced at it quickly and thrust it deep into his pocket before following the women from the room.

Less than a week later, just as Anne Weston was preparing to take the carriage into town, Eliza arrived at the house in a breathless rush, not waiting to be announced but running upstairs to the bedroom where her Aunt was tying her bonnet strings. Sullah was there; she was humming as she picked up discarded garments and folded them. She gave smothered gasp of horror as Eliza burst in; the contrast between two women could not have been more marked. One was serene, happy and glowing with health. The other was dishevelled, wan, emaciated and carried the familiar traces of bruising on her face.

Eliza threw herself into her Aunt's arms sobbing bitterly and it was several minutes before any coherent speech could be attempted. Anne sent Sullah to fetch water, sat her niece down on the bed and began to chafe her trembling hands. The younger woman gulped back her tears and scrubbed at her swollen eyes.

'Ser...servants at Fernleigh say it is the talk of Liverpool. You are to be married and are going away... Your whole household is going to the Colonies. Oh, Aunt,' she wailed. 'How could you?' The sobs began again.

'America has not been one of the Colonies for many years, as you well know,' retorted Anne briskly. She continued more gently. 'But yes it is true. Mr Barton and I are going to live in Georgia when we are wed.'

'But... but what about me? What shall I do? What will happen to me?' The wrenching sobs were threatening to resume.

Sullah, returning with the water banged the glass down on the bedside table, causing a few spilled drops to chase each other down the polished surface before dropping to the floor. It was typical of Mrs Bentinck's selfishness that her only thought was for herself and the slave sniffed her contempt. The girl had not given a moment's thought to her Aunt's happiness. She was rotten, rotten to the core.

Anne sprinkled cologne on a handkerchief and dabbed at Eliza's forehead, pushing the heavy, corn-coloured hair out of the way.

'You really must not take on so, my dear. Now that your husband has returned from Bristol, oh yes, my servants are every bit as busy as yours when it comes to picking up gossip, now that Henry is home things will surely improve. I am certain that Captain Stanton will need to join his regiment soon. Then, with my household and myself removed from Fernleigh you will have some respite. There will be the opportunity for you to get to know your husband better. Perhaps you can reach some under-standing.'

Eliza jumped to her feet, pushing away her Aunt's restraining hands and tearing off her cape. She pointed to her neck with shaking fingers and tugged aside the buttons of her bodice.

'The man is a monster. A monster I say. Look at me... Look at the marks. Now tell me that I should get to know him better. You do not know half of what goes on.' She tossed her head wildly from side to side. 'The moment he returned, his... his friends in the town could not wait to tell him that I had been entertaining a gentleman in his absence.' She paused for breath.

'Was it wise, Elizabeth? Everyone saw you. It is hardly surprising that your husband is displeased.'

Eliza's eyes slid away from her Aunt's concerned face. 'I have done nothing wrong. An old friend came to pay his respects whilst he was in the area. That is all. My sister-in-law was there for much of the time. We never dined alone,' she added defensively. 'I do assure you, Aunt, there has been nothing improper. Nothing.'

Anne Weston and Sullah exchanged glances. The girl's evasive manner, her insistent self-justification served only to increase suspicion. She looked from one hostile face to the other.

'You do not believe me, do you?' she spat. 'You pious creatures are all the same. Ready to think the worst. I saw the Rector's mouse of a wife as I was coming here. She crossed the street. That social nothing crossed the street. She did not wish to be seen with me.' Eliza strode up and down the room in temper, her colour high, her eyes flashing as anger replaced the self-pity. She halted in mid-stride, the blood draining from her face as she almost fell. Anne pushed a chair behind her knees and Eliza collapsed into it. Her breathing was laboured, her hands fluttered and perspiration gathered on her forehead.

There was a thunderous knocking at the door and a

251

distracted Daniel appeared.

'Mistress, you must come… At once… Miss Bentinck… Mrs Harrison, I mean… she is downstairs with a carriage. She says she has come to fetch…' He stopped as the two women moved aside to reveal the swooning figure in the chair. His eyes widened and he took a step into the room. Anne pushed him out, blocking the threshold. She turned to Sullah whose huge eyes had not left Daniel's face.

'Give her water. Bathe her face. Do not let her move. You, Daniel,' she pushed him again. 'Get the physician.' She squared her shoulders. 'I will deal with Mrs Harrison.'

As she halted at the door of the morning-room, Anne took a steadying breath and clasped her hands to still the unexpected tremor. She was more afraid of Mary Harrison than she was of Henry. There could be no doubt that brother and sister were both evil but the woman's behaviour had a detached calculation that chilled the blood. Anne was reminded of an animal that had once been hunted across the plantation in Jamaica. Most creatures will kill for food or if threatened, this rogue female killed for pleasure, leaving mauled carcasses in its wake for other predators to devour. It was not hungry, it was not threatened, it was a crazed beast that needed the chase, the torture, the kill. Anne shook herself free of the bloodthirsty images and pushed open the door.

Mary was standing at the window watching Daniel as he rode down the lane at breakneck speed in the direction of town. She turned slowly and smiled at Anne.

'Mrs Weston, how delightful you look. I regret that my first visit to you in your new home should be unannounced and in such difficult circumstances.' The charming voice dripped with honey and insincerity. Anne did not reply. Mary indicated the window. 'Daniel appears to be in something of a hurry. Nothing is amiss here I trust?'

Anne Weston placed herself directly in front of Henry's

sister and spoke quietly.

'Things are very much amiss, Mrs Harrison. My niece is most unwell and I have had to send for the physician. That is where Daniel was going in such a hurry.' She had the satisfaction of seeing a flash of consternation in the other woman's eyes before the hooded lids veiled all expression.

'What a pity it is that your summons should have been so unnecessary, Ma'am, for my brother has sent me to escort my sister-in-law back to Fernleigh Hall in the comfort of our own carriage. I fear that Eliza behaved rather impulsively this morning and rushed off in the cart, driving herself as I understand.' She gave an eloquent shrug of disdain. 'I must inform you, Mrs Weston, that your niece is becoming quite unpredictable. She is irrational and we are concerned as to her state of mind. She is much given to exaggerated speech and melodramatic claims. I am sure that my brother will summon a physician of his own acquaintance to attend his wife, should it prove necessary. Now, perhaps you will bring her to me?'

Anne bristled. 'My niece's bruises are not an exaggeration of speech, Mrs Harrison, nor are they figments of the imagination. Not Eliza's and most certainly not mine. She will not leave this house until the physician has pronounced her fit to travel. Now pray take your coach back to Fernleigh Hall and inform your brother that I will send word when his wife is able and ready to return. In the meantime, he can be assured that she is in good hands. I bid you good day, Madam.' She gave a distant nod and, without offering her hand, turned and left her visitor alone. Anne's heart was hammering in her chest as she climbed gratefully up the stairs, and she sighed with relief as she heard the front door slam.

In less than two hours, Anne was back in the morning-room with the physician, Andrew Stewart. He was a young man from Edinburgh who did not beat about the bush.

'She is in a bad way mentally but her bruises are superficial and there do not appear to be any more severe injuries. I have my own ideas about the loss of weight and fainting spells but she tells me that she has no appetite and is eating very little. I suppose that could account for her symptoms. Her listlessness is extremely worrying. In confidence, Ma'am, her state of mind is fragile and she is close to a crisis of nerves. A complete breakdown.' Daniel, listening shamelessly through the partly open door, drew a ragged breath. The doctor continued. 'Rest, quietness, nourishing broth and gentle drives in the country air. That is what I recommend. No excitement or worry. I also suggest that she should be temporarily removed from who-ever is the cause of those bruises. She is in no state to tolerate another beating. If you will send your servant back with me now, I will prescribe some powders to help her sleep. A good man that by the way, now, where was I? Ah yes. Young Mrs Bentinck needs sleep and peace of mind above everything.' Daniel scuttled away and was waiting in the hall with the physician's hat in his hands as Anne escorted her visitor to the door.

For the next few days the household at Everton Hill waited in trepidation for the wrath of Henry Bentinck to descend upon their heads but as time passed they began to relax. Finally, Sullah was able to inform her Mistress that word had come through from Fernleigh that Mr Bentinck had agreed to his wife spending some time with her Aunt, assisting with preparations for that lady's nuptials, and they were all greatly relieved.

Eliza's health improved and, even if she was still nauseous on occasions, at least she had lost a little of her frailty. Her figure began to fill and she recovered some of her zest for life. She was still engrossed only in her own affairs but had begun to take an interest in her appearance again and had become quite animated on their daily carriage-rides out into the countryside.

For Daniel, who acted as coachman, these outings were a mixture of exquisite delight and dreadful torment. He was relieved to see Eliza looking so much better, but was deeply concerned for her future when she would have to return to her husband's home. This interlude was a respite, not a solution. He was also desperately unhappy at the prospect of their departure for America, since it would leave Eliza totally unprotected. Of late, she had begun to notice him again, leaning heavily on his arm as he assisted her into the carriage, whispering her thanks, fluttering her lashes and bestowing gentle smiles in his direction. If a wicked voice inside murmured *she only looks at you in the absence of any other man,* the thought was banished instantly. All his dormant feelings were roused. His peace was destroyed and the problem of his identity reared its head once more. He allowed his devotion to shine in his eyes as they lingered on her face. Anne Weston watched in despair. Surely it was not about to begin again?

In the first week of February, a light dusting of snow covered the streets of Liverpool and, as the evening drew in, there seemed a distinct possibility of a heavier fall. Daniel, who had driven Anne and George Barton to a function at the Music Hall, decided not to return to Everton Hill but instead settled down on his box to wait. He huddled in his cloak with a blanket around his legs. His head drooped on his chest and he dozed. He opened one eye. Something had disturbed the horses; the animals stamped uneasily in the shafts. Daniel jumped down and went to the horses' heads. He stroked one silken nose.

'There, there my beauty,' he crooned. 'Rest easy.' He snatched at the reins as a passing drunk reeled into the side of the carriage and fell over cursing fluently. 'There,

there,' he soothed again as the startled animals pranced and skittered. He restored order and turned to look at the man who was leaning against the wheel of the coach. His legs were splayed out in front of him and his hat was sliding over his eyes.

Drunks on the waterfront were a common sight, but they did not usually venture into the more select areas of town and Daniel was surprised. He looked closely at the stranger. This was no inebriated sailor. His clothes were of good cut and quality. As he moved nearer, there seemed something oddly familiar about the man but the slave could not place him. Then the fellow's hat slid to the floor just as the harsh light of the moon appeared from behind scudding clouds. The absence of uniform had been mis-leading but there could be no doubt. The drunk was Edward Stanton. Daniel moved to assist him.

'May I help you, Sir?' he enquired, taking hold of Stanton's arm and hauling him to his feet. The Captain reeled away, peering blearily at his helper. He attempted to stand upright but tottered to one side as he swatted at the supporting arm.

'Itsh all your fault... You black heathen... Gettin' so's a gentleman ain't safe to walk the shtreets of thish town.' He lurched again and Daniel fought to suppress a smile. Stanton was enraged. 'Think I don't know your game, eh boy? Thinkin' to rob the Cap'n ain't you. Well, this Cap'n's got no money. Cash... cah... cashiered... thatsh me. Shtupid General's wife... Can't keep their mouths shut... thatsh the trouble with women... Can't keep quiet.' Suspicion clouded his features again. 'I know all about your sort,' he mumbled, tapping the side of his nose. 'Don't know what the place is comin' to. Shtreets full o' black heathens.' He leaned against the wall, shaking his head to clear the alcohol fumes.

Stanton's eyes narrowed as the moon re-appeared. He

suddenly seemed less intoxicated and pushed himself upright. His tone was still belligerent.

'I know you. You're Bentinck's man aren't you? From Fernleigh Hall?' He sniggered unpleasantly.

'No, Sir. I am nothing to do with Mr Bentinck. I belong to Mrs Weston and we no longer live at Fernleigh.' He turned away and made to clamber up on to his box. Stanton grabbed his jacket, pulling him down. The assault was so unexpected that Daniel almost fell.

'Such proper speech from a slave, "No, Sir. I am nothing to do with Mr Bentinck," so refined. Who do you think you are, boy? Don't ever turn your heathen back on me again. Do you hear me?'

Daniel stood still forcing himself to keep his eyes lowered as he felt his anger beginning to rise. His fists clenched and he bit back a retort, clamping his lips together in a thin line. Marcus' voice was in his head. *The man is drunk. He don't know what he is saying. He is trying to pick a quarrel. You knows it. Don't let him win. Don't let him rile yo', Daniel. Remember Jamaica. Don't yo' ever look a white bully in the eyes.* He felt the rush of blood receding. His hands relaxed and he continued to stare at the floor. A coach rumbled past the end of the street and in the distance a dog barked.

The slave's submissive demeanour, his lack of response goaded Stanton beyond reason. He forgot his own weakness. He forgot the darkness of the night. He ignored the other man's massive size. He prodded Daniel's chest, sneering as his victim took a step back.

'I know all about you. Think you're as good as anyone, don't you? Eh, boy? Father managed an estate in the West Indies, ain't that so? Shame about your ma though. What was she?' He sniggered again. 'A black slave whore. That was your ma. An' you think by talkin' fine and suckin' up to the womenfolk... You think you can be one of us.'

Daniel's huge hand shot out. He picked Stanton up by his jacket front and pinned him against the wall.

'You thank God that you are drunk or I would kill you for that,' he hissed. 'My mother was a good woman and was ill-used by the likes of you.' He released his hold and Stanton slid to the ground trembling in fear and rage. Daniel moved towards his seat on the box again.

'And is that why you tried to ill-use Eliza Bentinck, slave? Tryin' to get your own back?' Daniel froze. He turned to face Stanton and the other man blanched at the look in his eyes. 'Well... well... so I was told. It... it was in jest,' he blustered, trying to back away

Two huge black hands fastened themselves around his throat and he was again lifted off his feet. His fingers scrabbled against Daniel's arms. His eyes were staring in their sockets. A stream of bile erupted from his mouth and ran down the slave's face and hands. With an expression of unrelieved disgust, Daniel flung the man away from him and he crashed in a heap on the floor. Stanton drew in great heaving breaths as his adversary towered over him. The dark faced was twisted in contempt and loathing. A light shone at the end of the street and the sound of music and laughter floated out into the night. A few flakes of snow drifted down as Daniel climbed stiffly up to his seat and took the reins in his hands.

The Captain scrambled to his feet and, in an unexpected surge of strength, grabbed the head of the nearest horse, holding on grimly. He was suddenly almost sober. His eyes glittered and he screamed at Daniel.

'I know all about you. You think Eliza was fond of you. Carrying her back to your cupboard in the stables. Swearing eternal devotion.' Daniel gasped in disbelief, his eyes widening in horror. 'Put her on the sofa, didn't you? Oh, she laughed when she told me about it. You on your knees at her side. We laughed... Do you hear?... We laughed.' Daniel lunged with the whip, flicking it blindly over the horses' backs as he struggled to get away from the shrieking voice. The coach jerked forward and rattled down the street towards the crowd outside the Music Hall, and the whole time he was pursued by the demonic laughter behind him.

The carriage jerked to a halt at the end of the sedate line of vehicles waiting to take the gentry home. Daniel's breath came in shallow gasps and his head spun. The music, the chattering throngs all seemed distant. He tasted blood in his mouth as he bit through his lower lip. He smeared it away with the back of his hand, glad to focus on the pain. Snow settled on his head and bowed shoulders and crystals melted on his hands. His silhouette became a grey blur in the night.

He remembered nothing of the nightmare journey home through the driving snow. His mind was as numb as his ice-cold hands. He could not recollect drawing up in front of the Music Hall steps, nor seeing George Barton hand a smiling Anne into the carriage. He knew nothing of the rutted lanes, of the horses' struggles through the ever-deepening slush. No memory remained of the hours that he spent alone in the stables on their return to Everton Hill, as he again sought refuge from his grief by fiercely grooming the horses. He scrubbed the carriage until he was forced to strip off his shirt as it became drenched in perspiration, despite the plummeting temperatures outside. Tears mingled with sweat and dripped down his bare chest and arms, darkening the gleaming coats of the animals.

It was thus that Sullah found him. She did not know what had happened but she came to seek him out. She took the brushes from his unresisting hands, led him into one of the empty stalls and drew him down beside her into the warmth of the straw. She folded him in her arms and rocked him like a baby, crooning softly. Then she stroked his dark hair, murmuring incoherent endearments. She became conscious of a change in his breathing, of his gradual arousal. In the next stall, one of the horses rustled his hay and whinnied softly. Sullah smiled as Daniel moved towards her in the darkness.

CHAPTER SEVENTEEN

EVERTON HILL
MARCH 1795

The week before Anne Weston's marriage Eliza decided that the time had come to return to her own home. The attention being paid to her Aunt was beginning to irritate. Eliza found it difficult to tolerate the fact that she was almost ignored as a constant stream of visitors came and went, all entirely focused on the bride-to-be. She could also not fail to be aware that her reputation had been severely damaged. Her attendance in her Aunt's drawing-room caused considerable consternation. It brought all gossip to a standstill as the ladies of the town grappled with the social niceties of how to signal their disapproval of the young Mrs Bentinck without offending their charming hostess. George Barton was much entertained when stories of the ladies' discomfiture were relayed to him, but Eliza's sense of humour had long since deserted her.

She was neglected. No one had time for her any more. With the gradual improvement in her health, all sympathy and concern had evaporated. Her Aunt and George were absorbed in each other. The servants resented the extra burden of another demanding person to cope with and Sullah made no secret of her dislike, refusing even to acknowledge Eliza's presence in the house. It was most disconcerting. There was something different about Sullah. Something she could not put her finger on. Like Anne, the girl carried with her an inner radiance that could not be ignored.

Then there was Daniel. Eliza scarcely saw him and it was evident that he was avoiding her. If she came into a room he left it. If she went to the stables he was not there. A young groom took her riding, and Daniel could never be found if she needed something to be brought from town. Once, she had followed him into the empty kitchen. She stood close. He moved away. She looked up at him. He refused to meet her eyes. She tried every device in her considerable repertoire to attract him, even resorting to tears, but he would not be moved. Defeated, she had turned and left. Initially she was incredulous. He adored her. He had always adored her. She need only lift her little finger to bring him running to her side. What was wrong? In the wake of disbelief came curiosity, then irritation and then a cold, hard anger. There was nothing to keep her at Everton Hill.

There were other, more pressing reasons why it was necessary that she should return to Fernleigh Hall. Eliza knew that she was carrying a child. She suspected that it was Edward Stanton's baby but there was no way to be sure until the time of the birth. After all, Henry had only been in Bristol for a few weeks. Maybe no one could ever be certain? She knew that if she was not to be ruined she must return to her husband and convince him that he was indeed the father of the expected child.

There was nothing to be hoped for from Edward. He had left her, supposedly to return to his regiment, but she had heard the gossip and knew that he had been dismissed. He was apparently living in greatly reduced circumstances. As a married woman, Eliza had no money of her own and she had long ago lost her youthful enthusiasm for living in poverty with the man of her dreams. With experience she had acquired a healthy respect for all that a substantial income could provide. She was trapped. Once more she was faced with the choice of a life with Henry Bentinck or ruin.

The day of the marriage was blessed with fine weather. Winter had given way to spring. The trees in St Nicholas' Churchyard were in bud and the sun sparkled on the river, turning the murky waters of the Mersey into a dancing, white-capped background for the crowded shipping in the harbour. Boats jostled for space and the quays were thronged with people. After the initial commercial chaos caused by the onset of a European war, when the town was forced to issue its own 'promissory notes', trade had picked up again. Now, the waterfront was a hive of activity. Privateers, supply ships and military vessels all served to increase the prosperity of the port and put more money in the pockets of the people of Liverpool. The townsfolk always enjoyed a spectacle, and as Anne's carriage bowled along the Strand she was roundly cheered by interested spectators.

The carriage came to a halt outside the Church and Daniel, resplendent in new livery, beamed with pride as he assisted his Mistress out of her coach and began to clear a path for her through the good-natured crowd. He faltered at the sight of Eliza and Henry Bentinck who were just making their way into the Church, and his sharp ears caught some mutinous mutterings from those nearest to the door. The pair were clearly unpopular. He recovered his poise as he saw Sullah, in her new dress, holding a posy for Mrs Weston to carry. The Mistress smiled her thanks and the two slaves stood side by side grinning with delight as she passed into the Church. For the first time the phrase 'my woman' entered Daniel's mind. His eyes sparkled as he looked at Sullah, repeating the words in his head. 'My woman, my woman.' He liked it. He felt as though he belonged.

In the mêlée as the bridal party gathered outside the Church after the ceremony, Daniel became separated from Sullah who had gone to shepherd Miss Meg and Master Timothy towards the waiting carriages. A voice startled him and he turned to find Henry Bentinck, Mary and Eliza standing behind him. He inclined his head but not before he had noted Eliza's obvious good health, her re-discovered prettiness and Mary's elegant gown, designed to show off every inch of her fine figure. He fixed his eyes firmly on Henry's boots.

'So, in a few weeks you are on your way back to a plantation, I hear.' Bentinck's voice was harsh. 'It is as well for you that you are removing yourself from any contact with me or mine. I do not forget your insolence to both me and my sister at Fernleigh, nor the trouble you caused me when the other one got himself killed in the road like a dog.'

'Marcus. His name was Marcus.' The dark eyes were raised and glowered in Bentinck's face.

'Henry, leave it. Do not seek to provoke him. People are watching us, and God knows they can find enough to gossip about without adding fuel to the fire.' Eliza tugged at her husband's sleeve. He shook himself free.

'You carried tales to Blundell. I know it was you and the old fool chose to believe you. I was almost finished because of you, slave.' His lips drew back in a snarl. 'If it were not for the war in France… I would have been…' He stopped.

'We do not want to discuss issues of trade with the servants and certainly not here, brother.' Mary's voice cracked like a whip. Folk were listening. She threaded a firm hand through his arm and guided him away. Eliza followed, her hand clutching her bonnet as she cast a frightened glance over her shoulder.

Daniel stared after them. Bentinck's attitude to his wife had changed He was almost solicitous and she had lost that look of a cowed victim. And it was not just Eliza who was different. There could be no doubt that Bentinck had something to hide. The slave was aware, as was almost everyone in Liverpool, that fortunes were being made by Privateers in the European war. He also knew that any conflict provides opportunity for unscrupulous men to make a killing by selling weapons and trading with both sides. There had been whisperings on the quays about some of Bentinck's cargoes and rumour had it that important people in Mr Pitt's government were taking an interest in his activities. The slave shrugged. None of the Bentincks was his concern. Not any more. Not Henry, not his sister and not his wife. By summer, Daniel would be on his way to America with Mrs Weston... No, Mrs Barton. He grinned to himself. It would take some getting used to; everything would take some getting used to.

Someone slapped him on the back.

'Hey there, Daniel. They'll have you in the mad house if you stand there much longer with a daft grin on your face.'

'They ain't got a cell big enough for him,' called another man. Daniel laughed at their good-humoured teasing. He would miss these people. It had taken a while for them to accept him, but once they did their warmth and ready wit was infectious. He waved and set off to find Sullah amongst the throng of people and carriages gathered on the quay.

In the drawing-room of Miss Pimblett's house near Chester, three ladies looked bleakly at each other. Rosamund Beauchamp fidgeted uneasily. It was a companion's task in life to amuse but how, pray, could one amuse the likes of Mary Harrison? Miss Beauchamp was confused. She herself was impoverished and was reduced to taking paid employment in order to live. Mrs Harrison, Miss Bentinck as was, had been married to a brave military gentleman of the Irish nobility. She was Miss Pimblett's own niece and belonged to a most well respected family who were said to have come over from the low countries with King William. Her brother was the master of Fernleigh Hall, and yet Mrs Harrison was most definitely not a lady. Miss Beauchamp sighed and longed for the after dinner hour to be ended so that she might go to her bed.

Mary Harrison's lips twitched. She debated whether or not it was worth the effort to bait the companion but decided not to bother. The woman was either too stupid or too well-bred to rise to the challenge, and although her Aunt Pimblett was supposed to be profoundly deaf Mary was never sure just how much the old lady heard. She jumped as her Aunt's precise tones interrupted her reverie.

'It was kind of you to visit us, my dear. It is a pity that Henry was unable to join you on this occasion. Business with the war I expect.'

'Oh what a dreadful thing to be sure,' twittered Miss Beauchamp. 'The poor French King. I know it is a long time ago but it seems like only yesterday that those Barbarians cut off his head. And the Queen. It was just too sad. That poor, poor woman.'

'That poor, poor woman was the cause of half the trouble if you ask me,' observed Miss Pimblett, dryly. 'Women often are, I find. Would you not agree, niece?'

'Most certainly, Aunt,' bellowed Mary.

'There is no need to shout. I am not deaf. How is my nephew, by the way, and his pretty wife?'

'Henry is well, thank you, and Eliza is in an… shall we say… interesting condition.' A red flush stained Miss

Beauchamp's face and neck and receded leaving two blotches of colour on her cheeks. She opened her mouth to protest at this latest example of Mrs Harrison's lack of proper feeling but Miss Pimblett fixed her with a baleful eye. The old lady smiled as she turned again to Mary. She was enjoying the gossip.

'So they will not wish to travel. I see now why you came alone. I expect that life at Fernleigh Hall is somewhat tedious in view of your sister-in-law's condition. Also, the fact that Mrs Weston, or Mrs Barton as we must now call her, has taken up residence in her own establishment will not help the situation I am sure. When does that lady leave for the Colonies by the way?'

Mary did not even attempt to explain that the Colonies had, for some time, been an independent nation. She chose instead to describe the wedding in a wealth of detail and a pleasant half-hour ensued as the two maiden ladies heard about the dresses, the bonnets, the gentlemen's fashions and the crowds. They sighed in happy unison at examples of the devotion of the newly married pair. As Rosamund began to eulogise, in her turn, about the wedding of the daughter of an acquaintance, Mary allowed her mind to wander.

The decision to visit her Aunt had not been taken lightly, but the old lady had guessed aright when she suggested that life at Fernleigh had become stale. Eliza's condition could be cited as the ostensible reason for their isolation, but they all knew that they were still ostracised and that there would be no interaction with society. Mary was convinced that not even Aunt Pimblett's house could be as dull as her brother's home at the moment, and at least Chester offered the prospect of social contact.

There was another reason for her visit. With Henry about to become a father and with his fortune at the mercies of an unpredictable war, Mary needed to look to her own future. She now had scarcely any money of her own and needed to find another husband who could keep her in the luxury that she felt was her due. She had made a mistake with her first venture into matrimony. She would not make another. And then there was Aunt Pimblett. She had no dependants and would have to leave her fortune somewhere. Why not to her nephew's sister? Mary looked up to find the old lady's eyes fixed on her face and had the uncomfortable conviction that Miss Pimblett had read her mind.

The flustered arrival of one of the ancient retainers, her cap awry and her breathing laboured, provided a welcome relief. The maid bobbed unsteadily and addressed the lady of the house.

'There be a *gentleman* callin' downstairs, Mum. A gentleman!' So might Satan himself have been announced. Mary stifled a smile. It was probably Aunt Pimblett's doddering Parson looking for donations or maybe her equally senile solicitor. 'He says his name is Captain Stanton and he specially asked for Miss Bent... Mrs Harrison, Mum.'

Aunt Pimblett rose calmly to her feet and picked up her reticule. A well-bred lady was never surprised. She must ignore the lateness of the hour. She turned to her niece.

'I will come down with you, Mary. Perhaps you should introduce me to your... friend. If this gentleman is to be invited to my home it is as well that I make his acquaintance.'

'I did not invite Captain Stanton to come here, Aunt. Yes, I am acquainted with him. He is known to my sister-in-law and to my bother. He has visited Fernleigh Hall several times, but I repeat I did not invite him here. When I was in town yesterday I happened to come across a member of his former regiment and mentioned that I was staying with you.' Mary flushed as she recalled her flirtatious conversation with the attractive young officer. The fool must have seen Edward and told him that she was here. She felt uneasy. If Stanton had arrived at her Aunt's house the worse for drink, he would undo all her efforts to impress the old woman. She took a deep breath and followed Aunt Pimblett's rigid back down the stairs.

In the hall, Edward Stanton jumped to his feet and executed a perfectly judged bow in the direction of Miss Pimblett. It was with considerable relief that Mary's quick glance took in his immaculately polished boots, the exquisitely tied cravat and the impeccable cut of his coat and breeches. He had clearly come to impress and she watched, with admiration, the work of a practised charmer. It took only moments for her Aunt's frozen politeness to thaw and scarcely longer than that for her to regress into the blushing maiden of half a century ago. Such was the power of the gentlemen over Miss Pimblett's generation.

Within fifteen minutes, Stanton had obtained permission to call the following morning and take Mrs Harrison for a drive and had secured for himself an invitation to dinner for two days hence. He took his leave with the offer to regard Miss Pimblett's house as always open to him ringing in his ears. As she gave him her hand, Mary's eyebrow rose and she shook her head slightly in disbelief. His eyes gleamed before he turned his deferential attentions to his hostess. He again apologised for the lateness of the hour, but insisted that having only just discovered Mrs Harrison's presence in town, nothing would suffice but that he should immediately call to pay his respects.

Mary trailed upstairs in her Aunt's wake.

'Well, niece? This is a pretty kettle of fish, and you have not been here above a week. I was not aware that you had an admirer in Chester.' She smiled almost archly and tapped Mary's knee. 'Captain Stanton is indeed a most charming gentleman. Discharged with a war wound I believe he said, although he was becomingly vague about the nature of his disability. I do so approve of modesty in a man.' She sighed. 'You seem to have a penchant for attracting heroes, my dear. It is perhaps just a little soon after your sad loss for you to be accepting calls, but society is not what it was and you young things are so impatient. The Captain is clearly so very honourable in his intentions that I really can have no objection. Rosamund, ring the bell. I think that a glass of sherry is called for.'

Sipping the amber liquid and basking in the unexpected glow of her Aunt's approval, Mary stared at the fire. What would Aunt Pimblett say if she knew that the 'honourable Captain' had paid court to Henry's wife and sister both at the same time? That he had been thrown out of his regiment because of a liaison and was a penniless adventurer? She smiled to herself. She had no illusions about him. She took another sip of the sickly sweet wine. At least he was exciting, and her business with him had been rudely interrupted when Henry had returned to Fernleigh. Thinking back to those few weeks her eyes narrowed. He had courted them both but she had known that his preference was for Eliza's frail prettiness. Her lips curled. She wondered how far he had got with her pious sister-in-law. She had never left them alone at the Hall but she had her suspicions that Eliza may have visited his rooms. She shrugged mentally. It was unlikely. The girl had too little spirit for extra-marital adventures.

The logs shifted and fell, sending up a shower of sparks and disturbing their cosy reverie. Miss Pimblett got briskly to her feet, startling Mary and dragging her back to the present.

'Goodnight, niece. Come Rosamund. We have had more than enough excitement for one evening and we shall have much to do to prepare for our dinner-party.' Miss Beauchamp gathered up their belongings, simpered and scuttled out of the room in the train of her employer. Mary remained where she was, staring into the heart of the fire as the logs were slowly reduced to a heap of ash. Her face was full of shadows and her eyes glittered as the final embers turned to dust and the room grew cold.

Mary was preparing for dinner. She had chosen her gown with care and was pleased with her appearance. The carriage ride on the previous morning had been an unqualified success. Edward was at his most charming and she had enjoyed his flattering attention. She had quite forgotten how handsome he was and how plausible he could be. What a pity he had no money. He had been delighted to renew their friendship and had asked several questions about Miss Pimblett's fortune. She smiled grimly. It was as well that she knew him for what he was, or even she might be taken in. Giving a final pat to her abundant hair she went to receive her guest.

Halfway through the meal, Mary realised that Edward must have been drinking before he got there. Miss Pimblett had raided the remnants of her father's cellar, but a few glasses of wine would not have produced his strident tone, his florid face nor his slurred speech.

'The enemy was all around ush. Blasted Frenchies. Beg pardon ladies.' He hiccoughed. 'Half my men were gone. Couldn't shee anything through the shmoke.'

'Captain Stanton!' Miss Pimblett was indignant. 'Pray do not go on. Your exploits are most interesting but a lady's dinner table is scarcely the place to recount your adventures. I fear the excitement is becoming too much for Miss Beauchamp.' Stanton half stood and gave an apologetic bow before collapsing back into his chair. He signalled the maid to refill his glass. Miss Pimblett stared at Mary in desperation.

Her niece rose valiantly to the challenge. 'The meal has been quite delicious, Aunt. Pray give my congratulations to cook in the morning. The saddle of lamb was most tender. Was it not Captain Stanton?' He waved his hand in vague appreciation. There was silence.

Miss Pimblett tried again. 'I understand that you are acquainted with my nephew and his wife, Captain. Has Mary told you of their news?'

The man's bleary eyes struggled to focus. 'Newsh? What newsh?'

Aunt Pimblett became flustered. 'Ah well, yes. They are... Oh dear... It is rather delicate. Mrs Bentinck... A er... happy event is expected... A child you know. There is to be a child.'

There was the tinkle of broken crystal. A trail of wine ran across the table and dripped into Mary's lap. She stared at Stanton. Colour had suffused his face and receded, leaving him pale and sweating. He peered at his hand where it clutched the shattered stem of his glass, snatched a handkerchief from his pocket and wrapped it in a clumsy bandage around his fingers, trying to staunch the flow of blood. As the three women watched, he struggled to his feet, mumbling incoherently.

'Fine meal. My thanks. Musht go. Urgent engagement. Apologies, ladies.' He stumbled from the table, knocking over his chair in his haste.

Aunt Pimblett drew herself upright and addressed her niece in icy tones.

'I will order a carriage to be brought to the front door. Kindly ensure that your guest leaves my house at once. He will not be welcome here again. I also suggest that you arrange to return to your brother's home, Madam, and as soon as possible. I fear that the lifestyle here does not suit you after all. Come Rosamund.' The two old ladies left the room supporting each other. The ruins of their dinner-party lay scattered behind them in silent mockery of their efforts to entertain.

Mary could not move. She was stunned. There was no doubt in her mind. No doubt at all. Edward Stanton believed that the expected child could be his. Eliza was no innocent after all. Mary's scheming mind whirled. If Henry knew, he would have his wife put away. That much was certain. He might be tempted to keep the child, for no one could ever be totally sure as to its parentage. The timing of the birth would be critical. Henry had been absent for such a short time. The child could indeed be Stanton's but could equally well be his own. If, after the birth, Eliza was put away because of her infidelity then Henry would need someone to be Mistress of Fernleigh Hall. Who better to grace that position than his loving sister? Mary could continue to enjoy all the freedom that accompanied her widowed status whilst living a life of luxury under her brother's roof. There might be no need to find a rich husband after all, a husband who would constrain her, a husband who might well ill-treat her. She got to her feet as she heard Stanton's carriage rumbling away from the house. He was trouble and she was well rid of him. Aunt Pimblett was right, she should go back to Liverpool. Henry must be told of her suspicions, and the sooner the better. It was her duty. He had a right to know.

There was a new sense of peace at Fernleigh Hall and Eliza was reminded of her youth when all had seemed so safe and secure. She put a hand to her waist as she felt the faintest flutter, a slight stirring, gentle as the touch of a butterfly's wing. She smiled. If she thought of the reality of childbirth she was afraid but if she projected her mind to the future, when she might have a pretty daughter of her own, a tiny Eliza to dress up and take out, then she was happy. She sat back and laid down her needlework. It was delightful to have an excuse to be idle, to day-dream, to pretend.

Henry slid into the room and she started. He still made her nervous but she was no longer terrified of him. He had not visited her bedroom since the moment that he had learned of her pregnancy and he had become most solicitous of her welfare. The beatings of the past resembled a bad dream. To be sure, he often went to Liverpool after dinner and only came home in the small hours. She wondered about these excursions, but as long as he left her alone she was content. He would never change, she knew that, but if he committed his perverted activities out of her sight then she would not complain.

Now, he smiled down at her.

'Are you well, Elizabeth?' It was always his first question. His gaze dropped to her middle in proprietorial fashion and she shifted uncomfortably.

'Of course, Henry, I am in the best of health.'

'Would you like me to order the carriage to take you to Everton Hill? It has been several weeks since you have seen your Aunt. She will not be in this country for long now you know.'

Eliza shrugged. 'They are all so busy there, packing everything up. They have no time for me. And those children are so very ill-mannered and noisy; they give me a headache. I declare, that nursemaid gives them far too little supervision. My Aunt's servants leave a lot to be desired.'

Henry raised an eyebrow but said nothing; she had not always thought so. His wife read his mind and flushed, picking up her needlework again.

'Well, I shall leave you to your embroidery, my dear. You will have company again soon. That is what I came to tell you. My sister is coming home. I had word on the

Eastham Packet today. She will be here in a day or two. I will leave you to see that a room is prepared. I must confess that I am relieved that you will have company.'

He shut the door and Eliza stared through the window. The scene was the same but the peace had gone. Mary was coming back. She felt as though the bars of her prison were closing in once more. She rang the bell on the table at her side. She would have the fire built up. It was not warm in here. She shivered.

CHAPTER EIGHTEEN

FERNLEIGH HALL
APRIL 1795

Henry Bentinck looked up from his papers as the coach wheels crunched on the gravel in front of the Hall. Signalling to his shipping agent to take a seat, he stood to greet his sister. His heart sank to his boots. He heard the angry clatter of her heels as she crossed the hall and the irate tones as she dismissed the butler. The signs were unmistakable. A storm was about to break.

Mary swept into the library in high dudgeon, tossing her muff aside, tearing off an extremely becoming hat and shaking the dust from the folds of her travel gown.

'That man is insufferable, brother.' Her eyes blazed. 'His arrogance is unbelievable. I really do not understand why you keep him on as your groom. He… he insults me. Do you hear? If I threaten him with you, he sneers in my face. Why can you not dismiss him, Henry? What does he know about you?'

Her brother coughed, nodding in the agent's direction. 'You have not met Mr Clancey, my dear. Clancey, may I present my sister, Mrs Harrison. She has obviously had a tiring journey and appears to be somewhat overwrought.'

'Charmed, Ma'am, I'm sure.' The agent bowed over the extended hand and marvelled at the sudden change from storming virago to refined lady of the town.

'Perhaps you would wish to change your gown, Mary, and let my wife know that you are returned safely. She is upstairs resting before dinner. Clancey and I will not be long.'

'Indeed, Sir.' The ubiquitous agent rubbed his greasy palms together. 'I wish that all my clients were as well-versed in shipping matters as yourself.' He faltered as Henry gave him a blank stare. Bentinck had never responded to flattery. If he had talent, he knew it and saw no reason to be obliged to anyone else for pointing out the obvious. Besides, in his experience flattery was usually a precursor to a request for a favour. Clancey shuffled his papers and waited. His client truly had the coldest eyes that he had ever seen. He would be glad when his work at Fernleigh Hall was complete and he could put any connection with the Bentincks behind him.

The agent had been brusquely dismissed and Henry sipped his whisky as he awaited the summons to dinner. Mary bothered him. She had an air of suppressed excitement, a gleam of secret knowledge in her eyes. She had news to impart, that much was evident. What could have brought her home with such urgency? She had complained most bitterly about their dull existence at Fernleigh Hall; she had said that there was to be more fun had in the Parsonage. Now she was back and it was most unsettling. Henry had quite enjoyed the last week or so of marital harmony and he had no wish to see the even tenor of his personal life disrupted. There were sufficient problems connected with his business dealings to occupy his mind. He did not need his household to be disturbed. He had sailed a little close to the wind in his trading with the French and now Mr Pitt's Ministers were making enquiries about his activities. He had enemies both here and in London who would be glad to inform on him. He needed no further distractions. He looked at the clock, downed his drink and headed for the drawing-room where his wife would be waiting.

Mary and Eliza were sitting as far apart as decency would allow. His sister had a predatory look and his wife appeared fretful. She seemed relieved to see him.

'Is dinner ready?' Her voice was unnaturally high. 'Do let us go in. I declare that I shall faint if I do not eat soon.'

Henry was immediately solicitous. 'Take my arm. We can go in at once.' He led the way with Mary following behind, a faint smile on her face.

The crystal sparkled in the candlelight, the silver gleamed and the well-trained servants offered a selection of tasty dishes. Eliza, for all her protestations of hunger, merely toyed with the food on her plate as Henry tried to tempt her with the choicest morsels. Mary watched and waited. The conversation was desultory; gossip about the war, the weather, the delay in completion of the new Queen's Dock and finally, Henry turned to the topic of Mary's visit to Aunt Pimblett. He sat back, swirling the wine in his glass, satisfied, replete.

'So, Mary. Are you going to tell us what brought you back so soon from the delights of Chester? Is our Aunt's house even less exciting than Fernleigh Hall? Perhaps the military are all abroad? Is it a shortage of admirers that has brought you back to Liverpool?'

Mary ignored her brother and fastened her speculative gaze on Eliza's face. 'I met an old acquaintance of yours in Chester. He begs to be remembered to you.' Her sharp eyes took in the sudden tightening of Eliza's knuckles on the arms of her chair; she heard the quick intake of breath. Henry looked from one woman to the other. His expression was wary. He had never seen his sister look more dangerous. She continued to enlighten them. Each word was clearly enunciated and she relished the moment. 'Captain Stanton appeared to be quite overcome at the news that you are having a child, sister-in-law. How many weeks is it since he visited you? Not very long. I cannot think why he should be so concerned. Can you?'

Eliza clambered stiffly to her feet, her face frozen, her colour gone. She clutched at the table for support and turned a terrified gaze on her husband.

'I do not feel well, Henry. I shall go and lie down.' She gave a stifled sob and stumbled from the room.

Bentinck poured himself a drink and stood at his sister's side, towering over her. 'Mary, what is this about? What are you trying to do? Explain yourself. I am waiting.' There was no answer. His chest was constricted and his hand trembled as he looked into his sister's face. He knew! He knew but he needed to hear it.

He had had his suspicions after his visit to Bristol; Eliza had been surprisingly affectionate on his return. He had heard tales but had managed to convince himself that that the silly chit had merely been flattered by the attentions of the dashing Captain and then felt guilty because she had responded with a little decorous flirtation. Once Henry had got rid of the man, she had demonstrated her contrition in a most satisfactory manner. He had dismissed from his mind any thought that the liaison might have been serious. He knew his wife and she was not, in any respect, a sensual creature. Her notion of love was romantic not carnal and if truth were told, she found any activity in the marital bed distasteful. Eliza could never have committed adultery with someone she had only just met. She had only known the man a few short weeks. The idea was preposterous. It was quite impossible.

He glowered at Mary.

'Well, sister? Say what you have to say. What salacious gossip have you heard?'

'This is not tittle-tattle from those who know no better, Henry. There can be no doubt about this. None at all.'

'About what?' he shouted, glaring at her with wild eyes. 'About what exactly?' Mary's anger rose swiftly to meet his own. Why should he rage at her? She was doing her duty as a loving sister. It was that simpering bitch upstairs who should be the object of his wrath, not herself. She got to her feet and faced him defiantly.

'There is no way to spare you this, Henry. Captain Stanton believes himself to be the father of the child that Eliza carries. There is no argument. He practically admitted it, and in front of Aunt Pimblett too. She dismissed both him and me from her house. Our Aunt is not stupid. She knew.' Mary laid a consoling hand on her brother's arm her anger evaporating as speedily as it had arisen. 'I am sorry, my dear. I know what this child meant to you'

Henry's first emotion was disbelief.

'She would not. I know her too well. Her head is full of romantic nonsense. She hardly knew the man.' His eyes narrowed cruelly as he struck out at the bearer of the news. 'She is not like you, Mary.' He shook off her hand.

His sister's face became a mask of callous indifference. 'You are wrong, Henry. She did know him. He was her first love. I had it from one of his regiment in Chester. She was prepared to marry him and considered herself betrothed. She returned to Fernleigh to find that her father had given her to you. She was forced into the marriage with you to save the Broadwood reputation, but her heart was already elsewhere. You may have bought your wife, brother, but you could not buy her affection.' She stopped. She had gone too far.

Bentinck turned to a side table and put down his glass. His movements were stilted, careful, deliberate. The colour had drained from his face until he appeared bloodless; his eyes were grey pebbles, his lips an invisible line. There was a faint tremor in his voice.

'No one can ever be sure,' he whispered. 'The child will be acknowledged as mine.'

'And your wife?' insisted Mary. 'What of your wife?'

'I have no wife. Go to bed sister and stay there.' He turned his back and stood at the window legs apart and hands firmly clasped. He stared into the darkness of the garden. He stayed until he heard the door shut on the rustle of her skirts then his shoulders heaved and Henry Bentinck sobbed out his frustration and rage.

In the loneliness of her room, Eliza waited. The fire was out, but she had long since dismissed her servants with the instruction that she was not to be disturbed. She was aware that she had given herself away. She also knew that Henry's sister, for weeks past, had harboured a need for revenge because Edward Stanton had made clear his preference for Eliza's prettiness over Mary's own more obvious sexuality. Mary had a wish to see her sister-in-law disgraced and would make the most of this opportunity. In addition, the other woman had long held a grudge because of Daniel. The slave's physical strength, his impressive physique, his pride and indeed, the novelty of his dark skin and alien culture had whetted Mary's jaded appetites. He was different and had appealed enough for Mrs Harrison to make her desires known, but Daniel had chosen to devote himself first to Mrs Weston and then to Eliza herself. He too had rejected Mary's advances, and all because of Eliza. Henry's sister had bided her time and now she was in a position of strength. There would be no mercy.

Strangely, her fear of Henry was not so great. He had been a different man of late. It appeared that the child in her womb had changed them both. There was a new focus in Eliza's life. Finally something mattered more to her than her own gratification. She also had a serenity that had previously been missing in her character. There was nothing to be done about the past and the present must be endured for the sake of her child's future. That was now the most important consideration. Henry would know that she had been unfaithful and forgiveness was out of the question; it was not a part of the Bentinck make-up, but if she could only convince him that this child could possibly be his own flesh and blood then she might be spared the worst of his anger. So she waited, lying fully clothed on her bed, as the silence of the house wrapped itself around her.

It was hours later that a violent kick sent the door crashing back against the wall. Eliza's heart sank as she realised that Henry was drunk. Drunk in a way that she had never seen him before. Drunk beyond belligerence and ranting, drunk into an ice-cold anger that was infinitely more terrifying. He approached the bed, the blazing coals of his eyes the only spark in his livid face. He stared at her cowering figure. She drew the coverlet up to her neck with trembling fingers. The movement enraged him and he snatched it away, tossing it into a corner of the room.

Eliza folded protective arms over her stomach; the gesture was not lost on Henry.

'It is a little late for that, Madam,' he said. He leaned closer. 'So you loved Stanton did you?' His voice was a sibilant hiss.

'No, no, Henry. I swear I did not.' She babbled on incoherently. 'He meant nothing to me. Anything between us was over so very long ago. It was nothing I tell you. He… he was so very persistent and… and I was lonely. You were gone and I… He was tender and charming.' She battled valiantly for the future of her unborn child. 'It was nothing. Nothing, I say. You must believe me.'

He hit her hard across her face, first with the flat of his hand and then with the back. Her teeth rattled and blood spurted from her burst lip where his ring had cut deep into her flesh. The terrified girl shrank away from him.

'At least be truthful you whore. He was the love of your life. You wanted him. Why deny it?' He hit her again and a jolting pain shot through her cheekbone. Eliza began to sob, tears squeezing beneath her swollen lids, the salt stinging the cuts on her face, but she did not lift her arms to protect herself, they remained firmly clamped across her middle.

'I swear it meant nothing. If I had known that I already carried your son, I would never have let him near me. Your son, Henry. Your child. And have no doubt, whatever Mary has told you, that this is your child. You have to believe me.'

Through the haze of her pain, she registered the dawning uncertainty on his features, the need for it to be true. She grasped at the straw.

'Do what you will with me, but do not harm the child. The time of the birth will prove that it is your child, your heir.'

She had said the wrong thing. With a howl of rage he lunged at the bed. 'My child, is it?' he screamed. His lips drew back in snarling anger. 'Your actions have cast doubt on the paternity of my heir. He will never be free of it. You think that people will not talk? Do you imagine that the matrons in this town are incapable of counting in weeks and months? I will never be sure. All his life and I shall never know.' He was beside himself with fury.

Eliza closed her eyes to shut out the horror. Snatching up a decanter from beside the bed, he put the fingers of his other hand in the neck of her gown and tore it down to her waist. He smashed the neck of the bottle on the wall and Eliza flinched as shards of glass struck her face.

'No other man will ever look at you again,' he raved.

Finally she was driven to put up her hands to protect her face. 'No, please,' she begged in desperation. 'People will see. They will talk.'

The red mists left his eyes. 'No one will know,

Elizabeth. No one else will ever see.' With his free hand he trapped both her wrists together and drew the broken glass down her body in a thin line from neck to waist. Tiny beads of blood appeared. He laughed.

From her window, Mary watched as the crazed figure of her brother clattered down the front steps and set off, with a shambling gait, round the corner of the house in the direction of the stables. She pushed open the casement, her ears straining. Sound carried far in the silence of the night and she could hear the ringing of the horse's hooves as the animal crossed the cobbles of the yard. Henry's figure appeared from the side of the house, bent low over the animal's head, whip flailing as he urged the startled creature into a headlong gallop down the drive. He rode like a man possessed. The demons of Hell were on his shoulder. A bank of cloud suffocated the light of the moon and Mary's eyes strained in the darkness. He was gone. She drew a shawl about her shoulders. She would keep watch until he returned. He would need her then.

At the house in Everton Hill, Daniel slept fitfully on his narrow bed. His frequent bouts of gut-wrenching coughing echoed in the peaceful silence of deserted rooms. He was the only one left apart from a daily woman who would come in each morning. Anne and George Barton, together with Sullah and the children, had left that afternoon to undertake a final round of visits to relatives they did not expect to see again. The Mistress had given her household time off to call on their own families, leaving Daniel to continue the work of sorting papers and belongings that would need to go with them on their journey to America.

He had been almost relieved to see them depart. He was often tired, and was finding it increasingly difficult to hide the extent of his weakness from the others. Sullah was beginning to fret. The nature of their new relationship meant that she had become aware of the sleeplessness caused by his hacking cough. She had also once, to her dismay, caught a glimpse of blood-stained linen. The girl had tried to persuade Daniel to confide in the Missus so that medical attention could be sought but he would not have it.

'The Mistress is truly happy for the first time in years, Sullah. She is content and I will not be the one to bring her trouble.' He was insistent. 'It is nothing but the damp and the cold winter that we have just endured. The Mersey fog would give anyone a bad chest. A sea voyage and the warm air of Georgia, the feel of the sun on my back again, that is all I need. Now stop your fussing.'

She had seemed to be reassured and had left waving happily from the window of the carriage. Just once, as he had helped her up the step, her concern had threatened to overwhelm her. She had looked deep into his eyes, her own gaze dark and fearful.

'Yo' takes good care of yo'self 'til we gets back. Yo' hear me? Take care,' and she had made the almost forgotten sign against evil.

Daniel had laughed. 'Dear Sullah, still steeped in the old beliefs. Have no fear. You will not be gone for long. What could happen in such a short time?' He had stood smiling as the carriage jerked away and trundled down the lane, the shouts of Miss Meg and Master Timothy ringing in his ears.

'Goodbye, Daniel. See you soon. Goodbye.'

The 'Harrison' clock at the bottom of the stairs struck two. Daniel turned on his side pulling the rough blanket up around his head and trying to breathe shallowly through an open mouth. He dozed fitfully as the room was plunged from darkness into ghostly blue-white light and back again. He could hear the trees creak as the wind began to

285

rise. A storm was brewing. Somewhere an owl hooted. Eventually, the weight of total exhaustion overtook him and he drifted into a deep and heavy sleep.

Daniel jerked awake. Something had disturbed him. His ears strained in the hush of the pre-dawn glow of pearly light. He closed his eyes. He was so tired. There it was again. A scratching sound. It seemed to come from the front of the house. He dragged himself from the bed pulling his blanket around his bare shoulders, shuffled into Sullah's attic room that was located above the front door and looked out.

A bay mare, her empty saddle slipping to one side, trod delicately down the lane, stopped, snickered and turned her head. Daniel's blood froze. He had groomed that horse so many times. Dropping his blanket he ran to his own room, snatched up his breeches and hopped down the attic stairs, struggling to pull the trousers up to his waist. He swung around the banister on the main landing and hurtled down the final flight of steps to the hall. His breath came in great whooping gasps as clumsy fingers, suddenly useless, fumbled with the bolts. Throwing open the door he peered out into the gloom.

A thread of sound, a whimper, a sigh, whipped his head around to the side. Leaping down the two steps he dropped to his knees beside the limp figure huddled in the shelter of the wall.

'Dear God! What has happened to you?' He lifted her in his arms, flinching as she winced. Her head fell against his shoulder as he carried her inside kicking the door shut behind them. He hesitated, turned towards the drawing-room, looked at her ashen face and instead began to climb the stairs. He moved easily with his burden, padding along the carpeted corridor to the Mistress' own bedroom. He laid Eliza down on the coverlet and lit the lamp with shaking hands.

She had fainted and the pallor of her face stood out against her dark woollen cloak. Its folds were damp from the morning dew and Daniel unfastened the clasp at the neck to pull the heavy material off her. He drew the fabric aside and gasped in horror. The garment fell unnoticed to the floor. Bile rose in his throat as he backed away from the bed, old, long-banished pictures of his slave mother's mutilated body flooding his mind. Daniel gnawed at his fist, tasting his own blood. He turned away sickened, took a pace towards the door, hesitated and reluctantly returned. They were alone. There was no one else. He groaned and looked down at her mutilated body; the cuts were not dangerous but were deep enough to permanently scar the flesh. This was no frenzied attack. The assault had been carried out in a cold, calculated and deliberate act of vengeance.

Her eyes opened and the fog slowly cleared as consciousness was re-established.

'Daniel… Where is Anne?… Where is my Aunt?… I had to come… The child…'

He took the fluttering hand and pressed it in quiet reassurance. 'Please, Eliza.' He used her given name because that was how he always thought of her. 'You must not fret. You are safe here. Your Aunt is away, but…' The fear flashed in her eyes. 'You are safe,' he repeated. 'You are hurt but you will recover. There is no lasting harm done. We can bathe your cuts and make you comfortable. You must stay in this room until your Aunt and her husband return. It will not be too long. Eliza clutched at his hand, her vice-like grip surprising him with its strength. He soothed her as he might a fretful horse. 'There, there. You must rest. I promise I will protect you. I know who must have done this and I swear that he will not come near you whilst I am here. I will not let him hurt you.'

A knowing look slid into Eliza's eyes. She needed him

on her side.

'I just had to get away, Daniel.' Strands of damp hair tangled as she shifted her head from side to side. He smoothed them back with a gentle hand. 'Henry would have come back to hit me again. I know he would. I had to leave him. He might harm the child. He is mad. Mad I tell you.' Her voice rose and Daniel's throat closed in pity for her distressed condition. She needed his protection for herself and her unborn child. He could not understand what could possibly have driven Bentinck to do what he had done to his wife, but he would not be allowed to do it again. That was certain. He bent closer to the bed as her voice dropped to a whisper. 'He will try to have me put away. He pretends to have doubts about the child's parentage and is seeking revenge. He has listened to his sister and you know how she hates me. She has always hated me. She knew what he was doing to me. Her room is close to mine. She must have heard but she did nothing. She wanted to see him break me. I couldn't stay, Daniel. I could not.' She tried to sit up but fell back on the pillows.

Moments passed before she spoke again.

'He went out. I heard him ride away. I waited. It must have been for hours. When I recovered I crawled to the door. I don't remember getting to the stables. My knees hurt. So much of me hurts. I must have fallen so very many times. Bess is such a gentle creature. She knew. She stood still and somehow….somehow I managed to get the saddle on to her. I was so afraid that he might come back. I cannot recall how I got here, only that I was so relieved to see you.' The telling had exhausted her and she shut her eyes. Her breathing was laboured. He dropped to his knees beside the bed, laid his head on her hand and wept.

Later, much later, daylight crept into the room. Eliza screamed. Her body jumped. Her hands clutched her abdomen and her face turned a sickly shade of green.

Daniel stared as she turned her face towards him, terror in her eyes. She drew up her knees with a gasp and rolled on to her side.

'Oh God... The pain!' she panted. 'A knife... it is like a knife... The child... My baby... Daniel.' The last word choked on a second scream. 'A physician... I must have a physician... Get him...'

'But I cannot leave you alone. You are ill. There is no one...'

'Do as I say.' Her breath rasped through gritted teeth. 'If you do not get a doctor I will die. My child will die.' She bit her bottom lip, drawing blood, opening up her cuts. 'Get him for me. Take my horse. Go, damn you. Go!'

With a last despairing glance at her set face he stumbled from the room, down the stairs and out of the house. He snatched her mare's reins, tightened the girth, leaped into the saddle and kicked the startled animal into a gallop. They flew down the lanes towards Liverpool where the early morning workers gazed in astonishment as the half-dressed slave thundered past them. The town was just beginning to stir.

At Fernleigh Hall, Mary Harrison was jolted out of her doze by a thunderous knocking at her door. She had no time to respond before a grey-faced Henry lurched across the threshold. She had never seen a man look so ill and still be on his feet. His hair lay in strands plastered to his scalp and fell in lank, bedraggled tangles across his face. His hands and face were cut and bleeding and his soaked shirt was in tatters. He shivered uncontrollably and his teeth chattered with a violence that threatened to shake his staring eyes loose from their sockets.

He raised his whip, threateningly. 'Where is she? What have you done with the bitch?' The menace was unmistakable but Mary did not flinch.

'If you are referring to your wife, Henry, I have not laid eyes on her all night. I was ordered to come to my room and remain here and that is what I did.'

He collapsed into a chair. 'But she has gone. She is not here. I have searched the house. God knows how… When I left her she… But no matter. She has gone.'

He was not thinking clearly. Mary lowered her face until it was inches from his own. 'Her horse, brother. Is her horse in the stables? If her horse has gone, then we both know where she will be. She has gone to her Aunt's house. She has left you.'

Bentinck hauled himself wearily to his feet. 'She will be brought back. Until that child is born she will be in my house even if I have to put her under lock and key. She remains here with me.' He moved to the door.

'Where are you going, Henry?' Mary clung to his arm. 'You are in no state to go anywhere.' She reeled back as he thrust her aside.

'I am going to Everton Hill. If you want to help me then order the carriage and follow me there. She is coming home, sister. Make no mistake. I will get her and bring back if I have to drag her every inch of the way by her hair.' With a sudden burst of renewed energy, he flung open the door and almost ran from the house. Mary sighed, picked up her cloak and followed him. *Where would it all end?*

CHAPTER NINETEEN

LIVERPOOL
APRIL 1795

Daniel hammered on the door of the well-situated house which stood four-square on the corner of Strand Street. His mind was too preoccupied to take in the brass plate on the wall, the highly polished knocker, the pristine curtains and the general air of comfort which hung around the Doctor's residence. He beat his frantic fists against the stained glass panel set in the wood, becoming more and more impatient as anxiety threatened to get the better of politeness.

The door opened just a crack and two suspicious eyes beneath a crisp lace cap peered out at him. A diminutive figure in rustling black looked him up and down. The door was held in a firm hand.

'Aye. What is it ye be after?' The Scottish brogue was so thick that Daniel struggled to understand the question. 'Well, lad, are ye deaf or are ye daft? Do ye intend to stand there with yer great mouth open 'til Doomsday? Has the cat got yer tongue?'

'The Doctor, Ma'am. I beg pardon for my impatience but it is most urgent that I speak to the Doctor.'

The iron-grey eyebrows rose. The man's refined speech belied his scruffy appearance. Her manner thawed, but not sufficiently for the crack in the door to be widened.

'Aye, well, laddie, it is always urgent when folks come

to see the Doctor but he has not been in his bed for most of the night. He was called away to the Infirmary in the small hours. The wee mon is wearing himself out.'

Daniel almost managed to smile at the thought of the Doctor being referred to as a 'wee mon', but the urgency of his errand did not lend itself to humour.

'Ma'am, I assure you, it is truly a matter of life and death.' The slave's desperation pierced her tart exterior and the eyes were suddenly warm and compassionate. She held the door open wide.

'You'd best come in, laddie, and leave a message.'

'Thank you, but if the Doctor is not here I cannot wait. I must return to my...my Mistress. Will you ask him to call when he gets back? Tell him it is Mrs Bentinck who has need of his attentions. It is most urgent. Please tell him that time is short.' He turned to leave. 'Wait! I cannot believe I have been so stupid!' Rubbing a huge hand over his frowning face he turned back to the housekeeper. 'I had almost forgotten. Make sure that you tell the Doctor that Mrs Bentinck is not at home. She is not at Fernleigh Hall. She is staying with her Aunt, Mrs Weston... Barton, in Everton Hill. He knows the house.'

The shrewd old lady took in his unkempt appearance, his ravaged face, his desperation and his exhaustion. She nodded firmly.

'Dinna fret, lad. I'll give him the message right and proper. He won't be long away. He promised that he would come back here to break his fast before he goes to the Alms Houses up the road. I reckon the folks there will keep. I'll send him to Mrs Bentinck the moment he gets home.' Daniel nodded his thanks. Speech was beyond him as he attempted to suppress a choking cough. He climbed stiffly into the saddle, clicked his tongue and set off at a brisk trot through the increasingly busy streets. He clattered along Byrom Street, past the potent smell of the Porter Brewery and headed back to Everton Hill. Coming into the quieter roads, he kicked his heels in the mare's sides, clung to her mane and concentrated all his energies on staying in the saddle as the little horse gamely increased her speed.

Later he remembered little of his wild ride. The hooves beat a remorseless tattoo in his skull. *You must get back. You must get back. You must get back.* The mare snorted and tossed her head but Daniel hauled brutally on the reins and dug savage heels into her steaming flanks as he urged her on. The chill of the morning air dried the perspiration as it rolled down his back. He was not conscious of the cold and was unaware of the pain in his legs as he gripped the mare between his knees and bent low over her sweating neck. He was only mindful of the need to drag air into his tortured lungs and to stay in the saddle. Dizziness came in waves and the road seemed to rear up at him as it unwound beneath the flying hooves. He fought grimly against the nausea, gritting his teeth and clinging to the horse's neck. There was not far to go.

Henry Bentinck rode his exhausted animal gently towards Everton Hill. He was past tiredness now. The fierce urgency had left him. His mind was clear and he knew what he had to do. He intended to take possession of his wife, put her into the coach with Mary and escort her home to Fernleigh Hall. He would brook no interference from Mrs Barton and her husband; they had no jurisdiction over Elizabeth. She belonged to him and he would deal with her in his own way. A suite of rooms would be prepared for her at the top of the house and she would be confined there until his son was born. During her time of waiting he would make it known that she was suffering from a crisis of nerves, a breakdown in her health brought on by her condition. It was by no means uncommon. Eliza had always been emotional, so no one would be surprised. He knew a Doctor who, for a consideration, would be willing to certify that his wife was mad. After the birth she could be put away. He would supervise the child's upbringing himself. He would make his son in his own image and the boy's mother would be dead to the world.

Henry nodded his satisfaction, seeing the future laid out as he wished it to be. There was a thin line between insanity and reality and he had crossed that line many times in the demon-infested night that had just passed. He had travelled beyond rage, beyond despair, beyond reason. His agony was over and he was calm, calm with an icy self-control that bordered on the inhuman.

Approaching the front of the Barton's house he was surprised to find the door ajar. It swung open at his touch and he stepped into the hall. The silence was broken only by the ticking of the clock, insistently loud in the emptiness of the building. Bentinck stood still, scarcely breathing. His serpent eyes flicked from side to side and up and down. There was someone here. He could sense it. The hairs stiffened on the back of his neck.

'Who's there? Daniel, is that you?' The voice, caught on a sob, floated down from the first floor. Eliza! She was here. They had been right. Henry crossed the tiled floor on silent feet, his shadow flitting across the black and white squares. He moved stealthily up the steps but the creak of his boots betrayed him and a door on the landing was jerked open. His wife stood on the threshold.

She held the tattered remnants of her bodice together with one trembling hand; the other clutched across her middle as she shuffled towards him. The cuts and bruises stood out against the muddy-grey of her face. Her hair was in untamed disarray and her eyes were wild. She had aged ten years and the thought went through his mind, she is insane, she really is mad.

Her lips worked but no sound came out, then she shrieked at him.

'You wicked, evil man. You devil. You have done this. I am losing the child. I can't hold on any longer and it's your fault.' She screamed and bent almost double as the pain swept through her body. She straightened up again as the spasm passed, her breath coming in shallow gasps. 'Your child's life-blood is seeping away. Look at it, Henry.' She pointed a shaking hand at the pool of blood staining the carpet where she stood. 'I am losing your son and I am glad,' she hissed. 'Do you hear me? I am glad! How does it feel to kill your own son? How does it feel? You will never have a child on me, Henry Bentinck, never. I will die first.'

He felt faint; his head swam. The sweet sickly stench of blood was overwhelming. Gripping the banister he hauled himself hand over hand to the top of the stairs. He stared in fascinated horror as the blood spread around his wife's feet and flowed over the toe of his boot. And then he saw it. For one moment of sickening clarity, a black clot in the centre of the puddle pulsed with life. One beat, two and then it was still. An inhuman growl ripped from his throat and he lunged for Eliza, his hands rigid claws that closed around her neck.

In a parody of dance the pair rocked backwards and forwards, leaning, bending, their bodies inseparable. The red mist of madness was in Henry's eyes and Eliza's face was the featureless blur of nightmares. He knew only that this woman must die. She had betrayed him. She had killed his child. The talons that were his fingers tightened inexorably.

Eliza was scarcely conscious. She was haunted by her ordeal of the previous night, weakened by the loss of blood from her miscarriage and demented by the thought of her unborn child perishing in a slithering heap on the floor.

Blackness threatened to engulf her and she was glad to yield herself to unfeeling death. She dropped her hands from where they were clutching ineffectually at her husband's murderous fingers and went limp in his arms. Her breath was cut off and she felt the purple colour rise in her face. Her eyes were protruding from their sockets and her tongue swelled to fill her mouth.

Suddenly, her body jerked and her head snapped back. She gave a tortured gasp, a croak as a thread of air found its way into her windpipe. For a split second her eyes were able to focus and her brain was crystal clear. Henry was off balance. His foot had slipped in the slime of her blood and his grip on her throat was broken as he flailed his arms, trying to keep his feet.

She watched as he teetered at the top of the stairs. She watched as his boots finally found a hold. She watched as he came towards her again. With a spurt of super-human energy she lunged at him and thrust both hands in the middle of his chest. He swayed backwards. He half righted himself, leaning towards her with arms outstretched. He swayed forwards. She could have saved him. With clear deliberation Eliza laid her hands on his chest and again pushed as hard as she could. His face registered amazement as he staggered backwards, found no place for his feet and tumbled from the top of the stairs to the marble floor at the bottom, his body turning over and his head bumping on the steps until he came to rest with a sickening crack.

Horse and rider were close to collapse as the little mare shuddered to a halt and Daniel slid from her back, clutching the saddle for support as his legs threatened to buckle. His chest heaved but he seemed unable to draw air into his congested lungs. His mind was so confused that he almost failed to notice the other horse tethered to the gate. As he registered that Bentinck was in the house, his steps faltered. His heart began to thump and he stumbled up the front steps, staggering across the threshold.

Henry lay on his back in the hall, his feet resting on the bottom step and his head pointing towards the door. Four shuffling steps took Daniel up to the corpse. That it was indeed a corpse was never in doubt. The neck was bent at an unnatural angle, the sightless eyes were wide open and the arms were stretched out to the sides, the fingers of both hands curving inwards like a bird's claws. Daniel swallowed the bile in his throat and gazed down at the body of the man who had been his enemy. He had wished Henry dead so many times. He had sworn vengeance for the murder of Marcus, for the torture of Eliza and yes, for the injuries to his own pride. Yet, like all humanity, Bentinck was diminished by his end and Daniel had no joy in his passing. That he had fallen to his death was evident, and the slave raised his eyes to the head of the stairs tracing the path of the fall. A slight movement caught his attention. He cursed himself. *Eliza was still in the house. Was she safe? Where was she?*

Leaping over Bentinck's lifeless body he took the stairs two at a time. His eyes noted the intermittent smears of blood but his mind refused to accept the fact. At the top he stopped, horrified. The landing was a lake of blood, and at one side her shoulders convulsed was Eliza. She was half sitting and half lying in a huddle against the rail. She raised swollen eyes to his face.

'It is too late. The Doctor is too late.' He strained to hear her. 'The child is gone. It is dead.' She gave a hysterical giggle. 'Henry is gone. He is dead too.' The laughter vanished and another gale of sobs shook her.

Daniel's heart twisted. She was so thin, so pale, so very, very fragile. He took her hands and she clung to him in

297

desperation. He drew a deep breath. The question must be asked and he chose his words carefully.

'Listen to me. I need to know. Tell me what happened. You have to tell me before anyone comes.' He gave her a gentle shake. 'Did you kill him?'

She drew away, a knowing fear registering in her eyes. 'No! I swear I did not.' The words came in a rush. 'You cannot think so. He... he was coming into the house. I heard the noise and I got up and looked over the rail. He was climbing the stairs. He saw me. He... he seemed startled and he slipped. He fell.' She shivered. 'I could do nothing. Nothing, I tell you.' She was verging on the edge of hysteria.

'Did he attack you, Eliza? Did you have to defend yourself? No one would blame you.'

She struggled to her feet. 'How many times must I say it! I told you. He did not reach the landing. He slipped half way up the stairs. He lost his footing and the next thing I remember he was lying there and I knew that he was dead.' She began to sob and Daniel caught her in his arms as she threatened to slide back to the floor. She clung to him with a strength born of panic.

He held her against his chest. 'It's all right, Eliza. You are safe now. It will be all right,' he soothed. 'You must lie down. The Doctor is on his way.'

'Hen-r-y!' The drawn-out shriek filled their ears and rang around the hall. Mary Harrison was framed in the open doorway her face turned up towards them, her finger pointing in shuddering horror at her brother's body. 'You've killed him!' she accused. 'I knew you would, you murdering animal. Was it revenge for your friend or was it for her? Did you think she would have you if Henry was dead? Was that why you killed him? You murderer, I swear you will hang for this!'

Eliza sank to the ground unnoticed as Daniel's nerveless

hands released her. He stared aghast at the woman below, his denial sounding feeble even to his own ears.

'But I did not kill him. I did not. I was not even here when he fell. It was an accident.' He turned to Eliza who was struggling to her feet. 'Tell her! Tell her that I was not here. Tell her what happened.'

Her eyes avoided his face. She was terrified. No one would believe that it was an accident. Of that she was sure. Either herself or Daniel would be blamed. Mary wanted a scapegoat. She forced out the words.

'I cannot say what happened. I... I ... saw nothing. I was in my room. The baby... I was losing my child. I heard a noise and when I managed to get out of bed, Henry was lying there. He was dead.' She began to sob, 'I saw nothing. I was in my room I tell you.'

'And the slave,' hissed Mary. 'Where was he?'

'I don't know... I don't know.' She covered her face with her hands as her voice rose to a wail. 'Why are you asking me all these questions? I feel so ill. I cannot remember. I must have fainted. I don't know... I don't know.'

Daniel stared in stunned disbelief. He could not have heard aright. She was confused. He moved towards her.

'Get away! Get away from me,' she shouted.

'That's enough.' The commanding voice rang out. 'I am Doctor Stewart. I was sent for. What goes on here? Ye can hear the racket at the end of the la...' His eye fell on the man at the bottom of the stairs. He dropped on one knee, giving the body only a cursory glance. He looked around and asked again, his voice hard and insistent. 'What goes on here?'

Mary Harrison was the first to recover. She turned to the new arrival.

'The slave has killed my brother,' she accused. 'Henry had come here to bring his wife home. She had run away and you have only to look at the two of them to know the reason why. She is a whore… She's…'

'It is a lie! I came to see my Aunt…to spend a few days…but she was away. I was not to know. Then I began to lose Henry's child. I had to lie down. I could not return home. How can you say such things, Mary? I would never do anything… To suggest that I… Why, the man is a slave… No one could possibly believe…' Eliza was frantic. She began to sob again her beseeching eyes fixed on the Doctor's face.

He looked away. 'Go on, Mrs Harrison. What did you see?'

Mary had pulled herself together. She avoided looking at her brother's broken body. The reality of her own bleak future was beginning to seep into her mind. All Henry's possessions would now belong to Eliza and Mary would have nothing, no protector, no home, no place to go. The prospect of Aunt Pimblett's cold charity loomed large. With her brother's death Mary had lost everything. More importantly, Henry was the only person in her life whom she had truly loved, and in her grief the one emotion stronger than all others was a burning desire for revenge. The slave would pay. She drew herself up.

'Henry had asked me to follow with the coach. The men waited outside and I came in alone. We wanted no scandal, you see. I came in and they were fighting at the top of the stairs,' she lied. 'I saw the slave push Henry. It was a deliberate act. Look how much bigger than my brother he is, how much stronger. Poor Henry had no chance.' She covered her face with shaking hands as if to shut out the memory, but her voice carried on, clear, relentless, accusing. 'That man pushed my brother. Henry fell. I saw it happen. I will swear it.' She dropped her hands, threw back her head and pointed to the pair on the landing. 'I knelt by my brother. He was dead and when I looked up, that heathen had her in his arms. He was holding her. They did it. It was murder!'

Doctor Stewart looked from one to the other in frowning puzzlement. He got to his feet and climbed slowly up the stairs examining each of the treads and the blood on the landing. He halted in front of the sobbing Eliza.

'Mrs Bentinck, I need the truth. Did it happen as she said?'

'I have told you. I know nothing. Henry must have fallen... I was so ill... I still feel so weak... I swear I do not remember.'

Stewart turned to Daniel. 'Well? What is the truth? Did he fall? Was it an accident? Speak up, man.'

Daniel moved one step towards Eliza, holding out both his hands. 'Tell them,' he begged. 'Tell them, Eliza.'

'I cannot remember.' She lifted pleading eyes to his face. 'Do not ask me to, Daniel. I cannot be blamed. I cannot.' She turned to the Doctor. 'I remember nothing. I cannot help you.'

Stewart shook his head, moved to Daniel and tried again. 'Is Mrs Harrison telling the truth, man? You have to say. Dear God, they will charge you with murder! Do you not understand?'

Daniel sank to the floor, his back against the wall, his head dropping as he struggled for breath. A violent bout of coughing shook him. He looked up and his face was grey.

'Daniel,' Eliza sobbed. 'I cannot say. You must know I cannot. I don't remember. If you care for me... If you ever cared for me...' Her voice trailed into silence.

Daniel shuddered, conscious of the enormity of her betrayal. He resembled a wounded animal. He had idolised this woman; set her on a pedestal; worshipped her. Now, he tasted the bitter ashes of disillusion. He straightened his shoulders and lifted his head.

'I have nothing to say.'

There was a gentle thud and Eliza slid to the floor in a faint. Daniel did not look at her again. The Doctor pushed past him but the slave's gaze was fixed on Mary Harrison. Her features were twisted and her lips drawn back in a snarl of triumph. Daniel recoiled. In that moment, her resemblance to her dead brother was uncanny. She hissed her revenge.

'My footman will fetch the authorities and you will be taken away,' she gloated. 'You will hang for this day's work.'

Stewart made no attempt to hide his distaste. 'Aye, well, for now we need to see to your sister-in-law, woman. She has lost a lot of blood and must be put to bed.' He glanced at Daniel who waited in silent resignation. 'You have no cause to worry about him. He will not run away.' He picked up his patient and carried her into the bedroom.

Daniel remained on the landing. He was incapable of rational thought, yet afterwards could recall every moment in astonishing detail. Events, words, expressions, emotions were burned into his memory. He was aware that Mary had gone outside and returned with her footman. The man sidled through the door, his face alive with that mixture of horror, disgust and avid curiosity with which one human being always seems to regard the violent death of another. Daniel heard the rumble of wheels, the chink of harness and the clatter of hooves as the Fernleigh coach rattled away in search of some authority. He was startled by the loudness of the chimes of the hall clock as it marked the passing of another hour. And throughout it all, he was conscious of the malevolent hatred of Mary who finally edged past him and went reluctantly to tend Eliza.

Daniel waited in dumb disbelief until eventually Doctor Stewart emerged from the bedroom. There was sympathy in the Scot's eyes as he laid a gentle hand on Daniel's shoulder, drawing him along the corridor and pushing him into a chair in a dark corner of the landing.

'Something is not right. It makes no sense. They are lying, both of them. Mrs Bentinck insists that her husband did not come near her, but the man is covered in blood and it is not his own. It is hers. She says when she came out of her room he had already fallen, but his footprints are in the blood on the landing, the blood from the child she was miscarrying. Bentinck was up here at the same time as her. There is no doubt. Yet if that is the case, then the other one also lies. Why the man's sister should hate you so I cannot imagine, but it is there in her face. She is lying. They are both lying.' Stewart waited but still Daniel did not speak. 'You must tell the truth, man. I don't believe you had any-thing to do with whatever happened here but you must speak or I cannot help you. Was it an accident? What did you see? Were you even here when Bentinck died? Answer me, laddie.'

Daniel raised dull, expressionless eyes. 'I have nothing to say.' He struggled to control his cough, but his frame shook once more. He rested his head back against the cushion.

'They will accuse you of murder. Why are you protecting her? Can you not see?' In his exasperation the Doctor shook Daniel hard. 'They will hang you!'

The slave gave a twisted smile, spots of blood frothing on his lips. 'I do not think so, Doctor,' he said. 'There will not be time.'

Stewart stared at him in a moment of compassionate understanding. He patted the big man's shoulder sadly. 'No,' he agreed. 'You are right, laddie. You will not hang.'

In the darkness of the landing the two men waited for the authorities, the silence pierced only by muted sounds from the street outside, sounds which grew louder as vengeance closed in.

CHAPTER TWENTY

EVERTON HILL

APRIL 1795

Mrs Barton paced up and down the morning-room, anxiety churning her stomach and worry creasing her forehead. She sat in a chair and picked up her needlework trying to school herself to patience with little success. Muttering a curse as she stabbed a vicious needle into her thumb, she cast her sewing down and jumped to her feet. The restless movement began again until, giving up all pretence, she pulled the curtain aside from the window and peered out into the street below. She turned in response to a tap on the door but her shoulders slumped dejectedly as Sullah entered.

Like her Mistress, the slave was a picture of anxiety. Her recent concerns had pared the flesh from her bones and now, with this additional worry, the girl was almost gaunt.

'Has the Massa not come back yet, Missus? He sure is takin' a long while.'

Anne Barton frowned her displeasure. 'Sullah, I do not know what has been the matter with you these past weeks. You really must not be so outspoken. I know that since we got home yesterday you have been anxious, so are we all, but Mr Barton will return as soon as he has any news.' She had spoken more sharply than she intended and was immediately contrite as the young girl's eyes filled. She patted Sullah's arm awkwardly. 'Come now, my dear. This will do us no good at all and it does not help Daniel.'

At the mention of her lover's name, Sullah began to cry in earnest, wrapping both arms around herself and rocking backwards and forwards. The wailing increased to a high keening note and became more and more hysterical as Anne watched helplessly.

'Beg pardon, Ma'am.' The thick Scottish brogue of Andrew Stewart startled her. 'The door was open so I let myself in. Allow me.' The Doctor moved Anne to one side, stepped in front of Sullah and slapped her hard across the face. The girl halted in mid-scream, gulped in air and began to tremble as her legs buckled. Pushing her into a chair, Stewart barked at Anne over his shoulder. 'Water, Mrs Barton, if you please,' and the Mistress of the house ran to do his bidding.

Five minutes later, both women were sitting at the table and Sullah had recovered some of her composure although her teeth still clinked against the glass as she obediently sipped the water. Flicking up his coat tails and clasping his hands behind his back, the Doctor addressed himself to Anne.

'Forgive me for descending on you uninvited, but I only learned this morning that you had returned. I came as soon as I could. May I enquire, where is Mr Barton?'

'My husband has gone to Fernleigh Hall to discover what he can about what happened here. We arrived home yesterday morning and a friend of my late brother's, a town Alderman, called last night. We had no idea what had gone on and could not understand why Daniel had left the house unattended. We were told of the dreadful events and Mr Barton has gone to see my niece. I can scarcely believe it… But the Alderman said that you were involved… Perhaps you can tell us more? It has been most distressing. My niece's husband dead… and Daniel taken away… We do not know what to think. They say that Daniel killed him in a fight. Is that true?'

Andrew Stewart drew a third chair up to the table and sat down. He weighed his words carefully. 'Would it surprise you if that were so, Ma'am?'

'Well I… Daniel… He does have a temper and there have been incidents between him and Henry but… but no, I really do not believe that he would kill. Not deliberately. Not unless…' Her mind went back all those years to Daniel's treatment of the two men who had ambushed her in Jamaica.

'Not unless what?' Stewart asked.

'Not unless he or someone he cared for were threatened,' Anne murmured reluctantly.

There was a long pause, and the Doctor sighed.

'It would appear that Mr Bentinck came here to get his wife. She was in the house alone with Daniel.' Sullah's breath hissed between her teeth but Anne Barton motioned her to remain quiet. 'She was badly cut and bruised. She had been beaten and it caused her to lose the child that she was carrying. It is unclear what happened next. Mrs Bentinck cannot remember exactly but insists that she does not know how her husband died. Mrs Harrison swears that she saw Daniel attack her brother and push him down the stairs in a deliberate act. The man died from his fall, of that there is no question, but as to how or why he fell? That is open to doubt. I believe that neither woman is telling the whole truth. Daniel knows what happened but he will say nothing.'

Sullah's barely suppressed emotion finally burst out in a furious tirade.

'That Daniel is one great stupid fool. He is still took in by her pretty ways. I knows what he is like, 'specially around that Mrs Bentinck. An' as for that Mrs Harrison, well she'll say jus' 'bout anythin' to get back at Daniel 'cos he wouldn't go to her bed. Beg pardon, Missus.' The girl glanced apologetically at Anne Barton.

'Go on, Sullah. Go on.'

'Yes, Ma'am. Well, that one sure has had it in for Daniel for months. She promised he would pay for insultin' her.' She appealed to the Scot. 'Yo' can't jus' let her have him put away. Daniel didn't kill nobody. I just knows it.' One hand went to her belly in a universal, protective gesture, an action that was not lost on the Doctor. He nodded as the girl's wrath evaporated as quickly as it had arisen and two great tears coursed down her cheeks. She brushed them away with an impatient hand. 'What can we do? We has to do somethin'. We can't leave him in that there prison. If he stays behind bars he sure will die. Daniel has to be free.'

The Doctor looked from one anxious woman to the other and cleared his throat. He spoke gruffly, his fingers tracing a pattern of the polished surface of the table.

'I believe that there was an accident and that Mrs Bentinck was somehow involved. I also believe that Daniel knows what happened and will say nothing to deny the charge against him. He will stay silent to protect her.'

Tears poured unchecked down Sullah's face and Anne Barton got to her feet and moved around the table to take the weeping girl in her arms. She looked at the Doctor over the slave's head, concern etched into her face and a deep anxiety in her eyes.

'But he could hang?' The question had to be asked.

'Aye, he could Ma'am. But he won't.'

Sullah's face was lit by a ray of hope. 'Yo' mean that yo' can tell them how it was an' can get him freed?'

'No, my dear. I am sorry. If he won't help himself, I cannot go against him. No, there is more than you know. Daniel will not hang because he will be dead before he can be brought to trial.' Sullah flinched but the Doctor pressed on. 'He has a disease of the lungs... It is well advanced.

307

His cough… You must have noticed. He has only weeks to live at best. I know it and he knows it. He is going to die anyway and if he keeps silence, then young Mrs Bentinck can make a new life. If he speaks, he will still die and who can say what will become of her. He is an innocent man. What he is doing is truly noble and I will not seek to prevent it. I am sorry Mrs Barton and for you too, Miss, but there is nothing to be done. I had to come and tell you. You had to know.'

Bowing to Anne, Doctor Stewart took Sullah's cold hands in his own and looked into her swimming eyes. Her despair tugged at him and he hesitated, seeking to bring comfort.

'The child will be proud of him. There is to be a child, isn't there?' Sullah dropped her head. Stewart put one finger beneath her chin, raised her face and smiled. 'Does he know?' She shook her head dumbly as Anne Barton gaped from one to the other. 'Then go to him and tell him, my dear. Go to him, be brave and tell him he will have a child.' He smiled at the stunned Anne. 'Perhaps I should let myself out as I let myself in, Ma'am.' The door shut behind him.

For long moments after the Doctor's departure the two women stared at each other in silence, then, with a cry, Anne Barton swept the slave into her arms and they sobbed together.

'So much is clear to me now; the weight you have lost, your anxiety and indeed, your touchiness. Oh, Sullah, could you not confide in me? Did you think that I would not stand by you?'

There was a new pride in the girl's bearing as she pulled away from Anne. 'I wanted Daniel to be the first to know an' I did think that perhaps the Massa would not want me in America if he knowed that me an' Daniel had been bad. I knows how Daniel felt for Missus Bentinck an' I didn't want to say nothin' to nobody 'til we was away from here an' on our way. Then the Massa could not send me back an' Daniel would have to forget that woman. But now it don' matter no more.' Her face was bleak. 'Daniel, he ain't goin' nowhere an' if that Doctor man thinks I should go tell him 'bout the baby, then that sure is what I'll do. If yo' don't want to takes me with yo' well, perhaps someone in Liverpool will buy me an' I can stay near Daniel to the end.'

'Of course you will come with us, Sullah. It is what Daniel would want. Mr Barton and I will care for you and for Daniel's child. All that people on the new plantation need to know is that the child's father died of a lung disease before the baby was born. There will be no disgrace. As soon as it can be arranged we will both go to see Daniel and we shall tell him your news. Let us hope that it will bring him solace, for that is all that we can do for him now.' Arm in arm the two women left the morning-room and went upstairs to the nursery to take what pleasure they could in the companionship of Anne's two children.

In the deep silence of the night, Sullah perched on the window-sill of her attic bedroom. It had been a long and exhausting day, but sleep was impossible. Her thoughts were all with Daniel in his prison cell. She rested her burning forehead against the cold glass, seeking to ease her thumping head and gradually her heavy eyelids drooped. The maelstrom that was her mind threw up nightmare images of emaciated slaves chained together below decks in suffocating discomfort, far from the open skies. The face of her brother swam into focus, its features grey, the flesh lacerated as he pushed himself beneath her, lifting her clear of the towering waves. His feeble voice rang in her ears, 'breathe, sister. Breathe.' The sounds of her brother's last choking breath became the rasping of Daniel's tortured lungs. The rat-infested squalor below decks turned into her lover's dank prison cell. The rattling slave chains in her dream were chafing Daniel's skin as he lay in captivity.

A gentle tap on the door jerked Sullah awake and she slid thankfully from the window-ledge to collapse shivering on the bed. Anne Barton entered and set a candle down on the bedside chest. She held out her arms to the weeping girl.

'You cannot go on like this, my dear. You must take care of yourself now. Think of the child. Try not to worry. If you upset yourself it is bad for the babe.' She wiped away the slave's tears with her kerchief and laid her gently on the pillows. 'Sullah, I want you to listen carefully. Mr Barton has returned from Fernleigh and has spoken to both my niece and Mrs Harrison. He, like Doctor Stewart, believes Daniel to be innocent. He also visited the gaol, that is why he was so long away, and… you must be strong, my dear.' She took the dark-skinned hands in her own, gripping them hard. 'George had words with one of the town constables… It appears that the Magistrate has signed papers of charge. They have accused him of murder… largely because of Mary Harrison's evidence but also because, frankly, Daniel will say nothing to defend himself. He is to be indicted, and although Doctor Stewart will speak for him he is certain to be committed for trial. That means that he will stay in prison until the next Crown Court at the Assizes. I am sorry, Sullah. It could take weeks or even months.' By the time she had finished relating the sad state of affairs, Anne was as upset as her slave. For a long time the silence of the room was punctuated only by the sobs of the two women. They wept together. Mistress and slave, united in their grief and bound together in their love for Daniel and their horror at his plight.

Sullah sat up against her pillow. She scrubbed her eyes, sniffed loudly and swung her legs to the floor as her natural pragmatism reasserted itself.

'I thinks we both needs a drink o' that there coffee, Missus. I don' believe my Daniel would want us to take on so. If what the Doctor man says is true, then the good Lord will take him out of his misery soon an' he will be free. Bein' in that prison won't matter. What people think won't matter. Daniel will die anyways. If this trouble had never happened, he would still not have gone to America.' Her voice wobbled. 'An' he never would have seen this baby neither. But my Daniel, well, he lives in this child an' I'll surely always have part of him with me.'

'Wait, Sullah.' Anne's respect for the slave knew no bounds. The girl's lover and protector was accused of murder and would die in prison. She was about to be transported to a strange land half a world away where she would give birth to a fatherless child and yet somehow she had found the courage to face the future. For a moment Anne contrasted such bravery with the spoiled petulance and weak spirit of her niece, the girl who had brought such trouble on them all. She rose to her feet. 'The Master and I have been discussing things. We want to do something for Daniel. After all, if what we believe is true, he is taking the blame for my niece's wrong-doing. Whatever his reasons, he is saving my family from shame and disgrace and I owe him a great debt for that.' She paused, taking Sullah's hand. 'When we are able to go and see Daniel we will take with us a paper that will give him his freedom. You too, Sullah. My husband and I have decided. You will both be free.'

The girl rocked on her feet and Anne led her back to the bed. They sat side by side and for a long time there was no sound.

'Well, Sullah?'

'Missus... I don' know what... Daniel, he... It will mean so much... He will die a free man.' She burst into heartfelt sobs, and Anne Barton cried with her.

Finally the older woman gave a shaky laugh. 'We are neither of us doing this child of yours any good, you know, but I am just glad to be able to bring you some joy, my dear. There has not been much in your life.'

Sullah looked embarrassed. She fidgeted with her braided hair. She was feeling ungrateful and her words were hesitant, but she had to voice her worries.

'Ma'am, what 'bout me? If I is free, does that mean I have to leave yo' an' Massa Timothy an' Missy Meg? I surely think that I would as soon stay slave if yo' don't mind.'

This time Anne's laughter was pure delight. 'Do you think that we could ever manage without you? No, Sullah, things will stay much as they are. You will have the same duties but you will be paid a wage. You will be a servant not a slave. You may travel to America with us but if you choose to leave at any time, then you will be free to do so.'

The girl's face lit up with a radiance that brought a lump to Anne's throat. She bounced up and down in excitement.

'An' my baby? A child takes the standing of its Mammy. Is that right? So my baby will be born free?'

'Yes, Sullah. Your baby will be born a free citizen of America.' Shaking her head in stunned disbelief, the girl sank down on the bed again as her trembling legs refused to support her.

Her Mistress grinned. 'I think that I had better bring that drink myself or I fear we shall be here all night.'

Letting herself out of the door, Anne moved quietly down the passageway. She had only gone a few yards when she stopped in puzzlement. A gentle shuffling sound came from the room behind her and then a tuneful humming accompanied by rhythmic clapping. The noise was from deep in the heart of Africa; it was borne on warm winds and sparkling seas. Anne's face cleared. She had heard this before in Jamaica. Sullah was dancing. In her tiny room in the middle of a northern port the slave was celebrating in the time-honoured way of her own people. Her Mistress' eyes were damp as she hurried through the darkened house towards the kitchen.

Lying on straw in a corner of his cell, Daniel stared fixedly at the fragment of blue that was the sky. It was just visible through the tiny rectangle high up in the wall. He watched as the white clouds of a spring day criss-crossed the bars and formed chequered patterns of shadow in the filth on the floor. He tried to keep his head still, for every movement brought on another paroxysm of coughing which sapped his failing strength and drew hoots of derision from other prisoners in his vicinity. The sickness that had been a hidden part of his life for so many months was finally defeating him. His jaws ached from the effort of clamping his teeth together to still the tremors that shook his frame, and the fleshless bones of his spine were bruised from constant contact with the rough bricks of the wall. In the past week he had appreciated the gradual increase in warmth as the daylight hours lengthened, for although the sunlight never directly pierced his cell, at least it helped disperse the perpetual cold and damp that had almost been the end of him in his first days in prison.

As a man indicted on a charge of murder he was condemned to solitary confinement, a penance for which he gave grateful thanks. The fights, the raucous shouts, the bawdy songs and the curses of his fellow inmates frequently disturbed his nights but at least the racket was deadened by the thickness of the suffocating walls that shut out most of the light and framed the stale air. So he lay watching the shadows and allowed his thoughts to wander.

Daniel could not regret what he had done. He had acted with honour. He had protected the family name of the Mistress whom he had idolised since his youth. He had spared Eliza the disgrace a public scandal, and if his own death were to be hastened by his weeks in prison, then perhaps he had spared himself some suffering as well. He was calm; he supposed that he was even content. In this enforced period of inactivity he had finally discovered his own identity. The pretence was over. As Marcus and Sullah had tried to tell him so often, he was his mother's son. His father was unimportant in his life. His white-man's blood did not matter any more. For the first time he was able to accept who and what he was. He was, at last, comfortable in his own skin. Sullah would be pleased.

Sullah! There lay his only regret. He realised now how much he had come to depend on her simple wisdom and indomitable strength of mind, how much he valued her friendship and her selfless love. She was worth ten of Eliza. He knew it, but would never be able to tell her so. Life had dealt badly with Sullah but her spirit had never been broken. She had accepted her status with a dignity that was humbling. She was not debased by slavery; she rose above it.

A loud clanking of metal on metal announced the arrival of his gaoler and Daniel struggled to raise himself without setting off a coughing fit again. He was regularly brought food and fresh water by the guard who informed him that it had been 'commissioned' by the Bartons, though why anyone should want to waste good victuals on a murdering black heathen who was about to die anyway from either the hangman's rope or his corrupt lungs, was totally beyond Jeb Hacket.

'Yer breath'll stop one road or t' other. Nowt more certain,' he had observed with grim relish. 'Let's 'ope yer lives long enough not to cheat th' angman. A slave on th' end o' t' rope ain't what yer sees every day in these parts. A bit o' novelty 'elps pass time in 'ere. Yer'll draw a good crowd if yer gets t' th' Assizes, lad.'

Daniel had turned his face to the wall. He was grateful not to have to drink the brackish water and eat the rotten food that had been his introduction to prison life, but now, not even the finest delicacies could tempt him to eat more than a morsel or two and the alacrity with which Hacket removed the remains of his platter was an indication of who was gaining most from the Barton's charity. Daniel could not eat the food, but he was glad of the untainted water and thankful too for this daily evidence that he had not been forgotten.

It had come as a revelation to him just how many comforts could be bought in prison if money was available. Corruption was rife and regular payments to the guards ensured many privileges, including the offer of female company, although as Hacket pointed out with his gallows humour, 'A good tuppin' 'd put paid t' tha' breathin' fer sure, but it's not a bad way t' go.'

Now the gaoler had the door open and was carrying in a steaming bucket and a strip of coarse cloth.

'Visitors fer thee, lad. Tha'll need t' wash some o' that muck away. All that bloody coughin'. Tha'rt in a reet mess. Get a move on. Tha' 'asn't got all day.'Daniel was surprised. Apart from an early visit from an attorney, who had left in a tantrum in the face of the slave's obduracy, he had seen no one. He washed away as much of the prison filth as he could and waited for Hacket's return.

In a tiny room with a barred window sat Anne Barton and Sullah. The only furniture was a bare wooden table and three stools. George had not wanted his wife to go but she could not be persuaded to stay away. She knew that Sullah would need her. Even now, the slave was shivering as she listened to the clank of irons along the passageway. For Sullah it was a nightmare resurrected. The girl had been relieved that they were not to see Daniel in his cell, but nothing had prepared her for the sense of isolation that she had experienced as they entered the grim walls. She gnawed the knuckles of her hand and battled desperately against the panic rising in her gullet.

At Sullah's side, Anne Barton also strained to maintain her composure. She had previously had little sympathy for those who sought to reform prisons, believing that convicted felons had forfeited the right to any kind of humane treatment. Now however the thought of anyone, sometimes even women and children, in such a place filled her with horror. The brutality was evident as they crossed the women's court, the degradation complete. Screams and shouts came faintly from far away and the stench from the cells permeated the air that she struggled to breathe.

A massive door in the passage clanged shut and a key grated in the lock. Daniel shuffled into the room and collapsed on a stool, irons on his legs and wrists, dirty clothing hanging from his skeletal frame, shoulders slumped and hollow eyes sunk deep in their sockets. His rasping breath filled the space between them. He could not speak. The two women stared, Sullah's hand was bleeding where her teeth had pierced the soft flesh and Anne Barton's face was wet with silent tears.

'A few minutes, that's all tha' can 'ave.' The reminder came from Hacket as he folded his arms and leaned back against the wall, his bunch of keys clashing on the brickwork as he waited to earn his 'commission'.

Anne found her voice. She leaned towards Daniel but recoiled at the smell, then hated herself as she saw the pain in his eyes. She put out a tentative hand and touched the chaffed wrist above the irons.

'Oh, Daniel, what have they done?' She murmured. 'My

316

God, this is inhuman!'

'Yes Ma'am.' The sound was a mere whisper but at least she knew that he could hear her. He would be able to take in what she said. 'You must not worry for me,' he continued. 'I shall not be here long.' Daniel was shaking and almost fell from his stool. Hacket pushed himself off the wall but Anne motioned him back. There was not much time.

She held a paper in front of her servant's eyes. 'This is for you. It has been properly sworn. It says that you are now a free man, Daniel. Do you understand me? You are free.' For endless moments it seemed that Daniel had not heard. His expression did not change and then a single tear rolled down his grey face. It dripped off his chin and splashed on the irons that bound his wrists.

'That's it. That's all yer get.' Hacket came towards them.

'Please!' Sullah's desperate cry stopped the gaoler in his tracks.

'One minute then. One minute more. That's all yer can 'ave.'

The girl moved round the ugly table and dropped on her knees at Daniel's feet so that she could look up into his face. She took his hands in her own and covered them with kisses and her tears. The watching Hacket cleared his throat and turned away.

'Daniel, I is havin' yo' baby. Do yo' hear me? I is havin' yo child.' Daniel lifted his head, an expression of startled wonder creeping across his features, smoothing out the lines, easing his pain. 'An' the Missus has made me free too. My child, yo' child will be free born. The Massa is takin' me with them to America. Yo' son will be born there. An American. A free man.' She watched him anxiously. Had he heard? Did he understand?

Daniel stood upright, lifting the girl to her feet and Anne Barton wept unashamedly as Sullah held her man's hand

and laid it on her belly. The gaoler moved towards them and took his prisoner's arm. Daniel stared at the callused hand, raised his eyes to the man's face and Hacket loosed his hold and stepped back. With innate dignity the shackled man bowed to Mrs Barton, kissed Sullah's forehead in silent blessing, turned and walked unaided, with a firm step, back to his cell.

A warm June breeze filled the sails and the huge ship pointed her bows up river and slid away from the land as the bells of St Nicholas' Church pealed out across the Mersey. In the stern of the vessel, two women watched as the familiar landmarks began to blur into insignificance.

'He had a fitting end, Missus, didn't he? My Daniel would surely have been glad to see so many at his buryin'.'

'Yes, Sullah. He did indeed. All the servants from Fernleigh were there, even though my coachman told me that Mrs Bentinck had forbidden them to go. Many of those from the waterfront stopped too. I have seen dignitaries buried with fewer people to mourn their passing. The townsfolk came because Doctor Stewart has told everyone about Daniel's innocence and the people of Liverpool have ever been keen to see justice done. Even Jeb Hacket was there. Did you see?'

'Yes, Ma'am. He had a word. He done tell me that Daniel jus' went to sleep with no pain. I don't think I believes that but it surely was a kind thing to say.'

Anne Barton shivered as the wind strength increased. She moved away from the rail and went to find her husband and children. With a last long look over her shoulder Sullah put the town of Liverpool behind her and turned to face the open sea.

EPILOGUE

The first black President of the United States of America moved to the front of the podium to begin the inaugural speech. His voice soared above the crowd:-

'My great, great grandmother's grandmammy was once a slave. Her name was Sullah.'